The Power of Passion

Hunter rose from the water before her, and she looked at him dazedly. For the first time, she saw his body not as something that needed mending, but as a male body in the prime of beauty and strength. The rippling muscles beneath his smooth bronze skin fascinated her, the mat of black hair on his powerful chest filled her with a need to press her breasts against him.

When she looked at last at his face, a shuddering sigh escaped her lips. And when he reached down, her hands grasped his and she allowed him to pull her up.

His chest rose and fell strongly with his harsh breaths, and his vivid green eyes were alive with desire. "Siri . . . I'm not made of stone. I'm half mad with wanting you . . . Don't stop me this time, beloved . . ."

"I can't stop . . ." She heard the voice that was hers and not hers, and knew it came from someplace deeper than her mind. "I have to . . . stop." Her body, yielding, swayed toward him; her mind, trapped in chaos of its terrible conflict, fought the need to surrender.

Summer
of the
Unicorn

Kay Hooper

BANTAM BOOKS

TORONTO • NEW YORK • LONDON • SYDNEY • AUCKLAND

SUMMER OF THE UNICORN
A Bantam Book / April 1988

ISBN 0-553-25283-6

Published simultaneously in the United States and Canada

Bantam Books are published by Bantam Books, a division of Bantam Doubleday Dell Publishing Group, Inc. Its trademark, consisting of the words "Bantam Books" and the portrayal of a rooster, is Registered in U.S. Patent and Trademark Office and in other countries. Marca Registrada. Bantam Books, 666 Fifth Avenue, New York, New York 10103.

PRINTED IN THE UNITED STATES OF AMERICA

O   0 9 8 7 6 5 4 3 2 1

RUBICON

T he King was dead.

King Jason had been a hale and hearty man still in his prime, and no one had been prepared for his death of a sudden fever. The death of a king must always be traumatic for his country, of course, but never more so than when that ruler leaves behind him no children to inherit his crown. On Rubicon, the Morgan family had ruled for nearly ten thousand years, and although much of the governing remained in the hands of the elected Council of Elders, the ruling family wielded considerable power and was held dear by the populace.

Pacing slowly along a deserted hallway in the quiet palace, Tynan, Speaker of the Council, pondered the problem that his fellow Elders unanimously had placed in his hands. Grimly aware that his seat as Speaker could well depend on his solution, he was determined to satisfy everyone—no mean feat.

The people demanded a king, and were loud in their determination to see a Morgan assume the throne. The Council was also united in its determination that the

3

ancient ruling line remain unbroken. And the Court itself, though politically silent on the subject, felt a definite favoritism toward one of the princes. Tynan felt the same favoritism, and so it was inordinately difficult for him to be objective.

There were two princes, both legitimate Morgans, both of an age to rule. The problem was that they were the *same* age. They were, in fact, half brothers, born of different mothers. Jason's younger brother Darian, a scoundrel if ever one had walked, had married his betrothed with the full approval of his brother; three years later, he had persuaded his brother to reinstate the ancient law allowing male royalty a second wife. Jason considered it prudent to agree, since tests had shown that he himself would never father an heir; numerous offspring through Darian would ensure the succession.

But no one, least of all Jason, expected both of Darian's wives to announce their respective pregnancies on the same day. And since Darian, forever reckless, broke his neck out hunting before either of his sons was born, the boys' birth dates became of paramount importance: Since both boys were legitimately sired by the heir to Jason's throne, the oldest, by law, would rule after Jason.

The natural course of events should have solved the dilemma, since Elena, Darian's first wife, was by the best estimate of the Court physicians six weeks pregnant when she made the announcement, and Caprice, the second wife, eight weeks pregnant at that time. However, since a span of two weeks between two first childbirths must always be a dubious margin, no one dared to guess which child would enter the world first.

Brooding, Tynan paced slowly through the open double doors and onto the wide terrace. He stood gazing out over the peaceful, secluded garden of the palace, then sighed and rested his weight on the low stone balustrade. His black hawk's eyes wandered aimlessly for a moment, then became intent as he saw a man and woman walking some distance away. The man was tall and powerful, his black hair thick and shining in the sunlight. His head was bent attentively toward the older woman on his arm.

Caprice. The man beside her might well have been her contemporary rather than Hunter, her son, for Caprice still had the face and figure of a girl, and a girl's laugh. Her black hair was still too wild to obey the Court fashions, and her blue eyes still flashed with wicked temper often enough to startle the Court even after so many years. She was Queen, just as Elena was, though neither would ever rule because they were not Morgans born.

Fiery Caprice, who had been, Tynan knew, the wife of Darian's heart. There were those who still maintained that she seduced her prince, even some who claimed she possessed the legendary mystical powers of the Hillpeople, with which she had enchanted him. Tynan knew better. Darian had been ensnared by her beauty and spirit, but he had not been the victim of supernatural powers. Anyone witnessing one of their temperamental clashes, during which Caprice flung breakables at his head with abandon while Darian laughed and dodged skillfully, would have been conscious of observing a very typical marital drama.

Widowed before she could give her prince an heir, Caprice had lost her spirit for a time. But the birth of Hunter had renewed her life. And, though troublesome in most matters, Tynan reflected wryly, she had been rigidly circumspect regarding the birth of her son more than twenty-five years before. With a Court Wisewoman and two ladies-in-waiting in attendance, Caprice had delivered her son, seen to it that his birth was duly and punctiliously recorded, and followed the Wisewoman's advice in naming him.

Tynan sighed unconsciously, his black eyes expressionless as he watched Caprice and Hunter disappear on the far side of the garden.

It should have been simple. And it was ironic that Elena, the sensible bride chosen for Darian in his cradle, should have been the one to precipitate the complicated situation in which they were all now enmeshed. Elena, the quiet, reserved first wife, eclipsed in nearly every way by the more beautiful and lively Caprice.

Before Caprice was confined in childbed, Elena left the palace. As was the custom in her family, Elena had requested permission to return to her mother's house to give birth; the Council, requiring only that a Court Wisewoman and at least two other reputable witnesses attend the birth, assented. Scrupulously guarded and escorted, Elena had left the palace. No one could have foreseen that a band of Outcast soldiers, the seeds of what would become the People's Revolutionary Army, would attack the caravan.

None of Elena's escorts dared confess that the woman great with child quite possibly carried the next King in her womb; it would have meant sure death for Elena. The Outcasts, wanting only riches and women, took what they could, slaughtered the male guards, and carried off the ladies-in-waiting.

The Wisewoman, old and frail, died in the brief battle. And Elena, left alive in the wreckage of her caravan by men uninterested in her bloated body, began her labor far from any helping hands.

And far from anyone who could objectively record the birth.

Alone, she gave birth to her son. Alone, she managed to carry him back to the city and to the palace. She arrived, exhausted and so weakened by her ordeal that she was delirious, just three days after Caprice had given birth to Hunter. And Elena maintained that her son, Boran, had been born hours *before* Caprice's son.

There were no witnesses, and the Court physicians could not—or would not—decide which boy was oldest. And the greatest mark of uncertainty in the minds of all concerned was that Elena had declared her son's birth hour *before* knowing that Caprice had given birth on the same day. Yet there was no proof.

Jason, reluctant to set one nephew above the other, decreed that both would be raised in the palace, educated equally, provided for equally. Both would be trained in the duties of princes. And, when the time came, one would be chosen as the future King.

Being Jason, he would have chosen; he considered it his duty, and his responsibility. But Fate had taken the choice out of his hands. The fever had come upon him suddenly, drawing him down into a coma before he could voice his decision. He had never emerged from that coma.

And he left behind him two legitimate princes who could not occupy the same throne, and members of a Council on the horns of a dilemma.

Tynan sighed, aware that he was no closer to solving what he had to solve. There was no precedent. The oldest should rule, but if there was no means of determining birth time? There was no doubt both men were Morgans; the vivid green eyes were the distinguishing characteristic of the family, and both were taller than average, another characteristic. Equally trained and educated. Boran was more arrogant; Hunter more charismatic. Hunter was more popular with the Court and the populace, while Boran held many powerful people among his friends. Yet they were evenly matched in intelligence and skill, both capable of ruling and both eager for the throne.

As an interim measure, both Hunter and Boran had been named Regents, but neither had even nominal power while so named. Each commanded a legion of soldiers, as was the duty of a prince, but though they commanded their men neither could command their world. The Council would go on making the decisions which governed Rubicon. But the people were restless with their throne empty—and this was not the time for a restless populace.

The People's Revolutionary Army had gained a strong following during the past quarter century and was composed now of many young and eager people of all classes and guilds. They were agitated, ambitious, and careless with their young lives. After ten thousand years, Rubicon's natural resources had been strained, and the PRA's rallying call these last ten years had been "Expansion!"

Which was, Tynan reflected, all well and good, except that the PRA had set its sights on the only other habitable—and inhabited—planet in this solar system, Nidus. And the PRA wanted to conquer rather than share. The Council was struggling to prevent the PRA from becoming a political group with sufficient power to win a majority in the Council and declare war on Nidus, and to date it had managed the feat. But the Council of Elders was partially appointed by members and partially elected by the populace, and PRA supporters were growing in number.

Rubicon badly needed a king to heal the wound.

"Tynan?"

Rising out of respect for a prince and possibly the soon-to-be King, Tynan bowed slightly. "Your Highness."

"When will the Council vote?"

Tynan studied the tall man before him. Boran was the more aggressive of the two princes. "There will be no vote, Your Highness." And, intent and thoughtful, he watched the reaction to the news he imparted. Which prince? he asked himself. Which prince would make the stronger king?

"No vote? The people are calling for a new king, Tynan; they won't wait much longer."

"I am aware, Your Highness. But there is no precedent for this situation. If there were a vote within the Council, it would be an open vote, with each member's opinion made public." He watched that sink in, saw the shrewd, angry reaction.

"Cowards, the lot of you! So no one dares to choose their king?"

"We meet tomorrow to decide on a *means* of choosing," Tynan said, having just decided on this course.

Dryly, the prince said, "We could always fight for the throne." His tone was offhand, but there was something almost eager half-hidden in his expression.

Tynan shook his head slightly. "Our world is torn enough; watching our princes battle could upset the status quo."

"Give the rebels something new to yell about, you mean?" The prince considered that. "Perhaps you're right. But some test of skill—"

Neutrally, respectfully, Tynan said, "We will decide tomorrow."

The prince laughed and looked at the Speaker with a great deal of understanding. "They flung the decision at you, and now you'll fling it back at them. You are a politician born, Tynan."

Tynan stiffened almost imperceptibly. The Council had met in closed session; it seemed this prince had an ear inside that room. Reckless of him to alert Tynan to that. Or was it ruthless rather than reckless? This prince, at least, would know who decided for him—or against him.

Softly, the prince said, "I reward my friends, Tynan." Then, laughing, he turned and strode away.

Tynan stared after him, his lips pressed tightly together. Odd, he thought, but the disfigurement on Boran's left side that he had borne for so many years seemed more visible now. Like everyone in the Court and Council, Tynan had become so accustomed to Boran's scarred face that he was blind to it. But today he saw the terrible scars as if they drew his eyes like a magnet.

"It will be you, of course."

Hunter looked at his mother with laughing appreciation. "Certainly it would—were you to cast the deciding vote!"

Caprice, who was hardly ever still, twirled away from her son where he sat on a low stone wall. "You were first-born," she said firmly, her blue eyes very bright. "You were born in the palace, under the very eyes of a Wisewoman and two witnesses, and you were named according to custom."

"Elena says Boran was firstborn."

Caprice tossed her head. "Her! Oh, Hunter, she was fairly out of her head when she returned with her son! How could she possibly be certain what hour he was born? He didn't even get a proper naming, and what king could rule without that?"

"Boran," Hunter asserted dryly.

Caprice returned to sit beside her son, her lovely face suddenly grave. "Beware of him."

"He's my friend."

"He's your rival."

Hunter reached to take her hand, saying gently, "He's my brother. And he wants the best for Rubicon, just as I do. Whatever the Council decides, we will each honor the decision. As men and brothers, we can do no less."

"And when only one of you is chosen King? I know you will be honorable, my son, but what of Boran? He *wants* to be King; he hungers for the crown—"

"Mother, we both want the crown."

"You wish to rule as Jason did, wisely and well. Boran covets power."

"Mother . . ." Hunter said warningly.

Caprice looked at him, troubled. "I know you see only your brother and childhood friend when you look at him, Hunter, but he is so much more than that. Beware of him. Please."

Hunter patted her hand, his face relaxing in a smile. "All right, I'll take care. I suppose a mother's role is to worry."

"Yes." Caprice sighed almost unconsciously. "And the mother of a prince worries about many things. . . ."

Tynan, still brooding, found that his absent steps had led him to the locked, temperature-controlled room which housed the ancient books brought to Rubicon when their ancestors had settled here. He hesitated a moment, then used his key to open the door and went inside. Displayed with loving care in glass cases, the half dozen books reposed in the deep silence and cool atmosphere provided by the noiseless machines that preserved them.

Tynan moved among the cases, wondering idly if the ancient Councils had been wise in hoarding safely within the palace these relics of their beginnings on this planet. Some had been copied, of course, but those copies had been lost long ago, and the originals were now too delicate to withstand the process again.

Laying a long-fingered hand on the glass of one case, Tynan gazed down at the *Book of Fables and Myths* protected inside. Six, he thought bleakly. Just six books remained intact and preserved. All of them dealt with mythology and legend, as had all the books their ancestors had seen fit to bring to their new world.

Why? Tynan wondered, as he had so often wondered. There had been no books of factual history, or science, no studies of technology or sociology. There had been, at one time, a tattered star map showing the location of Earth, but that had disintegrated generations ago. The people of Rubicon knew their ancestors had left a planet called Earth, but they knew no more than that.

If there had not been so many technically trained people among the first settlers, Rubicon might well have become a primitive new beginning for the people, rather than the orderly and civilized society that had rapidly developed. Oh, there had been wars, of course, and struggles for power, and it had taken generations to establish a working society. But that was an astonishingly short time, given the nature of civilizations.

And the one dominant characteristic of all those first-generation settlers had been a total loathing of weapons; they had built cities and spaceships; their medical knowledge and equipment were highly advanced; the checks and balances of their governmental system were many and subtle and wise, so that society had developed swiftly in an ordered and peaceful manner.

For almost ten thousand years, no powered weapon had been made in Rubicon, nor were any allowed to be brought into the kingdom by visitors. Scientists and technicians were forbidden on pain of death to develop any device that could be used as a weapon. For almost ten thousand years, the only weapons on Rubicon were starkly simple or crude: knives, bows and arrows, spears, and the like.

And then the PRA had surfaced, and within a matter of years powered weapons were secretly purchased from off Rubicon, and the once-tiny band of people outcast for various crimes in the cities had become a force to be reckoned with.

The *Book of Fables and Myths*. Tynan looked down at it, frowning. Why had their ancestors brought so much of their legends with them, and none of their history? And why was he nagged by the feeling that the supporters of the PRA would immediately turn away from their group if they knew the answer to that puzzle? He shook the question away. He knew only too well there was no answer to be found.

And there was another question he must concern himself with now. Which man would be the next King of Rubicon? There had to be some way of choosing, or of

allowing the two princes to somehow make the choice
between themselves. His hand moved slowly over the
smooth glass of the case as he stared at the book. Mythology
and fable, stories and legends. Heroes and quests. . . .

Elena looked up from her sewing as her son entered
her bedroom. She was a small, thin woman with a pale,
heart-shaped face and expressionless blue eyes. She was
neatly dressed in plain colors, with no frills or ruffles, and
her hair was sedately plaited and wound round her head in
a coronet. Boran had often wondered if she wore her own
hair in the manner of the crown she could never have.

"The Council's stalling, Mother," he said, impatience
in his tone. "Nobody wants to crown their next king."

Softly, Elena said, "They must make a decision soon."

"Yes, but when?" He paced restlessly, frowning.

She watched him for a moment, her hands still in her
lap, then said, "You are the rightful King."

He laughed shortly. "Unfortunately, there's no proof of
that. Tynan, damn his soul, favors Hunter, but he isn't
willing to accept the burden of the decision. He's up to
something."

"Beware of him."

"Tynan? He's an old fool."

"No. Hunter. Beware of him."

Boran stopped pacing and stared at his mother. "Of
Hunter? Mother, he could no more harm me than he could
harm Caprice."

Elena's eyes were distant, unfocused. "There's a
strength in him, a power. He could be . . . will be . . .
your deadliest enemy. Beware of him."

Moving silently, Boran stood before his mother and
studied her with an intent gaze. "What have you seen?"

She looked up, and the distant look vanished. "A
beautiful valley," she said calmly. "A woman. A myth."

"What?" He knew his mother sometimes glimpsed a
distant future, but it was a secret shared only by the two of
them. Still, he had known her to be right too often to
disregard her words.

"Beware of Hunter."

"Ohhh . . ." She held his head to her breast, her body writhing uncontrollably, a little sigh of pleasure escaping her when she felt his teeth toying with a hard nipple. His tongue brushed the captured bud, rasping, and his hand slid down over her quivering belly to stroke the crinkly hair covering her mound. Her legs parted eagerly and her hips lifted, moving in a smooth, practiced rhythm to his touch.

She reached for his body, her hand skilled, but he laughed softly and pinned her wrists to the pillow above her head. He tormented her breasts and stroked the wet softness between her legs until she could only plead gaspingly, her body bucking with less rhythm now and growing, desperate need.

Only when she had become a wild thing did he roll over and cover her body with his, slipping between her legs and thrusting deep within her in the same movement. His rhythm was smooth and powerful, and the slick union of their bodies more heated with every stroke, until she arched beneath him and cried out in the strained, sobbing voice of release.

He didn't allow her the slow slide into limp peace, but continued thrusting in a quickening rhythm which soon had her writhing again. If she had been not a courtesan but a lady of the Court, with the long nails of fashion, she would have torn his back; as it was, her short nails left faint marks in his bronze skin as she raked it wildly. And when finally he buried himself in her with a groan, she had no voice left to cry out her own pleasure and could only sound her release in a shuddering gasp.

Ennea caught her breath at last and smiled, wreathing her arms up around his neck. "It's *my* role to pleasure *you*," she murmured.

"You have." He returned her smile, dropping a light kiss on the warm, rosy skin of her breast.

Since she was an experienced and skilled courtesan, Ennea knew that she had. She also knew that Prince Hunter was unusually preoccupied. "Sire—"

"Not when we're alone, Ennea. I told you that."

"It isn't proper."

He chuckled. "Neither are you."

Ennea accepted the compliment with a soft laugh, then rose on an elbow to gaze down at him as he moved to her side. "Proper enough to obey a command from my prince, at any rate. Hunter, what troubles you? The decision of the Council?"

He lay on his back, frowning. His big bronze body was gleaming from their exertions but, as usual, he was barely out of breath. Ennea found herself wondering, as she often had, if there was a woman on Rubicon who could lose him his constant, detached coolness. A skilled lover, Hunter both gave and found pleasure in his bedmates, yet he remained always somewhat remote, distant. Other courtesans had noticed and commented on it in their secluded quarters; Ennea knew very well that Hunter had never lost himself in passion as his bedmates invariably did.

He was kind and never hurtful, often voicing a sincere appreciation of female beauty and sexual skill. And the most beautiful courtesans and Court ladies had lain with him with a great deal of pleasure. A man of strong appetites, he rarely slept alone and never demeaned either a courtesan or a high-born lady by talking of his conquests afterward.

And he had not, unlike Boran, acquired a reputation for being volatile, difficult to please, or prone to abandon Court parties to dally behind any convenient bush or in an empty room with some woman who had caught his eye. Hunter was Hunter, always respectful and cool and kind and detached. He ignited the fires of passion in his bed, and was never burned himself.

"The Council?" Ennea repeated when the silence had lengthened.

Hunter stretched languidly, still frowning a little. "The Council won't decide," he said finally. "They'll find some means of determining between the two of us, but they won't decide. We will. Somehow, Boran and I will decide."

"A test of skill?"

"Perhaps."

As intelligent as any courtesan, Ennea knew when to allow a subject to drop. She leaned over him, smiling,

allowing her hair to brush against his hard, flat stomach.
"It's my turn to please you, my prince," she murmured, and
bent her head, her skilled fingers and lips bringing him
quickly erect.

He locked his fingers in her hair gently, moving to her
pleasuring touch. But she saw that even in the throes of
passion, his body burning, his green eyes remained cool.

Boran rolled off the woman onto his back, gazing up at
the ceiling with a preoccupied frown. "Send Terese to me,"
he ordered absently, hardly out of breath.

The woman he had left knew better than to waste a
moment in catching her own. Trembling, aware of the
soreness between her legs, she slid quickly from the bed
and gathered up her torn clothes, hurrying from the room
without pausing to dress. The guard at the door of Boran's
bedroom glanced at her, but said nothing.

Caltha didn't cry, but only because this had not been
her first visit to Boran. She hurried through the wide and
deserted halls of the palace until she came at last to the
wing reserved for the courtesans employed to keep the
princes and Council sexually satisfied. The guard there
quickly opened the door for her, and like his comrade, not a
flicker of emotion showed on his face.

In the community room of the courtesans' pavilion,
Caltha threw down her torn garments and swore with soft
bitterness. "He's in one of his moods," she announced to
the dozen or so women gathered in the room. "And he
wants you, Terese."

Terese, a dark, buxom woman barely out of her teens,
looked frozen for a moment. Then she moaned, "Not
again!"

Caltha, stepping into the hot bath already prepared for
her, spared the other a warning look. "I'll bet you won't be
the last tonight; he's as horny as he is foul-tempered."

Fearfully Terese asked, "Is he feeling cruel?"

Resting her head back on the lip of the bathtub, Caltha
grimaced. "For him, no. Compared to the Council and,
God knows, Hunter, he's brutal. And he's in the mood to
feel like royalty, if you please. Yes, Your Highness. No, Your
Highness." Caltha sighed tiredly. "I think I'll accept

Conrad's offer; there are worse things than being the wife of
a soldier."

Terese, being helped into a gossamer robe by two
other women, was already tense and afraid. "If you tell
Boran you've lain with Conrad, he'll have you thrown out of
the palace and Conrad demoted."

"I'm not so foolish. I'll tell Prince Hunter; he'll give me
a dowry and wish me well."

"Oh, I hope he's made King!" one of the others said,
and there were several voices of agreement.

Caltha shrugged. "Don't count on it. Boran's ruthless,
and he wants the crown. He'll get it somehow."

Terese smoothed her long, dark hair and glanced
nervously into a mirror. "How do I look?"

"Better than you will in a little while," Caltha said and
sighed.

Terese squared her shoulders and left the community
room, making her way with the quickness of fear down the
long hallways. She was admitted instantly into Boran's
chamber and moved gracefully across the room to the bed.
"Your Highness?"

He lay sprawled on his back, naked, and looked at her
broodingly. "Another whore," he muttered.

Terese almost winced, biting back a retort. But it was
difficult for her to hold herself silent. Courtesans were a
respected guild, highly educated and trained, and most
retired young with wealthy husbands. By the Council
members and other men of power seeking their services,
they were valued and treated well. From Prince Hunter,
they received nothing but kindness and respect. From
Boran, they received whatever he was in the mood to give
them, usually roughness and insults, if nothing worse.

Coldly Boran said, "If you come to me once more
wearing a robe my guard can see through, I'll purchase
your services for my soldiers. All my soldiers."

"Yes, Sire," she whispered. Yesterday, he had made
the same threat if she *didn't* wear the gossamer robe. He
was as ambivalent as the two sides of his face were different:
the right side angelic, the left hideously disfigured.

Boran's voice was abruptly gentle. "Did my guard leer

at you, Terese? Did he reach down to fondle himself when
he saw you walking toward him? Did you pause a moment
or so out in the hall to pleasure him?"

"No, Sire." She was trembling, hating him because he
caused it and because he saw it. Until recently, Boran had
not been cruel to his bedmates. Rough, certainly, but while
King Jason had lived, he had shown no sadistic tendencies.
Only since the death of their king had Boran shown such
arrogant contempt for the women he called to his bed. She
wondered if he would revert to his former brusqueness if
he were made King or if he would become only worse. And
what if he *weren't* made King?

"Take off the robe."

She unfastened the ties and allowed the garment to fall
away, standing naked before him. Boran's gaze roamed
insolently over her body, lingering at her breasts and the
mound of her womanhood with that strange intensity that
could arouse even as it repelled, and Terese felt her breath
grow short and slick heat dampen her sex. And thank God
or the devil, she thought, for that; at least she would be
somewhat prepared for him.

Boran sat up on the bed, and he was smiling. He
beckoned commandingly and, when she stood beside the
bed, leaned toward her to take one nipple into his mouth.
She cried out sharply when he bit down but remained
standing stiffly. Boran released the nipple and chuckled
softly.

"On the bed, whore."

Shaking, Terese climbed into the bed and, at his
deliberately crude gesture, parted her legs. She lay on her
back, wishing silently that she could feel as proud of her
calling with this man as with all others. He made her feel
like a lifeless female body designed only to host his swollen
member and drain it of its seed. Uninterested in the
pleasuring of trained courtesans, Boran merely used their
bodies.

He was between her legs, thrusting into her body
roughly while she forced her muscles to relax. Terese had
once attempted to respond to him physically, her lithe body
moving skillfully with his, but he had struck her face

brutally and commanded her to be still. So she lay now beneath him, arms and legs spread wide, trying not to tense at what would come.

He was well endowed, huge in fact, and he enjoyed knowing that no woman had ever taken him completely without pain. During these first moments he thrust only a part of his throbbing length into her; only when his excitement peaked did he lunge fully into her body. And her cry of pain triggered his release.

He rolled away from her, preoccupied once again. "Send Dacia to me," he ordered absently.

Shaking and supremely grateful she had gotten off so lightly this time, Terese slid from the bed.

Tynan sat alone in the Book Room long into the night, carefully turning the pages of each precious volume. He read quickly but thoroughly, renewing his memory of the stories, his agile mind gradually forming a possible solution to his problem. Not an ideal solution, but a workable one. If he could only find . . .

"Your attention, please." As Speaker, it was Tynan's duty to make the announcement to the Court and Council gathered in the tremendous Throne Room of the palace. He stood to the left of the empty throne, the other members of the Council behind him; the two princes flanked the throne, standing quietly, their gaze fixed intently on him. Tynan squared his shoulders and in a quiet but compelling voice addressed the members of the Court who were also gazing fixedly at him.

"The passing of our dear king has left Rubicon with more than grief to bear. His death left the throne empty, and left two princes equally qualified and able to wear his crown. You all know the reasons behind our dilemma; it is unnecessary to state them here and now. Suffice it to say that the Council cannot, in good conscience, choose between these men. And yet, only one may rule."

Tynan glanced at the princes, then returned his gaze to the waiting crowd. "We are a people who believe in legend and myth, as our ancestors taught us to believe. Though few in this room have ever seen the Books, all know the stories. And in those stories, time and again, the nobility of a man has been tested and proven by a Quest. It seems only fitting that now, with our world torn and our throne empty, we should turn to those stories for a solution to our desperate problem."

"Good, isn't he?" Boran murmured to Hunter.

Hunter glanced at his half brother and smiled a little. "They elected him Speaker."

Tynan paused a moment, not entirely for effect; he braced himself for the reaction. "Our king must be above other men. Stronger. Wiser. Compassionate without weakness. Decisive without ruthlessness. He must be the best possible man he can be.

"And so, the Council of Elders has on this day unanimously agreed that our king must be chosen by means of a Quest." He turned to face the princes. "Two one-man ships are being prepared in the spaceport. They are identical in every way, stocked and armed equally. Each of you will board his ship and leave Rubicon in three days. You will both search for the same thing. The first of you to return to Rubicon with the object of the Quest will be our next king."

A ripple went through the Throne Room that was visible as well as audible, approval on some faces, disapproval on others, and a question on all.

"I agree," Hunter said quietly.

Boran nodded. "And I."

They glanced at each other, the measuring, wary glances of men who are suddenly looking ahead to a bitter rivalry. And it was Hunter who asked the question.

"What do we search for?"

Tynan smiled. "A unicorn. The first of you who returns to Rubicon with proof that unicorns do—or do not—exist will rule this planet."

STYX

One

The sleek young stallion fought valiantly, with sharp hooves and strong teeth, his powerful hind legs lashing out again and again. Loath to give away the hiding place of the herd, he never once glanced toward the wide end of the valley and the cave opening hidden by brush.

Cannily evading the thrusts of the man's long knife, the stallion pinned his ears flat against his noble head and screamed his rage, dark eyes burning with a new and terrible ferocity. He lunged again, tearing flesh from the man's arm and tasting blood for the first time in his life.

The man shrieked in pain, clapping a hand to his arm and dodging frantically as needle-sharp hooves seemingly came from nowhere to send the knife flying. Triumphant, the stallion aimed a last and deadly kick, then whirled to confront the second enemy struggling to hold the slender woman who was fighting to escape him.

The woman was writhing within the big man's cruel embrace, the serene beauty of her face marred by fear. But not for herself. She saw the young stallion charging toward

23

them, and her velvety dark eyes were wild with terror and despair.

"No, Sasha!" she cried desperately.

But the stallion charged on, blindly intent on protecting the woman and destroying the enemy. So unheeding was he in his rage that he never saw the man's arm draw back suddenly and snap forward with vicious force.

And he never saw the long hunter's knife that buried itself in his snowy white breast.

"Sasha!" The woman's whisper was a breath of pure anguish. She was too far away to reach the creature in time, and the certainty of that knowledge tore at her. She slumped within the powerful arms gripping her, only the strength of an enemy holding her up.

Through tear-flooded eyes, she saw her beloved friend fall heavily to his knees and then on his side, crimson staining his pure white coat. She dimly heard the man's harsh laugh and dropped to her own knees as he released her.

And then, before she could give in to the grief-stricken rage welling up inside of her, a sudden trumpeting call rolled across the valley. The sound silenced the brute laughing behind her. The attacker whirled in a crouch to protect himself against an unknown threat.

Too late.

An older, more powerful stallion thundered from the nearby trees, head lowered and dark eyes flashing a killing fury. Before the enemy could do more than gape, he was lifted into the air with a force that would have broken his back even if the horn goring him had missed its mark. The limp body was tossed immediately aside and trampled beneath enraged hooves.

Only when the enemy was kicked viciously into the gorge and both bodies lost to sight did the older stallion's rage diminish. He whirled away from the canyon edge and hurried to the younger, fallen stallion and the woman kneeling beside him. The woman looked up with streaming eyes, her lovely face ravaged with grief.

Cloud's head lowered, his wise old eyes dimming with sorrow. He nuzzled the fallen body of his son once in a tender farewell, going down on his knees beside the woman. While they watched in helpless misery, the white coat of Sasha wavered and fell softly into dust, leaving but one trace of his life.

The woman reached out slowly and picked up the only tangible memory she would ever have of her friend, cradling the foot-long golden spiraled horn tenderly in her arms. In a sorrow too terrible for words, she looked at Cloud, seeing the blood staining his own golden horn and matting the flowing white beard.

The living commanded her attention.

Sighing raggedly, she rose to her feet, knowing that Cloud would remain for many days to come at the spot where his son had died. She could not lessen his grief or help him to find his way through this sorrowing time. She could only bring water from the Crystal Pool and wash the blood of his vengeance from Cloud's golden horn.

Wash away the stain . . . but never the memory.

Turning away, the woman opened her mouth and let out a piercing call for the herd. She waited for a moment until sunlight glinted off golden horns in the distance, then headed toward her cabin.

They were her friends, she was their protectrix—and she had failed them.

He was first to the City, traveling more swiftly, driven by the burning within him. No one looked at him for more than a moment as he passed, each pair of feral eyes skittering away from his mild gaze as if they had seen into the pit of hell. A path was cleared for him through the tumbled City, thieves, murderers, and worse giving way before him as if obeying an ancient instinct.

His ears were sharp; he heard whispers of the news he desired. He listened to the coarse murmurs of the City, and his path altered itself accordingly. Someone knew. Someone had found what he sought. He began searching for the Huntman known as King.

He regretted that it had been necessary to leave his energized weapons at the spaceport orbiting the planet, but it was a vague regret. The single law of this planet, imposed on it by the worlds nearby, was that there would be no further destruction here. The Huntmen could cut one another up as they pleased, but the planet itself had borne enough.

Life had become primitive here.

It did not matter to him. Weapons were only as effective as the man wielding them, after all. And he had no need of weapons. He was strong, well taught, and as wily as the worst of the hellions on this world.

He looked on them with contempt, these dregs of a galaxy. Not because they were killers, thieves, prostitutes in every sense of the word, but because they lacked purpose. They survived from one day to the next, plying their various filthy trades and then spending what they earned.

He had purpose. The years since leaving Rubicon had taught him much, and his determination was now an iron thing. He had three main objectives. And three within the three, for his first objective was a Triad: Age, Strength, Youth. The magical three. The powerful three.

First the Triad.

Then the talisman.

And with those, he would achieve his third objective. He would rule a world.

He found the Huntman he sought in a dark and filthy tavern, and spoke softly to him in a low voice that easily penetrated the coarse laughter filling the room. King looked up, frowning, and his face tightened when he saw the man standing over him. But the whisper had promised wealth, so he rose and followed the stranger out into the cool of approaching night.

No words were exchanged until they reached the house King had claimed for his own. And then it was King who spoke, avoiding any glance at that other face.

"You have a job for me?"

"No," the other said softly. "You have something for me, I believe."

King laughed harshly. "I sell only my services, stranger."

Pleasantly, the stranger said, "You will give me the horn of a unicorn which you have in your possession."

King stiffened, and his face went blank. He wondered at the other's knowledge but did not question. A small part of the horn he had ground to sell as a prized aphrodisiac, but most of it remained intact. "It's worth much," he murmured.

"Where is it?"

"What do you offer?"

The stranger smiled a terrible, twisted smile. "Your life, Huntman. That's my offer."

King reached instantly for the knife at his belt, but never grasped it.

"Huntman? Somethin' special, Huntman. Very rare. Drive the ladies wild. On my honor, Huntman—" It was a hiss, pleading, beguiling, cautious, reaching only intended ears.

Hunter Morgan turned an icy stare on the vendor, and the little man seemed to shrink in on himself like a collapsing air bag. He shrunk in size, in personality. The thin, reedy voice hastily apologized for the apparent affront.

"Not that you need it, I'm sure! No offense, Huntman!"

Hunter sighed impatiently, not bothering to explain that the offense had come, not from the vendor's offer of an aphrodisiac, but from the unsavory appellation of "Huntman."

They were the refuse of the galaxy, these Huntmen, scorned with distaste by every race save their own kind because they fed off death. They would hunt anything for anyone with a few gold pieces, and rarely did they return with a living trophy. Brutal, cruel men for the most part, they tended to congregate in cities like this one that had been abandoned uncounted centuries before by a more advanced civilization.

Which was why Hunter did not appreciate the vendor's salutation.

Still, he could hardly complain. This was a Huntmen's

city, known only by that name. Whores stood in doorways
wearing little, if anything, and called out lewd suggestions
to passersby, suggestions which were often accepted right
there on the broken rubble of an ancient sidewalk. Hunter
had threaded his way through a minor orgy some blocks
back, curtly refusing a drunken invitation to participate.

The strident sound of brawls could be heard from
nearly every building, shrieks of rage and pain mingling
with shouts of inebriated laughter. The heavy fumes of
intoxicants rose from snoring bodies sprawled in the gutter,
and many glassy-eyed individuals roamed the streets as if in
a dream, their minds the captive of potent brews from
diverse civilizations.

There were no controls. There was nothing even
remotely resembling law and order in a Huntmen's city.
Base law prevailed: Only the strong survived, and they did
so any and every way they could.

Hunter had never, in all his travels, encountered a
Huntmen's city until now. But he was strong. His distaste
for his surroundings did not show on his face. And as he
paused in the mouth of the littered alleyway where the
vendor stood, faint interest stirred to life in the cool,
guarded depths of his vivid green eyes. He paid no
attention to the small leather pouch which the vendor
clasped protectively in both hands, but studied instead the
wily, monkeylike face of the little man. Although the
vendor looked frail and frightened, Hunter knew that he
had to be both strong and smart to survive life in this city,
and most likely possessed information worth a gold coin or
two.

Keeping one hand firmly on the hilt of his long knife
and the other on the leather purse tied to his belt, Hunter
stared coldly down at the vendor. "I'm not interested in
your pouch, little man. But perhaps you can help me. I
heard rumors of a herd of unicorns somewhere nearby." His
sudden, bitter glance over his shoulder at the squalid city
crumbling all around him indicated that he had no expectation of finding the lovely pure white creatures anywhere
near this place. "Well?" he prompted harshly.

The vendor started. "Don't know nothin' 'bout that,"
he mumbled, panic flashing in his eyes as he realized that

the only way out of this blind alley was past Hunter's formidable bulk.

Hunter allowed the coins in his purse to jingle suggestively. "Think again, little man. And put a price on your tongue."

The greedy tongue licked dry lips as the vendor eyed the leather pouch tied to the large stranger's belt. He seemed to hesitate, then held out his own pouch desperately. "The most powerful aphrodisiac in the galaxy," he promised hoarsely. "On my honor, Huntman!" He hesitated again, adding almost in a whisper, "It's—from the horn of a unicorn."

Hunter, who had been about to coldly deny any need for an aphrodisiac, looked sharply at the vendor. "What did you say?" he demanded.

The little man swallowed hard, his Adam's apple bobbing nervously, and took a hasty step back. "The horn of a unicorn," he whispered constrictedly.

"I thought you didn't know anything about them," Hunter told him hardly.

It was not something Huntmen spoke of, but the vendor knew that his only way out of the alley was to talk. "They come in the summer," he promised, eyes shifting restlessly beyond Hunter to the crowd in the street. "Only in the summer. And only here. And they're guarded."

"Here?" Hunter repeated in disbelief.

Wincing beneath harsh skepticism, the vendor pointed hastily up and beyond Hunter's shoulder. "Up there somewhere. There's a valley, Huntman. Everybody knows there's a valley."

Since his trust of this little man equaled his trust of anyone in the city, Hunter clapped a strong hand on his shoulder to keep him immobile as he half-turned to look up above the shambling remains of once-tall buildings.

He'd seen the mountain on his trip overland from the coast, watched it growing as if with a life of its own as he'd neared it. It brooded above the city like a great sentry guarding whatever lay beyond it, black as hell except for the snow capping its peak. Brother mountains crowded close to its shoulders, spreading out in a line as far as the

eye could see and promising with jagged killer ridges and
peaks a dangerous passage. If ever man had thought himself
master of this world, the mountains stood in mute and
mocking denial, gazing derisively down on the butts of a
cosmic joke.

"Up there?" Hunter questioned briefly, turning back to
the vendor.

The little man, clutching his precious pouch against
the tattered remains of his leather tunic, nodded jerkily.
"It's called The Reaper. The mountain. It—it never gives up
its dead." He swallowed hard.

Hunter shook a bony shoulder. "And?" When the
vendor only stared at him pleadingly, he produced a gold
coin from his purse and dropped it into a grasping hand.
"And?" he repeated.

The vendor looked up at him fearfully. "They say
. . . they say that if you dig into the slopes, you'll find the
earth red, stained with the blood of men. They say The
Reaper kills for enjoyment."

"It's just a mountain," Hunter snapped, impatient.

"No, Huntman," the vendor whispered. "More than a
mountain. It lives. When the rain comes, it bleeds with the
blood of men who've died trying to master it. And
sometimes in the night, it howls like a soulless devil."

"The wind," Hunter scoffed.

The vendor stared up at him with faint despair. "It
lives." Then, as Hunter stirred impatiently, he hurried on.
"It guards the valley. Where the unicorns come each
summer. It allows no man to pass into the valley."

"Then how did you get the horn?" Hunter asked flatly.

Squirming beneath the hand holding him, the vendor
became abruptly still as the hand promised broken bones.
"A Huntman," he whispered, "brought it to me. The only
man The Reaper has allowed to escape its wrath. And not
even he escaped untouched. He—lost his tongue. He can
never speak of what he saw. And his eyes . . . are like the
broken windows of an empty building."

Hunter ignored the compelling imagery. "No one else
has returned?"

"No one, Huntman. Not unharmed. They try, in twos

and threes, to battle The Reaper. Each summer they try, because they know the unicorns are there. They hunger for the priceless golden horns. And they are never seen again, or else are found, broken and bleeding, on The Reaper's slopes. Or worse, they return as madmen with no voices to cry out their madness."

Hunter glanced over his shoulder again, looking at the brooding black sentinel. "It's only a mountain," he mused softly.

The vendor gulped. "And if you get past it," he said in a smothered voice, "the woman will destroy you."

"What woman?" Hunter demanded, turning keen attention back to the vendor.

"The Keeper of the unicorns." He made an ancient sign meant to ward off devils. "She's a witch, a sorceress, with eyes as black as The Reaper to drive men mad. They say she has silver hair and a siren's voice, and that she fights as a warrior fights. She's protected the unicorns for ten thousand years."

Hunter laughed shortly, and the vendor looked at him again with despairing eyes. "It's true, Huntman. Those The Reaper allows into the valley, she drives mad. She steals their minds and voices, so that they can never tell how they found her."

"What about this Huntman who brought you the horn? You say he lost his tongue. Is he also mad?"

"Not mad. But not whole. He lost more than his tongue in that place. He sits in his house, in the darkness, looking no man in the eye. He was not that way before he went in search of the valley."

"I want to see this Huntman, talk to him," Hunter said abruptly.

The vendor all but folded in on himself. "No!" he gasped, clearly terrified. "He'll kill me! I beg you, Hunt-man—"

Hunter dropped several gold coins into the vendor's instinctively grasping hand. "Go to him," he instructed briefly. "Tell him I have no desire for the unicorns or their horns. Tell him I wish only to prove that they exist. And tell him I'll pay well for his knowledge of that valley."

Dazedly, the little man stared down at the gold in his hand. "If—if he refuses to see you?" he whispered.

"Convince him," Hunter advised coldly.

"But—"

"Convince him. And be back here, at this spot, in three hours. With the answer I desire." Casually Hunter toyed with the hilt of his knife. "Be warned, little man. If you are not here with the answer I desire, you'll not see another sunset."

The vendor stared up at Hunter with terrorized eyes, nodding with a single gulp, then slid out of the alley and into the crowded street, disappearing in an instant.

Barely conscious of the strident sounds all around him, Hunter stood and stared up at The Reaper, feeling the first stirring of his excitement since he'd arrived at this godforsaken place.

He was not interested in the unicorns for the sake of their golden horns, but for the sake of their reality. For years now, he had traveled far to prove the reality of this particular myth—and gain his throne. But he had found no myths at all. On one world, he had discovered a living Pegasus, disappointed to find that the winged creature bore only the vaguest resemblance to a horse. On another he found a wizard, again disappointed to find that sleight of hand formed the basis of his magic.

And unicorns . . . He had seen goats with a single horn, gazelles, horses altered with man's aid to fit the myth. He had seen charlatans and fakers and tricksters.

He had not seen a unicorn. The creature had eluded him until he had all but given up hope of proving its existence. And yet it had been the stories of the creature told to him in boyhood that had kept him from admitting defeat. If unicorns existed, he meant to find them. Ironic, he thought now, if man's most delicate and beloved myth had chosen to reside in a valley high above the worst examples of the living . . . high above that breed of man in whom greed for golden horns far outweighed the fascination of dreams.

Hunter spent those hours of waiting inside the one relic of this planet's former civilization. A library. It had astonished him at first sight a day earlier, with its unbroken, polished windows and neatly swept marble steps. And curiosity had led him inside the huge building, where he had discovered a very old woman lounging behind a gleaming desk with her feet up on a stack of books and another on her lap.

Ancient, but far from decrepit, the woman had directed fierce blue eyes in his direction and snapped, "Huntmen aren't allowed!"

Standing very still and gazing warily at the huge—and illegal—blaster held confidently in the wrinkled old hand, Hunter made haste to disclaim the distinction. "I'm not a Huntman. I'm a visitor in the city."

"Look like a Huntman to me," she said, sniffing disdainfully.

"I'm not, I promise you."

"Come closer," she directed. "Slowly."

He did.

Keen eyes studied him for a long moment, and then the old woman relaxed her grip on the blaster and placed it on yet another stack of books at her side. "I don't get many decent visitors these days."

Hunter had just met Maggie O'Shea—a relic within a relic, as it were.

She had taken care of the library for most of her long life, "like my mother before me, and hers before her." Truculent, confident, and unafraid, she kept the Huntmen of the city at bay. And though her prime was years past, she still managed to keep the huge library relatively clean and almost dust-free.

Hunter had spent the day with her, at first fascinated, as always, by the unexpected and then charmed by the old lady's cheerful wisdom and tolerant attitude.

Seeking her out today as he waited for the appointment with the vendor—and possibly his destiny—Hunter was eager to question Maggie about the valley and the unicorns. Cut off though she was from the city by her own iron will, he had an idea that very little escaped Maggie O'Shea.

Calling her as he entered, he headed toward her

distant response and discovered her at last near the back of
the building. She was seated high on a rickety stepladder
between tall rows of musty-smelling books, the layers of
yellowed, diaphanous lace she habitually wrapped around
herself fluttering and drooping about her like the web of a
lazy spider in a gentle breeze.

Hunter stood with hands on hips and glared up at her.
"What're you doing up there, Maggie?" he demanded. "You
could fall and hurt yourself, and there'd be no one to help
you."

Maggie pulled the lensless wire-rimmed spectacles
down her nose—a "badge of office," she'd cryptically told
him yesterday—and stared at him over the tops. "Mind
your own business, young man."

"I'm making you my business," he said. "Come down
from there."

Closing the book on her lap and returning it to its place
on the shelf, she grinned down at him, her dentures
sparkling proudly. "Bossy, aren't you?"

"Come down," he repeated calmly.

Ostentatiously tucking a strand of gray hair back into
its flyaway coronet, Maggie gathered the lace around her
and descended the ladder with great dignity. Dignity
shattered, however, when she reached the bottom. "Well?
What d'you want now?"

"I want to talk to you. Is there any more of that acid
you call coffee, or did we polish it off yesterday?"

"There's more." With only one keen, searching look
betraying interest, Maggie led the way back through the
maze of tall shelves to the big desk near the front door.
Shoving two books, a feather duster, and one bedraggled,
long-suffering tomcat off her creaky old chair, she sat down
and gestured toward the archaic little butane stove placed
nearby on the inevitable stack of books. A battered copper
pot resided on one of the two burners, its contents
bubbling merrily.

Hunter rummaged through a low cabinet for the two
cracked ceramic mugs they had used the day before and
then poured some of the evilly strong brew into them.

"Where d'you get this stuff?" he asked, pulling forward

the hard wooden chair that was the only other furniture in the place. "I haven't seen it anywhere else in the city."

Maggie sipped the coffee and gave him a sly smile. "A ship brings it in for me from time to time," she explained.

Hunter winced at his first taste of the bitter coffee and stared at her with suspicions aroused by her bland tone. "What kind of ship?"

"A pirate ship," she murmured.

About to warn her of the danger of dealing with pirates, he belatedly remembered just where she lived. Sighing, he said instead, "I suppose you know what you're doing."

"Never doubt it, young man." She grinned at him, then wiggled the first two fingers of her right hand at him. "Smoke," she demanded.

"They're bad for you," Hunter said automatically as he reached into the pocket of his tunic for the package of cigarettes he had scrounged for her the day before.

Maggie accepted a cigarette and a light from him, puffing away with obvious pleasure. "Of course they are," she agreed gravely. "That's why they're still around after centuries. Now—what was it you wanted to talk about?"

Hunter didn't hesitate; he told her the entire story of his meeting with the vendor and of his quest to prove the reality of the myth.

Listening intently, Maggie nonetheless seemed a bit distant, the keen blue eyes, encased in their network of fine wrinkles, darkened and oddly sad. Hunter, his story told, gazed at her curiously and, prodded by intuition, avoided asking her point-blank if she believed in the valley and the creatures it supposedly contained. Instead he hovered around the subject.

"I can't understand why I haven't heard of the valley before," he mused, watching her without appearing to. "If the unicorns exist, that is. And if they live in the valley every summer."

Maggie stirred slightly, her darkened gaze shifting to the black and bitter brew in her mug. "Winter is long on this planet," she murmured. "Summer comes only once every ten Standard years."

"Why is that?" He was asking more to keep her talking than out of any real interest.

"Something happened," she said, still murmuring. "Natural or man-made—who knows now? It was a long time ago. A very long time ago. But whatever it was, it ripped this planet right out of its normal orbit and into a vast elliptical orbit. And now this planet is near its star for weeks only. There's a brief Autumn. And then Winter comes. It's long . . . and cold . . . and dark."

Forcing himself to remain patient, Hunter waited.

After a moment, she stirred again and this time looked at him fiercely. "Give it up, Hunter," she said flatly. "Don't go up there."

"Why?" he asked softly.

"Because . . ." Her voice trailed away and she looked back into her mug. "Because some things were meant to remain . . . dreams."

"Why?" he repeated, honestly puzzled.

Maggie looked at him for a long moment, her old, lined face entirely without expression. Then she shook her head sadly. "That's something I suspect you'll have to discover for yourself. Because the answer doesn't come from the mind, but from the heart."

Hunter grappled with this cryptic speech in silence and in silence dismissed it. His determination remained. "What about the woman? Do you know anything about her?"

"Only what I've heard."

"Which is?"

Maggie recited in a deliberate litany. "She's a witch, a sorceress, a warrior. She has silver hair and dark eyes and beauty beyond description. She guards the unicorns with a fierce, selfless devotion, and has done so for ten thousand years."

Sensing something behind the deliberation of her recital, Hunter looked at the old woman intently. "And what do you think about that?"

"I?" Maggie shrugged. "I think most of it is rubbish, Hunter."

"Do you believe the woman exists?"

"Yes."

"But you don't believe she possesses powers?"

Maggie's smile was small and odd. "Oh, I believe she possesses powers. I believe that the truth, my stubborn, misguided friend, will make the legend a shabby tale. I believe that this woman, this 'Keeper,' is a truly unique being with extraordinary abilities. And I believe most strongly of all that if you find her, and survive the finding, you may very well be the destruction of her."

Shaken, Hunter murmured, "I? But—how?"

She looked at him, her stare searching, intent, and then sighed. "You were born to destroy some woman," she murmured. "And your Quest brought you here. If you reach that valley alive, I can think of only one reason the Keeper would allow you to live. And that will destroy her."

"What?" Hunter demanded. "What reason?"

Maggie sighed again, her gaze dropping to the dregs in her mug. "What reason?" she muttered to herself. "An ancient, endlessly troublesome reason. The reason kingdoms have toppled and empires fallen. The reason behind many wars and countless deaths. And for the Keeper, an especially great danger."

He frowned at her for a moment. Then the frown cleared and Hunter laughed with a heart-whole man's scorn. "Love?"

She glanced up at his face with hooded eyes. "You don't believe in love, my young friend?"

He gestured back over his shoulder, indicating the squalid city all around them. "You can buy it for the price of a drink out there," he said curtly. "Anytime, anywhere."

She lifted a faded eyebrow at him, something infinitely amused stirring in her old eyes. "Is that love?" she asked mildly.

Hunter felt a bit embarrassed after his unthinking remark, silently berating himself for speaking so bluntly to this old, odd, but dignified woman. But there was that amusement in her eyes, that curiously veiled expression, and he felt strangely compelled to respond honestly to her question.

He shrugged. "The only kind I understand," he said briefly.

"Now, that isn't true, you know." She spoke with faint sternness, as if to a child showing a regrettable lack of intelligence.

"What?" he said, blank.

"That you understand no other kind of love."

Hunter stared at her. With careful lightness, he asked, "Have you become a seeress, old woman?"

"I've become nothing I haven't always been, young man."

She wasn't making sense. Hunter told her so. "And I don't know what you're driving at—if anything," he ended flatly.

Maggie sighed with long-suffering patience. "You had parents, young man?" she asked . . . but it didn't sound like a question.

"Of course I had parents." Hunter displayed no patience, long-suffering or otherwise.

"On a world far away?"

"Relatively far," he said dryly.

Coolly, she said, "And were you born for the price of a drink?"

He stiffened, then relaxed as her point finally sank home. "No, dammit, Maggie. I wasn't. My parents were wed. Happily so. From all I've heard, at least. I never heard that either complained."

"A love match?"

"So I believe."

"Then you are aware of a kind of love not for sale?"

"You've made your point," he said. "You don't have to keep beating me over the head with it."

"I think perhaps I do," she murmured.

He stared at her. "Maggie, I asked a simple question. Which was, if I remember, what reason you thought this Keeper would have for letting me live. You said it would be love, and that it would destroy her. Correct?"

She considered. "Basically."

"Another simple question, if I may?"

"Why not?"

Hunter ignored her amused tone. "Why would this supposed love destroy the Keeper?"

Maggie studied him for a moment in silence, her shrewd old eyes probing him. "Love is a powerful shield," she said finally, neutrally. "And a powerful weapon."

He pondered that. "You didn't answer the question."

"Did I not?"

"Dammit, Maggie!"

She smiled just a little. "So impatient. It's a reckless fault of youth, and a potentially damning one." She sighed, saying with sudden rudeness, "I'm an old woman and you're pestering me! Go away."

"No," he said flatly.

She stared at him, the frown gone as swiftly as it had come. Her old, lined face became abruptly benign, guileless. "Stubborn," she noted almost cheerfully.

He proved the force of her observation by saying stubbornly, "Tell me what you meant about love destroying the Keeper."

Maggie pursed her lips. "Oh, love in and of itself could hardly hurt her, young man. But love for you—or, for that matter, any man—certainly could. And quite probably would."

"Why?"

"I told you I believed she was a unique being."

"Yes."

"But you didn't listen."

"Maggie—"

"Oh, you heard. But you didn't listen."

Hunter ran the fingers of one hand through his shaggy black hair and stared at her, baffled. "All right. I'm listening."

"*Unique*," she said instructively, "can be defined as being the only one of its kind, being without an equal or equivalent." She frowned a little. "I forget which dictionary. Anyway, that's a clear definition. Yes?"

"Yes."

"Think about that."

He did. "So?"

She shook her head, clearly impatient with him. "You haven't realized yet. Think . . . oh, think. Imagine that there's a living unicorn standing here in the room with us. And realize that it's the only one of its kind."

Hunter thought, imagined. And the little boy who had dreamed of the horned mythical beast felt awe creep through him, the adult man. Slowly he said, "The only one. With no possible future for its race."

Maggie nodded quickly. "Like the Keeper."

He frowned. "She's supposed to be a woman."

"Let's say for the sake of argument that she's a very *unique* woman. With a unique heritage and a responsibility no other woman could bear. Let's say that her entire life, her being, is concerned with—and only with—guarding the unicorns and keeping them safe."

He nodded, accepting that.

"And man is the enemy," Maggie said softly.

"Not all men," he said without thinking.

"No?" She gestured, much as he had earlier, to indicate the city outside the library. "Huntmen live here, young man. Every Summer they assault the valley. Every Summer they attempt to kill unicorns. And only the Keeper stands between them and extinction. She knows only the men who enter her valley. Do you still believe all men aren't her enemy?"

Reluctantly seeing the truth, Hunter said, "She won't give her trust easily."

"She won't give her total trust until she loves."

"But . . . love will destroy her?" He shook his head impatiently. "We're going in circles. I *still* don't understand why you think loving a man would destroy her!"

"Because she guards the unicorns."

Hunter waited for the rest of the answer. But it didn't come.

"That's it?" he questioned. "Love will destroy her because she guards the unicorns?"

"That's it."

Hunter put his face in his hands, the muffled sound escaping him indicative of despair.

There was no answering flicker of amusement in Maggie's old eyes; she was troubled. "So much was lost," she murmured. "So many pieces of the story. You search for a myth you don't even understand. And, oh, the danger in that."

He lifted his head, glaring at her.

She was gazing intently down into her mug, as if the muddy dregs were whispering to her. Abruptly she said, "Why don't you return to your world, Hunter, and wear the crown you were born for?" He stiffened, hearing something new in her tone even more surprising than her words, something curiously powerful.

Carefully he said, "What're you talking about, Maggie?" Since princes were valuable to men who thought of ransom, Hunter had kept that part of his identity a secret— as, no doubt, Boran had.

"You left a kingdom behind you," she said almost idly.

Hunter kept all expression from his face. Lightly he said, "You're talking more and more like a seeress, old woman."

She looked hard at him, and that same elusively powerful *something* was in her old eyes. Her suddenly very, very old eyes.

Unaccountably, Hunter felt distinctly unnerved. "Don't tell me you believe in that garbage?" he questioned, less casual than he would have liked. "Crystal balls and the like?"

"I need no crystal ball, Hunter," she said mildly.

After a moment, he said, "You knew I was a prince. How?"

"Does it matter how I knew?"

"I . . . I think it does."

Maggie shrugged. "You wouldn't understand. Not now. One day, perhaps, but not now. It matters only that I know." She looked at him with those veiled eyes. "What would you say if I told you that I was very, very certain that you hold the power to destroy the Keeper . . . and the unicorns?"

"I wouldn't believe you," he said firmly.

"You think yourself so unworthy of love?" she asked blandly.

He started slightly, his mind hurrying to catch up to hers. Then he remembered. Love for a man would destroy

the Keeper. "What I meant," he said slowly, "was that I
wouldn't believe that I would . . . destroy her or the
unicorns."

"Obsession," she said obliquely, "is blind."

A sudden intense question forced itself up from the
depths of Hunter's puzzlement. "Who are you, Maggie?"

"If I told you I was a seeress?"

"I'd have a hard time believing that."

"Well, I'm not," she said abruptly. "More than that.
And less. Akin to that. But different."

The safe haven of the library seemed suddenly to
Hunter an uncertain, potentially dangerous place. His
warrior's senses told him that there was something here,
some power he couldn't fathom.

Maggie was smiling at him. "Like all men," she said
softly, "you scorn or fear what you don't understand."

"I'm not like *all men*," he denied, disliking being
labeled.

Unexpectedly, she agreed. "No, you're not like all
men. You left a kingdom filled with riches to go in search of
yourself."

"I'm searching for myth," he said instantly.

"You're searching for yourself, young man," she corrected placidly. "Whoever sent you on your Quest was
wise. You've found pieces of yourself here and there, and
your Quest is not now what it began as. Now you search for
a dream as salvation to your people, rather than merely as a
means to gain a throne. And you search, still, for yourself.
Oh, you'll find the myth first, I think. But you won't
understand it. You'll have to find all of yourself before you'll
be able to understand."

"You speak in riddles!" he snapped.

"Do I?" she murmured, studying him. She saw a man
in the physical prime of his life, strong and proud. She saw,
more clearly than another would have seen, the searching
look in his cool green eyes. She saw the level, inborn
command of those eyes, and the guardedness of too many
years of living with danger. And she saw, in the sharp-
honed stillness of his face, the look of rooted obsession,
blind obsession.

She wondered about the Keeper.

The Keeper would have to be strong.

She voiced a cool warning, watching his face for the effect it would have. "You'll destory all that you seek if you aren't careful. Very careful."

"I'm a cautious man," he said flatly.

Maggie wasn't happy with what she observed on his face. Oh, yes, she thought, the Keeper must be very strong!

"This possibly mythical Keeper we've been discussing. Does she exist?" he asked in a hard tone.

But Maggie would say no more. She sat there in silence, an old woman with old, wise eyes, gazing into the dregs of coffee brought to her by pirates. She said nothing, not even good-bye, and that disturbed Hunter more than he wanted to admit to himself.

He left the library with a strong feeling of disquiet, his mind toying with the enigma of its guardian. There was something about the old woman that was almost frightening. That odd, elusive power. And she knew . . . too much. She knew about a crownless prince half a galaxy away from his own world. She knew about a Keeper of unicorns she'd never met—or had she? Hunter wondered suddenly. Was that why she seemed to know so much about the woman who guarded the unicorns? Because she had been to the valley?

Hunter unconsciously grasped that possible answer with some relief. That answer was understandable, believable. Not impossible.

That answer made sense.

It was the other, elusive answer that was unnerving. Hunter didn't believe in magic. He didn't believe in killer mountains vested with human emotions. He didn't believe in ten-thousand-year-old women with the power to drive men mad. He didn't believe that an old librarian could gaze into the past or the future with stark clarity.

He didn't, in fact, really believe in unicorns. Not really. Not anymore.

So a crownless prince named Hunter threaded his way through the drunken, stoned, or just plain mad inhabitants of the Huntman's city, his mind wholly occupied with the possibility of finding a myth that he thought now he didn't really believe in. He retrieved his pack from the hiding place he'd found earlier, checking its contents carefully. It was all there. The threadbare clothing he never bothered to replace until it was completely worn out. He traveled lightly. And the ring was there. The ring he'd never worn.

He shouldered the pack and stood for a moment, gazing up at The Reaper that towered balefully above the city.

Killer mountains!

Indestructible Keepers destroyed by love!

It wouldn't take long, he thought, to discover if there was indeed a valley beyond that mountain. And a Keeper. And unicorns. Not long at all. Then he could shake the filthy dust of this place from his booted heels. Travel back overland to the coast, where he'd hidden his ship. Follow the next elusive trail to myth.

Because, of course, there was nothing but more war-blasted desert beyond that black mountain.

Nothing at all.

Especially unicorns.

Hunter shifted the pack more comfortably on his strong back and set out purposefully for the appointed meeting with a shifty-eyed vendor, and with a Huntman who had . . . perhaps . . . captured a myth.

King was a man with secrets in his eyes. He sat in an overstuffed chair by a cold and empty fireplace, the only light in the room coming faintly through dirty, uncurtained windowpanes. He ignored Hunter, as he'd ignored his entrance hours before and his persistent questions since.

Ignored him as one would ignore a buzzing insect.

Hunter had literally forced the monkeylike vendor to bring him here after the little man had arrived, terrified, at their meeting to whisper that King wanted no visitors. The vendor had led him to this small, unkempt house and then scuttled away, vanishing into the depths of the city. And Hunter, one hand guardedly on his knife, had walked boldly in.

As hours passed and his voice hoarsened by repeated questions, Hunter tried to gain some sense of his unwilling host. But there was nothing. King exuded no life-force, no sense of personality. He seemed a slate wiped clean, a flat, one-dimensional image without animation. No question won so much as a flicker of response from him.

But there were secrets and horrors in his eyes. Of that Hunter was sure.

He was a big man, nearly as large as Hunter, with a full red beard shadowing his craggy face and gray eyes as dim and impenetrable as dense fog. He seemed oddly unreal, the innate power of his muscular body held captive by utter stillness.

And Hunter wondered if the legendary Keeper of the unicorns had done this to him. And if so, how.

Finally, in desperation, Hunter stood between King and the cold fireplace which seemed to hold his entire attention, and quietly, clearly, told the Huntman a story about a world with an empty throne and two princes. And of a man who had discovered, in his quest for that throne, the vital necessity of myth, the need of his world for dreams. He told of the years since and a long search, sparing nothing of himself in his need to get through to King and learn how to reach that valley. He talked of the need of protection for the unicorns and of his desire to prove that they existed so that they could be granted that protection.

If there was myth . . . he had to find it.

Especially this particular myth, dreamed of in boyhood and revered on so many worlds . . . this myth that was the cost of a throne.

So immersed was he in the telling that Hunter didn't realize for quite a while that he had finally won King's attention. The Huntman was looking up at him, gray eyes still impenetrable but fixed on his face nonetheless. No emotion stirred the craggy face, but King was listening.

Stressing his intention to prove the unicorns' existence and disclaiming any desire to harm them, Hunter asked one last time for the secret to finding the valley.

The Huntman was still, his eyes watchful. Then,

abruptly, he gestured in simple sign language for Hunter to
come back in the morning.

Hunter hesitated for an instant, finally inclining his
head in reluctant acceptance. He had said all that he could
to convince King. Halting briefly at the door, he quietly
reminded the Huntman of one important fact.

"Only a few weeks of Summer are left. I don't have
very much time."

No sound or gesture answered him, and Hunter
turned away from the man whose haunted eyes were like
the broken window of an empty house.

Restraining impatience, tightly leashing hope, Hunter
passed the night restlessly. He was back at King's house the
next morning when dawn had barely lightened the sky and
found the older man on his feet but still coldly withdrawn.
Before Hunter could ask, King pointed to a roughly drawn
map lying on an otherwise bare table.

Eagerly studying the map for long moments, Hunter
looked up to ask suddenly, "Does she exist? The Keeper?"

Something very like pain tightened the big Huntman's
features for a brief moment. He turned away abruptly,
seemingly gazing out a dingy window and once again
ignoring Hunter's very presence.

Hunter looked down at the map, seeing suddenly
something he had missed in his first perusal. In the upper
right hand corner of the yellowed paper was shakily drawn
the universal symbol of danger: a skull and crossbones.

He sent a sharp stare toward the immobile man.
"Danger? From the Keeper?"

King made no move, no sound.

After a moment, realizing he'd get nothing more from
the man, Hunter quietly unfastened his money pouch,
laying it on the table before turning for the door. He sent a
last look at the still, silent figure of the older man, unable to
voice his thanks because of something he sensed rather
than saw. And what he sensed was a man on the rack.
Silently, he left.

Long minutes passed after the soft sound of the closing
door, then King turned from the window. He went to a
shelf, barren save for a small, cracked mirror. Lifting the

mirror, he stared for a moment into eyes with ghosts in
them. Ghosts of pain. Terror. Regret.

He swallowed hard and slowly opened his mouth,
gazing into the dark cavern where a gaping wound could be
seen.

King had no tongue.

He dropped the mirror to the floor and crushed the
shards beneath his boots.

Mother?
Daughter?
A man comes.
Men have come before, daughter.
But this man . . .
Is different?
Yes. He comes alone. He comes . . .
Out of greed?
No. Yes. A different kind of greed.
He searches?
Yes. For truth.
He hungers?
For truth.
Such men are dangerous, daughter. Take care.
Mother?
Daughter?
He has green eyes . . .
Take care, daughter.

He looked at the men with him, the Huntmen lured
here by promises of wealth beyond description. He was,
dimly, surprised that they had survived the journey into the
valley but supposed that greed could lend strength. They
were hardly a prepossessing lot. Still, he only needed tools,
and they would do.

"The sorceress knows we're here!" one of them hissed
fearfully. "She always knows."

"Not this time." Boran smiled faintly as he recalled a
plundered laboratory on a distant world and the secrets he
had found there. The amulet he wore around his neck was

one such device, designed to amplify his own considerable
psi abilities; the sorceress would not be able to sense his
presence, nor that of anyone near him. At best, she would
only sense a darkness, a blank spot in her valley.

Until he was ready to confront her.

The Huntmen looked at one another, and then at him.
Cautiously, one ventured, "She won't know?"

"If you remain near me, no," Boran answered, his soft
voice even and emotionless.

The Huntman who had asked the question felt a chill
crawl over his flesh. Boran wore a smile often, and spoke
softly, but there was something quietly horrible in that
smile and that voice. And he had not even seemed to notice
when one of the Huntmen had lost his grip on the rope
during their journey and had fallen, screaming dreadfully,
to bounce and tumble down the black slope of The Reaper.

"Hand me the glass," Boran ordered.

The Huntman fished it from his pack and handed it
over, taking care not to touch the twisted, constantly
beckoning hand. His flesh crawled again, and he wished
suddenly that he had remained in the city.

He thought it was safer down there. . . .

Boran studied the valley below, measuring with a
warrior's eye, seeking places of concealment and ambush.

First the Triad. Age. Strength. Youth.

He had the Strength, taken from King; only a tiny
portion of it was gone, but even that slight loss *was* a loss.

He wanted it all.

Fury reddened his mind for a moment until he caught
the scarlet wisps and dragged them behind mental doors.
No time for that now. He could bide his time until the
moment for fury came.

He needed power if his plans were to succeed; the
Triad was that power. As the possessor of the Triad, he
would be invincible. The craving for power surged within
him, hot and violent and pleasing. It traveled the twisted
corridors of his mind and spread a hellish glow.

Power. To take a throne and rule a world.

Power. To settle debts and even scores.

His right hand lifted to touch the side of his face.

Sensitive fingertips felt skin of a dead-wood hardness, furrowed and pitted; his cheek felt nothing of the fingers' touch. The left hand, curved stiffly around the glass, was as dead as half his face. Dead. Murdered. He didn't curse aloud, but oaths too bitterly felt for simple words coiled and writhed within him.

Power to settle debts. Power to even scores.

Two

Hunter slowly climbed the almost vertical side of The Reaper. He tried to use outcroppings of rock and sparse bushes as handholds, rather than depending on the rope anchored precariously far above him, because a cautious—and perhaps superstitious—voice within warned him that although The Reaper was not alive, of course, it was nonetheless malevolent. He had used a large rock to scratch curiously into the black surface of the mountain, oddly chilled to discover that the soil beneath was blood-red, as if with a deadly stain.

Shoving the eerie observation aside, Hunter paused for a moment in the long, hard climb, wedging himself into an unwelcoming niche to ease the strain in his arms. He rested there, gazing over the land spread out below him. The Huntmen's city appeared even more squalid, not even distance able to elevate it to something near beauty. Smoke from innumberable cooking fires rose like a dirty gray banner above the jagged tops of shorn-off buildings and hung listlessly in the air, defeated.

All around the bleak and barren city sprawled a landscape pitted and scarred after thousands of years of too much misuse, neglect, and war. A more ugly, inhospitable land ·Hunter had never seen.

Briefly and objectively, he wondered how in hell he expected to find a fragile and elusive myth just beyond these mountains. It was not only an unrealistic expectation, it was a ludicrous one. But Hunter had followed fainter trails in his quest, and since *impossible* had been his watchword from the beginning, he could hardly complain now.

Sighing, he took a firmer grip on his rope and pried himself from the niche, swinging free for a heart-stopping minute before his scrabbling boots found an almost invisible crack. Sweat trickled into his eyes, blinding him with a stinging haze. Sacrificing a moment of time and a bit of balance, he managed to wipe his eyes on the rough material covering his arm; the movement caused him to bang painfully against the rock and nearly lose his grip on the rope. Hanging there with his aching shoulder pressed against the unyielding stone, Hunter quietly and fluently cursed The Reaper.

But he kept going.

He was some sixty feet from his goal when a sudden gust of wind yanked him away from the cliff, pounded him against it twice, and then swept him sideways in a pendulum motion. Hunter cursed breathlessly, riding out the punishment with gritted teeth. He listened to the wind as it began howling all around him, remembering the vendor's comparison of the sound to a "soulless devil."

He fought the wind, fought it fiercely with every ounce of strength and determination he possessed. It seemed a living thing, snatching at him and taunting him shrilly as he climbed. It shrieked in his ears, first pulling him away from the cliff and then slamming him against it.

Then, abruptly, it was gone. Bruised, battered, his breath rasping harshly in his raw throat, Hunter climbed blindly for a few moments without realizing that the wind had abandoned him. It was only when his gloved hands reached the knot holding his rope around the peculiarly shaped jutting rock that he realized dimly he had won. He hauled his aching body the last foot, bracing his back against the rock and sitting astride the saddlelike doorway into the valley.

Automatically flexing his stiff fingers, he rested his forehead on an upraised knee for a moment, eyes wearily closed. Only when he had regained his breath did Hunter raise his head and look—with an inner warning to himself not to be disappointed—down into the valley.

Dizzily, crazily, time and space shifted. He was momentarily straddling two worlds and didn't know which was real. There was nothing gradual to acclimate the mind and spare the senses. No warning at all. Below on his right lay a barren wasteland. Below on his left lay paradise.

The Reaper itself was nearly as inhospitable on the valley side—but not quite. The jagged, blackened rock remained true for roughly half its height, the bottom becoming rolling hills dotted with flowering plants and covered with a carpet of brilliant emerald. A sparkling stream flowed lazily among the hills and out into the valley, forming a small lake.

Without realizing he was doing so, Hunter held his breath as he looked out over the valley itself and thought that if unicorns did exist, this surely must be the sort of place where they would be found.

There was an abundance of flowers and flowering plants, grasses waving gently in the clean-smelling breeze, and the happy sounds of birds chirping in contentment. Completely ringed by mountains, the valley was huge and beautiful and as rare in its setting as a diamond among dirty lumps of coal.

Squinting against the hot sun he was only vaguely aware of, Hunter searched all within his range of vision with the hungry eyes of a man obsessed. His gaze quartered the valley methodically, his first elation dimming when he saw no sign of movement other than plants and birds. Then he concentrated on the forest covering nearly half the valley, the far half, and the little lake which marked its beginning.

Around the lake were tall and stately hardwood trees,

their leaves the varied summer shades of green. Beneath the trees and bathed in patterns of sunlight and shadow was a small cabin.

Hunter focused on the cabin, his pent-up breath escaping in a soft sigh. His goal, he decided, was the cabin. And if a dark-eyed, silver-haired woman met him there with weapon or magic . . .

Briskly putting the incompleted thought from his mind, Hunter pulled his rope up, neatly coiled it, and then dropped it down on the valley side of The Reaper. Only then did he look down at what would be his path of descent, and the blood chilled in his veins.

A single glance around the valley had told him that this saddlelike doorway was, indeed, its only entrance, all else being sheer, concave cliffs far too high for any human being even to begin a descent by rope. But the sheer rock face below him was also concave, cut raggedly into The Reaper's base as if water had swirled angrily around and around the valley for aeons and then allowed lightning to blast narrow ridges and bottomless canyons in the rock.

Hunter realized wryly that he had let his first elation blind him to the hazards still ahead. He rested on his haunches for long moments, hanging on to his rope and leaning suicidally far out over the cliff edge. He could easily see the bottom sloping out, with wicked ridges boasting what looked like jagged shards of granite gradually turning into the gently rolling hills his eyes had first seen. His rope dangled just above one of those jagged ridges and far above the safety of the hills; he would have to traverse the last killing feet without the aid of the rope.

Assuming he got that far.

Leaning still farther out, he noted idly that the stream winding through the valley began as a wellspring pumped apparently from deep within The Reaper. He tried to get some idea of what awaited him between the top of the concave cliff and its bottom, but found that there was no way of knowing until he actually went over the edge.

So he did.

And as soon as he was hanging twenty feet from the top of the cliff, Hunter knew he was in trouble. Wasting no

breath or energy for panting or swearing, he kept his eyes
fastened on the razor-sharp rock that was even now cutting
into his rope with vicious speed. The unpredictable wind
that had dogged his ascent had returned, swinging his body
inward toward the rock wall and pinning it there; jagged
stone immediately began shredding the material covering
his knees and elbows, and he felt the muscles of his legs and
back protest in agony as he somehow managed to place his
booted feet firmly enough to push away from the cliff. The
wind fought him for every inch, and every movement he
made caused the rope above him to fray from its contact
with cutting granite.

Gritting his teeth until his jaws ached, Hunter used all
the discipline and strength at his command to ignore the
wind and the fraying rope as he began lowering himself
with reckless, inhuman speed. He didn't think of the rocky
coffin waiting below to cradle his broken body for all
eternity. He thought only of the unicorns, and the end, one
way or the other, of a long search.

He thought he would make it. After endless aeons of
straining muscles crying out for relief, he felt the lightness
in the rope that meant he was nearing the end of it, and his
sweat-blinded eyes turned toward the bottom and the end
of an agonizing race.

Then, abruptly, he was out of time, perhaps out of life
itself, because the rope gave way and he was falling, falling
into the mouth of a hungry, rocky hell. Instinctively he
tried to turn his body, tried to land on his feet with at least
an even chance for survival. But there was still no time, and
no room at all to turn in because the first touch of rock was a
brutal blow to his head and Hunter knew no more.

He thought he woke once or twice, thought he fought
his way up through swirling black mist and fiery flashes of
pain. He forced leaden eyelids to lift, seeing a crimson haze
and understanding with a vast indifference that it was his
own blood he was looking through. He felt nothing now, no
pain and no cares, only a vague sort of curiosity. Blackness
claimed him again.

The second waking—if waking it was—was accom-

panied this time by a pain so great that it wrung a hoarse
groan from his lips. Again he forced reluctant eyes to open,
the earlier crimson streamers gradually washed away by
tears of agony until he could see sunlight. He was conscious
of icy water flowing all around him and of rocks digging into
his body like the points of a dozen knives.

Some logical part of his mind unmaddened by pain
told him that he was in shock and losing blood fast. And that
same ruthlessly disinterested voice told him that he didn't
really see a golden spiral waving with hypnotic slowness
before his eyes. Ignoring the voice because he wanted to,
because he was unwilling to die without *knowing*, Hunter
tried to turn his head to see the unicorn that would prove a
child's dream. A sheet of white-hot agony made every other
pain he had ever felt before a pleasure, and the blackness
took him.

From a very great distance, he idly noted that the
water was cold and the sun hot. There was silence broken
only by the soft chirp of birds. And then there were other
sounds, faint and puzzling sounds. Scrabbling sounds like
hooves on rock, and a sweet, familiar, grassy smell accompanied by warm breath on his face.

And then there was a voice, a voice that was gentle for
all its violent, angry words, and musical beyond belief. He
tried to fight his way back up through the blackness because
he wanted to meet the voice, but the effort seemed to drive
the lovely sound away, and Hunter felt a strange grief that
he would never know that face behind it. Something
touched his shoulder, something warm and firm, and his
skin tingled pleasantly. The pain faded until it was somewhere on the fringes of himself, and as it went the void of
its leaving was filled with a sudden implacable determination.

Hunter was dying; he knew that the retreat of pain
meant the retreat of life and the coming of Death. And he
refused to accept it. His mind was clear and cold. He
gathered together every scrap of will, every thread of
determination, flinging both into Death's face with a savage
laugh that emerged from his throat raggedly and brought
back the pain.

He clung to the pain fiercely, embraced it, welcomed it because it meant the retreat of Death. He sank beneath the waves of pain, exultant because Death had given up its hold on him.

———————

Boran watched almost constantly. From his vantage point there was an unobstructed view of the valley below. He could not see far into the forest, of course, but he could see the cabin.

His breath had quickened at first sight of the herd, but he had made no move toward the valley. When he saw the sorceress, his fingers went ivory-knuckled around the spyglass. Holding his mind carefully blank, he watched throughout the day, studying as many of her habits as possible. She moved among her charges, a touch here, a pat there. She played a brief game of chase with the smallest of the herd.

He watched that one a long time.

The sorceress left his sight for a while, reappearing on the far side of the valley; he realized she was patrolling watchfully. He noted she carried no weapon. No *visible* weapon, at any rate.

He watched until night fell and a lamp flickered within the cabin. Then he rose, stretching cramped limbs, ignoring pain. He was very good at ignoring pain. His hand lifted to touch the hard left side of his face, fingers tracing the deep, immovable furrows that had replaced once-firm, pliable flesh. Almost lovingly, his fingers probed.

Some men, through the passage of time, forgot their reasons to hate. Boran had not, and he would never forget.

Boran had not been certain what form his revenge would take until he had focused his spyglass on the sorceress. The perfect, unmarred beauty of her face rose before his mind's eye now as he fingered his own petrified flesh, tracing the hardness where it began above his brow and ended at the base of his neck.

How different her skin would feel! Like golden velvet. He imagined that soft skin beneath his touch. He thought of that lovely face flushed with anger, then pale with horror and revulsion as his heavy body covered her helpless one.

He saw her black eyes wild with terror and pain and grief as he destroyed her. Destroyed her ability to guard her charges. Destroyed her most precious possession. Destroyed her beauty.

He wondered if Hunter knew just how vulnerable the sorceress was to maleness; it was possible, but not probable. He himself had found that bit of knowledge on a distant world Hunter had not visited. Only a virgin could hold the trust of the unicorns. Only a virgin. . . .

There were worse fates than death.

Then he frowned a little. Was there a better way? Taking, after all, was easy. To persuade the sorceress to give, however, that was another matter. Boran fingered the amulet around his neck and then glanced toward the men crouching around the low fire. Silently, he commanded. And watched as one of the men stood up, turned three times, and then sat down again. There was no expression on his face, and the others showed no awareness of what he had done.

Boran smiled. Her mind would be stronger than these, of course, but not so strong that he could not control it.

Yes.

His chuckle, an incongruously pleasant sound to emerge from the distorted lips, was soft in the still night air. Such a lonely place, this valley. And so many long and lonely Winters she must have faced. But if she allowed Hunter to live . . . if she accepted his presence in her life because of his desire to find myth alive and walking . . . then perhaps she would remember those lonely winters.

Boran smiled. Yes. But he had to be cautious. The sorceress had power. He would have to control her carefully, search for the strengths and weaknesses of her mind.

Standing in the darkness, he pondered the possible emotional state of the sorceress. Her valley had been seriously threatened only once this Summer; she was probably complacent. On her guard, but not inordinately so. Hunter would become the first chink in her defenses, and Boran had only to wait, and watch it happen.

The second day of watching brought Hunter to the valley.

Boran watched through the spyglass as the sorceress emerged from the cabin very early, and he heard the eerie whistle she sent winging across the valley. He saw the herd turn instantly for the forest—all except one. The one, obviously the oldest and leader of the herd, stood firm. The sorceress was very still—Boran felt a tickling near the back of his head and strove to build his wall higher—then she turned abruptly, clear anger and worry in every line of her slender body, and followed the leaderless herd into the forest.

She returned to the meadow later and stared at the motionless leader. More tickling; Boran ignored it. It was clear to him that the single unicorn refused to follow some order of the sorceress, and he frowned as he realized that she did indeed know there was a threat to the valley. He wasn't concerned that his presence had been discovered, but her ability to be forewarned disturbed him; he would have to be careful.

He would have to remember that particular power, try to discover if he could somehow confuse or cloud that ability. He could. Of course he could. The amulet would be his tool to accomplish it.

He watched her go back into the cabin, watched the leader cross the valley and disappear behind a jumble of boulders, then raised the spyglass and began searching across the valley where King's path lay. It was nearly two hours later that he saw Hunter reach the saddlelike crest of the path.

Boran saw every move Hunter made. He saw the man sit for a moment, recovering from the climb, saw with pleasure his bruises and exhaustion. He watched him begin the descent into the valley and saw instantly that the descent was doomed.

He saw Hunter fall.

Bitterness rose sickly in his mind. No. That death would steal half his revenge. He cursed softly, tonelessly, his good eye fixed to the spyglass, staring at the motionless, broken body cradled by granite. He swore at gods abandoned long ago and far away for depriving him of half his revenge.

Then his good eye blinked and stared more fiercely into the lens. The leader of the herd had approached the broken body—and it stirred faintly. Boran held his breath. Not dead! Not yet. He watched the leader turn and move away, its speed uncanny as it raced toward the cabin.

Boran followed the creature with his glass, seeing the sorceress emerge from the cabin with one hand held to her head as the leader reached her. She swayed slightly. Then she straightened her shoulders, her beautiful features angry and pale. She followed instantly as the leader turned and both made their way toward the fallen man.

He felt hope rise in him as he watched the sorceress bend over the broken body, watched her quickly fashion a litter from strong limbs and strips of cloth fetched hastily from the woods and the cabin. He saw the leader submit quietly to being hitched to the litter bearing the unconscious man, and followed their progress back across the meadow to the cabin.

When the walls of the cabin finally hid the little drama from sight, Boran sat back and lowered the glass. He would have to wait now, wait and discover if the sorceress's powers could yank a man back from death. Wait and find out if she would use those powers to save an enemy.

Boran hoped that she would, for he could think of only one reason why she would do something so alien to her life and responsibilities. And that reason boded well for his plans.

If Hunter lived.

Three

The ceiling was heavily beamed. Hunter studied it thoughtfully for moments or hours, his mind a limbo in which nothing but the ceiling mattered. It was a good ceiling, he decided finally, and having come to that decision, he abandoned it. Tentatively he allowed his senses to reach for more information, unsure if he were ready to absorb it. A bed. He was in a bed and warmly covered with heavy quilts. The scratchy feeling told him that he was naked beneath the covers, a fact which disturbed him on some deep and utterly male level. The constricted sensation around his head seemed a sure indication of a bandage of some kind, but Hunter felt no pain. Only an intolerable weakness.

Fighting the weakness, he made a single attempt to push himself up on his elbows, a bitten-off groan of frustration emerging from him when his arms refused to support him. He released a stream of smoking curses, relieved to note that his tongue was still capable of speech.

"Cheerful when you wake up, aren't you?" the Voice questioned coldly.

Through sheer effort of will, Hunter managed to raise his head a few inches, and quick hands banked pillows behind him for support. He stared up into eyes as dark and, at the moment, just as malevolent as The Reaper.

Silver hair fell in a shining a curtain to her tiny waist, framing a face that was as delicately beautiful and fragile as the crystal flowers he remembered from a faraway world and a distant past. Her brows winged upward, like her huge eyes, lending her a mysteriously feline gaze. And her face had the serenity of a cat's, the proud and sure confidence of certain self-knowledge. In spite of the fierce anger of her dark eyes, there was a gentleness in her that Hunter could sense more than see.

Though tall and slender, her body was ripe with the rich curves of womanhood, and the black garment which covered her from neck to knees emphasized rather than concealed the fact. The garment had full sleeves caught tight at the wrists and fit like a second skin everywhere else. Lacings ran from her waist to her throat, leaving a crisscross pattern of black over creamy golden flesh and the shadowed valley between her firm breasts. The pants were tucked into boots made of some woven material.

Weak though he was, Hunter felt a flush of sensation, his numbed body coming to life with a will of its own as his loins swelled and hardened. His tongue tangled in his throat as he stared up at her, the assurance of nearly thirty years disappearing and leaving him as speechless as a schoolboy.

The lady made up the lack. Easily.

"You've been out for three days," she told him, her cold voice a startling contrast to her gentle face. "And just as soon as you can stand up without falling on your face, you're out again. Out of my valley. Do you understand?"

Hunter blinked, trying to reconcile the icy voice with the picture of delicate beauty standing before him.

"Do you understand?" she demanded again fiercely.

"Yes," he murmured.

"How strong do you feel?"

Before Hunter could attempt an answer, the lady bent

forward and calmly swept the quilts from the bed and from his naked body.

Being a man, there was no possible way for Hunter to hide his body's reaction to the lovely woman, and she could hardly have missed seeing it. He was a big man in every physical sense, and his manhood was boldly erect with desire. But she said not a word, and her face changed neither expression nor color. While he felt the rush of heat to his face and silently, uselessly, commanded his body to obey him, she merely turned aside for a brief moment to pick up a bundle lying on a stool next to the bed. Then she composedly began to dress him in his clothing.

He nearly groaned aloud at the touch of her cool, firm hands and clamped his back teeth together fiercely in an effort to control a wild, raging hunger. He quite literally lacked the strength to obey his body's need, but that did nothing to diminish the throbbing arousal. He was going to disgrace himself if she didn't stop touching him, he realized, with the astonishment of a man who had never lost control in his adult life. Desperately he tried to think of anything but her hands.

Hunter would realize later that she had repaired the ravages his journey had inflicted on his clothes, but for the moment he was occupied only with inflamed senses. She pulled him into a sitting position on the bed, leaving him dizzy, weak, and furious at his own helplessness. Brisk, businesslike, and matter-of-fact, she inserted him into undergarment, pants, and the full-sleeved shirt which looked whiter than it had in quite some time. She didn't hesitate to touch any part of his body, and Hunter forced himself to concentrate on a formula for spacial navigation, reciting coordinates while he stared fixedly across the room at the stone fireplace. Then she pulled him to his feet.

And if she hadn't caught him with a slender and amazingly strong arm, Hunter would have fallen flat on his face.

Silently, while he cursed softly and breathlessly, she lowered him so that he was sitting on the bed again.

"Want these off again, or shall I leave them on?" She gestured at his clothes.

"On," he answered hastily, aware of the constricted tightness of his trousers but unwilling to chance her hands on him again.

The woman banked pillows at the head of the bed and deftly arranged him against them so that he was half sitting before pulling the quilts back over his now-clothed lower body. He stood head and shoulders above the average man and weighed correspondingly, and she handled his body, he thought with astonishment, as if he were a child.

It was a peculiar sensation. And not at all welcome.

"Tomorrow," she said suddenly, flatly. "You'll leave tomorrow." Then she turned away.

Hunter fought against a final wave of dizziness, shaking his head slightly to clear it. He reached up with a probing touch to find that his head was indeed bandaged. But there was no pain. Anywhere. Except in his achingly full loins, a pain caused by her rather than by the fall. He couldn't remember seeing a bruise or a scratch on his body, which puzzled him greatly. Surely he should have been a mass of cuts and bruises, to say nothing of broken bones? The pain had been everywhere. . . .

Pushing the memory and the question aside, he looked up, his eyes following the woman as she moved around the cabin's single room. And she moved with eerie grace, with the smooth, coordinated, uncalculated rhythm of motion perfected. She made not a sound, her booted feet touching the hardwood floor as though they were the soundless pads of a stalking predator. Hunter shifted uncomfortably, astonished by his unusually instantaneous arousal but understanding the cause.

God, she was beautiful! He hadn't seen her like on a hundred worlds, and he had never wanted a woman as he wanted her.

She crossed back to him as he watched, and he silently accepted the cup filled with water she had drawn from a wooden keg in one corner. He noticed that she avoided, now, any touch, and that her eyes had closed down to something hostile and coldly guarded.

He drank the water gratefully, feeling relief as the parched membranes in his throat relaxed, loosened. And watched as she went over to stir something in a black cooking pot over a low fire in the rough stone hearth.

The silence bothered him. Badly.

"You probably saved my life. I want to thank you," he ventured finally, his voice sounding unnaturally loud to him.

"You can thank me by leaving," she responded curtly, without turning to face him.

Hunter stared at her perfect profile. Haunting beauty. No wonder the Huntmen thought her a sorceress. "I came here to—"

"I know why you came."

"I'm not a Huntman," he said quietly, and was ignored. He tried again. "I came to find the unicorns—though not to harm them," he added swiftly. "My name is Hunter Morgan and I . . . I just want to find the unicorns." The last words were hopelessly inadequate, he thought, but it was difficult to address half of a beautiful face. Quite deliberately, he lowered his voice to a drawl he had been told was quite charming. "What's your name?"

Somewhat to his surprise, she replied, "Siri."

"A lovely name. For a lovely lady."

She tossed him one scathing, contemptuous look, and Hunter immediately felt very small. *So much for your vaunted charm, fool!* Still smarting beneath the sting of his earlier embarrassed helplessness and the vulnerability of his desire, he nonetheless refused to give in to anger. Evenly, he said, "You are beautiful. Incredibly beautiful. And I'd think the same even if I weren't trespassing in your damned valley."

He thought he saw her shoulders stiffen and then loosen in an oddly defeated movement, but couldn't be sure. Restless in spite of—or perhaps because of—his weakness, Hunter was determined that this beautiful, cold woman would talk to him. He was certain that the coldness was a facade; the underlying gentleness he sensed had to be the real Siri, and he wanted to know that woman, wanted to know her with an intensity that surprised him. It was more than desire for her,

Shock tactics, he thought. "I saw a unicorn," he said

flatly, hazy memory fueled by inner certainty and flung at her, and this time he was positive that she tensed and then slumped in defeat.

"Cloud," she said almost inaudibly.

Hunter felt tension steal through his own body. "Cloud?"

Siri abandoned her cooking, half-turning to face him and leaning against the stone hearth. Her arms hung loosely at her sides, the posture giving the man a still stronger sense of her defeat. "Cloud. He leads the herd. He found you and guided me to you. I knew you were here, but I didn't know where."

"How did you know I was here?" he asked.

"I felt your pain," she said simply, the cold mask of her face at odds with the gentle, tired voice.

"You—" He stared at her. "You felt my pain?"

She nodded.

Feeling himself on treacherously unsteady ground, since he was not a believer in magic or in psi, Hunter abandoned that point. "Cloud leads that herd? How many?"

"Ten," she said bleakly. "Just ten now."

Hunter felt suddenly shaken. "Ten? You mean only ten exist?"

"Only ten." Her voice became hard and embittered. "Men have hunted them, you see. Down through the ages. Hunted and killed them for their horns, because they believed the horns possessed magical properties of one kind or another. Hunted and caged them for their rarity. And Unicorns cannot live in captivity."

"But they must breed," Hunter muttered, unwillingly affected by her words.

"They breed. But Unicorns live many years before they reach the Age of Mating. And here in this valley, they mate during one season and give birth during the next. In the Summer. Once every ten Standard years. And during that short, precious time, men die trying to get into this valley. Some die inside the valley, and some kill Unicorns before they die."

Abruptly and unexpectedly, Hunter was brought up

short, not because of what she had said about the unicorns, but because of what had been revealed by her words. He had no idea how old she was or if she had spent her entire life in this relatively sheltered valley, but her knowledge—"Standard years?"—of the world outside this tiny one made her either inexplicably wise, very well educated—again, inexplicably—or else perhaps what rumor and legend had made her out to be.

No, Witch, sorceress, warrior, Keeper, human or inhuman—whatever she was had to be explained by rational means. And in spite of his excessive interest in myths, Hunter was a rational man. He did not like puzzles.

"Where were you born?" he shot at her suddenly.

She looked at him for a long, silent moment, and Hunter had the peculiar feeling that she was unsurprised by the change of topic because she knew very well the mental twists that had brought him to it. And her dry words confirmed his feeling.

"Thinking of the legendary Keeper of ten thousand years?"

"Yes," he said slowly.

"There have been Keepers for more than ten thousand years," she told him, "And if you have your way, Morgan, I'll be the last of the line."

It didn't occur to Hunter until later that she had not answered his original question. Instead, he felt compelled to defend himself. "I've told you. I don't want to harm the unicorns. I just want to prove that they exist."

"Why?" she asked flatly.

"Because . . ." His voice faltering, Hunter wonder if his reasons could be explained to this woman with the cold, beautiful face and suddenly fierce voice. The reason that had sent him on his Quest would sound selfish and arrogant: *Because I want a throne*. And the other reasons he had discovered only during the Quest would sound, he thought, foolish: *Because my world needs to know if the substance of the dream exists*.

She didn't give him a chance. Turning back to the cooking fire, she reached for a bowl on a shelf beside the hearth, using a ladle to fill it from the cooking pot. She carried the bowl and a spoon across to him. "Eat," she ordered.

Holding the bowl and listening to the hungry growls of his stomach as the appetizing scent of an unidentifiable soup rose to his nostrils, Hunter watched her return to the fire for a moment and then seat herself in the single chair at a rough wooden table before the hearth. He tasted the soup tentatively and, pleased with the unusual spicy flavor, got down to eating in earnest.

But he didn't take his eyes off Siri. He watched her draw forward a stack of what looked like large playing cards and briskly shuffle them before laying out a cryptic pattern on the table. He watched her stare down at the cards for a long, still moment, her face oddly altered into something tight and suddenly fearful. He watched her sweep up the cards, shuffle again, and again lay out the strange pattern.

His soup finished, Hunter tried to talk to her. But Siri ignored him as if he were no longer in the room. She repeated the same sequence over and over, the strain in her face growing stronger with each repetition. Hunter was curious at this transformation, but he felt languid and sleepy despite the continued aching fullness of his loins, and his curiosity gradually dissolved.

Siri heard the man's voice quieten until there was silence, and she didn't have to look over at the bed to know that the sleeping mixture had done its work. Had he been aware of being drugged, she knew that he would have claimed she'd put him to sleep to avoid his questions and speed his recovery—and he would have been right. But only as far as it went.

Relieved to be able to drop her mask of coldness, Siri propped her elbows on the table and rested her face in her hands. Why, she asked herself bitterly, had he come as he had? If she'd been able to confront him for the first time before the awful injuries that had left him weak and helpless, meeting strength with strength, there would have been no need for a mask. She would have been fiercely angry and hotly defensive of her beloved charges. She would have quite possibly killed the man.

Instead, Cloud had led her to the broken, bleeding body of a man who had, in his unconsciousness, laughed raggedly, with a strange defiance. And something had turned over within her breast, tempering her anger at his intrusion into her valley. Bitterly aware that she could very well be destroying any hope for the future of the herd, Siri had gritted her teeth and used every ounce of skill at her command to save the man's life.

She should have let him die. Siri knew it, and the knowledge was as dry and bitter as dust in her mouth. Hunter Morgan was obsessed, and a man obsessed was a dangerous and deadly force. He had claimed to have no intention of harming the herd, and she believed that he meant that. But the knowledge he would inevitably carry from the valley would sound a death knell for them just as surely as if he struck the killing blows with his hands.

And there was more, she knew. Though her contact with men had been infrequent, she knew about male needs. The Huntmen, their brutal, half-fearful hunger for her obvious in their thoughts, had always disgusted and repelled her. What they wanted was possession, bestial and uncomplicated, and the images in their minds had sickened her.

But Hunter Morgan . . . From his mind, she had caught images similar—and yet vastly different—from those of the Huntmen's minds. His body had swollen in bold need, and she had known what he wanted of her. But he hadn't thought of stark possession, of merely relieving his needs in her body or of gaining any kind of control over her. He hadn't thought of destroying.

He had thought of mutual pleasures, of senses alive and bodies seeking a completion, a merging, a passionate union.

And her body *had responded to that*. She had felt a drawing sensation deep inside her, an abrupt, unfamiliar heavy ache. Her breasts had hurt suddenly, her heart thudded wildly, and an unknown hollowness throbbed between her legs. For the first time in her life she had been wholly, completely aware of her body as distinctly different from a man's, as female and yearningly incomplete.

And, oh, the terrible danger in that!

Drawing a rasping breath, Siri uncovered her face and stared down at the cards spread out before her. With a smothered curse as violent as any the man had uttered, she swept the cards up and dealt them out again. And again. She stared blindly down at the pattern that repeated itself no matter how many times she dealt. They had never lied to her, the cards. Never. And because of what they now stubbornly told her, Siri felt a sudden terrified desperation. She had to get him out of her valley; he presented a double threat to the herd—and to herself. Because the cards never lied.

She and the man would be lovers.

Forbidden! Outcast!

Coming to her feet in one smooth motion, Siri crossed the now-silent room to stare down at the sleeping man. She prayed to an unknown deity to give her the strength to kill this man, but long moments brought a slump of defeat and the hot pressure of tears walled up and trapped somewhere in her heart.

It had taken her three days to recover from the drain of energy needed to save Hunter Morgan's life, three days in which she had barely moved to seek the sustenance of food and water and to make certain that he was healing. She had even left the Unicorns to fend for themselves, something she had never before done. And if she had not been so weary, she would have realized then that this man's life meant more to her than it had any right to. Too much to kill him now, even though it quite probably meant the destruction of the Unicorns and of the only life she had ever known.

She wondered, dimly and on some remote level of herself, what it was about this man that had reached down and touched something inside her. She tried to look at him with the disinterested, faintly distasteful gaze of someone who had no choice but to accept an unwelcome guest for a brief time, tried to see him with the clarity of unthreatening objectivity.

He was a big man, with powerful arms and shoulders and a great barrel of a chest tapering to a leanly muscled stomach and flanks. Long legs promised endurance and strength, and his virility was as potent and obvious as any stallion's. She bent quickly to remove the white bandage around his forehead, noting with the satisfaction of a talented healer that not even a scar remained to bear witness to the terrible gash she had found leaking away his life's blood. Then she continued to gaze at him. His thick black hair was a little shaggy, raggedly cut, framing a face that was lean and filled with a compelling strength. Awake, he had the cool, level gaze of a man accustomed to command, and the curiously vivid green eyes, at the moment hidden from Siri, were alive with intelligence.

A man that women would call handsome and men dangerous, Siri knew. A man who had begun his Quest with the fixed intention of seeing it through. A man who would not easily be dissuaded from that intention. A man who was more than a threat to her peace.

"Leave," she whispered haltingly to the sleeping, unaware presence. "Go back where you came from, before you destroy us all. You *won't* be my lover! I won't let you. The herd would die without me, and you'd take me away from them. You'd destroy the trust. Please leave. . . ."

Whirling suddenly, Siri left the cabin, because it was time to patrol and because it was past time to stop staring down at Hunter Morgan.

She sent a reassuring whistle to Cloud as the stallion lifted his head, and stood for a moment at the edge of the lake, watching the rest of the herd graze in the tall meadow grass. Ten. Only ten now. And only two due to foal this season. Maya, the strikingly beautiful mare who was Cloud's most beloved mate and a vanishingly rare ivory color, and Teen, who was mated to Crom, Cloud's second son.

Sighing unconsciously as she watched the herd, Siri lovingly considered each creature in turn. Cloud, long white beard flowing as he turned watchful eyes on his family. Maya, close beside her mate, still graceful on her feet despite the extra weight of the foal to come. Crom and Teen off to one side, the young stallion anxiously nuzzling his mate and clearly concerned by her first pregnancy.

Sighing this time with familiar exasperation, Siri shifted her gaze to the spirited battle going on nearby. Storm, Cloud's eldest son, arrogant to a fault, was being angrily pursued by his fiery and barren mate Fancy. And Siri didn't have to see Heart hurry to Cloud's side to know that the young and gentle filly had found herself unexpectedly cornered by Storm, who wanted a second mate.

Looking at frightened, bewildered Heart, Siri ached inside. Heart would have been Sasha's mate next Season— had he lived. But Sasha had died weeks before, and poor Heart, still grieving, was both too young and too frightened to accept the attentions of Storm or to understand Fancy's jealousy. Only the fact that Fancy was too wise to turn her ire on Heart made the situation bearable. And only when Fancy matured enough to share her mate would there be peace.

Cloud trumpeted abruptly, commandingly, his rusty call quieter these days since his favorite son had died, and the squabbling between Storm and Fancy ceased immediately. At once, Fancy sidled up to Cloud coquettishly, as she always did, soothing Cloud's temper by apologizing prettily. Storm merely stood off to one side, gazing at his father and his mate with the overbearing eye of the heir soon to be crowned.

Biting her lips, Siri looked worriedly at Cloud. Older than the valley, and filled with the ancient wisdom of his race, Cloud was her special friend. She loved him deeply, and to see him now, the proud arch of neck and tail gone forever since the death of Sasha, hurt her unbearably. Listless, responding little even to the anxious nuzzling of Maya and the frightened closeness of Heart, Cloud watched over the herd as he'd always done, but rarely bothered to chastise Storm any longer.

But Storm's mother, Shree, an old and dignified matron, nipped her wayward son's gleaming white rump fiercely, and Storm danced away in ludicrous surprise. Weeks ago, Siri would have laughed aloud at Shree's clear despair at her son's misbehavior; today it didn't even spark a smile. She watched with an unfamiliar weariness as Shree briefly nuzzled Cloud and then comforted the frightened Heart, who was her daughter.

Siri felt something bump her abruptly, nearly sending her sprawling, and she laughed for the first time in days. "Rayne!" she exclaimed, finding her balance and staring down at the forehead rubbing frantically against her hip. The first foal of the Season, lively and inquisitive Rayne was constantly trying to alleviate the fierce itch of her newly emerging horn. Siri helpfully scratched the delicate white forehead, looking smilingly down at velvety dark eyes half-closed in blissful enjoyment. Then little Rayne, her long legs still not quite steady, trotted away to check on the whereabouts of her mother, gentle Dawn, Cloud's third mate.

Siri looked back at the herd, seeing each creature as an individual with a personality uniquely his or her own, and her weariness returned. Only a few more weeks. If she could protect the herd for only a few more weeks, the Summer would be over. The Winter would be long and cold and lonely, but at least she would have the satisfaction of knowing that the herd lived.

If she could keep them alive for the next few weeks.

If Hunter Morgan didn't destroy them all.

If the cards were wrong . . . just this once.

She took a deep breath and turned away to begin her patrol, wondering dimly if she had the strength she would surely need in the coming days. The man had to leave the valley. And he had to leave with a vow of silence somehow extracted from him. Which left Siri with a bitter choice of three alternatives, the first of which she already knew to be fruitless: She couldn't kill him. So she had either to chance his leaving with full knowledge of the Unicorns and their reality and whereabouts, or else she would have to allow him to stay until she could convince him that they should remain as they were: a treasured myth. And she was almost willing to risk his leaving with full knowledge.

Because if he left with that knowledge, at least there was a chance that no one else would be able to find the valley, or would survive finding it. But if Hunter Morgan remained for any length of time, there would be no chance, no chance at all for the Unicorns.

Unless the cards were wrong. . . .

When Hunter awoke, the cabin was lighted only by the low fire in the hearth and by a lamp sitting on the table before it. He was clear of mind and immediately aware that he had slept for some time; it was night and the silence of the room was broken only by the crackle of the fire.

He sat up slowly, relieved that some of his strength had returned, and banked the pillows behind him as he stared across at the occupied chair by the table. Siri sat there, still and silent, staring into the fire without her mask of coldness. Instead, her lovely face brooded worriedly over some inner dilemma. The strain, oddly enough, made her all the more beautiful, and the man watching felt a lump rise in his throat.

What, he wondered, could etch this portrait of despair? Then she looked over, saw he was awake, and Hunter spoke quickly before the coldness could descend over her delicate features.

"It's no use now; I've seen what lies beneath the coldness." He was surprised at the husky sound of his own voice, at the instant renewal of desire. And he felt a brief moment of superstition, of unease. Perhaps she was the sorceress, the witch, the siren he had been told she was. Perhaps, like the Black Widow of legend, she had been born to ensnare men and drain them of manhood and life.

Then his rationality asserted itself. No! Absurd. She was a hauntingly beautiful woman, and she naturally stirred his senses; it was no more than that.

She looked at him steadily for a long moment, then turned her eyes back to the fire. "There's more soup if you want it."

"No, thanks," he said, sudden realization in his tone. "I seem to have lost a day or so since the last bowl."

She shrugged. "Only a few hours."

"You drugged me." It wasn't a question.

Siri shrugged again without looking at him. "You needed the sleep."

"And you needed the silence?"

She didn't smile at his faint attempt at humor. "You still need sleep. And it's late."

Hunter sighed and decided to employ shock tactics again. It had worked the first time, he thought. "Where do the unicorns live in the long Winter?"

"Go to sleep," she said flatly.

"How long have you been their Keeper?"

"Go to sleep."

"Have you lived in this valley all your life?" He watched her hands as they rested on the table and saw the knuckles whiten.

"Go to sleep." Her voice was growing tauter by the moment.

"How did King come by that horn?"

At last, he got results with his tactics.

Siri leapt to her feet, the chair overturning behind her, and whirled to stare at him. Her dark eyes were wild with despair. "Ask me no more questions!" she cried violently, crossing the room to stand by his bed. Her breasts were heaving with the deep, ragged breaths she took and Hunter, stunned by her reaction and mesmerized by the wild beauty of her, could only stare up at her and feel his body throb.

"Can you stop and think for one single moment what your very presence here is doing to me?" she demanded desperately. "Can you see past your damned obsession and realize that you threaten what I love most in the world? Isn't there some *part* of you that understands that? I'm the Keeper of the Unicorns, and I'm the only thing—*the only thing*—standing between them and extinction!" Her voice dropped to a hoarse whisper that hurt Hunter's throat. "Damn you. I should have let you die. I should have—" Abruptly, she turned and stumbled away, flinging open the cabin door and disappearing out into the darkness.

Hunter sat in total stillness, staring after her. He felt as if he had wounded something fragile, picked it up and brutally shaken it, and the feeling confused him. He hadn't intended to hurt her with his question of how King had come by the horn— And then he remembered. Closing his eyes abruptly, Hunter winced. She'd talked of the past and of the men who had killed unicorns in order to take their golden horns, and he understood then that one of the herd had died to provide King's horn.

Did she believe that he intended to kill one of the creatures in order to obtain the proof he wanted? And then, for the very first time, it occurred to him that he would have to obtain proof of some kind; his word of the creatures' reality had to be accompanied by tangible evidence. Wasn't that the point of the Quest? Hunter didn't want to think about it.

And, as it happened, he didn't have to at that moment, for his attention was caught by a dream. The dream came into the cabin through the open door on tiny hooves and long, unsteady legs, its huge velvety dark eyes surveying the cabin without, apparently, noticing the immobile, watching man. It turned its small white face this way and that, tasted the rough wooden bolt on the door with curious lips and small white teeth. It came farther into the cabin and stared at the low fire warily before rubbing its head against a table leg, rubbing fiercely and giving a soft little grunt of seeming relief. Then it turned its head.

And Hunter, staring in still, utter fascination, saw the emerging golden horn, no longer than his thumb, in the center of the unicorn foal's forehead.

There was absolutely no movement in the cabin. The foal was frozen, staring with wide, panicky eyes at the man in the bed. And the man was looking in wonder at a myth come to life.

Then there was a confused rattle of tiny hooves on floorboards, a white blur shooting through the door, and silence.

Hunter was still in the same immobile pose when Siri came through the door quite some time later. He watched her close the door and rap the bolt home before crossing to the table.

"I saw one of them," he said bemusedly. "A baby unicorn. It came inside the cabin for a moment."

Siri looked at him, then blew out the lamp. In a darkness lighted only by the dying cook-fire, he saw her move over to the far wall, where a low, wide shelf had been turned into a makeshift bed. Silently, her movements barely visible and making no sound at all, she got into the bed.

His bemusement clearing then, Hunter remembered how she had looked when she had left the cabin—and how she had looked when she returned. Her face had been white and strained, her eyes red-rimmed from tears. And he was appalled that he had done that to her.

"Siri . . . Siri, I'm sorry," he said into the darkness. "So sorry."

Utter silence answered him.

Exhaustion had drawn Siri into a deep and dreamless sleep, and the night had brought counsel. There would be no more tears. She would never have been able to keep the Unicorns and herself alive for any length of time at all had she been either weak or indecisive; Siri was neither. The momentary weakness of tears, she assured herself firmly, had been the result of weariness and the shock of the cards' prophecy.

That was past.

For the present and the future, it was necessary that she employ all her strength and will in order to preserve her beloved Unicorns. It was the only thing that mattered. And as she patrolled the valley after leaving the man still sleeping, Siri cleared her mind of everything but her duty. She greeted the herd as they emerged from the forest and watched them for a few moments before continuing on her way.

At the Crystal Pool, she found most of the valley's other inhabitants sharing a morning drink. They were restless and uneasy with the man's presence in the valley, and seemed comforted by Siri's arrival. She sat down on a boulder and watched them, smilingly listening and responding to the varied sounds of greeting.

The pair of snow leopards roared at her, ruffling the feathers of the mated lyrebirds strutting nearby. The male snow wolf nudged his mate and both turned bright blue eyes to Siri for a moment with faint welcoming growls before resuming their drinking. Albino tigers and lions drank companionably side by side with sand cats, white-tailed deer, and bears. A pair of giant Pandas rumbled greetings, looking at Siri with button eyes. Perched on low branches, drinking from the pool, or soaring overhead were peacocks, white eagles, swans, and dozens of songbirds.

And tumbling all around Siri were cubs and chicks and babies of every kind, all squeaking and chirping and growling for bellies to be scratched or feathers smoothed.

Siri scratched and smoothed, and gained a certain peace. And she silently and knowingly put her fate in the lap of the gods. She would impose her will as far as she was able; not even she could demand more of herself. There was, after all, a boundary beyond which she simply could not see . . . even if she shuffled cards forever trying to peer into a misty future. The boundary was there, and only the gods knew in certainty what tomorrow would bring.

After a while she rose and went deeper into the forest, compelled by some need she could not even name. Something was pulling at her, and yet the farther she walked the less conscious she was of the feeling. She went deeper, where it was dim and quiet, and then sat on a fallen log. Very slowly, the tenuous peace she had gained became stronger, surrounding her like a cloak. Her warrior's senses dulled, her instincts for danger faded.

And when a man stepped out of the trees, she looked at him, curious and unthreatened. He had the face of an angel, she thought, and lovely green eyes. For a moment, just an instant, one side of his face seemed to waver, like heat off a rock on a summer's day, but then the faint distortion was gone.

He had the face of an angel.

Mother?
Daughter?
Can the cards lie?
No. No, my child. They speak the truth.
Then what will I do, Mother?
You must decide that.
If . . . if the prophecy is fulfilled, will there be another Keeper, Mother? Will the Unicorns survive?
There is no time to prepare, daughter.

Mother . . .
You must make the choice, daughter.
Must there be a choice, Mother?
I am sorry, my child.
Green eyes . . .
So sorry.

Four

Hunter woke to silence and emptiness. He pushed himself up on his elbows, pleased to discover his strength was returning so quickly. Looking around the cabin, he saw no sign of Siri, and decided quite abruptly that he would face her next time on his feet.

It was easier in thought than in deed, however.

When he had picked himself up off the floor, Hunter managed to keep on his feet by hanging onto the bed and then onto the table by the hearth. Crossing the distance between the two left him sweating and trembling. He leaned on the table and wiped his wet brow with a shaking hand, hearing only his rasping breaths in the morning silence. He was just beginning to wonder if he could make it around the table to the single chair when Siri returned.

"By tomorrow, you'll be strong enough to leave."

Hunter turned so quickly he would have fallen had she not swiftly crossed the distance between them and caught him in her strong arms.

And he promptly forgot everything but the slender resilience of the body substituting its strength for his own.

Ebony eyes looked up at him with a sudden startled awareness, gazing out of a face too delicate to belong to a warrior. His heart lodged somewhere in his throat, choking him with its pounding, even as morning sunlight lanced through the window to turn her hair into a blinding silver halo. She seemed tiny and fragile, yet bore the larger part of his weight with no visible strain.

But she trembled suddenly.

Fascinated, he watched her lips part on a soft gasp, and strength drawn from a well of desire aided him in standing suddenly taller and straighter. His hands found her shoulders, ignoring the slight resistance of tensing muscles to pull her closer. The arm she had thrown around his waist tightened almost convulsively, and he felt the hand resting on his chest shaking.

He gazed deeply into her eyes, even after the first touch of lips, seeing and marveling at the tiny sparks of purple fire nearly hidden in the blackness of her irises. He lost himself in the pools of dark velvet, searching instinctively for something to ease the new, unfamiliar aching emptiness inside of him. Her lips warmed and bloomed beneath his, her lids slowly lowered, and Hunter was only distantly aware of the purely male rush of satisfied triumph.

Her breasts were firm against his chest, their tips turning to hard buds of desire. Her loins were pressed to his, yielding, fitting him so well, and a scalding rush of passion swelled his own loins achingly. And his need for her was so powerful, so intense, he wanted to sink down to the hard floor with her and lose himself in her yielding woman's body until she would never be rid of him. The heat of her intensified, and he felt that he wrapped his arms around a pure white flame that branded him indelibly. Her mouth was hot and sweet, and his tongue possessed it with a demanding passion that she responded to instantly.

But even as he pulled her closer, even as he felt her fingers curl into his back, tension was filling the body he held. A strange, broken cry escaped her lips as she jerked away, leaving him half-leaning against the table behind him. Across the room with no sound to mark her passage, she stared at him as one might have stared at a demon from hell.

There was terror in her eyes.

"Tomorrow." The single word emerged strangled, hoarse from her lips, and she quickly cleared her throat. "Tomorrow," she repeated, clear and flat this time. "You'll leave tomorrow."

"I don't think so." Hardly aware of doing so, Hunter leaned back against the table, gripping its edge with white-knuckled fingers as he listened, from a great distance, to the sound of his own voice. He couldn't take his eyes off her; he watched as her full breasts rose and fell unsteadily, erect nipples straining through the fine cloth, a feverish heat burning in her ebony eyes.

"You'll leave!" *Forbidden! Outcast!*

"No." He had never in his life wanted a woman as he wanted her, the aching throb of desire in his body threatening to tear him apart. Visions of Siri writhing in like desire beneath him, her long legs wrapped around him, her heat drawing him deep into her body, filled his mind until he could scarcely breathe.

Siri crossed her arms across her breasts, defensive, wary, desperately ignoring the hot tremors weakening her body. "I won't let you destroy the Unicorns," she said as evenly as she could manage. "I won't let you destroy me. You'll leave my valley, dead or alive."

"Could you kill me?" he asked softly, huskily. "Would you?"

She looked at him with eyes too hot and aching to produce tears, fighting for every scrap of control at her command. "I could," she said, lying for the first time in her life. "I would. Understand this: Nothing—*nothing*—will prevent me from defending the Unicorns. I'd destroy this world to save them."

The quiet, even tenor of her voice convinced him as no outburst would have, and Hunter tried to rein his desire as he carefully worked his way around the table and sat down. This time, she didn't help him. He couldn't believe she meant to deny her own desire, but pushed that aside for the moment to deal with the threat she had made. "You'd kill

me?" he probed, disbelieving. "When I have no intention
of harming the unicorns?"

Siri laughed shortly. "You'll destroy them."

"I only want to prove their reality," he protested, a
lingering hoarseness making his voice rough. "Is that so
wrong?"

"Is it so right?" she countered fiercely.

Hunter was honestly bewildered.

She took a step toward him. "Who gave you the right
to destroy other men's dreams?" she demanded. "Who set
you up as a god and decreed that you would determine
reality for all men?"

Again, Hunter shied away from thinking thoughts that
would ultimately bring down the walls of his resolution.
Deliberately, he changed the subject. "What frightens you
the most, Siri? That I'll destroy the unicorns? Or that I'll
teach you to love me?"

She jerked as though he had slapped her, her face
altering in a second from fierce to shocked, and then going
totally expressionless. "If you knew anything at all about
love," she said without emotion, "you'd know that it isn't
something which can be *taught*. And if you were less
arrogant, you'd realize that I could never feel anything but
hate toward anyone wishing to harm the dearest friends I
have in this world."

Hunter chose to respond to her first statement and
ignore the second. "Perhaps love can't be taught," he said,
"but I didn't imagine your response a few minutes ago. You
want me, Siri. You want me as much as I want you."

"You're wrong." Siri fought down panic, willing nothing to show on her face. *Forbidden! Outcast!*

"Am I?" Hunter smiled slowly. "You were burning in
my arms, and you're still shaking with desire now. Do you
think I don't know, can't see?" He was arrogantly certain of
her response. "You'll be mine, and we both know it. In
time."

In that moment, Siri very nearly could have killed
him: For his certainty in the face of her confusion. For his
strength in the face of her sudden weakness. For his
arrogance in claiming her as his. And for the knowledge of

her own womanhood, burning with a hollow need inside her, which she should never have been forced to confront.

For all his verbal arrogance, Hunter was not at all certain of himself. Or of her. He wanted her, yet his own mention of love bothered him. He enjoyed sexual pleasure, and because on his world those pleasures were valued by men and women alike, he knew very well how to please a woman. He wanted to think of Siri that way, as just another hunger to be fed, as a warm body pleased by him and pleasing him, but there was more to it than that, and he was uneasily conscious of that fact.

Hunter had never loved a woman. In the beginning he had deliberately blocked off a part of himself in order to avoid just such a complication in his life, and the years had done nothing to alter that resolve. But holding Siri in his arms had left him with an ache which was not only the pain of unsatisfied hunger but something deeper and stronger. He wanted to hold her again, wanted to run his fingers through the silver silk of her hair. He wanted to feel the softness of her lips beneath his, feel her supple body mold itself to his.

But more than that, more than anything, he wanted to set them in a different place, a different time, and do away with a barrier he didn't understand. The unicorns.

Watching silently as she worked at the hearth preparing their morning meal, Hunter tried—honestly tried—to see the creatures as she seemed to see them.

He could not.

Granted, they were mystical, magical creatures, myths come to life. But they were just *animals*. Flesh and blood. Oddities of nature perhaps, like camels, giraffes, elephants, and a hundred other curious animals. *Man* had made unicorns something else, something special in his eyes. *Man* had woven stories into legends.

And if they died?

The question floated gently into his mind, demanding an answer. And Hunter shoved it violently away, because he refused to believe that in proving their reality he would be destroying them. "I don't want to hurt them," he said, hearing the words with a sense of surprise, for he had not meant to speak aloud.

Siri placed a food-laden plate before him and, oddly, smiled. A sad smile. "I know."

He looked at her. "But you still believe I'll destroy them?" he asked.

"Yes."

"Why? *Why?*"

She sat down on the raised stone hearth, her own plate resting on her knees. For a long moment she was silent, weighing the arguments which sprang immediatetly to her mind. She was strongly aware that convincing Hunter would take time, knowing that obsessions were difficult, if not impossible, to uproot. And it had come to her only moments before that by being fiercely argumentative, she was only reinforcing his own firm beliefs. Her best chance of success lay in calm reason, and accepting that did much to soothe Siri's strained nerves.

One step at a time.

The Summer would be over soon.

She would impose her will on the cards' prophecy, and on this treacherous awakening of her body.

The Unicorns would—*would*—be safe.

One step at a time.

"You plan to tell people about the Unicorns?" she asked neutrally.

Hunter stirred uneasily. But he *had* asked, after all. "Yes."

Siri nodded. She stared down at her plate, then lifted her clear gaze to meet his. And strove to ignore the faint, hot tremor that spread through her body whenever she looked at him now. "If you tell people, they'll come to see for themselves. They'll build a road over The Reaper or blast a tunnel through it. Someone will realize there's wealth to be made, and build a gate to collect it from the visitors. And people will come and stare—even if they do no worse—and marvel. And the Unicorns will be in a cage, one with the appearance of freedom, but a cage nonetheless. And Unicorns cannot live in captivity. So they'll die."

"They can be protected," he objected.

"They are protected," she said softly.

Hunter looked down at his food and began to eat, unable to meet the unwavering certainty in her gaze. "This is good," he murmured, changing the subject quite deliberately.

Siri inclined her head slightly in thanks, eating her own food with sober attention.

An absent realization rose in Hunter's mind as he ate. "You're a vegetarian," he noted.

"Of course." She hesitated, then added, "Unicorns aren't the only creatures in the valley, but all live in peace here."

"Carnivores?" he queried suddenly.

She nodded.

"Then it can't be very peaceful. Carnivores kill to survive."

"Not here."

Hunter stared at her. "Then how do they live?"

Siri met his eyes with an odd, bemused surprise, because the question had never occurred to her. And uneasiness stirred inside her. She had never wondered about that. Why? And why did the question disturb her now. "They survive."

"How?" he pressed.

"They're cared for."

"By whom? You?"

She put her plate to one side, frowning a little. "I watch over them," she said slowly. "I signal them to hide when the Huntmen come. But they feed at night."

"Then how can you be sure they don't kill for food?"

"You don't understand." Siri struggled for words to explain a way of life she had always taken for granted. She felt unsettled, disturbed. "The number of creatures in the valley is—controlled. I'd know if any were missing. Babies are born in the Spring and they live here throughout the Summer. In the Fall, they're . . . taken. Only the mated pairs remain in the Winter."

"*Taken?* You mean killed?"

"No, no!" She gestured slightly. "They're *taken* . . . to other worlds. So that their numbers will increase."

"Who takes them?" Hunter asked blankly.

She frowned at him. "Does that matter?"

He pushed his plate away, surprised by such passive acceptance from her. "I think so."

Siri looked at him, puzzled. "Why?"

Hunter answered with a question. "Doesn't it bother you not to know where the animals are taken, and who takes them?"

"No." But it did bother her, for the first time. No one had ever asked questions of her, or of her life in the valley, and it had never occurred to her to question what was. "No more than it bothers me that the Unicorns are taken each Fall. I know they're cared for, and will return." She made her voice firm, certain. Yet now she wondered.

"*How* do you know?"

"I know."

Frustrated, Hunter ran his fingers through his hair. For such a clearly intelligent woman, Siri had peculiar blind spots. Because she had grown up here in this secluded valley? He wondered, then, if her birthright as Keeper quite simply precluded questions; was her seemingly passive acceptance as natural to her as his curiosity was to him? "Are they taken by someone on this planet?" he asked, wondering if she was truly alone but for the animals.

"Of course not," she scoffed.

"Then *who?*" he snapped.

Still unsettled, Siri felt the rise of her own temper. But she concentrated, asking a mental question and bothered because she had never asked it before. The answer rose in her mind, easing her anxiety. "In ancient times they were called the Guardians," she explained, relieved to have an explanation for him. She searched mentally through these new memories, looking for more information. "They sought to . . . to maintain a proper balance. When your race and others all but destroyed some creatures, the Guardians stepped in to prevent extinction." She felt triumphant. There *were* answers.

A little puzzled by her inwardly turned gaze and the curiously stiff way she spoke, as if by rote, he ventured cautiously, "You mean *no creature that ever lived in myth or reality is extinct?*"

"Of course not."

Hunter found this answer almost impossible to believe. He had certainly come across supposedly extinct animals thriving on planets other than those that had seen their creation, but he had merely supposed it to be the result of parallel evolution on similar planets. That was, after all, a scientifically sound explanation.

But myths? He had found none on hundreds of worlds, disappointed time and again by failure. He had found beauty here and there, enough so that his disillusionment had not been total, but no myth had stood before him to prove that the beauty of dreams still lived.

Until he had found this valley. And unicorns.

But there were other myths. "Pegasus," he said suddenly.

She had no difficulty in following his thoughts. "No."

"No? You mean winged horses really don't exist?"

"I don't know," she said reasonably. "They don't exist here. I'm sure they exist somewhere, though. They're too beautiful not to."

He ignored the opinion, reflecting with a sense of relief that at least there was one creature still relegated to myth and legend. His own emotions should have told him something then, but Hunter was not yet ready to examine his deepest dreams. His attention was caught suddenly as Siri stared past him at the open door; she spoke even as he swiftly turned his head.

"Rayne."

A tiny white muzzle, one ear, one black eye, a minute golden horn; Rayne was peering around the rough doorjamb with a curiosity stronger than her fear of Hunter.

"Rayne," Siri said again softly. And then, to Hunter, "Don't try to touch her when she comes in."

One step, then another. Rayne kept her bright, wary eyes on Hunter as she cautiously moved toward Siri and the piece of bread her mistress held out in invitation. She stretched out her small face, nostrils quivering, then took the last few steps in an awkward, long-legged trot. The bread was snatched by gleaming little teeth and an itching forehead was rubbed furiously against Siri's shoulder.

Hunter stared, enchanted. A glimpse of a horn seen through pain-clouded eyes; a shadowy glimpse of horned mischief; neither had prepared him for the reality seen in daylight and sanity.

They were real. *Real*. Until that moment, he had not fully believed.

"My God," he said quietly.

Rayne whirled, the rat-a-tat of her hooves loud in the stillness of the cabin as she shot through the doorway.

"She isn't accustomed to the sound of a man's voice," Siri explained.

Before Hunter could respond, another sound filled the air. It held him spellbound in its very uniqueness, and chills of awe chased one another down his spine. Window-panes rattled as the sound sliced and tore its way through the cabin. Echoing, reverberating, it tangled among the trees outside and rose in a crescendo that was as eerie as it was powerful.

Hunter stared at Siri as the sound died away. "What—?"

She was still gazing toward the doorway. "His trumpeting used to shake the whole cabin," she murmured, as if to herself. "But not anymore." *Because a man killed his son.* She could feel hostility rise in her and welcomed it; she couldn't allow herself to relax with *this* man because he *was* a man . . . and dangerous. She looked at him, and when she explained, her voice was tight. "That was Cloud. He was disturbed when Rayne went out so fast."

"You mean he used to—uh—trumpet louder than that?" Hunter asked incredulously.

Siri nodded. "He's old," she said abruptly, and there was pain and bitterness in the tightness of her voice now. "He . . . he won't be back next Summer."

Hunter was puzzled by the abrupt hostility in her eyes but decided to ignore it. She always seemed to become angry and defensive when discussing her unicorns. It was, he supposed, a natural reaction. After a moment, he pushed himself to his feet. "I have to see them. Together. All of them."

"You're not strong enough to make it outside," she said emotionlessly.

"I can, if you'll help me." He looked at her, not too proud to ask for her help but very aware that she had little reason to give it to him.

Siri returned the look. "I helped you once before today," she reminded him flatly, and both of them, for different—and similar—reasons, tried not to think of what had occurred after the helping.

He hesitated. "That won't happen again. I promise."

"I wish I could believe," she said, "that a promise means the same thing to you as it does to me."

Hunter took a deep breath. If only compromise would keep him in the valley, he was willing. For now. "I promise, Siri, that I will never again take advantage of your helping me. My word of honor." He had to regain his strength. Quickly.

Siri's instincts told her that Hunter meant what he promised, but those same instincts warned her the less touching between them the better for her peace of mind and her future. But she had her anger and bitterness, and that was a shield of sorts. She took a deep breath in her turn, focused a mental question and sent it winging to Cloud. The immediate and firm answer surprised her.

"Odd," she murmured. "Cloud agrees."

Hunter looked bewildered. "Agrees?"

"That you should see the herd."

"You *asked* him?"

"Of course. He leads the herd. It's his decision."

"*How* did you ask him?"

Siri stared at him. His questions, his ceaseless *questions!* "I just asked him," she snapped.

"But you didn't say anything."

So that was it. She had forgotten that most beings outside the valley were not telepathic. Or—had she ever known? She felt unsettled again. "Mind-touch," she said stiffly. "It's how I talk to Cloud."

"Only Cloud?" Hunter wondered why he was even asking; he *still* didn't believe in psi.

"Only Cloud." Siri rose to her feet and stared down at him. "And before you ask—no, I don't know why it's only Cloud. I never thought to ask him that."

"You accept a great deal on faith, don't you?" he murmured as she came around the table and offered a shoulder and arm for support.

She didn't answer.

They moved out of the cabin slowly, with Siri supporting a good half of Hunter's weight; she didn't complain and seemed under no strain at all. As for Hunter, he set his mind firmly on unicorns and blanked out the feeling of deceptively delicate bones beneath his hand.

But that was almost impossible. Her arm was strong and supple around his waist, and he was burningly conscious of her breast pressed to his rib cage. Only the promise he was determined to keep prevented him from crushing her against him. He couldn't take advantage of her help.

The sunlight was nearly blinding after the dimness of the cabin, and he couldn't see much of anything for a few moments. Siri eased him down onto a rough wooden bench beneath a towering tree, releasing him almost immediately and stepping back to watch his reaction. Hunter neither moved nor spoke for long minutes.

They stood grouped in a little half circle between the cabin and the tiny lake, ten pairs of dark eyes watching him with varying degrees of wariness. Cloud and Rayne were the only ones Hunter recognized, the foal because he had seen her clearly and the stallion because great age was apparent in the length of his beard and horn. Enchanted, Hunter identified two more stallions—both young—and five mares, one of which looked considerably older than the others and one which looked very young.

He realized that he was equating these creatures with horses and guessing at age as he would have with a horse, but instinct warned him not to get into a discussion with Siri about the ages of unicorns. He didn't think he'd believe her answers.

He put his questions aside for the moment and just concentrated on looking his fill. They were beautiful creatures! All had snowy white coats except for one breathtaking mare of an ivory color; she moved with ponderous grace, her swollen belly evidence of an approaching foal. Another slightly younger mare—he didn't doubt his guess, though he knew he was still judging their ages by comparison to horses—was also clearly in foal, the young stallion at her side anxious to the point of absurdity.

The other young stallion looked arrogant and impatient; he was obviously the raw and untried crown prince. At his side stood a young mare that looked as if she were prancing even standing still; she was trouble on the hoof, Hunter decided firmly.

Unconsciously, he went on assigning personalities to the creatures.

The youngest mare save Rayne remained close beside the oldest mare, her delicate face timid and frightened, her eyes nervous. The old mare was dignified and watchful, and clearly protective of what was obviously her daughter. And Rayne's mother kept a gentle eye on her lively foal, seemingly content with the alien man's presence because Cloud had agreed to it.

Cloud. He was taller by a hand than either of the younger stallions, his snowy beard reaching to his knees and his golden horn half again longer than any in the herd. His dark eyes were old and wise, the intelligence contained there a near-tangible thing. He returned the man's steady gaze, his own filled with calm, with acceptance. Hunter realized dimly that here was a noble creature for whom life held no surprises. Cloud would always instinctively, innately . . . understand.

Hunter was only vaguely aware of Siri's soft voice beside him.

"What do you see?"

"A . . . family," he murmured, and listened as she continued to speak quietly.

"The ivory mare is Maya; she carries Cloud's foal. Probably his last offspring. The anxious stallion is Crom; his mate is Teen. Crom should lead the herd after Cloud, but he isn't a Leader. Storm, the arrogant one, will lead next, if he can ever learn to manage his mate Fancy. Heart is the timid filly. Beside her is Shree, Heart and Storm's mother. And Dawn is Rayne's mother."

Hunter stirred for the first time, tearing his gaze from the herd to look at Siri. "Odd. As soon as you named them, I could pick them out."

"What's odd about that?"

He gestured helplessly. "With a word or two, you gave them—individuality."

Siri looked at him steadily.

"No." Hunter shook his head. "One animal is pretty much like another, and I refuse to believe—" He broke off. He could not deny that only moments before he had recognized the distinction of personality of each unicorn. He turned to look back at the herd and froze, finding himself staring at a tiny white muzzle only inches away. Rayne had crept up in silence and now stood perfectly still, her small body quivering as instinct urged her to run and curiosity compelled her to remain. She stretched her neck cautiously, nostrils flaring as she absorbed the man's scent. Velvety lips tested the texture of rough cloth and then lifted higher as she chewed meditatively on a mouthful of shaggy black hair, long lashes blinking over bright dark eyes.

"Hello, baby," Hunter said softly.

Rayne took a step backward, her mouth still working after tasting his hair, her dark eyes watching him. She snorted softly and shook her head, pawing the ground with impatient little digs.

Holding his breath, Hunter slowly lifted a hand and stretched it toward the tiny golden horn. He touched the satiny fur of her forehead, scratching gently until the foal relaxed, and then touched the minute horn. And, curiously shocked, he felt the blood pulsing beneath his fingers. He drew back and stared at the foal and at her living horn. She returned his stare, her own humanly quizzical, then turned and trotted back to her mother.

"The horn . . . there was a pulse," Hunter muttered.

"When a Unicorn dies," Siri said quietly, "only the

horn remains. The body falls into dust. But the horn lives on as if all the energy of the body were drawn into it after death. And it glows for a very long time."

Hunter turned his head to look at her almost blindly. "Magic?" he asked, hearing the harshness of his voice.

She sat on the ground, wrapping her arms around her upraised knees. "What *is* magic?" Shrugging, she gazed off toward the herd. "Something not completely understood? By that definition, I suppose magic is as good a word as any. But why does it have to be defined?"

"Man's quest for knowledge," Hunter said automatically.

Siri nodded a little, but she wore a taut smile. "Man? You mean men like you—and the Huntmen?"

"They aren't like me," he protested.

"No? You're all human. You all sprang from a single world uncounted centuries ago, didn't you?"

He looked at her, intrigued by the curious complexities inherent in her. Accepting so much on faith, and yet with obvious knowledge of other worlds. "Maybe some of us did," he admitted. "But not all of us. There are humanoids on many worlds, who developed independently just as my ancestors did."

"On your home world?" She felt a sudden curiosity, and told herself it was because she needed to know about Hunter and his people in order to discover the best way of persuading him to leave her and the valley in peace.

"No. No, my people live on a world they traveled to generations ago."

"Which world did they leave?"

He shook his head. "They fled from a war, or some natural catastrophe; they chose not to preserve that part of their history. All I know—all any of us know—is that they called it Earth."

She turned her head and gave him a strange, searching look. For the moment, it seemed her hostility had vanished. "I see. And man's quest for knowledge? Is that what drove you to leave your world?"

He was silent for a moment, and then spoke slowly. "When my people left their home world and went into space, never knowing if they'd survive long enough to find a habitable planet, they left so much behind. All their history. Only their knowledge and their mythology survived. They used their knowledge to build a new world for themselves, a new culture composed of bits and pieces of what had to be memories of their history. A simple society on a planet that was at first hostile to them. They held tight to their myths. Ancient heroes and adventurous quests. Magical creatures. They were careful to preserve those."

"Why did you leave?" she asked again.

"It started out as a simple Quest," he said. His mouth twisted faintly. "I just wanted to find a unicorn. Myths were once so important to my people—so important that they chose to take that part of themselves to a new world." An innate caution kept him silent about the rest. "It was only that, at first."

"Only that?" An odd question, she thought, disturbed.

He frowned a little. "I—yes. All my life, I had been fascinated by myth."

"And then?"

Hunter was gazing at the unicorns, but he was seeing something else. He was seeing what he had seen for years in his travels. "I found other humans on other worlds with no memories of their beginnings," he said softly. "As if our entire race had been driven from its home world and scattered out into space. They had their myths, though. My myths, and my people's. They were all *the same*. Dragons. Pegasus. Centaurs. Pandora's box, and divine beings, Fates and Muses, demigods like Hercules, heroes like the Argonauts and Odysseus.

"They were all there. On dozens of worlds whose technology ranged from the primitive to spacegoing, I found the same mythology. And almost all had been altered, either minutely or greatly, to fit the needs of each world. But the names remained the same. And only one myth survived *exactly* the same way on each world. Unicorns. Always, they represented purity and grace and wisdom and strength."

Siri waited, watching him.

"Oh, I found humanoids with no mythology at all. And

in each case where a world had forgotten or contained no myth, no dreams of beauty, the societies were dying. They were in chaos, at war, destroying themselves. They had forgotten how to dream, and they were dying of the lack."

She listened, realizing that he had not grasped the importance of that, but curiously unwilling to point out what he had not yet discovered on his own. He had to understand for himself, she knew. Somehow, he had to understand.

He looked at her, his expression that of a driven man, a fierce and determined man. "My world is losing its myths, Siri. Do you understand? My grandfather saw it happening; my father saw it happening; I see it happening. Generation by generation, they are increasingly losing the ability to dream. Forgetting the legends of their past. And that beautiful, simple society is beginning to lose the threads holding it together. In another few generations, my world could become like those others: in chaos, destroying itself."

"So your Quest," she said softly, "is to save a world. By presenting to them myth alive and breathing?"

Intensely, he said, "They need to see that dreams are *real*! They need to know that."

She returned her gaze to the herd, thinking. An important Quest, she realized. But he did not yet understand why his solution to his world's problems was based on a fallacy. And she could not explain. "Could it be that easy?" she asked softly.

"Easy?" He laughed shortly. "I've spent years searching, Siri. I've been drawn into wars against my will. I've been stranded on hostile planets, captured by antagonistic cultures, forced to participate in rituals and customs I barely understood. I've had to learn new responses, new languages. I've had to fight for my life when that was never what I wanted to become adept at."

She pushed aside her sudden curiosity. "I didn't mean that your Quest was easy. I meant could it be that easy to mend a torn society? What would you show them? A horse with a horn?"

"A unicorn." He stared at her. "A dream."

He had to understand for himself; she couldn't force

him to see the truth. "And destroy my valley for your world."

"*Your* valley?"

She rose to her feet, absently brushing dust from her pants as she gazed at him. "My valley. I'm the Keeper."

"Was it always your valley?" he probed cautiously.

"I was born the Keeper."

He hesitated, then decided to press for at least one answer while she seemed amenable. "Were you born here in the valley?"

"In a manner of speaking."

"What? What does that mean?"

Hands on hips, Siri stared down at him. "It means that I was born inside The Reaper, Hunter. Now, do you want to sit out here while I patrol, or would you rather go back inside?"

"I'll stay here."

She nodded briefly, glanced toward Cloud as if sending a silent message, then struck out through the trees.

Hunter watched until he could no longer see her, then turned his baffled gaze to the black sentinel brooding high above the valley. *Inside The Reaper?* How could that be?

The unicorns were grazing peacefully now and more or less ignoring him. He watched little Rayne trot over to the small lake, dip her nose into the water briefly, then spit out a mouthful with an irritated squeal. Distracted from his thoughts, he watched as Dawn lifted her head and nickered softly and her foal answered with another squeal before darting through the woods in an awkward baby gallop.

Hunter noted that the foal had followed Siri's path, and he waited for nearly ten minutes for her return, his mind working keenly. When Rayne trotted back to the herd, her long legs were wet all the way up to her body.

Nodding to himself, Hunter looked back toward the lake. He followed the lake's feeding stream with his eyes until he could barely pinpoint its origin in the wellspring low on The Reaper's slopes. "A mineral spring, probably," he murmured aloud. "The water's undrinkable." He looked toward the trees and the path Siri and the foal had taken. "There must be another stream."

He filed the information away in his mind and watched the unicorns, dazzled by their grace and beauty . . . and the strength of their personalities.

A kind of pattern was established during the next few days. After breakfast, Siri would help Hunter out to the seat in the shade where he could watch the unicorns. She would then leave on her "patrol," returning from time to time apparently to keep an eye on him. Sometimes she would stay for a while, telling him more about the unicorns and avoiding any mention of herself and her past. There were flashes of hostility, moments when she looked at him grimly, but for the most part she was virtually emotionless. She prepared meals for them, efficiently stripped Hunter of his clothing once—entirely against his will—so that she could clean his garments, and generally treated him rather like a bothersome houseguest on sufferance.

Grimly, Hunter waited for his body to recover its strength, exercising gradually more and more each day. He meant to abide by his promise to Siri; he would never again take advantage of her helping him. Instead, he meant to stand on his own two feet, meeting her strength with his own. And he meant to make his desire reality: He and Siri would be lovers.

As for Siri, she was counting each sunrise and sunset as bringing her closer to the end of the Summer—and the safety of the Unicorns. She tried in vain to keep her thoughts focused on that goal and off the disturbing presence of Hunter in her valley and in her home. Tried.

He haunted her awake and asleep. Driven by the necessity of protecting the Unicorns, she had no choice but to consult the cards daily, and each time the prophecy remained the same: She and the man would be lovers. And as the days passed, she became less and less certain she could impose her will on that prophecy. Her body's response to his was an ever-present thing now, and it was difficult for her to hide that from him.

But she tried, fiercely, to do just that. She couldn't allow him to see awakening instincts and senses, because she knew from what she had learned about all men that he too would reach out for what he wanted without counting the cost to her.

To do him justice, she was almost certain that he honestly had no idea of the single inviolate taboo in her life, and it was something she could not tell him. *Cruel of the Guardians,* she thought more than once, *to impose that structure on Keepers. We may not know the physical love of a man, and we may not explain to him why we cannot.* The one immutable law of Keepers was that she could not live outside the valley. Outcast, she would die.

He didn't know; she couldn't tell him; and the cards predicted that it would come to pass.

And something new had entered the cards' prophecy. Something that puzzled and alarmed her. Green eyes again. But this time there were *three* green eyes, one of them so hazy and indistinct she could barely see it. She didn't know what it meant.

Hunter woke with the uneasy feeling of something being wrong. The cabin was lit only by moonlight shining through the windowpanes, and as he pushed himself to his elbows and let his eyes follow the shaft of light, he realized what had disturbed him. The shelf Siri had made into a bed for herself was empty.

Stronger now, he had no difficulty in getting up. He didn't bother to reach for the shirt lying nearby but went to the door wearing only pants. He opened it softly and went outside. A glance upward showed him that the moon had risen, its light spilling brilliance over the valley. It was easily as bright as day, but the light was eerily white and each object cast a stark shadow. The lake was glimmering darkness, the tall meadow grass still and silent, and nothing stirred in the night.

Until . . .

Unconsciously holding his breath, Hunter saw two shapes emerge from the trees, two white creatures of such purity that their snowy coats seemed to glow with translucence. Dimly he realized that he was watching Storm and Fancy, the arrogant prince and his flighty princess, but identities didn't seem to matter. What mattered was the result.

In unison they moved around the lake, side by side and in perfect step. They circled the water, gliding, making no sound. Then, on the far side of the lake, they began to move about each other. Heads dipping and lifting, tails flying proudly, dark eyes gleaming, they performed a minuet to the music in their souls. Each pirouette was flawless, as though an invisible rider guided and signaled. Each arch of neck and swish of tail was music in motion. They were ethereal, luminescent shadows without substance. They were myths alive only in dream, visible only to the heart. And they breathed the mist of fantasy.

One by one, other glowing forms joined the two by the lake. Each performed a different dance in the moonlight, from Cloud's stately expression of age and wisdom to little Rayne's awkward, curiously moving and joyous comedy of youth. They all danced, in silence and breathtaking beauty, and Hunter watched, mesmerized.

He suddenly realized that Siri stood by his side, and he turned his head to look down at her. She was smiling a smile as ethereal and luminescent as the creatures' dance, and Hunter wondered if he were really asleep and dreaming.

"You should feel privileged." Her voice was soft, only a breath of sound. "The Unicorns dance only when they feel safe and secure. And only once in a Season. One other man in my lifetime has seen the Dance."

"Who?" he asked breathily.

"My father."

Hunter stared at her for a single moment out of time, then followed her gaze as she turned to watch the unicorns.

They danced on, seemingly oblivious to the watching humans. It went on for hours, until gradually, one by one, all but the original pair faded into the trees. Storm and Fancy danced alone until the moon began to set between two mountain peaks on the far side of the valley. Then they too faded into the woods. The moon vanished from sight, stealing the brightness of a false day just as the sun began rising and splashed orange-pink light to replace what the moon had stolen.

Hunter turned to Siri, hoping that the smile he had seen on her face was not as rare as a unicorn Dance.

And it was not.

She looked out across the valley, the dreamy smile still curving her lips. Her eyes were a smoky, mysterious gray, holding only faint glints of the impenetrable black to which he was accustomed. The golden sunlight bathed her delicate features with a radiance Hunter had never seen on a woman's face. He was every bit as mesmerized by her as he had been by the moonlight Dance.

"The first time I saw the Dance," she murmured, "my father was with me. I was very young, and the night seemed to last forever. The Unicorns seemed to dance just for us."

"How many times have you seen the Dance?"

She stirred slightly and looked up at him. "Three times. Just three." She turned and went into the cabin.

Hunter followed slowly, sitting down in the chair by the table as she began to prepare breakfast. Watching her move with the almost eerie, uncalculated grace that was peculiarly hers, Hunter tried to take his mind off the instant responses of his own body. But it was almost impossible, and had been growing more so every day. He shifted restlessly. "Your parents?" he probed.

"My father's dead," she told him.

"I'm sorry."

Siri looked at him as if wondering why he was sorry, then turned back to her work. "I don't remember him very well," she mused conversationally. "I remember that he was a big man with broad shoulders. I remember that he loved my mother. That's what killed him, in the end. He loved her too much."

Hunter was puzzled. "How could that kill him?"

"He drowned," Siri said, as if that explained everything.

She seemed to be in an unusually fey mood, her expression still dreamy and abstracted, and Hunter decided to take advantage of her apparent willingness to talk. "Saving your mother?" he ventured.

"Of course not," she scoffed. "He didn't listen to Mother. She'd told him that he couldn't do it, you see, and for a long time he believed her. But then I suppose it just got to be too much for him. Loving her. And one day he went in after her."

"Went in?" Hunter sought to find a binding thread in the conversation and silently admitted failure. "Where was she?"

"On the bottom."

Hunter ran his fingers through his hair. "The bottom?"

"Of the sea," Siri told him, looking at him in a very puzzled way.

He knew how she felt. "She was on the bottom of the sea?" he questioned.

"Yes."

"Is your mother—alive?" he asked cautiously.

"Of course."

Hunter grappled silently for a moment, finally expressing himself with a shrug of defeat. "I don't understand. Your father drowned because he went in after your mother, who was on the bottom of the sea. But he didn't go in to save her? And she didn't die?"

Siri nodded, clearly finding it odd that Hunter didn't understand. Realization suddenly hit her and she smiled. "My mother *lives* on the bottom of the sea. She's a Mermaid."

Hunter heard the rest through a haze. At least this shock distracted his mind from desire, he thought.

"Mother says its the tragedy of loving men rather than Mermen. A man can never resist a Mermaid, but he can hardly grow gills and sleep with her in her sandy bed. And it's sad, because the more he loves her the more likely he is to drown trying to be with her."

Through his haze, Hunter saw her frown.

"It has given Mermaids a very unfair reputation, too. A Mermaid can't stop a man from following her into the sea; she can't stop him from loving her. It's her curse. And Mother . . . well, she cried for a long time after my father drowned. I remember that. She'd been asleep, you see, and hadn't realized he was trying to be with her until it was too late."

"You don't have fins," Hunter observed, keeping his voice steady with an effort. And then he heard her laugh for the first time. It was an incredible laugh, husky, with the innate music the unicorns had danced to.

"Don't be ridiculous! I could hardly have fins when my father was a man. And I couldn't have been the Keeper. That's why Mother chose a man instead of a Merman. It was her turn."

Rubbing absently at the faint ache between his eyes, Hunter wondered which was the greater madness: What she was saying—or the fact that he was *listening* to what she was saying. "Her turn?" he managed, watching, with utter fascination, Siri cooking before the low fire.

"It was time for a new Keeper to be born," she explained, frowning down at the cooking pot. "And since the gift of Sight is always given to Mermaids, the Keeper must be the child of Mermaid and man."

"The gift of sight?"

Patiently, she said, "The Keeper must be forewarned of any possible danger to the Unicorns. Surely you can understand that?"

Hunter wanted to tell her that nothing in this absurd conversation made the slightest sense to him, but he didn't dare to interrupt the flow of information or set fire to her temper. "Of . . . course. How did your mother know it was time for another Keeper to be born?"

"The Keeper at that time was old," Siri said briefly. "She died after my first Summer."

"Then you aren't ageless," he murmured softly, finding and holding on to the one apparent hard fact she had revealed.

She looked at him, amused. "The legendary Keeper of ten thousand years again? No, of course we aren't ageless. But it's an understandable mistake, born of confusion more than anything else. We all have light hair and dark eyes, you see."

"And each Keeper is a woman?"

"Yes. A girl-child is always the offspring of man and Mermaid."

Hunter wished silently that she would stop using the word *Mermaid*. Like any word naming an impossibility, it became more familiar and reasonable with repetition. But that was one myth he had never believed in. Never.

Siri went on. "A woman must be Keeper; it's one of the reasons Mermaids are responsible for bearing Keepers."

Hesitating briefly, Hunter finally asked a blunt question. "And do Keepers ever—mate?"

She stiffened immediately and turned her head to stare at him. Impenetrable black was replacing the dreamy gray of her eyes. "No."

"Is that a rule?" he asked with forced lightness. "Something taboo? Or just personal choice?"

"It doesn't happen," she said flatly. "Ever."

The easy companionship of moments before was gone; Siri was on her guard and wary, and Hunter regretted that more than he was consciously aware of. He tried to make up lost ground but couldn't seem to comletely drop the subject.

"You mean you're expected to live your entire life up here all alone except for the animals?"

"I was born for this."

Anger grew within Hunter, an anger all the more unruly because it was based partly on selfishness. "You're young, vital, beautiful," he said harshly. "It's a waste, Siri. A waste of life!"

Siri drew up to her full height and turned away from her cooking. She was abruptly a goddess of silver and ebony fire, an avenging spirit filled with a fury he had never seen in a human face. Very softly, intensely, she said, "I live each Summer with Unicorns. I protect and guard them, and I see them Dance. I heal them when they're sick and fight for them so that blood will never taint their horns and their souls. I protect the seeds of *myth* from man's unholy greed! And if you can't see how worthwhile that is, I'll stop wasting my *time* in trying to convince an insensitive, obsessed *brute* to find some shred of wisdom in his tiny mind!"

She left the cabin with the stride of a warrior.

Hunter rose and followed, halting at the open door, staring after her as she disappeared along the path into the woods. A jumble of thoughts and emotions skittered through his mind. No matter what he thought of her life, he had driven a knife into the very heart of what she was, and he wanted to go after her and apologize for that.

But what he had done could not so easily be put right; she was justifiably angry and quite possibly hurt, and neither emotion would be quickly forgotten. He also knew that an apology from his lips would not ring true, because he was suddenly aware that he hotly, fiercely resented the unicorns for their vitally important place in her life.

His final tearing realization was that he was helplessly, hopelessly in love with a woman who claimed to be the offspring of a man and a Mermaid, who claimed to be telepathic, and who had committed her very existence to the lonely preservation of a myth.

Hunter looked toward the lake to see the unicorns huddled in a restless, uneasy group and staring at him warily. Living dreams, symbols of ageless fantasy. And a symbol of hope for the dying world he loved.

They represented the fulfillment of a Quest that had taken years and had sent him to worlds scattered throughout the galaxy, a Quest that had begun as a means to a throne and had over the years become a man's driven need to save his people.

Very quietly, he said, "I could learn to hate you."

Five

"You're going to see the sorceress again?"

Boran turned to stare at the Huntman. Pleasantly, he said, "That is hardly your affair."

Con, chosen to speak for his fellows only because his fear of this place and this man lent him a certain courage, stiffened his narrow shoulders and tried to meet the man's gaze. "You promised us wealth," he said. "Days are passing, and we only sit and wait while you meet the sorceress. We have a right to—"

Casually, Boran dealt a backhand blow that sent Con staggering back. The green of his good eye was bright, and there was enjoyment in his twisted smile. "Your only right is to live while I allow it," he said. "Obey me, and you will have your wealth. Disobey, and I will kill you. Is that understood?"

Con wiped the blood from his mouth, his gaze now fixed on his dirty boots. "Yes," he whispered.

Boran glanced from man to man, using his mental powers to instill an even greater fear in each of them. He watched them cringe away from him, pleased. Then, dismissing them from his mind, he turned and left the camp.

His abilities were growing day by day, and his control over the sorceress was now virtually complete. Summoned to him, she came each day, friendly and happy to see him. He had worked carefully to blank her mind on each visit, so that while she was with him she had no memory at all of her charges or of Hunter healing in her cabin. And once she left him, she had no memory of the meeting.

Boran was pleased with the results, but he was surprised to find that his own interest in Siri was growing day by day as well. Cut away from her moorings of duty and responsibility, she seemed very young and eager. Fascinated, he searched the girl who came to him for the strengths of a warrior, the complexities of a Keeper. And he found strength in her, and intelligence; but more, he discovered a girl on the threshold of womanhood who looked at him with awakening eyes.

And because he willed it, she saw a man with the face of an angel, a man she was beginning to feel a hunger for.

They met deep in the forest, far from the grazing unicorns. Each time as she first turned to face him, there was a flickering instant of hesitation in her expression, a momentary confusion. He would feel a pleasant leap of his senses, and an increased concentration that was becoming automatic. And he enjoyed most of all his control over her.

"Boran!" Her face would brighten, confusion gone as he allowed her to remember their previous meetings.

She was lonely.

"Hello, princess!" He enjoyed that too. His own private joke.

"I'm not a princess!" Always, the same laughing response.

"Then what are you?" He watched the confusion settle briefly over her features as he tested his control.

"I'm Siri." Confident again.

Laughing quietly, the day's game over, he sat down beside her on the fallen log. He always made certain she was on his right side and was careful never to touch her with his left hand; the mind control was solid, but he was aware that she would likely feel his petrified flesh if she touched his left cheek or hand. It was, he knew, far easier to control the mind than the physical senses.

"Who are you, Boran?" she asked today.

He mused over that for a moment. "I? I am a seeker, princess. A seeker after—justice."

"Has someone wronged you?" she asked anxiously.

He smiled at her, aware that she was looking at the profile of an angel. "If so, it was long ago in the past and unimportant today."

She was still disturbed. "Friends share pain, don't they? Aren't you my friend?"

"Of course I'm your friend, Siri," he assured her. "And if there were pain, I'd share it." He smiled through the lie. "What of your pain?"

"My pain?"

He kept his voice soft, almost hypnotic. "You must be so lonely."

"I . . ." She frowned a little, purple eyes clouded. "I feel . . . alone. I dread the coming of Winter." She shook her head. "Am I . . . alone in Winter? Will you go away?"

"I'm afraid so," he murmured. "I'm just a visitor in your valley, princess, a traveler pausing to rest for a while."

"I don't want you to go." She looked at him in entreaty. "The Winter is long and cold. Why do I stay here? Why don't I leave this place?"

He looked on his creation with fascination. She was rootless, innocent, puzzled. No past, no future—except what he allowed her. In his control of her he found a taste of the power he craved, and it was addictive.

"Your roots are here," he said finally.

"I may not leave, then?"

"Your roots are here," he repeated. She looked so sad that he reached and took her left hand in his right one. "And I'm here for now," he whispered, allowing his desire to creep unthreateningly into her mind. He was using his mental powers to create and nurture a physical response, and when her eyes darkened and her lips parted, he almost laughed aloud in triumph.

Siri left the forest and stood gazing out over her valley. She frowned a little as she absorbed the peace all around her. There was no danger; her patrol had revealed nothing threatening. But she felt unsettled. She looked down at her left hand, puzzled because she could almost feel the pressure of fingers around her own.

And that hand lifted to her breast as her frown deepened. Her breasts felt sore, heavy, the nipples erect, and she had an unnervingly sensual feeling of aching and dampness between her thighs. Disturbed, she mentally calculated, assuring herself that she was at the beginning of her Moon-cycle and would not bleed for two or three weeks yet.

She didn't want to face the knowledge that Hunter was doing this to her, making her so often aware of her body and these new and troubling, dangerous feelings. But she had to face this truth, because she awoke too often in the night now and lay listening to his deep, even breathing, feeling the memory of the imprint of his mouth on hers, his big, hard body pressed to her own.

Useless to try and pretend to herself that this was not happening. Useless to deny what was. But the feelings bewildered and terrified her, because they were so often beyond her understanding and control.

She shook away the feelings, desperate. It was Hunter, she decided, preying on her mind. And the strained atmosphere between them heightened her senses painfully. He had tried to apologize to her, but she had simply refused to hear him. And she refused to see him. She left the cabin early each morning and returned late at night. She put out food and water for him, but ignored him otherwise. He was almost completely recovered now and quite able to take care of himself.

Silence had built an impassable wall between them.

Siri squared her shoulders and ignored the sudden feeling of loneliness. *She* could not alter what she was, but *Hunter* could. She would not allow that. Life in the valley went on, despite the presence of a man she refused to talk to.

Life went on.

Restless, at loose ends, and filled with the consuming anxiety and powerful desires of a man in love for the first time in his life, Hunter began exploring the valley more out of a hope of encountering Siri than from any real curiosity. And, though too troubled to have room in his heart for enchantment, he nonetheless felt a growing sense of awe at the increasing evidence that it was, indeed, an enchanted valley.

The weather was always perfect; if it rained at all, it was only a gentle predawn shower leaving sparkling moisture on greenery for the sun to use in creating minute rainbows. And the animals . . .

Giant pandas, snow leopards, white tigers, dodos, lyrebirds, peacocks, Albino wolves, eagles—each animal declared extinct by science for centuries. And there were animals with no place in history unless it was in the history of mythology, the mythology of human and nonhuman worlds: The sand cats of Marcos III with their multicolored fur, six-inch fangs, and ridiculously shy little growls; the gyres of Delta Omicron with their feathered bodies and almost-human faces; the apelike shrelots of Lotar . . . and a dragon.

Hunter had discovered supposed "dragons" on other worlds, finding them to be only reptiles representing a quirk in nature low on the evolutionary scale and far more timid than their legendary fire-breathing brethren. And he had finally been forced to accept the assertion of science that it just wasn't possible for a living creature to breathe fire without artificial aid.

Until he was nearly roasted by a yawn.

Stepping back hurriedly from the mouth of the cave he had been about to explore, Hunter stood for a moment and eventually decided that hallucinations weren't *hot*. He fought a purely instinctive urge to find a weapon and slay the beast, reminding himself that this valley was peaceful. He looked up at the blackness of The Reaper towering above him, then carefully peered around and into the cave opening.

The dragon was big. *Huge.* The cave entrance was three times Hunter's height, and it looked like a tight squeeze for the dragon. The creature was a bright, shiny green, with purplish, wicked-looking spines running from its small pointed head down along a wide back and long, pointed tail. Its tail was neatly coiled around its large, cumbersome body and, as Hunter watched in astonishment, the dragon yawned another stream of fire, this one too small to shoot outward from the cave.

"You're not possible," Hunter said slowly.

The dragon made an abrupt snuffling sound and turned large, black, deceptively unthreatening eyes onto the intruder.

Hunter was too fascinated to draw back again. "You'd have to have a throat and mouth made of Pyroceram," he said, arguing with reality.

As if it understood, the dragon opened its mouth in another tiny yawn, this one conjuring only a faint spark. But the small flash was enough to show Hunter that the dragon's mouth *was* lined with something very like the material that shielded the nose cone of his ship.

Drawing back, Hunter stared blindly in front of him and decided very sanely that the line between reality and impossibility was becoming very fine indeed. He turned away, halting when he saw Siri.

She was standing a short distance from him, arms crossed and lips twitching with a smile she was trying hard to hide.

Completely forgetting the wall of silence, Hunter jerked a thumb toward the cave interior and asked, "Is that a dragon?"

Siri nodded mutely.

"You didn't tell me there was a dragon," he said accusatorily.

"I didn't think you'd believe me," she offered politely.

Hunter stared at her. "Dragons," he said decisively, "aren't possible."

"Of course not."

"They were created out of nightmares by fearful men who didn't know what was over the horizon."

"Yes."

"They are an evolutionary and scientific impossibility."

"So I've heard."

He blinked. "You aren't arguing with me."

"No."

"Why not?"

Siri gestured slightly. "If you'll turn back around and look inside the cave, you'll see why. Bundy presents a much more convincing argument than any I could offer."

Hunter's eyebrow rose. "Bundy?"

"Yes."

"Who'd name a dragon *Bundy*?" he wondered.

"I don't know. He's always been Bundy."

"Always?"

Very gently, Siri said, "Dragons *are* ageless."

Hunter stared at her.

Siri began to laugh, a startling girlish giggle, and Hunter was fascinated by it. Seeking to hear more of that enchanting sound, he continued along the same lines.

"I didn't believe *Mermaids* and now you toss in a dragon? Will I find a centaur lurking in the rocks? Hydra occupying another cave? Cyclops?"

She was smiling at him. "Only if you want to see them, and look with your heart."

He grappled with that for a silent moment, then demanded, "Can I see Pegasus?"

"Sorry."

He snorted. "Some enchanted valley *this* is."

Siri began to laugh again.

Hunter bit back what he wanted to say then, knowing that the words would sound utterly fatuous. So he just thought about how lovely she looked when she laughed. But it wasn't enough somehow, and unable to stop himself this time, he blurted, "I've missed the sound of your voice."

She appeared to freeze, her eyes widening in the transitional shock of laughter to stiffness. Before she could turn away, as she showed every sign of doing, Hunter spoke huskily.

"Siri . . . I don't like living in a desert."

She was baffled by his words.

"Without your voice," he said soberly, "without your company, this valley might as well be a desert."

After a long moment, wary indecision and something that might have been longing flickering in her eyes, Siri turned away. "I have to go," she murmured. "Teen's foaling."

Quickly falling into step beside her, Hunter fought to keep his voice grave and unthreatening. "She's foaling now?"

"Yes. In the glade."

Deciding that although Siri seemed a bit uncomfortable with his presence, at least she hadn't asked him to leave her alone, Hunter silently vowed to tear down the wall between them even if he had to do it brick by brick. So he tightly reined the impatience of his body for hers, assuring himself that their time would come. Soon.

"Do you have to help her?" he asked, partly out of interest and partly out of his determination to keep her talking.

Siri shook her head. "No. And there are no Huntmen coming, so the glade doesn't have to be guarded. But I like to be nearby, just in case."

He nodded, then said abruptly, "I've seen the other animals."

"I know."

Hunter was unsurprised by her quiet comment and merely nodded again. "It's incredible. I feel as if I'm looking through books, one of history and one of myth. Living books." He looked down at her to find that she was smiling again, and the sight made his heart perform a peculiar flip inside his chest.

"And the animals went in two by two," she said softly.

"Yes." He frowned a little. "There was a story, an ancient story, about the beginnings of . . . Earth. A great flood, and the animals were saved in mated pairs. Like this valley. A new beginning for everything."

"For everything," she agreed.

Silently, they followed a winding path through the woods near the dragon's lair until they encountered eight calm unicorns standing near what looked like a huge, impenetrable thicket of brambles. And the two-legged newcomers were very nearly run over by a ninth frantically pacing unicorn.

Dodging Crom's lowered horn, Hunter stared in astonishment for a moment, then burst out laughing. "He's pacing! He's actually pacing."

Siri smiled a little. "It's his first foal," she explained. "He's concerned about Teen."

"Concerned?" Hunter choked on a final laugh. "He's pacing the edge of a nervous breakdown!"

Taking a seat on one of a cluster of small boulders, Siri murmured, "Well, stop laughing at him."

Hunter dodged a second pass of the blindly pacing Crom and hastily made his way to the relative safety of the boulders. Sinking down beside Siri, he inadvertently brushed an arm against the fullness of her breast and heard her soft catch of breath even as he clamped his teeth firmly together. His arm burned, and he stared across at the thicket with a fixed gaze.

Did she have any idea how violently she affected him? She never seemed to notice, although he often found himself shifting uncomfortably like some rutting stripling with his hormones in chaos. He had even awakened once gasping from an erotic dream of Siri—something that hadn't happened since he was half his present age.

He had never forced himself on a woman, but Hunter was increasingly conscious of pounding temples and the straining ache of his loins, and he knew he was dangerously close to abandoning control.

Hanging on grimly, he cast about in his mind for something casual to say. "Are you really the daughter of a Mermaid?" he asked suddenly.

"I really am."

"Incredible."

Siri stole a glance at her human companion, seeing a lean and dangerous face that was as beautiful as a male face could be. *The face of an angel.* She blinked, frowning. Angel? Where had that thought come from? There was nothing at all angelic about this man. His features were rugged, and if the razor-keen look of rooted obsession had

softened somewhat, still she had the uneasy feeling it was
only because he now hid that part of himself from her.

The moment of humor at Bundy's cave aside, he still
wore the coolly level, direct gaze of command, and she had
seen his first instinctive reaching for a weapon no longer
strapped to his hip. *He's a warrior,* she reminded herself.
*He laughed at Death, as only a man who has faced that
before could do.*

She wondered, briefly, what kind of world had produced such a man. He was so unlike the Huntmen! A
peaceful world? He had mentioned a "simple society." Had
his travels since leaving his world taught him a warrior's
skills, or did his simple world still require a rite of passage
for its young males? What had he said? That he had learned
to fight for his life? He had the indefinable look of
command, the almost arrogant air of a man of importance
stamped in his carriage, in the tilt of his head.

Siri blinked, startled to realize where her thoughts had
gone. Why was she thinking of things outside her experience? Of other worlds and important men? This valley was
her world!

For the first time, that thought was a hollow consola-
tion. He had somehow awakened a part of her mind with
his ceaseless questions, forcing her to think in a way she
never had before.

She sighed without intending to, and nervously looked
away when he turned his head and met her stare with a
smile. *He's a man! And men betray to get what they want.*
Gazing toward the glade and the miracle of birth it
contained, she saw instead green eyes with a profoundly
disturbing heat in their depths. She couldn't let down her
guard, couldn't allow him to shake the foundation of her
life, of all she was— The cards' prophecy abruptly superim-
posed its symbolic image over the green eyes in her mind,
and Siri bit her lip.

He wanted her, and she knew his need was growing
stronger. Sometimes the images in his mind caught her
unawares, dimly shocking but exciting as well, arousing her
body with a suddenness that stole her breath. He was
healed now, strong and powerful, and she was terrifed by

her growing response to him and his regained strength. Could she fight him if he attempted to take her? Or would her own body betray her?

Forbidden! Outcast!

Her breasts hurt, and Siri unconsciously covered them with her arms, leaning forward to hide from him the evidence of what he was doing to her.

"Baby unicorns take their time making an entrance into the world," Hunter noted as hours passed and the glade remained silent but for the muffled thudding of Crom's hooves.

His voice recalled her from a distant, worried place, and Siri looked at him. She saw that he was absently scratching Rayne's itching forehead and knew that neither he nor the young Unicorn was aware of the bonding that was taking place between them. It was little Rayne's first Summer, and she had not yet learned to fear men; though the instinct to be wary was deeply rooted, the Unicorn was learning to trust one man at least.

Siri knew that wasn't good, but she felt helpless in the face of it. The danger . . .

Hunter nodded toward the calmly waiting unicorns. "They'll remain here as long as it takes?"

"As long as it takes," she confirmed, clearing her throat quickly of huskiness. "Especially now with the herd so small, the birth of a Unicorn is an event the rest of them truly cherish, because it means a continuation of their ancient bloodlines."

"Do they know that?" He looked at her curiously. "I mean—are they consciously aware that they're the only ones left?"

"They know," she replied very softly. *Sasha, his pure coat stained with his life's blood; Cloud enraged and then grieving when only a horn remained of his son . . .*

Hardly aware that the tiny chin of a baby unicorn rested on his knee, or that he scratched the base of a minute golden horn, Hunter continued to gaze at Siri. "I want to understand why you think they should remain legendary," he said guardedly, conscious of the wall keeping them apart. "They're beautiful, enchanting creatures; why should only a handful of men know that they exist? Why should the sight of a unicorn Dance be denied to men?"

Siri linked her arms around her knees and stared broodingly at the herd. "Because if dreams were real, there would be no magic in them."

Hunter shook his head. "*I* know they're real—and it's still magic to me."

"That isn't what I meant." Would he understand? She had to *try*. "Unicorns are creatures of *dream*. And because of that, they've been endowed with only the best and most noble of traits. A Unicorn is untainted by the realities of harsh existence. Unicorns are symbols of good luck and prosperity, of wisdom and purity. They live in forgotten valleys and enchanted forests, and drink from crystal pools.

"Don't you see?" She turned her head to stare at him, willing him to understand. "To a man with no soul, a Unicorn is only a horse with a valuable horn. But to a dreamer, a Unicorn is magic. A dreamer has no need to give flesh to his dream, and a man with no soul has no right to the dreamer's vision."

Hunter looked down at Rayne, his thumb gently stroking the living golden horn. "But to know they're real—"

"—would only turn them into just another of nature's oddities," she swiftly interjected, "like camels, elephants, and giraffes. Creatures with a logical, scientific place in the order of things. There would be no magic about them anymore."

She tried to think of some analogy that would make the truth clearer to him. Slowly she said, "When men first looked into the skies and saw tongues of fire lighting darkness, they were terrified and awed. For many ages on many worlds, comets and meteors were omens of good luck or bad; some were named gods. Then science explained a natural phenomenon, and the majority of beings never again even looked up at a tongue of fire in the sky. Because it had become a rational phenomenon, a fact. No longer was it a night wonder.

"That can't happen to the Unicorns. They *must* remain

myth—a vision for dreamers. Their reality would destroy that vision . . . and them."

Abruptly Hunter asked, "Which man am I, Siri? A soulless man? Or a dreamer with a vision?"

"I—don't know." She looked at him, baffled. "Enough of a dreamer to see the vision . . . and enough of a soulless man to demand its reality." She felt suddenly hurt, aching. *For him.* "The tragedy is that I believe you'd come to hate yourself one day for destroying a dream. And it would be too late then. Myth would be forever dead to you."

He gazed into her ebony eyes, feeling her certainty tugging at some basic knowledge within himself, some truth he had never faced. And refused to face now. "I set out to discover reality," he said tautly.

"At what cost?" She could feel the frustration, the anger gnawing at her. "Fantasy is just as vital as reality, don't you understand that? We need *both.* And on your world, the people don't need a myth explained, made 'fact,' alive and paraded before them! They need to believe in a *dream.* If they've lost that capacity, nothing will give it back to them, Hunter. *Nothing.* Because the ability to dream comes from *here!*" She struck her breast with a clenched fist, her eyes fierce.

Through lips that felt numb, he said, "They need to believe that dreams are real."

Siri turned her gaze away from his, and her voice was a rasping sound of discouragement. "You just won't see. Destroy your myths, Hunter, and then see what's left to dream of."

"Siri—"

"Did you really go in search of reality? Or did you go in search of your own soul, hoping to discover the soul of a dreamer? Did you really want to find Unicorns? Or did you want only a confirmation of man's ability to dream?"

Before he could respond, Hunter looked up and saw a proud Teen emerge from the thicket through an opening he hadn't noticed, a wobbly, hornless foal at her side. He heard an indrawn breath from Siri and was vaguely conscious of holding his own breath, but his entire attention was taken up by the baby tottering about inspecting her relatives.

If Rayne was joyful youth, this new addition to the herd was uncertain infancy, her long legs bending at odd angles and her huge black eyes filled with an eternal puzzlement. She turned her snow-white face this way and that, wary of straying too far from her mother's side but clearly intrigued by life as Teen led her—in an oddly formal little ceremony—from one of the herd to another, beginning with Cloud and ending with Crom, the father who had finally stopped pacing and now looked at his daughter with something very like terror.

Quietly, responding finally to Siri's challenge, Hunter said, "I'm not . . . sure any longer what I wanted."

Her sigh held the sound of reluctant understanding. "The path to any truth begins with questions, not answers," she said. "At least now you're asking yourself questions."

"And what about you, Siri? Will I ever understand you? You've lived your entire life in this valley virtually alone, yet your knowledge spans history and distance. You understand reality, yet speak of myth and impossibilities with reason and certainty. You've devoted your very life to a Summer that comes only once in ten Standard years." He paused, adding almost inaudibly, "You're a witch, a sorceress, driving me mad—"

"I'm no witch!"

"You are!" His laugh was rough, unsteady. "You've bewitched me, maddened me until I can't think, can't do anything but love you and hunger for you like some enchanted fool."

His words caused a part of Siri to close down, to shut itself off from the rest of her. It was the part of her that had ached and worried, the part that Hunter had awakened from a sleep meant to be lifelong. And she was glad that it was, however briefly, locked away and hidden within her. She got to her feet, expressionless. Without a word, she walked over to greet the new arrival to the herd.

"How I love you," Hunter murmured to himself, watching her among her beloved unicorns.

The cabin was quiet. Siri stood before the fire, stirring the beginnings of a stew, and Hunter sat at the table peeling and slicing vegetables with his long hunting knife. They had remained in the glade for hours, and the subject of his feelings toward the unicorns and toward her had not been mentioned again. Now the valley was bathed in the moonlit peace of night, and the two people within the cabin talked warily, as if any misstep would bring about disaster.

Because both knew it would.

They talked carefully until Siri could stand it no longer. She looked at Hunter. "You're healed now," she said abruptly, the smooth stiffness of before becoming something jagged. "You can leave the valley."

His hands stilled, and he looked up at her. "No. I can't."

"You have to leave," she said steadily.

"I can't, Siri."

Siri felt the rage of desperation welling up inside her. "You can! You've found your damned truth—the Unicorns live! Now go and start a plague of death with your truth!"

"Siri—"

"Go! Leave my valley!"

Hunter cursed softly and began to rise to his feet. With his entire attention focused on the need to remain here and somehow win her heart, he completely forgot about the wicked knife in his hand. It caught his forearm in an instant, cutting a deep and ragged tear in tanned flesh. Scarlet blood immediately splashed onto the table, and Hunter gasped in pain.

Whatever the turmoil of emotions inside her, Siri was instinctively, innately, a healer. Swiftly she leaned across the table and clamped a hand over the bleeding cut, automatically calling on her energies to heal.

Hunter's first thought was that she was simply halting the flow of blood with pressure, but then the pain in his forearm faded to nothing, and he realized that something else was happening. She removed her hand. Blood no longer spurted. It didn't drip or smear. It didn't even stain. Because there was no blood. No blood, no gash in the flesh, not even a *dent*. Only a faint pink line fading even as he looked at it and being replaced by tingling warmth.

Silently, Siri found a cloth to clean the knife and wipe away the splashes of scarlet on the table.

Hunter stared down at his arm for a long moment. "When I first woke up," he said slowly, looking at her now, "I was puzzled. No cuts or bruises or broken bones. That fall should have killed me, but it didn't." Siri had returned to stirring the stew, and he stared fixedly at her profile. Her beautiful, remote profile. "And you told me that you . . . felt my pain. You're an empath, a healer!"

Siri said nothing.

"True healers are almost as rare as—as unicorns. It's the one psi talent there can be no disputing." He saw then that her face was pale, her eyes oddly dimmed, and a sudden realization brought horror. "Siri, how badly was I injured when you found me?"

She turned slowly toward him, feeling her energies building up once more and remembering against all intention the first days after finding him and the dangerously low level of those energies then. How desperate she had been to save him. And how desperate she was now for him to leave her forever. "You were dying," she said briefly.

"It takes something out of you when you heal, doesn't it?" he asked hoarsely. "You give your own life-force. You endangered your life by healing me, didn't you?"

"I'm a healer," she said flatly, turning back to the fire.

"And I was an enemy," he countered slowly.

Siri didn't want him to wonder about that, didn't want him to question her motives. "I'm a healer," she repeated. "It's instinct."

"I owe you my life." He had said much the same words before, but now he understood just how much he really did owe her.

"Then repay your debt," she whispered harshly. "Leave my valley!"

"Anything but that. Ask anything else of me, Siri."

She felt so alone, so terribly afraid. She could ask him never to betray the Unicorns' existence, but unless he left the valley soon the promise would mean virtually nothing. His very presence here would destroy them all. *Was* destroying them. She closed her eyes. "Leave. Please. Just leave me in peace."

Hunter rose from his chair and moved around the

table, standing before her and gazing down into shimmering ebony eyes. "I love you," he said tautly. "I can't help but love you."

"You'll destroy us." Her voice was still so low that Hunter could barely hear her words.

"I don't want to destroy. I want to enrich your life, Siri. I want to show you the wonders possible between two people who love."

"I don't love you." She heard her voice as if from a great distance, hollow.

"I think," he said softly, "that you fell in love with a stranger just as I did. Because there was no other reason to risk your own life in saving an enemy."

She saw him now for the enemy he truly was. Not just another man after the Unicorns, but a man who could very well destroy the entire herd and herself with it. And somewhere deep inside her, near a heart that had beat only for Unicorns, the conflict that had raged almost without her notice exploded into her consciousness with a force beyond reason.

I love him.

He'll destroy us all.

Siri had believed that she knew pain in all its forms. She had felt her own, his, the Unicorns'. She had felt minor pain and tearing pain and dying pain. But she had never felt anything like this agony.

Numbed by it, holding Fate at bay with so little strength left to her, she said steadily, "I won't be your lover."

His hands found her shoulders and held them without force. "Siri—"

"I won't be your lover."

"Why?" he pressed. "Why are you fighting what I know you feel? Siri, we need each other."

"I need the Unicorns." She said it as though it were a talisman to ward off evil.

Hunter began to draw her toward him, intent on showing her just how much they needed one another. But the motion died almost before it was born. Fear leapt at him from her eyes, a terrible fear. And he saw something else in the shimmering darkness of her eyes, something which touched something inside him that had never been touched before and stopped the instinctive male demand to have done with words.

She was taut, a live wire stretched too tightly for safety, and the danger of devastating implosion burned in her eyes. The sharded brightness of a soul in torment shrieked behind the stillness of her face and, somehow—without really understanding—Hunter knew that to push her now would be to irrevocably lose her.

He sighed, a ragged outrush of compelling emotion. Lifting a hand from her shoulder, he cupped her cheek gently, without demand. "I'm not going to give up," he said quietly. He watched his words sink into her, felt the faint shudder of some rigidly controlled feeling, and wondered in an unfamiliar discouragement how he could ever come to understand the enigma that she was.

Siri stepped back carefully, her cheek burning as if with a brand of possession, and fought to keep her voice steady. "We'd better finish preparing the meal. It's late and—tomorrow won't be a good day."

Hunter frowned down at her for a moment, finally going back to his chair and continuing to prepare the vegetables. He was silent for a while, but curiosity and an instinctive worry got the better of him. "How do you know tomorrow won't be a good day?" he asked finally.

"Huntmen."

"How do you know?" he repeated. And wondered, suddenly, if Boran had found this valley. But, no, that was unlikely. If Boran were here, he would certainly make his presence known.

"I told you before. The Keeper must possess the gift of prophecy; the cards told me." She felt cold, and wondered where the calm voice was coming from. "Danger. And that means Huntmen will violate the valley sometime during the day tomorrow."

Pondering the word *violate*, Hunter asked, "What will you do?"

"Kill them," she said bleakly, "if I can."

Hunter froze. "You shouldn't have blood on your hands," he said in a rough voice.

For the first time since he had laughed at Death, she heard the voice of the warrior. "Why not?"

"Because . . ." His first word trailed off as he tried to collect the jumble of his thoughts. "Because you should know only love and laughter," he said finally. "Not blood and violence and brutality."

"You keep forgetting. I was born to this."

"No." He laughed harshly. "I don't forget. I just can't understand how any god or gods—or whoever the hell you answer to—could expect you to face such ugliness every Summer of your life!"

She turned to look at him. "No, you don't understand. No god or gods compel me, Hunter. No one *expects* anything of me—except me. I could have chosen not to be Keeper; a child born to be Keeper is always given the choice. I made my choice. I've never regretted it." *Liar!*

"And during the Winter?" he probed. "When the winds howl and the snows come and darkness falls? Is your choice worth the long, cold Winter?"

"The Summer of the Unicorn is worth anything. Anything." She felt torn in two, and wondered if she would ever be whole again.

He watched her turn back to the fire and sighed unconsciously. She was no fanatic to be ignored, or fence sitter to be coaxed to the "other" side. She was a woman committed to her choice and to her way of life. And Hunter didn't know how to fight that—or even if he should. Except that her refusal to become his lover was all tied up with her commitment and with the unicorns, and that was something he had to fight.

Searching for words, he said, "Couldn't you have a life, a family of your own and still take care of the unicorns in the Summer?"

Siri fought a shudder of fear and longing, and didn't answer for a long moment. "The Keeper of the Unicorns," she said finally, "is just that . . . always that . . . and only that. They are my first loyalty, and must remain so."

"Then you sublimate everything that you are to them and their needs. Don't you matter?"

"No."

Her immediate, quiet answer left Hunter shaken. "But you're a being in your own right, deserving a life to meet *your* needs!"

Siri turned to collect the vegetables and drop them into the cooking pot. She didn't look at him, but she responded. "And suppose that I did have a—a family. Don't you see that once my loyalties were divided, as they would be with a family, my effectiveness in protecting the Unicorns would be halved? There would be levers to use against me. Hostages to fortune. And one day I'd be forced to make a choice between the Unicorns and the flesh of my flesh."

"Not necessarily," Hunter said quickly.

"No?" She leaned back against the rough stones of the fireplace and gazed at him steadily. "Suppose I—I had a child. And suppose that a Huntman learned that, and took my child hostage. Suppose that he held a knife to my child's throat and told me to tell him where I'd hidden the Unicorns or watch my child die." Her dark eyes were quiet. "What would I choose, Hunter? The death of my child? Or the death of the last herd of Unicorns?" She shook her head slowly. "I don't have magic. I can't stop time, or bewitch a knife from the hand of a Huntman. And I can't—I won't— make that choice."

She turned back to the fire.

Hunter thought of a child, Siri's and his, realizing only then how much he wanted to see her grow great with their baby. But he forced himself to think through what she had said. And felt cold. For the first time, he began truly to understand not only the depth of Siri's commitment but also her reasons for refusing to become his lover. And his love for her was new enough and fragile enough to spark the resentment he felt toward the unicorns, yet he was at odds with her beliefs and his own uncertainties. The unicorns deserved to live. Siri deserved to love.

Or was that only his selfish desire speaking?

No. No. Siri deserved to love. It was a basic need to love and be loved by another, and not even the preservation of unicorns . . . But unicorns were wondrous creatures; only eleven of them existed, with only one more foal due this Summer. No one had the right to destroy them; she had convinced him of that, at least. But . . .

They chased themselves around in his mind, the arguments, one balanced immovably against another. The unicorns. Siri. His love and the possibility of hers. Save the unicorns or save a child unborn. But need it come to that? Was there not some way of preserving both? Was it written in blood that a Huntman would destroy any child of Siri's? Was it a fate to be averted only by depriving Siri of the love of her child, the love of a man?

No guarantees. No way to be sure that a child could be protected.

She was right: Divided loyalties would make her less effective in the life she had chosen. But the life she had chosen, barren and lonely for ten years at a time, was brightened only by brief Summers in the company of unicorns. And even in that joyful time, she was forced to kill, to stain her hands with blood and her soul with violence.

In his heart, Hunter couldn't feel that the result was an acceptable balance. Nor could he condemn the unicorns. He could, in fact, see no way through the dilemma. If he remained, his own desires—and possibly hers—would torment them both. And if he left, his heart would remain forever rooted in this valley.

He couldn't leave. He would find *some* way of resolving it. There had to be a way . . . but he didn't know what it was.

He hadn't realized that his sense of defeat showed in the slump of his shoulders, but when he looked up, he found Siri gazing at him for the first time with eyes as soft as black velvet.

"It isn't easy, is it?" she asked almost inaudibly.

"What?" he murmured, lost in her eyes.

"To see all sides. To realize that no single action stands alone. Each act causes or affects another. And so we make choices. We choose to act, or not to act. We choose to think of the results of our actions, or not to think. And we stand by our choices."

"No matter what?"

Siri wished she could heal the agony inside her, wished it with all her heart. She half-closed her eyes, hurting. "No matter what," she whispered.

"I didn't choose to love," he said. "But I do love you. And if I left this valley now, I'd never be whole again. It would be a life worse than none at all. That's a choice *I* can't make, Siri."

Siri felt the conflict within her rage even more intolerably, until she wanted to cry out. The slump of his broad shoulders, the dark pain in his green eyes, the sudden haggard set of his features told her more than words ever could. And her commitment to her valley and her Unicorns swayed on its foundations. She felt sick with confusion and an aching need, left with nothing but the tatters of what had once been certain knowledge.

She had healed the wounds of his body even while she knew he was her enemy, had allowed him into her life even with the memory of King's betrayal still fresh in her mind. She had fought to keep anger alive, and bitterness, and certainty.

And it was all sliding away from her now, treacherously unsteady beneath her feet. The valley was no longer enough. The Unicorns were no longer enough. And Winter was so long.

Siri turned back to her cooking, feeling a shiver pass over her. Winter . . . It was so lonely in the Winter, so cold. Even most of the Huntmen in the city abandoned this world in Winter. And there was a long period in Winter when only the pale moon shed light on the cold, lonely valley.

She would have food and shelter. But no companionship except for the animals. Nothing to brighten the darkness.

Siri felt a hot tear drop onto her hand and stared down at the gleaming moisture. *This was her choice*. And because she could not alter that choice, she allowed her sudden bitterness to focus on Hunter. Love wasn't something that had been intended for her, and desire was a fire never meant to be set alight. She was born never to know a man's touch, never to bear a child, never to leave this valley.

And in that moment she could hate him again. Not because he was a man, but because he was a green-eyed man who had stolen her heart and destroyed the certainty at the center of what she was.

Hunter woke in the middle of the night, as he had once before, acutely aware that Siri wasn't in the cabin. She had insisted that he continue to use the one real bed, saying the shelf was too narrow for him, and they had turned in shortly after their meal, the silence stretching between them in a painful tension.

Now she was gone.

He rose, pulled on his shirt and boots, and left the cabin. The night was a mirror replica of the night the unicorns had danced, white moonlight splashing the valley with brightness and utter stillness filling the air. But the unicorns weren't dancing; they were grouped near the cabin, some lying and some standing, and watched the man passing through their midst with sleepy, accustomed eyes. Hunter automatically counted heads, realizing that Cloud wasn't among the rest. He stood for a moment, thinking, then looked for and found the faint path leading through the woods—the path he had seen Siri take so many times.

Following the path as quietly as possible, Hunter was aware of the stillness of the valley and the darkness of the forest; he was finding his way more by instinct than sight. Gradually, though, he began to sense a lightening in the darkness. Then he realized that he was approaching the source of water he had assumed lay in this direction; he could hear the gurgle of water, and there was obviously a clearing ahead.

Unconsciously slowing his steps, Hunter made his way carefully among the trees until he came upon the clearing. It was as bright as the light of the moon would allow, and a crystal pool lay like a glowing gem in its center. Water tumbled over a cluster of tall boulders on the far side of the clearing, dropping in a fall to splash into the pool. Flowers, their brilliant colors oddly visible in the whitewashing light, grew in a profusion all around, and the circling trees loomed overhead like stoic guardians of the night.

The trees weren't the only guardians, however; Cloud stood near the waterfall, his luminescent purity shining like a beacon. He was still and quiet, his dark eyes fixed on the crystal pool.

And in the pool was Siri.

She stood with her back to Hunter, submerged to her hips and obviously naked. Her long silver hair hung down her back, shimmering in the moonlight as she tilted her face, eyes closed, up to the heavens. Her arms lifted, splashing sparkling water over her face and shoulders. Abruptly, she sank beneath the surface, rising almost immediately with a faint gasp as cold water streamed over golden flesh. Gently defined muscles rippled beneath her skin as she swung her wet hair back, each movement an unconscious illustration of grace perfected.

Hidden in the shadow of the trees, Hunter watched, spellbound. He didn't breathe, intent only on gazing at a different and even more bewitching moonlight dance than that of the unicorns. His body ached with need, and his heart ached with the beauty of her.

She bent forward in a shallow dive, disappearing briefly beneath churning water until the moonlight found her quicksilver form in the crystal depths. Her unique heritage lent her a breathtaking elegance in this particular habitat, an easy confidence that made each flowing stroke music in motion. She was all rich curves and delicate lines, a nymph to tempt the gods into leaving their lofty realm for enchanting earthly pleasures.

It was not a sight which a purely human and intensely loving man could easily resist, and Hunter was conscious of no godlike restraint. His body was all too human, as was his need for her. But what he was most conscious of was the fragility of the moment. She was beautiful beyond his wildest, deepest dreams of beauty, and vulnerable as he'd never before known her to be. Exquisite in the natural adornment of moonlight and crystal water, she was every bit as ethereal as the glowing myth standing guard over her, and just as elusive.

Hunter wanted to join her, to be a part of the magic, to hold her in his arms and in the certainty of his love. But the myth guarding her was the wall between them, and he had found no way past it.

He watched and, in watching, branded the moment in his mind and heart for all the eternities of what would come. He etched an image of loveliness in moonlight, knowing that, in the end, it could very well be all that he would hold of her. And he was anguished, because it was as though he attempted to hold moonbeams or starlight in cupped hands.

It wasn't enough, and the emptiness of it was a pain he had never known before. He would have given his life to never have experienced that agonized, hollow emptiness. Yet a part of him was glad that he had known it this once.

Calling on every shred of willpower, Hunter turned away before Siri could sense his presence, aware of leaving some vital part of himself at that pool. He could feel it tearing from him, pulling with every step he took away from her. Blindly he walked back to the cabin.

And fell into bed and into sleep, to dream of Siri.

Naked and laughing in a crystal pool.

Glowing in moonlight.

Holding out her arms to him . . .

———————————

Boran watched Hunter move off toward the cabin, then turned his gaze back to the pool. He was concentrating carefully, because he dared not reveal his presence to the mind-adept unicorn; he had tried to reach out to that animal's mind and had encountered a surprising wall.

So. Where the unicorns were concerned, he could blank his presence, but could not control. He would remember that.

He watched Siri swim in the pool, and felt impatience at her unicorn guard. He wanted to go to her now, wrap her in his mindspell again. Naked, she was vastly tempting, and he toyed with visions of her lying beneath him in a bed of flowers. He had little doubt that she would succumb to his

charms while safely enmeshed in his mindspell; he had
spent his time with her to good effect, subtly manipulating
her growing feelings for Hunter toward himself.

He glanced toward the distant cabin, remembering
what he had gleaned from Hunter's mind. That one, he
thought, was near the edge; he had certainly fallen under
the sorceress's spell. And Boran felt in Siri's mind a tearing
confusion, an uncertainty for the first time. Was the woman
who had been born never to love a man herself on the
edge?

Boran realized his teeth were gritted and forced
himself to relax. There was time yet. And he meant to be
first. He would charm the sorceress into spreading her legs
for him, he decided. And when he was inside her tight
passage, the precious maidenhead torn, her body writhing
in furious passion beneath his and her power over the
unicorns gone forever, then he would allow her to see him
as he really was.

He could picture that so vividly in his mind that he was
forced to block his thoughts with care; it would not do for
the sorceress to sense his presence.

Hardly aware that he was stroking the petrified flesh of
his left cheek, Boran absently moved to widen his legs as
the ache in his loins intensified. She would be beautiful in
surrender, of course. And her virginal body would hold his
manhood with the tight heat only a first coupling ever
provided.

Boran half-closed his eyes, smiling. He enjoyed seeing
pleasure turn to pain, enjoyed watching the primitive,
animal passion in a woman's face turn rigid with fear.

But the sorceress . . .   He would take his time with
her.

He could feel, even now, the slender purity of her
body in his arms. Her full breasts swollen and rosy with
need, the nipples hard buds that would taste of honey.

Boran hardly heard the low rasp of his own breathing,
and only the amulet around his neck and an automatic,
unconscious control kept his presence a secret from those at
the pool. Bracing himself against the tree, he reached down
his good hand and adjusted his trousers, allowing the

aching flesh freedom from the painful discomfort of straining cloth.

He saw Siri in his mind, tumbled among the colorful flowers, their delicate blooms crushed and fragrant beneath her writhing body. Saw her long golden legs part for him, the arms beckon. He saw her witch's eyes blackly purple and passionate, her smile feline, her voice a siren's. And he felt the silk of her hair, the satin of her flesh.

He could feel her cradle him with strong, seeking limbs, hear her whispered desire. He could see the silver-furred triangle of her sex, feel the wet heat of her need for him. His eyes closed now, breath rasping as he leaned against a rough-barked tree, Boran imagined how it would be.

He watches her head move restlessly, soft moans escaping her perfect lips. He tastes the sweetness of her mouth, and his tongue rasps the sensitive hardness of her pointed nipples. He guides her hand to stroke his manhood, feeling soft fingers surround and caress the turgid flesh even as his hands fill themselves with her breasts.

And as passion builds he caresses her body, guiding her patiently until she is a wild thing, feral in her need, writhing and pleading. Then he spreads her legs wide and lifts them high, his demanding manhood probing her wet flesh, seeking entrance. He feels her slick heat surround him, the taut membrane barring his way—only for a moment. Hears her startled, hurting but passionate cry when the barrier gives way and he thrusts deeply into her once-virginal passage.

He feels her tightness and heat, feels her legs close about him as her hips lift with instinctive need. Feels the soft quivering flesh of her belly against his, the demand of her hard nipples against his chest. And, watching her blindly seeking face, he luxuriates in the sensations while be braces himself above her and thrusts powerfully.

She moans and whimpers, clutching at him with hands, gripping with legs, her belly rippling with every movement, the blood flush spreading rosily over her swollen breasts and up her graceful throat. Her mouth open, eyes glazed.

He moves faster, thrusting, plunging deeply into her welcoming heat, holding a tight rein over his own desire in order to drive her mad with hers. And he can see her face tense in a mask of need, see her eyes widen, feel the coiling, spreading tension of a female body poised on the brink of a small death. And then, in that flashing instant, he drives his body into hers with punishing force, as deeply as possible, causing her to lose her breath in an animal grunt, and as he holds himself buried in her, he brutally rips away the wall he has built in her mind.

Between one heartbeat and the next . . . she *remembers*.

Her eyes widen now with horror, with mind-numbing anguish, and the hands that sought his body in passion now push frantically as she struggles, broken cries escaping beautiful lips twisted in an obscene parody of passion. Terrified by his seared face and single gleaming eye, by the twisted, petrified hand cupped stiffly around her cringing breast like the dead thing it is, she screams again and again, animal cries of agony, her body twisting frantically to escape him.

But she's impaled, pinned in place by his heavy weight as he laughs and bucks on top of her, and pours himself into her, violating the sanctity of her chaste womb forever. And as he withdraws his spent member from her body, he forces her to remember that she *invited this*. She was willing, passionate. She gave herself to him.

And he looks down on her, limbs spread limply in the crushed flowers, the gleaming silver triangle of her sex marred now by her own blood and traces of his seed, and he laughs as he sees the terrible anguish in her face, the knowledge of what she has lost to him. . . .

Boran steadied himself against the tree, his hoarse, panting breath finally easing. He turned his gaze to the pool where the sorceress casually dried her naked body among the flowers, unconscious of the watcher in the woods.

"You'll surrender to me, princess," he whispered.

"You'll willingly spread your legs for me. I'll brand you mine before he has a taste of you. And when I've finished with you, there won't be much left for him. But you'll enjoy it, princess. For a while."

He stood in the concealing darkness of the forest and absently adjusted his trousers, watching as Siri and her unicorn guardian set out for the cabin.

"Soon," he murmured.

Six

Hunter opened his eyes and said, "But there's no sea." He grappled with his own words silently; they made no sense. *Piece together reality,* he told himself firmly.

He was in bed. In the cabin. Alone. The narrow shelf she'd made into a bed for herself was empty. Morning sunlight shone through windowpanes.

Ah. He'd been asleep, then. Presumably dreaming. About the sea. Hunter closed his eyes with a frown, flipping through the pages of his subconscious looking for the dream. Siri in a moonlit pool, he remembered suddenly, naked and beautiful. Laughing. Just beyond his grasp. He'd reached for her, and then— There had been no pool, but Siri had stood by his—bed?—dressed and holding a basket. Her lips had moved, forming words. She was going to get seaweed, he should sleep.

Seaweed?

"But there's no sea," Hunter murmured, opening his eyes. Satisfied with having unraveled a puzzle, he didn't really notice at that moment just how big a puzzle he'd been left with. Instead, his mind occupied with the reality of last night and the dream which had followed, he linked his hands together behind his neck and stared at the heavily beamed ceiling, thinking of Siri. Lovely Siri.

There existed, he knew, few things or beings which remained "beautiful" irrespective of opinions governing standards of beauty. A rose was lovely—unless one was allergic, when it became an instrument of torture. The view from a mountaintop was usually breathtaking—unless one suffered from vertigo, when sickness and dizziness blinded one. And a lovely woman was considered lovely by some— but not by others.

Musingly, Hunter thought of the possible reaction if Siri were to walk the corridors of some busy spaceport with her graceful warrior's stride. He pictured her at diplomatic balls, royal banquets, and merely wandering through some of the better-known tourist cities. And he knew that she'd cause a first-class riot wherever she went. Hers was truly that rare beauty, that curiously charismatic aura which would inevitably halt conversations in midsentence, draw all eyes, and cause the unwary to slam head-on into certain immovable objects such as walls.

Hunter chuckled to himself, picturing that likely series of events. Then he sobered, realizing that quite probably Siri would never leave this valley, and that the only other beings aside from himself who would ever see her beauty would be men too soulless to appreciate it.

Beauty to drive men mad . . .

Yes, the Huntmen would see her in that light, because she stood fiercely between them and a source of gold—the unicorns.

One thought led to another, and Hunter found himself exploring, as he had countless times, the bond between her and the mythical creatures she guarded. The unicorns trusted her with their very existence; the trust they felt for her was a tangible, visible thing, glowing in their dark eyes and evident in each gentle nudge. And Siri returned that love a thousandfold.

Hunter stirred uneasily, restlessly in his bed. Was it possible for Siri to love a man with that riveting, selfless devotion? Or had she given all that she had to give to the unicorns?

Abruptly, a new and startling thought occurred to him, and Hunter sat bolt upright. He had missed it! Bombarded with unicorns, Guardians, Mermaids, and dragons, he had somehow missed a possible solution to the entire problem!

Siri entered the cabin just in time to hear him say triumphantly, "The Guardians!"

"You awaken very strangely," she noted dryly, crossing the room to place a basket on the table.

Impatient with this trivial aside, Hunter fixed his gaze on her. "The Guardians. You said no creature that ever lived is extinct; the Guardians wouldn't allow the unicorns to die!"

She looked at him, her ebony eyes veiled. "Which two would you have them save?" she asked softly.

"What?"

Her voice still soft and emotionless, she said, "*If* the Guardians were to offer their protection, only a mated pair would survive to be the seeds of a new herd. That means that nine Unicorns would have to die first. *If* the Guardians stepped in."

Hunter felt elation drain away. "But . . . the Guardians *would* step in, if necessary?"

"No."

"Why not? They save the other animals."

Eyes still veiled, voice still soft, she said, "Yes . . . they save the *animals*. And I don't know how to make you understand that Unicorns aren't animals. They're a race of *dreams*. Dreams are created and nurtured in the hearts of men, and dreams live or die *in the hearts of men*. Hunter . . ." She sighed and shook her head. "You should see that more clearly than I. For me, the Unicorns began as reality; for you, they began as dream."

Hunter took a deep breath, still fighting to see, to understand. Because if he didn't understand, there was no way he could find his way past the wall between them. "And the Guardians won't save a dream?"

"Dreams are what men make of them."

"And women are the keepers of dream?"

Siri looked at him, conscious of a flicker of warmth in the coldness of her pain. "You're close," she murmured. "So close to understanding."

"Help me." It was half command, half plea, needing.

"I'm trying, Hunter." She sank down in the chair, gazing across the room at a man with this terrible need to understand, searching within herself for something that would help him, perhaps help them both. "Each race," she said slowly, "has purpose. A reason for being. For mankind, the purpose is building, growing. For womankind, the purpose is nurturing. And millions of years of evolution never change those very basic traits. In Nature, the traits of each animal balance out those of other animals. Meat-eaters help control the population of plant-eaters. Insects pollinate flowers; flowers provide food."

"And unicorns?"

Siri groped for words. "Unicorns . . . are the proof that mankind, for all his technical and scientific advances, can still *dream*. Can still cherish a myth *as* a myth, with no need to prove or disprove it." Very softly, she said, "The Unicorns know their own origins. Do you know what they believe?"

"What?" Unconsciously, he lowered his own voice.

Siri smiled. "Like any race, they possess . . . legends of their own, and a Creator of their own. They believe that their Creator was a gentle dreamer, who came upon the twisted horn of a gazelle one day, and dared to make of it a legend. And that gentle dreamer was a man, a man who endowed his creations with the traits he idealized . . . in women."

Hunter listened, fascinated and curiously moved.

"He molded them," Siri went on softly. "He gave them grace and strength and heartbreaking beauty. He gave them a trumpeting call that could be heard for miles. And he gave them their Dance. He made them gentle and kind. And he chose as their homes cool, shaded forests and sunny valleys."

She looked down at her hands, folded atop the table, then back at Hunter. "Once, Unicorns felt no fear of man; how could they when their own Creator was a man? But they were shy, elusive creatures. They lived in peace, harming no living thing. And men came, because they valued golden horns above dream. And they killed. Can you imagine the devastation, the heartbreak, for the Unicorns? A race they revered as gods came to kill them."

Hunter nodded, trying and failing to swallow the lump in his throat. Her words evoked images too painful to forget easily.

Siri nodded in her turn. "So they went into hiding. Heartbroken and stunned. Unicorns no longer peopled forests and valleys. Mankind was not yet ready to release his dreams from his secret innermost heart. And while the dreams were hidden, the Unicorns were, too. They learned to fear man.

"But their Creator had idealized women, and the Unicorns did as well. In time, only a woman could win the trust of a Unicorn. And when men began using . . . maidens . . . to trap Unicorns, even that instinctive trust became a hard-won thing." Almost inaudibly, she said, "But what's hurt them the most, what's nearly destroyed them time after time is that they've had to kill men in order to survive." Ebony eyes fierce with the rage of grief, she stared at Hunter. "How would you feel if you were forced to kill, again and again, your image of God just to survive?"

Siri rose to her feet jerkily, needing to move because stillness was abruptly unbearable. "Do you know why Cloud acts the way he does now?" she asked unsteadily, memories rushing in to add to her pain and confusion. "Why he's listless and why his eyes are heartbroken? Because his son was brutally killed by a man, and because Cloud killed that man in the first rage he's ever felt in his long life. His horn and his soul are stained with the blood of his god and *he'll never be able to forget that!*"

Driven by an instinct not to be probed or ignored, Hunter left his bed and crossed the room swiftly to her side. He drew her into his arms, intent on comforting and nothing else, unaware that it was the first truly selfless action of his entire adult life. "I'm sorry," he breathed. "I didn't know, Siri . . . I didn't understand."

Too overwrought to be conscious of the chemistry

between them, Siri blindly reached for the comfort he
offered. His body was warm and strong, offering a shelter
and an anchor she'd never needed before. She felt the
steady beat of his heart beneath her cheek and the soft
intimacy of his breath stirring her hair. Her arms went
around his waist briefly, holding him because in that
moment, for the first time in her life, nothing else was so
vitally, compellingly *real*.

Siri didn't cry. But for a moment—a single split second
out of time—she wanted to relinquish burdens that had
never before felt heavy, and needed to turn her back on
responsibilities that were tearing her apart. In the last days,
she had learned the bitter weight of the burden of responsibility and wondered what life would be—could be—like
with total freedom. For a moment. Then, torn by bewilderment and anguish, she drove the rebellious emotions back
into hiding. Total freedom didn't exist; she knew that. And
her life was the one she had been born to.

Hollow comfort. That talisman no longer worked.

She drew away from Hunter gently, eyes veiled as she
gathered the reins of her control tight. Turning away from
him, she picked up the basket and carried it to a small
work-shelf by the hearth. She said nothing, because there
was nothing to say and because she didn't trust herself to
speak.

Hunter, obeying once again instincts that seemed to
grow stronger and more certain with each passing moment,
followed her lead and said nothing. He returned to the bed
to find and don his shirt and boots, then came back to the
table, intending to offer his help in preparing the morning
meal.

That was when his earlier, unnoticed puzzle loomed in
his consciousness abruptly and demanded a solution.

"*Seaweed?*"

Siri half turned at the blank query, eyeing Hunter with
a somewhat strained smile. "You are an odd man. You
awake with strange words on your lips and seem prone to
store information in your mind until you decide to study it."

"There's been too much to absorb all at once." He

defended himself reflexively, then blinked. "What information?"

"I told you I was born inside The Reaper."

"I remember."

"And that my mother is a Mermaid."

Hunter winced. "That, too."

"Then isn't it reasonable that a certain inference should be drawn from those two facts?"

"Nothing is reasonable in this valley."

"The question stands."

He stared at her for a moment, then cautiously sat down in the chair. Cautiously because the fine line between reality and impossibility had grown fainter. Again. "Are you trying to tell me that there's a . . ."

"Sea inside The Reaper. Yes."

Carefully, Hunter said, "Seas beneath mountains aren't unknown, but it's impossible for a mountain this far inland to hold a saltwater sea. The ocean is hundreds of miles away."

Siri leaned back against the hearth and folded her arms, staring at him patiently. "Unicorns are impossible. Dragons are impossible. Mermaids are impossible. You're quibbling over a sea?"

Hunter rubbed a thumb along his jaw, nodding slowly. "Forgive me," he murmured. "I forgot to whom I was speaking. And where I am. Of course there's a sea. It only stands to reason that there's a sea."

"I thought you'd get the point."

"Does the ocean feed the sea?" he asked curiously.

Siri had turned back to her meal preparation. "Yes. There's an underground river from the ocean to The Reaper."

Hunter was busy coming to several realizations. "The lake. It isn't mineral water; it's seawater. That's why the unicorns won't drink from it."

"Yes."

"And your mother . . . um . . . lives in The Reaper?"

"Not really. She comes to visit. But it's a long journey through the river, and she misses the other Merpeople if she's away from them too long. And for most of the Winter, of course, the Merpeople have to remain in the deepest part of the ocean because it's so cold."

Merpeople? Hunter wondered distractedly; the meaning, he felt, was clear, but the very concept bewildered him. "Is she here now?" he asked finally.

"Yes," Siri responded, feeling restless. She could hardly dismiss his questions now after having decided to answer them, but her veneer of serenity was painfully thin.

"Can I meet her?"

"No."

"Why not?"

"Several reasons."

"Which are?" he asked, impatient now.

"One: You'd have to get past Bundy, and since he was born to guard that passage, I doubt you'd be able to. Two: My mother avoids men because of the loss of my father. And three—" She turned to face him, forcing a smile. "Do you really want to fall in love with a Mermaid and drown?"

"Would I?"

"Of course."

Hunter struggled with that for a moment in silence, trying to remember the stories of Mermaids. There were gaps in his knowledge, because his people had lost or forgotten so much of their mythology.

Patiently, Siri said, "I told you about it once before; it must be one of the things you haven't chosen to think about yet."

He remembered then that she had told him something about her mother's race, and agreed silently that either he must have dismissed what she'd said or chosen not to hear. He wanted to hear now, though.

"Mermaids," she said casually, "are irresistible to men. It's where the legends of a 'siren song' originated; Mermaids sing because they're almost always happy, and their voices are so beautiful that men are compelled to follow the sounds into the sea. And any man who once beholds a Mermaid will be enchanted and bewitched for the rest of his life. It's a madness."

"I could resist that," Hunter said.

Siri smiled. "Just as Unicorns were born out of gentle dreams of beauty, so Mermaids were born out of man's primal desire for the perfect enchantress. She's beautiful with an eerie, compelling beauty. She's sensual in a way no human woman could ever match." Siri spoke with detached, analytical certainty, as if she were discussing an immutable law of nature.

Hunter frowned at her. "Who taught you all of this?"

Shrugging gently, Siri turned back to her cooking.

He looked at the graceful lines of her body, feeling his own throb with ever-present desire.

"One day," she murmured, mincing the seaweed with a large knife, "you're going to realize that not everything has an explanation. And that sometimes it's better that way."

"You mean you?"

She glanced over her shoulder, her eyes still veiled, and her delicate face tightened. "No one asked questions before you came. I—I understood my life before you came."

He felt his pulse quicken. "And now?"

Siri watched her working hands again, struggling with the fury of her emotions. "Now . . . I don't know."

"Siri—"

"Will you return to your world?" she asked quickly.

It brought him up short, but after a moment he answered. "I've found what I set out to find. And my world needs to know their dreams are real." There was still some part of him that was unwilling to explain exactly why he'd left his world, about his Quest, about the throne. He hesitated, then said, "Come with me, Siri—"

"Your knowledge won't help them."

"I have to believe it will," he said evenly.

For the first time in her life, Siri was encountering a problem that none of her abilities could solve, and that shook her more than she would have believed possible. *Mother, you told me I'd always be strong! Mother? I don't feel strong anymore.*

There was no answer.

"What will you take back to your people as proof?" she

asked unsteadily. "A horn you'll have to kill to claim? A living Unicorn who will die long before you reach your world?"

"No! No, Siri. But there must be a way!"

"There is no way! You ask for proof of *dream*! And like all men, you'll destroy to get what you want."

"I'll destroy nothing!" He was on his feet suddenly, and the frustration inside him exploded painfully. "I've seen destruction, Siri, horrors you can't even imagine! I've seen what happens to worlds when wars tear them apart. I've seen plagues, and famines, terrible natural disasters.

"Have you ever been to Marcos III, Siri?" He was taunting her now, but couldn't stop himself. "You have sand cats here from Marcos III. I've walked on that world—what's left of it. It was a human world once, but their beautiful civilization was shattered by a war with another planet. No one remembers what started the war, but no one could stop it. And Marcos III was laid *waste* by a war no one wanted!"

She turned to face him, numbed by his outburst and yet mesmerized in a strange way by what he was telling her. He was pacing the small cabin violently, his lean face taut, the vivid green eyes turbulent with memories. And his deep voice was quick and sharp as he talked, edged with the impotent fury of a terrible despair.

"And there's another world on the far side of the galaxy, near my own. They were an offshoot of my people once long ago. The planet they found was already inhabited by a nonhuman race, extraordinarily intelligent. A dying race. And do you know what they were dying from, Siri? Pleasure. They had devoted all their vast technology to the art of physical pleasure. They had built machines which stimulated their senses, and over the aeons pleasure had become pain. The humans discovered what had happened, but too late. They were already addicted to their host world's pleasure machines. If you visit that world now, do you know what you'll find? A dead planet, with a dead race still hooked up to the machines that killed them!"

"Hunter—"

He went on, unhearing. "And then there's the Tarus

system. Not a human system, but then humans aren't the only fallible beings in the galaxy. The Tarus race on all three of their habitable planets is winged, but they can't fly. They forgot how, you see. And, too late, they're grieving over their loss. When their species envolved beyond the primitive, they began to structure their society, and flight became a privilege that was granted to few. By the time they had achieved spaceflight and had spread to three worlds in their system, they could no longer fly without their machines. And now their young are trying desperately to fly, and are killing themselves by the thousands because they don't know how.

"But we were talking about destruction, weren't we?" His eyes were glittering. "There's a plague on Mars. Mars . . . an old name my race brought with them into space. New Mars, they called it for a while. A red, dusty planet hot as hell. Humans settled there. And they deliberately destroyed the technology that brought them to their new world. They destroyed their spaceships, and since that group was composed of people with few technical skills, they effectively destroyed their ability to leave that planet. And they found out too late they had stranded themselves on a world that would destroy them. When they began having children, they discovered their plague. Ninety out of every hundred children born die within a month. Ten are immune. And it happens with each generation; the immune parents have found that they can't pass on that immunity to their children. There's no cure. The plague is indigenous to Mars; the spacegoing worlds nearby have quarantined the planet. Those humans are dying, and there is no way for them to leave the world that is killing them."

Almost whispering, Siri said, "No wonder you searched for beauty."

Hunter had stopped pacing, and now leaned forward to grip the table with white-knuckled fingers. "Beauty? Yes, I found beauty here and there. And do you know where I found it? On the worlds where mythology was still valued. Only on those worlds. Human or nonhuman, it didn't matter. If mythology lived, societies lived and prospered.

But on the worlds where the people had abandoned their myths, civilizations were dying. Wars. Plagues. Technology advancing at a far greater rate than the wisdom to use it."

"And your world—?"

"I told you." His face was hard. "My world is losing its myths. Forgetting them. There are a few books, preserved because they're too delicate to be read or copied. And my people are forgetting. After generations of a simple civilization, some on my world have rediscovered the art of making weapons and making war. There's a nonhuman world near mine, and we have a peace treaty with them. There hasn't been a war—yet. But there will be. The young revolutionaries of my planet have begun to resent the greater natural resources on that other world, and they want to conquer it. Our king and Council have tried to hold the society together, but the young aren't interested in remembering ancient heroes and daring quests; they want to experience *greatness* firsthand. They want the excitement and *glory* of war."

Hunter slammed both hands down on the table, and the sound was like a thunderclap. "*Glory!*" He laughed harshly. "They've known nothing but peace all their lives, and yet they want war. They want something that will destroy them. I have to show them the beauty of dreams, Siri. I have to help them to remember their mythology." *I have to claim a throne.*

After a moment, she said very quietly, "I think there's something you haven't considered, Hunter. What if you're wrong? What if your culture isn't dying because myth has been forgotten? What if myth has been forgotten because your culture is dying?"

Slowly he sank back down in the chair, gazing at her with an arrested expression in his eyes. "No. Myth will save my world. It has to."

Out of her own pain, out of her own need to find some sense in this new confusion, Siri discovered a possibility. Should she tell him? Yes. He had to know. "You said that some catastrophe sent your people out into space."

"Yes."

"And that they abandoned their history, and claimed their mythology."

"Yes. So?"

"Then perhaps what's happening to your race is natural. Perhaps there's a cycle which must be completed again and again while they evolve."

"What are you talking about?" He was taut, impatient. Still unsettled by the possibility that in discovering myth alive and breathing he was no closer to helping his people, his world.

"What sent your people out into space was the eve of their own destruction. They stood on the brink of an extinction they had brought on themselves, and out of that horrible moment, they brought their mythology. Perhaps they must face that again to reclaim myth. Each time their technology advances, they begin to lose myth. Only when they nearly destroy themselves as a race do they reclaim it."

Hunter was frowning. "I tell you, we don't know why they left their home world. Probably a natural disaster of some kind—"

"No."

"How can you know? It was thousands of years ago—"

"More than ten thousand years ago. And I can know, Hunter. Because I know the dawn of your history. It's as much a part of me as the Unicorns are, because the Unicorns were born long before your race left the world they all but destroyed."

"Siri—"

"Don't you see?" She seemed to be gazing into something very far away, and an odd little laugh escaped her. "No, of course not. How could you? Your people abandoned all that they were along with their blasted world."

"See what? What are you talking about?"

She looked at him with sadness in her lovely eyes. "Climb The Reaper and look out over this planet, Hunter. See what your people did to their Earth."

"What?" It was a breath of sound, shocked.

"You've come home. Did you never wonder why the Unicorns lived here in Summer? Why they mate and give birth here? Here on this blasted, barren world? It's because this is their home. Their roots are here, their origins. *This* is Earth, Hunter."

He sat in a numb silence, his mind whirling, hardly conscious that she had returned to her cooking as if aware that he needed to absorb this.

Earth? He remembered all the desolation he had seen on his trip overland from the coast, the pitted wasteland of this world. Long-dead cities moldering in silence, ancient buildings little more than rubble. This planet was virtually a wasteland, and after ten thousand years . . . How must it have looked on the eve of its destruction? What vicious progression had led humans to turn their very world into the hell they had feared for all their thinking history?

Siri set a plate piled high with little golden cakes on the table, then went over to the water keg. She carried two cups back to the table, saying nothing. A jar of golden honey, forks, and plates were brought. She fixed her own plate, pouring honey over the cakes, then retreated to the hearth with her meal.

Automatically, Hunter began to eat. After a few bites, some unnumbed part of his mind realized what he was doing. "I've been eating these cakes every morning; I never realized they were made from seaweed. They're delicious."

She looked at him, hearing the lingering shock in his voice. Should she have told him? He deserved to know that he had come home, she thought wearily. He had found his myths and his roots on a world all but destroyed and abandoned by his people ten thousand years ago.

Returning her gaze to her plate as she ate silently, Siri tried to make sense of it all. *I love him.* Why? He was a man, like all the men who had hunted Unicorns for so long. And if his search was for a different reason, the results would still be the same. They would die. She would die. And his myth would die on the world that had seen its birth.

For the sake of the Unicorns, she wished for Fall, and yet she had never before dreaded the approaching loneliness of Winter as she did now. She felt so cold.

She rose and began clearing away and cleaning up after the meal, and Hunter got up to help. Obviously searching for something casual to say, he finally commented, "I saw that pool in the woods." He sounded preoccupied.

"The Crystal Pool. It's beautiful, isn't it?" She welcomed the unthreatening topic.

"Yes. Especially with all the flowers around it."

Siri went very still for a moment. She turned slowly and looked at him where he leaned against the rough stones. "You've been exploring at night."

"How did you know that?"

"The flowers. They're Moonflowers; they only bloom at night."

He held her gaze steadily. "I saw them at night. Last night."

Siri didn't change color or expression. "I see. You didn't announce yourself."

"I . . . didn't want to intrude."

She nodded almost imperceptibly. Siri wasn't the least embarrassed that Hunter had seen her unclothed; it wasn't an emotion she was familiar with in regard to clothing, because that was a learned rather than instinctive emotion and her minimal contact with humans had spared her that. Siri knew only that her body was hers just as Hunter's was his—clothed or unclothed made no difference.

She couldn't help but wonder, though, what she would have done last night if he had announced his presence. If he had touched her, held her. Her body ached with new feelings, and she wanted to cry out against them.

"I have to patrol," she said abruptly. "I'll return before midday."

"May I come along?"

She shook her head. "I'd rather you didn't."

Hunter stood in silence and watched her leave the cabin, hoping she'd look back but knowing she wouldn't. And he was right.

He felt drained by his earlier outburst and by the shock of her revelation, holding on to his growing love for her as the only thing that was certain. Having found her and the unicorns, he couldn't now feel that his Quest had been in vain, and yet he grappled with the possibility that he might not be able to help his people.

The Council of Elders had been wise in sending their princes on a Quest, Hunter had come to realize these last years. Were he to return to Rubicon and occupy the throne, he would be a better king now for the experiences of the Quest. And he had seen enough to be utterly certain that his world was slowly dying, and that their only hope was the resurrection of myth and dream. But how could he return to them something so elusive?

And what of Boran? He had not seen his half brother since both had left their planet years before, though he had often sensed—or thought he had—Boran's intensity in unguarded moments. Had Boran found a trail to follow to this valley? Could both of them have found their way here in the vastness of the galaxy? And if Boran did come, would he remain only long enough to take a dying unicorn's horn before returning to Rubicon and the throne?

Hunter pushed that question away, knowing that it could not be dealt with unless and until Boran came. He knew only that he wanted the throne, wanted to help his people. And with every day spent in this valley he was less and less certain that he could help them.

Perhaps one man could not, after all, summon the future.

But even with that leaden knowledge within him, he had to believe that he could summon his own future. And his heart told him that his future lay with Siri.

The unicorns stood between them.

He was dimly aware that there was an alertly waiting part of his mind—or his heart—just beyond his reach, a part that held some key to understanding her, this valley, mythology. Memory, instinct, deeply buried racial knowledge—he couldn't see it clearly enough to define it. But it existed within him; he knew it, and she knew it because she kept trying to help him understand.

Some germ of truth. Some innate ability to see, to realize what it all meant. Some *reason* that the Council had sent him away from his home and the responsibilities he'd been born to, in search of myth. Something more than a throne.

What was it?

Frustration gnawed at him relentlessly. He had a sense of standing at the edge of a precipice, with dark emptiness around him. There was a chasm, a gulf of ignorance and blindness and lost knowledge to cross, and she waiting for him on the other side. He *felt* that. He had to build a bridge with the understanding that was locked elusively inside him, but it remained tauntingly just out of his grasp. His mind remained stubbornly dark. He hadn't yet learned to reach with his heart and use that true sword to pierce the blind layers. His heart yearned for dream, but his mind, his educated, inflexible mind, denied any need for dream to exist as dream.

He was angry, rudderless. He couldn't help his people, couldn't even help himself. The future of his life's happiness hinged on his own understanding, and it eluded him cruelly.

He was still standing there long moments later when a unicorn's impatient baby hoof scratched at the door. Hunter smiled faintly despite himself; it had become a habit of little Rayne's to come in for a visit each morning after Siri left to patrol. She had apparently realized that Hunter was a soft touch when it came to saving tidbits from breakfast.

He went to the door and let Rayne in, leaving the door open behind her in case one of her occasional panics came over her. But she was happy and affectionate this morning, even more so than usual, perhaps because of the new addition to the herd. The newborn filly—the herd had christened her Joy, Siri had told him—was much the center of attention, and Rayne must have felt slightly eclipsed.

Instinctively, Hunter understood and sympathized with the displaced feeling, and he tried to make it up to Rayne. He sat in the single chair and fed her bites of the morning's golden cakes, dipping an occasional piece in honey, to the foal's blissful enjoyment. He scratched her itching horn and talked to her softly and gazed into bottomless black eyes so eerily like Siri's.

When Rayne finally trotted from the cabin some time later, Hunter found himself restless. He paced around, looking at without seeing the room's simple furnishings. And then he saw.

One bed. One table. One chair.

He stared at that chair for a long time. It grew in his eyes, looming ever larger and larger in importance. One chair. A place for one. A place for only one.

A life intended, shaped, for only one, with not even the simplest conveniences set aside for any other.

No place for any other.

Slowly, he turned away, moving to the shelf by the hearth. He lifted his long hunting knife, sliding it from its sheath and staring down at the gleaming blade. Then he slammed tempered steel home in rich leather and strode purposefully from the cabin.

This time, Boran summoned her even more deeply into the dark privacy of the forest. Watching her last night, he had grown more impatient, and in the dark hours before dawn he had decided to test his mindspell's limits. The conflict in her mind was growing stronger with every passing hour, and he knew that the time for him to act was now; if he wasn't careful, Hunter would get in before him and steal what he intended for himself.

He was confident that he had charmed the sorceress. She was his to do with as he wished. So he summoned her again. And when she arrived, he was stretched out on a soft bed of moss, boldly naked.

Control was easy now, and when she stood over him she was completely under his mindspell.

"Boran?"

"It feels wonderful," he murmured. "Try it for yourself." He heard a rustling sound and opened his eyes, pleased to find that he had guessed correctly. Raised in the solitude of this valley, she had no sense of modesty, no feeling that clothing was emotional protection. He watched while she undressed.

"You have a lovely body," he remarked casually, feeling his loins tighten and swell.

"Have I?" She was pleased.

He waited until she was lying beside him, then raised himself on an elbow to gaze down at her. Eyes closed, she stretched like a cat, her lithe body supple.

"It does feel good," she murmured.

Relaxed, he reached out his right hand and laid it over her breast. "The body understands pleasure," he told her, moving his palm in a slow circle over her hardening nipple.

She opened her eyes and smiled lazily at him. "That feels good too."

"Yes." He leaned over and licked the hard bud gently, then drew it into his mouth and sucked, his tongue rasping. He could feel her shiver with pleasure. Lifting his head, he gazed down on the wet nipple, then smiled at her. He was concentrating hard, all his energies focused on relaxing her, making her compliant and aware only of her sensual feelings; he didn't allow himself to think of his true motives at all.

"I can teach your body to feel wonderful things," he promised softly. "Will you let me do that, princess?" Gambling that his mindspell was strong enough now, he allowed his twisted left hand to stroke over her flat belly. And he discovered that to be correct when her smile remained undimmed, trusting.

"I like to feel wonderful things," she confided.

"Good," he murmured. "Then just lie there with your eyes closed, princess, and feel the pleasure."

He caressed her breasts gently, carefully, and her sighs were music to him. Her warm flesh tasted sweet, and he concentrated fully on the swelling mounds. He licked around her pointed nipples slowly, tracing the areolas, flicking the hard tip, and then drawing the erect tissue into his mouth and sucking strongly.

Siri murmured something in the back of her throat and shifted restlessly.

Boran didn't try to part her legs yet, but his hand trailed down over her quivering belly slowly until he could stroke the triangle of silken hair. He could see her thighs tighten in a reflexive movement, but her eyes remained closed and she sighed softly.

Even as his own body swelled and throbbed and desire sought to cloud his mind, Boran remained alert, his attention fixed on her, on the soothing, seducing thoughts he was sending to her mind. He caressed her slowly and expertly, watching her skin flush with sensation, her breathing quicken, her body shift subtly in sensual discomfort.

"Open your legs for me, princess," he whispered, probing gently with his fingers while his twisted left hand rubbed methodically over her breasts.

A faint, troubled frown flitted over her features, but when his fingers discovered the slick flesh they sought, she caught her breath and her thighs slowly widened to permit the caress. Boran stroked her delicately, barely aware that his own breath had quickened, that his own heart pounded as wildly as the one beneath the flesh his lips caressed.

He wanted to make it last, wanted to watch her while passion caught her in its merciless toils. But his own body raged, and the patience he had imagined last night shattered. With a groan, he rolled over to cover her body, his legs forcing hers wide apart, his aching manhood probing stiffly.

Her eyes opened, and she gasped. "Boran—what are you—no, don't—"

"Pleasure, princess," he muttered harshly. "I promise you pleasure. Let me in—let me show you—"

"No!" Her face was changing even as she struggled, the serenity and sensual hunger of his mindspell disappearing. And her purple eyes were darkening with anger and a wisp of awareness. "No, I won't! The Unicorns—"

He knew then, even through the haze of passion, that he was losing his control of her. And for an instant, trapped in the toils he had wished for her, he very nearly gave in to his own consuming passion. But rape was not what he wanted. He wanted her willing, wanted her to give to him what no man had been given in ten thousand years.

The virginity of the Keeper of the Unicorns.

And the strength of that desire overbore the aching of his body. He went still above her, staring into her eyes commandingly, focusing every atom of his will. Siri went still as well, gazing up at him with blank eyes and a face suddenly wiped of all feeling.

In a strange, suspended voice, she said, "I can't do

this, Boran. Forbidden. I would be Outcast . . . I would die."

He was shaken by her strength, by her ability to penetrate the veils of his mindspell to voice those words, and he concentrated even more on controlling her. He steadily shored up the wall he had built in her mind between knowledge of him and the awareness of her precious unicorns, but for the first time that wall felt unsteady to him.

And he realized then that this taboo was indeed a powerful one, because the near breaking of it had wrenched her from his control. The knowledge was bitter, but his explosive rage brief. He had just moved too quickly, that was all. She would surrender to him. She *would*.

Slowly, still maintaining the fierce control, he moved until he was beside her again. And he carefully probed her mind for the memory of this attempt, working to neatly remove the knowledge. Her face became serene again, and her eyes closed.

He reached out and stroked her body with a steady hand, undemanding now. And he held her mind captive in a limbo as he murmured, "You will be mine, princess. If I have to mount you with all the roughness of a stallion with his mare, I will take you. But I want you willing. You'll be a mare in season, my love, and more than ready for me."

He rolled over onto his back, fighting for the control not to take her now, willing or not. "Get dressed," he ordered harshly, still holding her mind caged.

Her face blank, Siri rose and got dressed, her movements automatically graceful. And Boran watched, his hunger growing. "Legend says I'll have your power when I have you," he murmured. "I'll have what no man has gained in ten thousand years. I'll have the power of your witch's mind, and your virgin's blood will make me even stronger."

She stood, face blank, awaiting his command.

"I'll have my revenge. And I'll have the Triad," he said to himself. Then he ordered her to return to her other life and watched as she vanished into the forest.

He remained where he was for a time, frowning up at

the trees. Whether she were willing or not, taking her virginity would accomplish a part of his plan—why did he hesitate? Why did it matter that she be willing?

Boran lay and cursed slowly.

———————————

Siri returned to the cabin just after noon, tense and preoccupied. She felt unsettled, all her senses unusually alive and aware, troubled by something she couldn't see clearly and didn't understand. And troubled by the coming confrontation with Huntmen. She thought that the violent emotions of the morning had probably driven the cards' prediction from Hunter's mind, but she could not forget.

Returning to the cabin after her swim the night before, she had found Hunter deeply asleep and had consulted the cards again. Again, they had predicted Huntmen violating the valley late today. That prediction had been made before and would, should she survive this day, be made again. It had not frightened her.

But there had been more to the prediction. A smothering blanket of darkness and pain had blinded her ability to see further than the coming of Huntmen; the cards had prophesied something so blackly agonizing that she simply could not see it.

That frightened her.

It frightened her because what she could not see she could not control; whatever was meant to happen *would* happen. It would be impossible to impose her will on events she would not see until their occurrence.

It frightened her and there was no one to turn to in her fear. She dared not lay that burden on Hunter's shoulders; whatever his ability to carry it, the responsibility was not his, and she was terrified of taking that first step toward giving in to her feelings for him. And her mother, confined by what she was to the sea beneath The Reaper, could not help.

She was frightened and confused and tired, and for once—just this once—she wished that there was someone she could turn to and say, *It's enough. I'm tired. You take over now.*

But there was only Hunter, and she couldn't reach out

to him. Greater than her fear of the Huntmen and the darkness they brought with them like a plague was her fear of what would happen if she reached out to Hunter.

She would never be able to let him go.

Siri's first Summer in the valley, at the age of three, had been spent with her parents. She had met the Unicorns and watched the old Keeper, but had understood little. During the long Winter, she had understood more. Her second Summer had marked her coming of age at thirteen, had seen her first gritty battles of protection, her first kills in defense of her beloved Unicorns.

Her third Summer was tearing at everything she was. Her certainties were no longer certain. Her loyalty was no longer whole. Her heart no longer belonged solely to the Unicorns. And a womanhood of the flesh, something she was never intended to know, loomed just within reach.

She had never been meant to love a man . . . but love a man she did. She had never been meant to ache in the night for strong arms to hold her . . . but she did. And she should never have been asked to make the choice Hunter and his love demanded of her. But he and his love demanded.

She was lost.

Torn, bleeding from the inner wounds of certainties tearing away, she stood near the cabin with bowed head for a long moment. Then she looked up toward The Reaper—and beyond. To lands she had never seen, worlds she knew only by the cold facts of their existence, peoples she had never seen nor heard. Oh, she knew them all in a sense. She could assign each world its place in the galaxy, could have drawn a map for Hunter that would have been accurate to the last star. She could speak the languages of peoples she'd never met face-to-face—and never would meet.

But she had never, could never, *feel* them. Would she know how to laugh at their humor? Would she know what roused them to anger or compassion or love? Would she be able to interpret the smile on an alien face as being one of amusement, or pity, or tenderness? Would she see the reason behind customs developed for individual peoples and places?

No.

Bitterness rose in her throat, choking her. *Why me?* she cried silently to an uncaring universe.

Hunter had walked upon alien worlds, mixing among their vastly differing peoples. And he had done so, she thought, without realizing what a precious gift that was. And then he had come here, into her life, this man from a distant world but whose racial roots were here just as surely as hers were, and he had opened doors that tormented her. She was bound to this valley and this life, and she felt cheated.

Cheated.

She would never walk on a distant world. She would never even be able to see the ocean of this world. She was tied to the life a child had chosen, and nothing could ever alter that.

She didn't blame Hunter for her sudden bitterness; she could not be certain that his coming here had roused all these feelings within her. Perhaps she would have realized one day without the spur of his questions and demands. But he had come, and demanded, and questioned.

And she now craved the sounds of her own footsteps treading on alien soil.

Hunter saw the change in her the moment she walked in. He didn't know if her patrol had changed her or if he were simply seeing more clearly now after his struggle with a bewildering and emotional morning—but he suspected the latter.

Her great black eyes were as dark and empty as the outer reaches of a cold, dark space, empty with an iciness that came straight from the soul. There was no anger in her, and the coldness was not directed at him but simply emanated from her as though the very core of her being were ice. Despair clung to her like a leech, sucking the life out of her. And a bitterness alien to her very nature twisted the gentle lips. She seemed in another world, one which was terribly unfamiliar and a threat to her.

"What is it?" he asked immediately, alarmed.

She looked at him, aching with love and pain. "Nothing." Her voice was normal, shockingly so. "Nothing's changed." *But everything had changed, and there was a sense of time rushing past, things out of her control.*

And then she saw the chair.

It stopped her in her tracks. There was nothing particularly special about the chair. It was roughly made, the pieces of it notched and fitted together with accuracy but little beauty. It was functional and looked to be no more and no less comfortable than the chair that had been in the cabin as long as Siri could remember.

There was only one difference. This new chair was built a bit larger, a bit stronger. Built to hold more weight. Built to hold a man.

And Siri knew what it meant, knew what Hunter was telling her. He had found her life within this cabin shaped for one—herself. He had taken one small but vital step in changing that. By building the chair, he had made a place for himself.

She looked at him with hot eyes. "Leave. Please leave."

He shook his head slowly. "I can't. And if I did—what would change? You can try to wipe me out of this valley. Burn the chair. Erase every footprint I've left in the—Earth. But I'll always be here, Siri." It was the raw, aching sound of truth, the tethered wildness of a spirit and heart captured by an immutable certainty.

Siri looked at the chair and at the man who would destroy her, and wondered vaguely if Fate had meant to be unkind or if she herself had paved her road to hell by saving, beyond all reason, the life of a stranger and an enemy.

What does your world look like, Hunter? Are your Winters cold and bleak as they are here?

"I'm more yours than my own," he said slowly, holding on to that certainty. "I belong here. I belong to you."

But you have walked on other worlds. You weren't cheated. "I belong to the Unicorns."

"Why does it have to be one or the other?" he asked

intensely. "I'm not trying to take you away from them—I know they need you. But *I* need you, Siri! I don't want to hurt the unicorns, and God knows I don't want to hurt you. I just want to love you."

"You can't."

"I do!" He was willing her to believe, to understand.

She looked at him almost blindly. "I can't escape what I am," she murmured. "I çan't . . . love you." *But I do! Please, someone tell me what to do!*

He stepped forward suddenly and caught her in his arms, wild with the driven impatience of a man in love. "You can love me," he said gratingly. "You do!"

"No—" She had struggled in his arms once before, but there was no strength left in her for that now. No physical strength, and precious little will. But even with her confusion and longing tearing at her mind, she was dimly conscious of other emotions and sensations. As if the faint memory of some half-forgotten dream flitted through her mind.

He fitted his mouth to hers in utter possession, his tongue driving deeply to twine with hers, and Siri felt a shocking pleasure jolt through her body. She was only indistinctly aware of her hands pressed between them against his chest, the fingers curled into the palms until her nails bit into the skin. She wanted to stretch her fingers wide and touch him, but her knowledge of what was forbidden to her was desperate enough to keep her hands frozen in fists of resistance.

Forbidden! Outcast!

His powereful arms drew her closer, one hand sliding down her back to her hips, and she felt another shock as the swollen hardness of his manhood pressed against her. An aching tingle began in her breasts, spreading outward like ripples in a pool, and there was something distantly familiar in the sensation—but different. There was an elusive memory of the physical sensations, but not of the terrible yearning that came from her heart as well as her body.

Longing . . . No! Outcast.

But her body remembered. Yet how could her body

know of these feelings? Blankness. There was a blank place in her mind, a walled-off place. Hands on her body . . . Forbidden! A restless heat rising . . . a heavy ache between her legs . . . an intolerable need . . . Forbidden! Hunter kissing her with a demand she couldn't resist, couldn't fight, the hard male strength of his body pressed to hers, her own body yielding, helpless in a desire beyond reason. Forbidden!

Hunter's love. The Unicorns.

"No!" It was more moan than word, anguish rather than protest. And she found the strength, somehow, to break free of him. She stumbled away, her legs shaking, heart pounding, her breathing ragged as she grasped the back of a chair for support. And she half-closed her eyes when she looked down and saw that the chair was his.

Hunter swayed on his feet when she left him, the force of his need nearly overwhelming him. God, but he wanted this woman! And she wanted him; blind and deaf, he still would have been certain of that. Why was she fighting him? He tried to rein the fierce needs of his body, the ache in his loins a throbbing threat to his control.

"Siri—"

She was struggling for control, terrified at the weakness of her own body. If the strength of a ten-thousand-year-old taboo hadn't been so great . . . And there had been something familiar in her body's response, but—it was gone now.

"You want me," he said then, his voice hoarse.

"I can't change what I am," she whispered.

"I'm not asking you to change!"

She straightened slowly, her shoulders squaring. And she looked at him with dry, hot eyes. "Asking. Demanding. But *I can't change what I am!*" Without another word, she went to prepare their midday meal with shaking hands.

After a while, her hands steadied. Her heart stopped pounding and she could breathe again. But her fear didn't lessen, and the black foreboding was heavy in her mind.

She couldn't change what she was, but Hunter could. And she couldn't tell him that change would destroy her, couldn't explain, because it wasn't for telling.

Mother?
Daughter?
Help me, Mother . . .
I cannot, child.
Mother . . .
Beware, child. And be strong.

Seven

His failed possession of Siri had enraged Boran more than he liked. He lost his temper with Con and one of the other Huntmen when he returned to camp to hear mutters of discontent, and took a great deal of pleasure in nearly breaking Con's jaw. Only the awareness of his slipping mind control enabled him to stop short of actually cracking bones in his fury.

He stood swaying a little, staring down at Con where the Huntman sprawled and nursed his bruised jaw with a shaking hand. Another Huntman began to speak, and Boran knocked him flat without even thinking about it.

Slowly, though, he began to regain control over his temper. His earlier lust, lacking the completion of the act with Siri, had transformed itself into physical rage, and he felt calmer once that tension was dispelled. His mind settled into its normal alert and methodical state, and he decided the time had come for action of a different sort.

He had yet to see the sorceress in battle, and he wanted to know her strengths in that area. It would be useful, too, to discover if Hunter had healed entirely. He frowned a little, recalling Siri's abrupt resistance just short of penetration. Was there something he had overlooked, some part of her mind he was unable to reach into and control?

No. No, it was merely the ingrained taboo honored for ten thousand years. She would not easily give up her virginity. But if her strengths were further tested? If she were forced to be violently active in defending her beloved unicorns from the the threat of Huntmen? Would that not strain her abilities, weaken her strength?

Yes.

He looked at the Huntmen. Dull weapons to be thrust by a strong arm. Still, there were more in the city, easily recruited by promises of gold. And he would be absent from the valley only a day to bring more Huntmen here.

Con had risen to his feet, still nursing his jaw. Sulkily, he said, "We're tired of waiting, Boran."

Boran smiled suddenly and was amused that they shrank from that more strongly than from a blow. "No more waiting," he told them pleasantly. "We move against the sorceress and her lover. I know her weaknesses now. You will do exactly as I command."

The midday meal was a silent and strained one. Siri was tense, preoccupied, her manner stiff, and wary eyes studied Hunter from time to time. She ate without feeling hunger, her mind fixed rigidly on the coming confrontation and the blackly agonizing darkness she couldn't penetrate.

What was it? Not the end? Fear clenched inside her, holding her heart in a fierce grasp. No, she wouldn't let it be the end! The Unicorns *would* survive. Nothing else mattered. She didn't matter. He didn't . . .

Hunter. She looked at him, her eyes sliding away almost instantly. Damn him. Damn him for *mattering*. Her heart thudded against her ribs, hurting her as fear tangled with her love for him and rose in her throat. Was that it? Was that the blackness she couldn't penetrate? Was his vital importance to her causing the anguish she could feel lying ahead of them?

And she sent a prayer to nameless, faceless gods to spare her a choice she wasn't strong enough to make.

I can't choose! Choosing them would mean his death. And so much of me would die with him. Choosing him would destroy the Unicorns . . . and me.

"Siri?" His voice was deep, hesitant. "I—I want to help defend the unicorns. When the Huntmen come."

So he hadn't forgotten after all. She rose and carried her plate to the work-shelf, barely aware that he'd done the same. *Maybe there will be no choice,* she thought bleakly. Seeing the possibility of her own death in the cards' black prophecy, she was torn yet again by a sudden desire to tell Hunter where the Unicorns would hide. If she were to die, would Hunter protect the Unicorns until another Keeper could take over? Could she trust him that far?

Did she dare take that step? No Keeper had ever asked for the help of a man, had never wanted or needed it, and she knew in her heart that the asking would be her first voluntary step toward destruction. She would be admitting that she trusted him, that she cared enough to trust, and after taking that step she would never be able to go back. Her resistance to trust, to . . . love . . . was half her strength; once she abandoned that part of her will, how would she find the necessary courage to fight Hunter's desire—and her own?

Once trust and love were freely given, could even the power of a ten-thousand-year-old taboo prevail over the relentless and chaotic need of an all-too-human body? Could any promise or vow stand against that?

Siri squared her shoulders. She wouldn't love him, she refused to love him! If she didn't admit it, refused to say the words, it wouldn't be real. It wouldn't really exist. But she could trust him. She had to take every possibility into account, prepare for every eventuality; and the cards had never before prophesied such a black and terrible danger. And if she were to die on this day, there were yet weeks of Summer to leave her beloved charges vulnerable. She *had* to ensure their survival—even if that meant giving her trust to a man.

But not her love. Never her love. She could feel it, but

keep it safely undeclared in her heart. Safe. So that it wouldn't interfere with her vows and promises, and so that he couldn't use it against her.

"Leave," she said suddenly, harshly, giving him a last chance. "Leave now. Today. This minute. I won't be responsibile for you."

"You aren't,, he said instantly.

Siri turned her back on him to walk to the open door, staring out over the peaceful valley. His refusal to leave left her with few choices, few alternatives. There was no longer time available for thought, for finding acceptable answers. She could only use every resource at her command to fulfill her own trust and guard the Unicorns.

It was all she could do.

"They're coming," she said in a voice deadened by defeat. She was so afraid. "I don't know how many. But they're strong. And determined."

Hunter watched her, sensing from how she spoke that these Huntmen posed a greater threat than any she'd known. A part of him understood that he was somehow responsible for that greater threat, but it only made him more determined to help her. "Let me help, Siri."

She turned suddenly to face him, her back against the doorjamb. The sharded brightness of something rent into limitless, elusive pieces was in her dark eyes, some resolution or decision set aside in terrible pain for the first time. "I can't ask you," she said flatly.

"You don't have to. I want to help, Siri. I need to help."

A sigh, shuddering and heavy, escaped her. "Then you have to make me a promise—two promises."

"Anything." He realized in that moment, jarringly, that Siri would not again ask him to leave the valley. On that point, at least, he had won. But what had she lost? What had his victory cost her?

"First, you must promise never to reveal the Unicorns' hiding place. Never. Your word."

"My word. I promise you, Siri. I won't betray your trust." He felt elated by her request. She trusted him. It wasn't love—but it was a beginning.

Siri met his gaze fiercely, unsettled and afraid because she saw that he understood in some way the importance of her trust. Would he try to use that against her, use the knowledge to get what he wanted from her? And could she fight that? "And you must promise that should I not survive this day, you will do everything in your power to protect the Unicorns until another Keeper can take over—even if it means returning to this valley next Summer to guard them. Your word!"

Coldness, icily desolate, replaced his elation. He heard his own voice emerge hollow and mechanical. "What have you seen? What has your Sight shown you?"

He saw a faint quiver disturb her tightly held mouth. "Give me your word."

"Tell me!" he demanded.

She shook her head slightly, her eyes never leaving his. "Nothing I could speak of. Something I—I can't really see. Perhaps death. I may lose today."

"You can't die," he said, and it was a desperate denial.

Abruptly, she held a hand out between them and reached with the other to pull back the tight cuff of her sleeve. On the golden flesh of her forearm, hidden from him until now, was a ragged scar. She held his eyes again when they lifted to hers. "Cut me and I bleed. I can't heal myself, Hunter, not the way I healed you. I'm as mortal as you are."

"You can't die!" he repeated between gritted teeth, his words shaped by an unconscious determination to hold reality at bay for the first time.

Her black eyes were fathoms deep. "Yes. I can die. I told you before—I'm no sorceress. No witch. In fighting the Huntmen, I have only my hands, my wits, and the weapons I fashion for myself. No magic."

"You've always won before." It was a last protest against truth, whispered in pain and denial.

"I may not win this time."

He reached out suddenly, needing to hold her, but Siri stopped him with a hand lifted to his chest. Just that. No force, but he went still, feeling that hand and seeing the rejection in her eyes. She wouldn't be held by him. Not now.

Hunter let his arms fall to his sides, staring into her eyes. He wanted to stand between her and any threat, protect her, cherish her. And she would have none of it.

She'd told him more than once that this was her birthright. Told him in pride and determination. He could no more stand between her and danger than he could allow her to protect him. It was her right to protect the creatures entrusted to her, her right and her choice. To offer her his protection would be to belittle her and everything she believed in. He could only offer help.

She wouldn't even allow him to comfort her.

"Your word," she said steadily.

"You have it," he said in a heavy voice. "I'll keep the faith, Siri. If I survive and you . . . don't, I'll protect your unicorns."

Siri saw that he was pale, his features haggard, green eyes dark and curiously lost. Her hand fell slowly. "Thank you."

He smiled just a little, and one hand lifted to touch her cheek so briefly that she didn't have time to draw away. "For what? You won't even let me carry your sword."

She knew what he meant and felt a flicker of respect for him in this. He was strong enough, and more than willing, to fight for her, she knew. But also strong enough to fight with her, and that meant more to her. "Just knowing you'll shield the Unicorns makes me stronger," she told him.

"I only hope it makes you strong enough."

There was no answer for that, except time. "We should hide the Unicorns now. We'll also have to gather forage to place in the cave with them; I have a feeling this battle will last longer than any other."

Hunter followed her from the cabin, trying not to flinch from a possible future in order to deal with the present. "Cave? You mean the dragon's cave?"

"No, not Bundy's cave." She sighed, apparently at odds with her valley's peculiar reality. "If they could be hidden there, everything would be much simpler. But dragons and Unicorns are ancient enemies; not even they know why any longer. I've never known a Unicorn to go near Bundy."

"But if they could—?"

"Dragons are guards. Always. As you observed, they were created out of man's fears of what might be just over the horizon, and so a dragon's purpose is to guard. Sometimes they guard treasure, sometimes they guard a more defenseless race than themselves. Bundy guards the sea within The Reaper because the Mermaids live there while they bear and raise Keepers. Dragons always guard Merpeople, because they're gentle and defenseless."

"But not unicorns."

"No. Unicorns aren't defenseless, except against men and then only by choice. Cloud's told me stories of the ancient times; Unicorns were fierce in battle then. It was before the Guardians or Keepers, and before man had disillusioned them. Only a dragon could defeat a Unicorn, and then only rarely."

They were walking toward the woods, following the unicorns that were already moving along the path to the Crystal Pool. Hunter thought about her words for a moment. "Yet the unicorns and Bundy live here in peace?"

She nodded. "Because Bundy remains in his cave and the Unicorns respect his domain."

"Another easy solution shot to hell."

Siri smiled a little. "Indeed. If Bundy were Keeper of the Unicorns, they'd be well protected. But he isn't."

Hunter looked down at her as they walked, and reached suddenly to grasp her hand, retaining it even when she would have gently pulled away. And even that small resistance rubbed salt in an aching wound. Why did she fight him? "I know you're allowed to touch, Siri, even if you can't love! You've touched me before this."

After a moment, he said, "Your hand's cold."

She wanted to tell him her heart was cold as well, but concentrated instead on the preparations they would have to make. And tried not to think of how warm and strong his hand was, of how naturally her fingers had twined with his.

The twilight world of the forest, shaded and quiet, closed around them as they walked. The murmur of the spring ahead grew louder, the faint splash of the little waterfall became a rushing gurgle as they neared. And the unicorns, like the forest, were silent and subdued.

"They know, don't they?" Hunter asked.

"Cloud's known as long as I have. It's a bad omen for the herd, Huntmen coming so soon after a birth. They're worried."

Hunter pushed aside yet another chilling presentiment of death, forcing his mind to practicalities. "What weapons do you have?"

Siri glanced up at him. "Few." She touched the long knife at her belt with her free hand. "This. A bow and arrows, a couple of spears. And there are traps, snares to be set around the valley."

He sighed. "Damn."

"The Huntmen will be armed little better than we."

"Well, at least the odds will be fairly even."

She stopped suddenly on the path, staring up at him. "You have to remember something, Hunter. The Unicorns will be hidden. The Huntmen know I always hide them. Alive, one or both of us could reveal the hiding place, and the Huntmen know that, too. What they aren't sure of is how long the Unicorns can remain hidden; for all they know, it could be for the rest of the Summer."

"So they won't want to kill us both," Hunter said slowly.

"If they're smart, no," she said evenly.

"Torture?" he guessed in a taut voice.

Siri shrugged and began following the path again. "It's a possibility."

He wasn't deceived by her casual tone, nor was his mind diverted from the possibilities her words had conjured. The thought of Siri bleeding and broken, in an agony of the Huntmen's creation, horrified and sickened him. He swallowed the bile rising in his throat, but couldn't swallow the fear.

On a world called Argosy, humans had evolved into a martial society, and one of their greatest joys was the conquering of other worlds. They had raised torture to a fine art, competing among themselves to see who could keep a captive alive the longest while systematically destroying the body. Hunter had seen. He had seen shapeless forms devoid of all but the last faint flicker of suffering consciousness. He had seen the travesty of life flesh could be reduced to. . . .

"They could capture you," she said softly, not looking at him.

"I'd prefer a clean death," he said, the fear for her still choking him.

"So would I," she said even more softly.

Nothing more was said for a long time. They followed the path and the unicorns past the Crystal Pool, Hunter noticing that the Moonflowers were closed against the day, no longer colorful or mystically beautiful. The path branched just beyond the pool, one way leading to Bundy's cave, the other becoming fainter and fainter until it disappeared. But the unicorns continued moving through the forest, finding their way through brambles and thickets where there was no path to betray their whereabouts.

They emerged, finally, to face the sheer, black-rocked cliff of The Reaper's base. Brambles and thickets grew here too, nearly hiding the spring bubbling from a narrow crack in the rock. It was here that the Crystal Pool's clean water found a source, the little spring forming a narrow stream which wended its way through the forest.

Hunter searched the cliff thoroughly, the unicorns' quiet waiting telling him that they had reached their hiding place. This was the wide end of the valley, The Reaper spreading out two arms of black rock on either side of where they stood almost as if it sought to protect what would remain here. But Hunter saw no opening, and looked at Siri quizzically.

She nodded toward one of the bramble thickets. "Behind the brush." And freed her hand from his gently to begin pulling the loose brush aside.

He helped, discovering only moments later that a narrow opening did exist, virtually undetectable, behind the brush. As Siri slipped through the opening, he followed, conscious of Cloud's presence close behind him and hoping that the unicorn would take care with his long horn.

"How—" Hunter began, hastily lowering his voice as

echoes threw the word back at him firecely. "How is it that The Reaper holds a saltwater sea and springwater as well?"

"You'd have to ask The Reaper that," responded her voice from in front of him in the narrow cave.

"I should have guessed. Another thing to take on faith."

She heard the harsh rasp of his voice, but realized that there was nothing she could say to ease his tension. They both had to get through this day as best they could.

Before anything else could be said, they emerged from the tunnel and into a huge cavern which was, incredibly, almost as bright as day. Hunter blinked, his eyes adjusting from the darkness of the tunnel, and, when a horn nudged him gently, quickly stepped aside to permit the entrance of the unicorns. He realized that the moss growing all over the walls emitted an odd, yellow glow; the stuff grew so thickly that it brightened the entire huge room.

There were piles of forage and other signs of the unicorns having stayed here many times before. And this chamber, which appeared to possess no side tunnels or rooms, held a small and apparently deep pool of clear water.

Stalactites projected downward from the ceiling, eerily like the unicorns' own horns, and the air was fresh and clean. Hunter watched as the creatures came in and wandered about, noting again how subdued they were; even Storm and Fancy, usually spirited, were quiet. And both Rayne and the new foal, Joy, were obviously nervous, remaining close to their dams' sides.

Siri was checking over the piles of forage, frowning to herself. Then she returned to the tunnel mouth and Hunter's side.

"We'll have to gather quite a bit—enough to last for a couple of days at least."

Hunter followed as she went back into the tunnel. He waited until they emerged into daylight before asking, "Do you really think they'll have to stay in there that long?"

"As long as there's a chance, we have to be prepared for it."

The trip back to the cabin this time was silent and

swift; Siri seemed more conscious of time passing. Once inside, she unearthed a couple of large woven sacks, handing one to Hunter and taking the other herself. They went back out into the meadow and he followed her example in using his knife to cut the tall grasses and place them in the sack. It didn't surprise him to note that she used her knife with expert ease.

Both worked swiftly, and their sacks were nearly filled when he asked abruptly, "When?"

She squinted briefly up at the sun. "Couple of hours, I think. We'll have to hurry."

With both sacks filled, Hunter reached for hers. "I'll make the first trip," he offered, and she nodded, bending over to continue cutting the grass.

His trip was quick and so was the second. The third trip was made by both of them, since Siri decided it would be the last and, hopefully, provide enough. The unicorns would eat sparingly, she told him, because they knew as well what was happening.

Hunter emptied the sacks on top of what had already been brought, turning just in time to watch Siri saying a silent good-bye to the creatures she loved.

Just in case.

He watched as she went from one to the other, a gentle, lingering touch for each velvety neck. When she reached Cloud, restraint shattered, and she threw her arms around the old stallion's neck with a smothered sound, her forehead pressed against his powerful jaw.

Whatever she said to the old Leader, she said silently, and Hunter, watching with a sudden lump in his throat, wondered dimly how many times they had gone through this wrenching farewell. The remainder of the herd stood still and quiet, even the frightened, nervous foals. And only a faint gentle rumble broke the silence; it came from Cloud's throat and was, Hunter realized, a whisper of his rusty trumpeting.

Loath to disturb or intrude, Hunter found himself sending his own silent farewells to the herd. He realized in that moment that finding them had not been enough, that he wanted them—deeply, passionately wanted them—to live. And he accepted at least a part of the burden of their survival, whether Siri willed it or not.

He would protect them with his last breath.

She came away from Cloud, moving blindly past Hunter and into the tunnel. With a last look into the wise old eyes of the stallion, Hunter followed.

They emerged into the sunlight and Siri immediately began piling the brush in front of the opening. After a quick look at her, Hunter helped. Her eyes were dry, but hot, and her taut jaw spoke of gritted teeth and utter control.

He ached for her.

The last tangle of brush in place, Siri straightened and gestured to Hunter. "There are a few traps and snares on this side of the valley to be set," she said evenly. "Then we'll get out the weapons and set those snares on the other side of the valley."

They were occupied for some time with the traps, which consisted of the type of snares used to capture or kill animals. Pits, looped vines, trees bent to await a spring; all were cunningly placed and set, all promised a swift death for the unwary.

Tonelessly, Siri explained each trap exactly on both ends of the valley, making certain that Hunter was familiar with each one. And it wasn't until they'd set the last trap and begun working their way back toward the forest that he realized why she'd been so thorough.

Halting suddenly on the almost imperceptible path they were following, he said harshly, "You *believe* you're going to lose!"

She stared off across the meadow for a moment, then lifted her eyes to his. Haunted eyes. "I have to be prepared."

Holding tightly to two long spears in one hand, he reached out the other to grasp her shoulder. "No, it's more than that. It's something you've seen, or something you feel." Words tumbled from him, darkened by fear, gnawed by anxiety. "Siri, you can't *be sure!*"

"No, I can't," she agreed quietly. "I can only be ready—for whatever happens. You must see that."

She saw herself then, saw herself frozen in anguish as a knife was held to Hunter's throat. And she wasn't ready, could never be ready for that. Hunter or the Unicorns. She had to choose. But she couldn't choose. She couldn't make that choice. No god, no Huntman, however inhuman, could demand that choice of her. But a Huntman would, she knew that despairingly. No! Better she should die. The Unicorns would be safe with Hunter. Somehow, she had to prevent that choice! And she prayed again, desolately, that she be spared that choice. Anything but that. . . .

Hunter reached for her abruptly, chilled by the emptiness of her eyes. "Siri . . ."

She backed away jerkily, grace dissolved. She couldn't let him touch her, couldn't accept comfort—not from him. "We don't have much time," she managed to say tautly. "We'll find cover at the edge of the forest. Best not to be caught out in the open, at least until we can judge how many come this time and where they'll come from."

His jaw tightened. "All right."

"And we'll find food enough in the woods."

He nodded.

They walked quickly, shoulder to shoulder, not speaking. Siri was disturbed by his taut silence. She fingered the quiver of arrows hanging from her shoulder, trying to think of something to say to ease his mind.

Her instincts and intuition told her to keep up a conversation between the two of them, allowing no time for other emotions to tear them apart. They couldn't afford that now. She followed her instincts determinedly.

"We're lucky in one thing. By the time they get well into the valley, it'll be nearly dark. They'll probably make camp near the edge of the woods. We'll be able to get their number, and may even manage to draw one or two away from the others."

"Divide and conquer?" he asked.

She heard the continued tension in his voice but ignored it. "It's worked before."

"How do you plan to draw one or two away from the others?"

She shrugged a little. "I'm not strongly telepathic

other than communicating with Mother and Cloud, but I *can* read strong thoughts and create an . . . an uneasiness in the mind of a man. Depending on the man and his strength of mind, it sometimes causes him to leave his fellows and go in search of what bothers him."

"And then?"

"And then I'll lead him into one of the traps or kill him myself," she said.

"I can do that."

"No."

"Siri—"

"Hunter, you don't know the forest the way I do. I've done this before and I know what I'm doing. If two leave the camp at the same time, I'll need you to follow and handle one of them; if one leaves, I go alone while you stay and watch the camp."

He swore softly.

"Hunter—"

"All right! I see the sense in your plan, but don't ask me to like it."

Siri was silent.

After a moment, he said, "You said that sometimes you can read strong thoughts."

"Yes."

"From me?"

Siri weighed her words carefully. "From you, I sometimes receive . . . images. Not clear thoughts, but the images of them. Clear images."

Hunter remembered some of his thoughts, remembered just how often his hunger for her had filled his mind. Unconsciously he winced, and began to understand how she could fear rape. "Is that why you're afraid I'd force myself on you?" he asked roughly.

With all her senses strained in awaiting Huntmen, Siri had no difficulty in picking up images from Hunter now. Her breath caught, and she felt her body responding wildly, as always, to his desire. Striving to hide that reaction from him, she said, "You don't think of force. Except . . ."

"Except when I wonder how long I can control my need for you," he finished, grim.

"Yes," she whispered.

"I love you, Siri. I would never do anything to hurt you."

"You're a man. Men take what they want."

After a moment, he said, "I can hardly blame you for believing that, with only Huntmen as your examples. But all men aren't alike, Siri. The differences are as vast as the number of grasses and plants in this valley. Strong men, weak men, selfish and unselfish, brutal and kind, intelligent and ignorant. All of them are different."

Siri understood what he meant. There was even some part of her that believed that whatever his own doubts about control, Hunter would never force himself on her. And there was, she knew, more danger to her in that knowledge. If he attempted to possess her with all his physical strength, her very nature would rebel and she could possibly fight him. But if he seduced instead, in caring and hunger, could she fight that?

She pushed the thoughts away, desperate to postpone that confrontation as long as possible. Gesturing as they passed the cabin, she changed the subject. "Huntmen won't go in there, at any rate."

He accepted the change. "Why not?"

"They think I'm a sorceress, remember? As far as the Huntmen are concerned, that cabin is cursed. I've never yet seen one cross the threshold."

Hunter smiled just a little. "You do have a few special weapons in this war, don't you?"

"A few. Their fear counts for a lot."

"That reminds me." He sent a sidelong look at her as they entered the woods. "What about the madness? I heard in the city that any who escaped this valley were driven mad."

She frowned. "Madness? It isn't my doing. I suppose the few who escape alive are held to be mad because they rave about what they've seen here."

After a moment's thought, Hunter agreed silently with her reasoning. After all, if he left this valley raving about dragons, unicorns, lyrebirds and snow cats—not to mention

Guardians and Mermaids—he'd fully expect someone to clap *him* rather quickly into a chamber for the mad.

Then he remembered. "The Huntman, King. I met with him. He couldn't talk."

"He could when he left the valley." Siri had halted and now crouched down to peer through the underbrush in the direction of the meadow. "We can wait here; we can see without being seen by them." Hunter felt perplexed and uneasy. If King had not lost his tongue in the valley, where had he lost it and when?

Propping the spears against a fallen log, Hunter gestured toward the thickening depths of the forest. "What about from that direction?"

She sat cross-legged on the ground and looked up at him. "From that direction, we have an alarm." She whistled shrilly, and was immediately answered from half a dozen places deep in the woods.

Hunter nodded as he sat down beside her. But not touching. "So the birds keep watch."

"All the animals do. They're forbidden to kill in the valley, but they help all they can."

"Forbidden by the Guardians?"

"Of course."

"Have you ever *seen* a Guardian?"

"No."

"Then how in hell can you believe in them?"

Siri was finding it difficult to meet his eyes, all too conscious of his emotions and her own. She tried to fight her own awareness, and her body was tense with the effort. "I believe in them because I see the evidence of what they do. I believe in them because they *are*. Can't you understand that?"

"No." He looked away, also having trouble with his feelings. "A race of gods? That is how you describe them, you know. A whole race of superior beings."

"And is that so impossible? Are you so convinced that mankind is the superior race of the galaxy?"

After a moment, he shook his head. "No. I've seen other races that are wiser, more stable. But a race of *gods?*"

"Your word, not theirs. They are Guardians, protecting the diverse life and mythology of a galaxy."

"Do they protect you?"

Siri looked down at her hands clasped loosely, seeing the tension there. Always, they returned to her. To her place, her responsibilities, her life. "No."

"You're the only one of your kind, aren't you?"

"I'm the only Keeper in the valley."

He looked at her, trying to keep his mind on the conversation and off everything else. But she was so beautiful . . . "Are there other Keepers, then?"

"I don't know."

"On this planet, perhaps?"

"I don't know." She glanced at him. "Why don't you call the planet Earth?"

He countered her question with one of his own. "Do you hate my ancestors for destroying this world, Siri?" Even now, it was hard for him to say it, hard to accept that his ancestors did indeed destroy this world. But he believed it. What she had said about the unicorns returning to their world each Summer to mate and give birth had convinced him.

"I don't hate anyone."

"Not even the Huntmen?"

"I hate what they do. I hate their greed and brutality."

"Do you hate me?"

She watched her knuckles whiten.

"Answer me, Siri! Do you hate me?"

"No."

"You trust me?" He was intent, concentrating on discovering the cause of her resistance to him. Nothing else mattered in that moment, not Huntmen or danger or her own obviously growing strain. He had to know.

"To protect the Unicorns if I die, yes."

He didn't want to think about that possibility. "Do you believe that I love you?"

"I believe that you believe it."

"But you don't believe it's true?"

I don't want to believe! "It doesn't matter."

"It matters to me, dammit!" he snapped. "I love you, Siri; I want to know if you believe that."

She drew a deep breath and let it out slowly. "It doesn't matter," she repeated slowly. "I can't change what I am."

"You're a woman," he said as he'd said before. "And no one could expect you to spend your entire *life* existing for a Summer that comes once in ten standard years! You need human companionship, Siri, love—"

"How do you know what I need?"

He gazed at her steadily, willing her to meet his eyes; and when she did, he spoke with utter certainty. "I know because I felt you respond to me with need. *Need*. I saw it in your eyes, felt it in your body. Your heart was pounding, Siri, and you couldn't breathe—just like me. I've seen you try to hide it. I've watched you turn away from me, and—cover your breasts with your arms when they would have shown me your desire."

"Stop," she whispered.

He held her eyes fixedly. "No, I won't stop, because what we feel for each other is important. It's *rare*. Love isn't something you ignore, or throw away; you can't pretend desire doesn't exist. I don't know what your precious Guardians intended for you, but they couldn't have believed you would spend your life up here alone."

"It's been that way for ten thousand years." She was still whispering, but the silence around them made her voice clear. "Keeper after Keeper, inviolable, alone. I was *born* to protect the Unicorns."

"That was before you saved the life of an enemy, Siri. Before you responded to me with need. Before you gave me your trust."

She flinched as though he had struck her, feeling the awful throb of yearning, the chaos of confusion. "I can't change what is," she whispered.

He was staring at her, and his love and need made him implacable. "I can," he said quietly. "I won't leave the valley, Siri, and I won't give up. I'll share you with the unicorns, but I won't lose you to them. Your Guardians can strike me down for interfering with their grand plan, but they can't make me stop loving you. Not in this life."

Siri tried to escape the snare of his intense green eyes, and found it impossible. "You'll destroy me."

Hauntingly, Maggie's words echoed in his mind. *"You were born to destroy some woman . . ."* And he reacted to that sting and to Siri's painful whisper with suppressed violence. "Why? How? Dammit, *how?*"

"I was never meant to love."

The lost note in her voice caught at his heart, and his frustration was a terrible thing. "If you were never meant to love, then why were you given the capacity for it? There's so much love in you, Siri, so much caring; what kind of cruel being could demand that you never explore the absolute limits of your caring? Don't you see? Love is innate to you; it's as natural for you to care as it is for you to breathe!"

Achingly conscious of her inability to explain fully, Siri tried to explain what she could. "I was never meant to love a man."

"Why not?"

"Man is an enemy."

He reached out suddenly, covering her left breast with one large hand. And he held her eyes, watching them widen as she went utterly still, feeling her heart thudding unevenly and hearing the sudden rasp of her breathing as her nipple hardened beneath his palm. He fought an instant surge of his own desire, concentrating on what he had to say. "Enemy?" His voice was deep, hoarse. "Your heart is beating for me, Siri. Your body is responding to my touch. I'm a man, but not your enemy—and you know it. Your body knows it."

Siri couldn't breathe, couldn't pull away from him. The warmth of his hand caused her breast to swell and harden, and she could feel the tight throbbing of her nipple. And more. The ache between her thighs was suddenly so sharp she almost cried out with it, and a molten heat filled her body. She had an almost overpowering urge to push herself more strongly into his hand, to grasp his other hand and put it, too, on her body.

She wanted to fall back on the ground and feel his heavy body cover her, join with her, possess her until the terrible hurting need was satisfied.

I can't do this. Her lips moved stiffly to shape the

words, but there was no voice. Only a whispery, raspy, aching sound. And her eyes, her lovely eyes, were a deep, rich violet color—and agonized. "I can't do this." This time, the words had a voice. A voice that was thick, suspended, anguished.

And for the first time, Hunter saw her tears. They trickled down her ashen cheeks, welling up from the bottomless depths of her eyes as if some inner barrier had been ruptured.

Slowly, his eyes locked with her suffering ones, he withdrew his hand. And then he pulled her into his arms, holding her tightly in an embrace that demanded nothing. Bewildered, he understood only that his insistence was tearing her apart for some reason she could not, or would not, explain.

This was not the time, he knew, to continue pushing her, even if he still had the will to do so. And for the first time, he lacked that will.

Eight

A distant shout promising danger tore them apart as both reached instinctively for weapons. Siri was back on balance as that threat became obvious, and her tears dried slowly. There was not even time to feel relief in being able to shy away from her feelings one more time. They stared intently through the underbrush, both tense and alert, both, if not forgetting, at least pushing aside the turbulent emotions they felt.

"There," Hunter said softly.

The Huntmen came slowly, making their way through the tall meadow grasses and gazing around them warily. They were armed with crossbows and knives and loaded with backpacks. Four of them came to a halt a few yards from the cabin, holding a low-voiced conversation among themselves as they gazed at it.

Siri's head was tilted, her face taut, listening with more, it seemed, than just her ears. Then, softly, she said, "They know you came here, Hunter; your interest in the valley was noted with curiosity in the city before you left.

They're wondering if you're still alive and, if so, why. They're thinking you may have found more than Unicorns here. They're thinking that maybe—" She broke off, a quiet, unconscious sound of disgust escaping her and her head jerking as if from a blow. The eyes she turned to Hunter were dark and unreadable. "They're putting themselves in your place."

Hunter felt the tension of gritted teeth. "I can guess what they're thinking," he said, adding bitterly, "No wonder the touch of a man is something you fear!"

How could she respond to that? She couldn't tell him that his touching itself brought no fear, but rather her own betraying reaction to that touch; she was forbidden to talk about the one absolute taboo of her life. In any case, by responding at all to his bitter comment she would only be keeping the wound raw between them. And that couldn't be, with danger upon them.

Siri returned her gaze to the Huntmen, satisfied that they were occupied with unloading their packs and posed no threat for the moment. She didn't want Hunter to dwell on his thoughts, didn't want to confront that terrible pain yet again. And somewhere on the edge of awareness, she recognized a blankness in the valley, a place she couldn't see or feel. It bothered her.

Seeking anything to distract them and keep the silence from growing unbearable, she said finally, softly, "Your people will have to find their dreams for themselves; do you understand that now?"

"Not entirely," he divided his attention between the Huntmen whose rough voices and coarse words shattered what should have been the peace of nightfall and Siri's closed face, so near and so distant.

"You can't help them find what must live in their hearts."

"Then my search has been for nothing."

She heard the pain in his voice, and the innate healer in her had to respond to it. "No search is ever fruitless. You found much in yourself, I think. And you found the beginnings of your race here."

"Yes, I found that." His voice was harsh. "I found that

my race destroyed a world, along with most of its history. I can return to my people in triumph, can't I, Siri? I can return with a validation of our greatness as a race. Look what we've done! We killed the world that bore us! We wiped out a million or so years of our evolution and history, choosing not to remember how we almost destroyed ourselves."

She kept her eyes on the Huntmen's camp. "Is that why you said you would stay here?" The question was a difficult one, and Siri wasn't sure she really wanted to hear the answer. "Because you believe as your ancestors did— that painful truths should be cast aside? Don't you realize that your people should confront their history?"

"How?" He laughed shortly. "I have no proof, no evidence to hold up before them. I can only tell them what I have learned, and there's so much I don't know, so many pieces still missing. I can tell them we destroyed our world, but not when or how. What good will that do?"

After a moment, Siri said, "Knowledge is a resource, a valuable thing. The Guardians would have preserved it somehow. If you are meant to return that knowledge to your people, you will find it intact."

About to object to her faith in her Guardians, Hunter had a sudden thought—and a chill of awareness. Was it possible? Slowly, he said, "In the city, there's a huge building filled with books. Thousands and thousands of them. I never looked at them, but . . . If this is Earth, those books have to be *about* Earth, and more than ten thousand years old. And there's an old woman, Maggie, who guards the library. Preserves it. She said that her mother also perserved it, and hers before her."

Siri wasn't surprised. The information made perfect sense to her. "A Guardian, perhaps. Or a Keeper. She must be preserving the knowledge of your race, Hunter."

Hunter stared at her, conscious of awe, and of his missed opportunity. "I was so near. I could have opened any book and learned more about my people. I could have found the missing pieces of our past, and all the forgotten myths and legends." And now Maggie's uncanny perception made sense, he realized, her seeming understanding of so much she should not have known. If she were a Guardian or, like Siri, a Keeper, then she was indeed something very special.

"You can still do that. You can take your people's lost knowledge back to them, Hunter." She looked at him. "Do you believe now that your quest was for nothing?"

Hunter's mind was whirling with the possibilities, and he felt a new certainty in himself.

"You'll go back, now," Siri said very quietly. "You have an important reason to go back."

He looked at her, and something inside him was breaking suddenly. Whether or not he gained the throne, he did indeed have to go back to Rubicon. "I can't leave you."

"You have to. You must complete your journey." Only her simple faith in any part of her Guardians' work enabled her to speak calmly and quietly; the thought of him leaving tore at her like a vicious animal. "It was meant that you find your people's history, because you did. And meant that you return it to them, because you can. It's your destiny."

"Come with me." His voice was deep, cracked.

"I can't."

"Siri—"

"I can never leave this valley."

"The unicorns won't need you in the Winter."

"I can never leave this valley."

He heard the truth and certainty in her voice, but was unwilling to admit defeat. "Then I'll come back," he told her fiercely, uncaring in that moment that his decision, should Boran not have survived the Quest, could leave Rubicon's throne empty for good. "I'll take the knowledge to my people and then return here as soon as I can."

Siri wondered if he would. She felt cold. Returning her attention to the Huntmen's camp, she said, "We'll have to wait until they settle down for the night before making a move. Are you hungry?"

"Yes," he said, and both of them knew he was talking about much more than food.

She ignored that. "I'll get something," she murmured and slid away through the forest.

Darkness fell, only a faint light provided as the moon rose. Siri found and gathered late fruit from the trees and showed Hunter how certain roots, when carefully peeled, provided a crunchy, satisfying meal.

They talked only occasionally, both preoccupied and troubled. Both aware of the desire that words would never conquer. And they listened to the sounds of intruders as the Huntmen fouled the clean valley air with their coarse voices and crude laughter.

"Did the cards foretell my coming?" he asked her once.

"Yes. A green-eyed man, hungry for truth."

Memories, some indistinct and some clear, jostled his thoughts as he remembered back to his first day in the valley and his delirious moments of awakening. "I saw Cloud, I think, before you came. You didn't hide the unicorns?"

"Yes, except for Cloud. He refused to be hidden with the rest that day, and wouldn't tell me why."

"No wonder you were angry when you found me."

"I was angry from the moment I knew you were coming."

He nodded, then frowned. "It seems odd that he would have refused you. And his attitude toward me . . . He accepted me very quickly, considering how many others have come here to hunt the unicorns."

Siri also frowned. "Yes. Very unusual. But I'm sure he had his reasons. Now that I think about it, I remember that the old Keeper told me once that Cloud sometimes knows even more than the cards."

"What could he have known? That I didn't come here to harm them?"

"I don't know." She was still frowning. "Something similar has happened only once before. Cloud asked me to trust King—and he wasn't even disturbed when King took Sasha's horn and left the valley."

"King didn't kill Sasha?"

"No. That happened before he came, at the beginning of the Summer."

It was a subject never discussed between them before,

and now Hunter knew the answer to something that had puzzled him—why Siri had trusted the Huntman enough to enable him to steal the horn. Because Cloud had asked it. His mind took up her musing, and he thought about that before he said finally, "If it hadn't been for that horn and King, I probably wouldn't have come up here. I'd heard rumors of unicorns nearby, but I was so disgusted by what the city itself held that I was on the point of leaving when a vendor offered me what he claimed was an aphrodisiac made from the horn of a unicorn. That led me to King."

After a moment, Siri said slowly, "Cloud could have known your destiny; the Unicorns have a stronger awareness of the Guardians and their purposes than I ever could. Perhaps Cloud knew that your time here was a part of your destiny. His wisdom is so old, and so certain."

"It's amazing that he'd want to help any of my race."

"The race that created him? No matter what else happens, they never forget that."

It was a humbling thought, but Hunter nonetheless felt unsettled by the implications. "I don't know that I like being a pawn of fate," he said finally.

Her eyes wandered toward the Huntmen's distant fire. Her gaze sharpened, probed. Then she was rising soundlessly to her feet. "Wait here," she murmured and melted into the darkness of the forest.

Hunter turned a quick, hard stare toward the Huntmen, his heart lurching as he counted only three forms huddled about the fire. It took every ounce of willpower he possessed to keep him seated and watching the camp, and even then his ears and his mind focused and strained toward the forest behind him.

Where was the fourth? Had Siri prodded him away from his fellows, or was she, as a warrior, simply taking advantage of the Huntman's recklessness?"

Hunter gritted his teeth and waited. Long silent moments. The valley was eerily quiet. When would the Huntmen notice one was missing? The moonlight dimmed abruptly as clouds scudded across it. The valley possessed its own safeguards, perhaps, spreading darkness in a tactical blanket. Where was Siri? She had only a knife and—

A sound? His imagination? The faith, keep the faith. His love, his need to protect, could not stand between her and what she must do. Never that. Never that.

Where was she?

A Huntman stirred, glanced toward the woods. Hunter's heart caught in his throat, his body tensing in readiness. No. No, even at a distance, he saw the uncaring shrug and the lapse into stillness. A long time now. Too long. Much too long. His heart was ticking away an eternity of moments. There was a desperate, swelling need for more time with her. But the cards . . . *damn* the cards! Goddamn them. Any god. Every god. If the price were his soul, he'd buy more time with her.

Where was she?

The camp was restless. More glances toward the woods. Anxiety and fear coiled and writhed icily in Hunter's belly, crawled like a snake in his veins. The camp's small fire danced mockingly before his fixed gaze. His vision tunneled, the forest closed in behind him, hugging his back like some softly chortling, lunatic presence. The Reaper loomed high above, unseen but felt, heavy anger at the Huntmen's escape from it creating a palpable sense of oppression over the valley.

Anxiety coiled tighter and tighter, constricting his breathing, squeezing his heart in gripping talons. She was protecting the unicorns— No. A *race* of mystical, magical, ancient people. *The Unicorns*. She was protecting the Unicorns. It was what she was bred for, born to.

Her right.

Her choice.

Another Huntman rose, hitching at the belt and knife he wore, bravado in the gesture of scorn for his companions' uneasiness. Harsh, mocking laughter. And then he was striding boldly toward the woods.

Hunter rose to a crouch, his eyes following the second man. But he'd promised not to interfere unless two left the camp at the same time! Every instinct fought against that promise; only the awareness that his presence could fatally distract her caused him to ease back down, staring toward the silent, still camp. Chafing against the bonds of waiting. Listening. Hearing only the gloom of the forest and the silence of the meadow and The Reaper's brooding anger. Smelling the fear of the Huntmen, and their greed. Feeling Death on the wing somewhere behind him in the forest, dressed in the deceptively gentle feathers of a Keeper of the Unicorns. Tasting the bitter bile of his own fear for Siri, thick and hot in his throat. Feeling the slow, heavy, constricted beat of his heart. Sensitized by tension, his flesh tightened and chilled and crawled. His eyes were hot and rasped dryly against the lids.

Insanely disjointed, scenes tumbled past the focus of his mind's eye. His own dimly remembered battle with Death. Siri standing stiff and angry by his bed . . . reading cards before the fire . . . spitting in fury and pride when he had belittled her life . . . soft-spoken and musing after a Unicorn Dance . . . instinctively healing a jagged cut from a careless knife . . . cold with fear after a prophecy she could not or would not see . . . agonized by his insistent desire.

Ahhh, God, how he loved her!

Then he heard the cry. Muffled, it nonetheless raised the hairs on his scalp and the nape of his neck. The cry of an animal, brutal and sharp, in pain and fear.

Before Hunter could even absorb the sound or his own rapid, fearful response, she was just suddenly *there*, moving with the predatory silence of a warrior, and Hunter's spring-coiled tension found release in a draining rush of relief. He caught her fiercely in his arms, holding on tight to the flesh-and-blood reality of his love.

Siri drew back, surprised that he would worry about her and too unsure of her own control to remain in his arms for long. She was wary of touching him, nervous that there was too much between them to allow even a simple touching. And she felt the shock and building anger in him even before his fingers lifted to touch the already livid bruise high on her cheek, barely seen in the darkness.

"It's nothing," she said. "Not even intentional. He just struck out blindly and I got in the way. By morning it'll be gone."

Hunter felt her drawing back, and his hand fell to his side. "You said you couldn't heal yourself; this won't be gone by morning."

"I can't heal myself, but I do heal quickly."

He looked at her, barely visible in the darkness. Woman, warrior, Keeper. A gentle, protective touch for the Unicorns, a wary, unwilling passion for him, death for the Huntmen. An easy wisdom at odds with unknowing innocence. Battle skills warring with healing ones. The stoic strength of Winter coexisting with the freedom and beauty of Summer.

She didn't know how incredible she was.

How inexplicable.

How magical.

It was the warrior, the fascinating, intriguing warrior, who brought him back to more dangerous thoughts. Her eyes and mind probed the distant camp before she said, "Neither of the others will venture away, I think, until morning. They'll keep guard tonight. We can't get close enough unseen to use the arrows or spears."

"So we wait," Hunter finished.

"And we'd better sleep while we can; tomorrow will be a long day, I think."

"I'll take the first watch," he said instantly.

Siri didn't protest. Nor did she protest when he remained close beside her as she stretched out on the ground and settled herself. The last thing she saw before sleep claimed her was the shadowy image of his profile.

And she dreamed about him. Dreams which had nothing to do with Huntmen or Unicorns or danger or the knowledge of something forbidden. Dreams about unfamiliar, longed-for things. Dreams about a kind of love she was never meant to know.

He had done a fine job, he decided complacently, in wiping all knowledge of himself and these last days from the Huntmen's minds; the sorceress would have nothing to be suspicious about if she read their minds. He hid and watched, paying close attention to her methods.

Boran was impressed. Granted, neither Con nor

Stovin had been strongly skilled or particularly fierce, but the sorceress had dispatched both neatly and with almost no noise.

From his position deep in the forest, he reflected on her skills, and on her courage. It would be, he thought, a pity to break the spirit of such a woman. But necessary, of course. He began working his way cautiously toward the other side of the valley. At first light, he planned to return to the city and recruit a second group of Huntmen; they would be required for his final assault against the valley and the sorceress.

And Hunter.

And when his tools were safely in the valley and hidden, he would summon the sorceress to him again. She would be weakened after her battles. Weakened enough so that he could seduce her completely this time.

He pondered then, not for the first time, his inability to discover within her mind the hiding place of the unicorns. Like the taboo preserving her virginity, that knowledge seemed rooted deeply, and she would not give it up. But once he had taken her precious virginity, he was certain her mind would be so shattered he would have no difficulty in tearing that knowledge from her.

Still moving cautiously, he thought idly that it would be pleasant to force Hunter to watch him destroy the sorceress. Tied helplessly, he would be an attentive audience. And it would likely drive him mad, due to his fatuous *love* for the woman, to watch her mindlessly succumb in wild passion to another man, and an enemy at that.

Boran chuckled softly deep in his throat, absently stroking the front of his trousers as he walked. What an enjoyable scene that would be! Hunter struggling against his bonds, shouting his rage and anguish, while his chaste ladylove was willingly spreading her legs for another.

Hardly conscious that this near-constant state of sexual arousal was unusual for him, Boran put distance between himself and the others before finally giving in to his building need for release. He found a secluded place on the far side of the valley and made himself comfortable after casually dropping his trousers around his ankles. And the soft little chuckle continued to rumble from his throat as he half-closed his eyes and focused his mind on the scene he had conjured.

Hunter would be bound close by, of course, with an excellent opportunity to see it all. And Boran would have total control of the woman's mind, ordering her to strip away her clothing and watching while she obeyed. He might even comment crudely on the various parts of her body as they were revealed. Then he would lay her down close to the bound man and discard his own clothing before beginning to caress her pure body.

How Hunter would fight to free himself! And the agony he would feel when the woman moaned frenziedly in her passion! Would he scream in his rage as her slender hand boldly stroked Boran's turgid member? Would he curse savagely when she begged in complete abandonment for his possession? And would he go utterly berserk when her legs parted and her slick virginal opening eagerly accepted his swollen organ?

Boran's chuckles had become panting gurgles, and he changed the fantasy scene suddenly to allow for a greater punishment to Hunter.

He would take her like an animal, he decided. On her hands and knees, rump jutting, moaning like any bitch in heat. He would fondle her dangling breasts and the smooth curves of her buttocks, and then nudge her legs farther apart and mount her. He would linger over the act of deflowering her, letting the other hear her moans of need, allowing him to watch the first slow moments of penetration. And when her maidenhead gave way beneath the force of his sudden lunge, he would laugh as he heard two animal cries of anguish—one male and one female.

And while both of them cried with the pain, he would hunch over her body like any rutting animal, pounding into her tight passage, hauling on her breasts. And then he would strip the walls from her mind just as she was beginning to enjoy it again, and her horrified writhing body would draw forth his seed in a jetting rush of pleasure.

Boran caught his breath finally, becoming aware of his surroundings again. It occurred to him vaguely as he cleaned himself and adjusted his clothing that for a second time he had given in to the need for release with no female body to accept his heat. It was faintly disturbing, but no more.

The sorceress would take him soon.

He was regretful that such a scene as the one that had so recently given him pleasure would not actually take place. He reluctantly doubted that his control over the sorceress could withstand the presence of Hunter. She was far more likely in such circumstances to break free of his mindspell. He could rape her, of course, but he still wanted her willing—which meant that Hunter would not watch it happen.

But it didn't really matter. Hunter would know soon enough just how thoroughly she would be destroyed. And there was a great deal of pleasure in that.

. . . and he was hunched over her body like any rutting animal, pounding into her tight passage, hauling on her breasts . . .

Siri woke with a start, her body aching and cold, and she realized that her first yearning dreams of Hunter had become something else, something terrible and painful. But even as she tried to recapture her nightmare, it was fading away, until finally she could remember none of it. All that lingered was a sense of disquiet, an unnerving blankness where something should have been visible.

Her internal clock told her that hours had passed, and she watched Hunter for a few moments while he remained unaware. He was relaxed but wary, ceaselessly vigilant as he watched the Huntmen's camp. And her disquiet faded as she became totally absorbed by his face. A hard face, a face with much experience stamped upon it by time. A face that had known battle, known rage and fear and driving purpose. A face that softened suddenly as it turned toward her, the green eyes lighting with pleasure.

Without even realizing she spoke aloud, Siri murmured, "You are a beautiful man."

Lips softened in a smile that was startled and amused. "Sleep," he said quietly.

But Siri sat up in one fluid motion, unsettled and embarrassed by her own words. "We divide the watch," she reminded.

"Siri—"

"I'm fine, Hunter. And you need rest as well as I do."

After a moment, he stretched out as she had done, pillowing his head on one arm. He watched her for a while; she could feel his gaze even though she kept her own attention fixed on the Huntmen's camp. But soon she knew from his breathing that he slept, and her eyes moved as though pulled by a lodestar to gaze at his face.

No beard growth.

She thought about that for a while, her attention divided between his face and the Huntmen with the automatic awareness of a warrior on watch. Her mind, needing to be busy, toyed with the thought of Hunter's nonexistent beard. She hadn't thought about it before, sharing in a way his trait of not thinking about some things until she was ready to, or had the time to, or was curious enough.

Men grew beards, she knew; the Huntmen were nearly always bearded. Yet Hunter had not shaved since coming to the valley. She formed the question in her mind and then released it, tossing it into her subconscious where the deep well of knowledge her mother and the old Keeper had provided lay waiting. And she waited, content in the certainty that knowledge handed down from Keeper to Keeper and enhanced by the wisdom and learning of her mother's racial memories would provide the correct answer. And it did.

Growth retardant.

She weighed the new phrase in her mind, understanding the meaning of the answer provided. Of course. Hunter had traveled the stars in his search for myths, and he was a man who would choose the convenience of an injection to halt beard growth rather than the daily ritual of shaving. Of course.

Had Hunter been privy to those few moments, much that he found confusing in Siri would have made sense. That the knowledge of three races—Unicorn, Human-

Keeper, and Merpeople—reposed deep in her mind Siri
knew, but it was a matter-of-fact knowing and nothing she
found surprising or worthy of comment. The transference
of that knowledge had occurred early in her childhood, a
painless, interesting process, leaving her with a well to
draw answers from should questions trouble her.

From generations of Keepers came the instincts of
warrior, protector, and healer, the knowledge of herbs,
food-gathering, and tracking an enemy. From the Merpeople's galaxy-encompassing racial memories came knowledge
of what lay beyond this valley and planet, the sciences and
technologies of man and beings other than man, and the gift
of Sight. And from the Unicorns came a history that their
own creation had bound to mankind's, and the wisdom and
learning of a people known only as Guardians who traveled
beyond man's scope and saw what was to be seen.

In a vague sort of way, Siri understood that the
knowledge was hers only to be used sparingly and passed
on, called when needed but never drawn in totality from
the well. A part of her understood that the well held the
horrors of the bloody wars, destruction, and evil that
Hunter had seen so much of, but that was a part meant only
to be passed on so as not to be forgotten. That there would
one day come a need for such knowledge she did not doubt;
that certainty had been placed with her just as the
knowledge had.

But that was for a distant, unseen future, and another
Keeper, perhaps. It troubled her no more than her own
possession of the knowledge troubled her. A fact of her life,
and real as she knew reality.

Siri frowned a little, though, and looked again at
Hunter's face. How her life had changed! The simplicity of
her existence had been challenged by his coming, and
there was a part of her that could not regret that. There
were more questions now than answers, questions her well
of knowledge had not been meant to cope with. Yet she had
learned.

She had learned that all men were not, could not, be
her enemies because he was not. She had learned that the

Unicorns felt privileged to have Hunter with them, and deeply grateful; here was one of their gods who was *not* bent on hunting or killing them, and they felt that to be an affirmation of their faith that man would one day reclaim his myths and dreams.

She had learned that her body had needs unknown to her until now. And she had learned that neither her unique heritage nor her inborn responsibilities could spare her the painful awakening of her female flesh.

She had learned to love a man.

And she knew then that, despite everything, she would not have chosen to repeat this Summer with his presence wiped away. She felt immeasurably older, painfully wiser, and more human than ever before. She was Keeper—but she was also woman, and women were no more perfect than the male half of their race. Cut, she would bleed; bleed enough, she would die; and nothing of that had changed except her own awareness of her mortality.

At the beginning of the Summer, she had been perfect in her certainty. Arrogant, strong, confident, selfish in her possessiveness of the valley and the Unicorns, unmoved by the dark history of this planet and its peoples, uncaring of other races and other worlds. As much obsessed as he had been.

And then he had come. Questioning her certainty. Mocking her arrogance with his own vital determination to save a world. Moving her with his pain and shock, forcing her to feel the near-extinction of a race and its struggles. Appalling her with his memories of countless worlds and wars, of races dying and dead. Shaking her confidence, splintering her obsession.

Mother?
Daughter?
I'm different, Mother.
Yes, child.
Was this intended for me?
I cannot answer, child.

Does it have to hurt so, Mother?
I'm sorry, child.

Siri was distracted then, in that moment of communication, by the blankness she felt. It hovered just beyond the fringes of her awareness where she couldn't touch it. A wrongness in the balance of things. A blankness where something should be seen. It was there, and she felt that there would come a need for knowing that wrongness, but she couldn't grasp it. And there was a sense of time slowing and then speeding, of events that would stretch painfully the space of heartbeats.

Chilled, she looked at Hunter's sleeping face. His obvious strength comforted her somewhat, and there was not even a faint shock that she could now look to someone else for a strength to add to her own.

Dawn came to the valley. A gray, troubled dawn, its arrival heralded neither by bird nor beast. The cloudy sky lightened reluctantly, slowly, dropping a thin mist over the meadow and the stirring Huntmen.

She looked down, about to call gently, but there was no need. He was awake and gazing up at her. And his features held such an expression of love and tenderness, it made her throat ache.

"I was afraid I'd dreamed you," he said softly. "I'm always afraid to wake up now for fear you were only my dream."

Siri heard her brisk warrior's voice suggesting breakfast as he sat up and saw her hands reaching for the fruit they had saved, feeling divided from that warrior because another part of her had changed. Could her life ever be the same again?

"Siri—"

"There's something wrong." She tried not to think of what had not changed. There was still Hunter. There were still the Unicorns. There was still the dark foreboding of a choice she would die not to make.

Hunter glanced toward the Huntmen, assuring himself they were still at their camp, then looked back at her, waiting.

Siri shook her head. "I just don't know. Huntmen always bring imbalance to the valley, a sense of wrongness. But there's more this time. A—a blankness somewhere. As if I'm looking right at something I can't see."

"The cards?"

"No. This is me." She chewed on her lower lip unconsciously, staring off toward the Huntmen moving stiffly and cautiously as they built up their fire and prepared a silent morning meal for themselves.

Hunter gazed at her taut, seeking face and felt the growing battle-tension of her slender body. He almost wished that he *had* dreamed her, because she would be safe in his mind and she would never be as safe as he wanted her to be in her lifetime.

Born to keep and protect the Unicorns.

He waited stoically for the resentment, the jealousy to gnaw at him. But it didn't come. He realized then that his final understanding and acceptance of the Unicorns as an ancient and mystical race had healed the hurt of knowing she could never learn to love him as she loved them. They were in her heart, her mind, her very soul; everything she was bound her to them with a tie nothing could destroy.

He had come so close to losing her so many times. Words wrongly spoken. Intentions misunderstood. Actions that would have driven her irretrievably from him halted just in time. In his arrogance and insensitivity he had hurt her more than once, and angered her frequently.

If he could somehow win a part of her love, it would be enough. Sharing her with the Unicorns would be enough. And if the knowledge of being second in her heart would haunt his dreams and solitary moments, then he would live with that.

If he could only win some part of her heart.

A brief touch on his arm. "Hunter?"

He looked at her, forced a smile. "Can't read my thoughts?"

She was gazing at him, intent, sober. "Even if I could, some thoughts aren't meant to be read."

He was saved from having to respond when the Huntmen took up weapons, left packs behind, and began to

move cautiously in their direction. And the warrior he
loved was moving instantly to gather her weapons, then
lead the way as they faded back into the forest. And it was
the warrior who saw and was troubled by the Huntmen's
unnatural woodcraft.

"They know too much," she whispered to Hunter.
"They learn to hunt in the warrens of cities, not the silence
of forests; they know too much!"

"They guessed what would be here," he reasoned.
"They prepared for the valley."

Siri tossed the useless puzzle into the winds, her mind
turning to strategy. "They're keeping to cover; we can't use
the arrows or spears with so great a chance of wasting them.
I'll have to draw them out first."

As they continued moving stealthily among the trees
and screening brambles, Hunter voiced a rapid protest.
"They've lost two men; they'll be quick to fire now.
Especially at you, since they fear you. I'll draw them out."

"You're my edge, Hunter," she told him firmly. "They
aren't *sure* you're here in the valley and alive. We have to
use that surprise eventually, so why not now? If we're
quick, we can get them both."

He growled a reluctant agreement, his respect for her
strategy growing as they reached the clearing holding the
Crystal Pool and he realized what she had in mind.

"They're coming this way," she noted quickly. "I'll get
down behind that rocky rise on the other side of the pool
while you move around behind the Huntmen. We'll wait
until they're well into the clearing. When you see me
stand, get the one nearest you. I'll take the other." Then
she was moving swiftly and silently around the pool toward
her hiding place.

Hunter faded back into the woods, rapidly finding a
vantage point where he halted and strained every sense in
listening, in pinpointing. It was a sense other than hearing
which found the enemy, a sense honed by survival battles
on distant worlds over many years. He instantly shifted
position on soundless feet, pleased to note a moment later
that his instinct had not been at fault; a Huntman passed,
unsuspecting, where he'd stood heartbeats ago.

Knowing in his mind and his body how to measure another man, Hunter followed and studied them, creeping more silent than a whisper in their very bootmarks. He let his instincts probe, his senses reach out fully and carefully. And what he found in them was only greed, bestial anger, and a fear born out of their ignorance.

And the strength of determination.

He watched as they drew nearer to one another, their tactical sweep of the forest narrowing as they moved toward the Crystal Pool.

He might have killed at least one while following, but dared not take the chance of losing one of his two spears in striking at an unsure target. Any miscalculation on his part could mean a greater risk to Siri—and that was something he would not even consider.

It was obvious that these Huntmen mistrusted the path through the woods, equally obvious that they were men determined to find what they sought.

Even if it meant bearding a sorceress in her den.

They reached the clearing at last, moving with the innate caution of frightened men. Carefully, they stepped from the cover of trees, stiff and wary, their own bravado now mocking them as the peaceful pool and apparently quiet and unthreatening clearing met their eyes. Another step. Another.

Hunter readied his spear, marking his target before allowing his eyes to search out the rocks where Siri hid. As quickly as he was ready, she rose into view, arrow nocked, bow arm drawing back expertly.

His own arm snapped forward, the spear released to fly straight and true to its target. He knew the surprise was complete, even as he saw them lurching for cover and weapons with panicked eyes and frantic bodies, confusion leaving them with nowhere to turn. He faded instantly back, his eyes coolly noting his target sprawled face down, with half the length of the spear jutting from the rough leather tunic.

Both his eyes and his ears followed Siri's arrow singing through the air, a brief song for the short journey it made before finding its destination in the chest of the lunging target.

Neither of the enemy had managed to use his own weapon.

Hunter thought of Siri rising from those rocks, silver hair flowing about her shoulders as if it possessed the living intent to enchant.

Even in the brief instant granted him to see her, the impressions the Huntmen must have felt had crashed through him. How extraordinarily magnificent she was! Black-clad strength and grace, black-eyed savagery and power, and the beautiful face and perfect womanly body of a goddess. Rising out of nowhere in silence and purpose.

Death wedded to Beauty by sorcery.

Hunter took a deep, full breath, his first in what felt like a very long time. God, she was glorious! Like no woman he had ever known, she embodied all the very best of womankind. Strong and wise, knowing and innocent, beautiful and gentle, passionate in her temper and vulnerable in ways he didn't understand. He felt humbled suddenly that this woman had trusted him with the secret knowledge of the herd's hiding place, had allowed him to help her defend her beloved Unicorns.

Siri was waiting by the pool, smiling when she saw him, her eyes the bottomless, serene black that was not battle. "You're good with spears," she noted admiringly, nodding toward his fallen victim.

"You're better with the bow," he returned, his voice husky from emotions still swirling within him. Then, conscious of her searching look and unwilling to bring about the return of her inexplicable pain by reminding her of his love, he changed the subject carefully. Nodding toward the bodies, he said, "We leave them?"

Siri nodded. "The animals will take them to the gorge and leave them there."

Remembering the almost bottomless canyon at the far end of the valley, Hunter decided it would make a fitting resting place for the Huntmen. In battle, there was no feeling for the shells left by the enemy.

Nine

As they went about releasing the Unicorns and trying to restore the valley to normality, Siri wondered. She was troubled by her continued unsettled feeling of blankness in the valley. She wondered why the black agony had not materialized. And lastly, she wondered why they were unable to discover any of the Huntmen's weapons.

They'd gone first to free the Unicorns; by the time they'd passed the Crystal Pool, the two bodies had been taken away by the animals. The speed of that was unusual, but Siri decided that the animals had just acted more quickly today. At the Huntmen's abandoned camp, there was nothing but a circle of charred ground and four worthless, empty packs. There had been no opportunity for her to take the weapons of the two she'd slain in the forest during the night, and now those bodies had also been taken away by the animals.

Hunter didn't seem concerned by the lack of weapons; he was clearly too relieved that nothing in the valley had been destroyed to worry about anything else. And even though he could hardly know what was normal under these circumstances, Siri shared his relief and finally pushed aside her troubling thoughts.

And it wasn't until after their noon meal that she realized the blankness was gone. She reached out with her mind, probing, and found nothing but peace and quiet in the valley. And even though she was relieved by that, she was still troubled. She was also uneasy to find that with the valley restored to normality, she had nothing to keep her mind occupied with things other than Hunter and her own feelings.

Every instinct she could claim told her there would be an ultimate confrontation between them, and her tension grew as she realized he was watching her more intently than ever, and that he, too, was obviously conscious of passing time. They both knew he would return to his world; neither mentioned that subject. But Summer was waning, and although there would be a brief, cool Fall, Winter would make travel to his ship impossible.

He would have to leave before Winter.

"Siri?"

She halted at the door, then half-turned to look at him. "I'm going for a swim," she said, her inner restlessness apparent in her voice.

"May I come?"

With a shrug, she left the cabin. A vague instinct warned her that it was not wise to accept his company, but Siri didn't understand why. In the cabin or at the pool, what difference did it make?

She began to understand when, reaching the pool, she pulled off her boots and stood to unlace her bodice. Her movements were casual and automatic—until she glanced up to find Hunter standing nearby watching her. Nimble fingers became awkward suddenly, and she felt heat flush through her body. Frowning, she worked the stubborn laces until she could shrug out of the top half of her garment, then bent over to pull the clinging material down over her hips and legs and step free of it.

Without looking at him again, she moved slowly out
into the cool, clear water of the Crystal Pool.

Hunter was barely aware that he was removing his
own clothing slowly, unable to take his eyes off her. He had
seen her in this pool once before, but at night and from a
distance. Now she was so close, and the filtered sunlight
dappled her golden body with light and shadow. His
physical response to her was instant, and he swallowed
hard as he followed her into the water.

The wellspring water should have been icy, but was
instead cool and refreshing. It should have chilled his ardor,
but he realized that little, if anything, was capable of that
now. In the middle of a blizzard, he would be hot with
wanting her.

Gritting his teeth, Hunter struck out through the
water, trying to release tension in physical activity. But he
was starkly aware of the caress of the water over his skin,
and of his body's pounding, throbbing need. He couldn't
take much more of this, couldn't go on fighting himself. For
the first time he was very much afraid that he would
completely lose control and force Siri against her will.

He swam with powerful strokes, forcing his body to its
limits, desperate to attain some measure of control. Hardly
aware that she had slipped into the shallower area to give
him room, he swam blindly, fighting to block out the
intensity of his need, trying to exhaust himself.

Siri, trembling, watched him. Though she was not
tired herself, her breathing was as ragged as his, and her
heart pounded. She felt shaky and weak, and her body was
hot. She located a flat stone under the water and waited
there, feeling the waves of Hunter's passing lap over her
breasts, feeling his thoughts battering her. She drew her
knees up and put her arms around them, half-consciously
rocking a little and almost moaning aloud with the aching
fullness of her breasts.

The images in his mind tormented her; his struggle to
control himself pulled at her like a lodestar. He fought
himself and she fought them both, and her battle was no
more successful than his. The taboo in her mind grew
wispy, insubstantial; her will seemed to flow from her grasp

as though a barrier inside her had ruptured. She felt the scalding trickle of tears and wasn't even sure why she was crying, except that she hurt.

Hunter rose from the water before her, and she looked at him dazedly. For the first time she saw his body not as something that needed mending but as a male body in the prime of beauty and strength. The rippling muscles beneath his smooth bronze skin fascinated her; the mat of black hair on his powerful chest filled her with a need to press her breasts against him, and the swollen fullness of his loins made her own ache emptily.

When she looked at last at his face, she felt something inside her quiver tensely and then, suddenly, yield. A shuddering sigh escaped her lips, and when he reached down, her hands grasped his and she allowed him to pull her up.

"I can't stand anymore," he said in a thick, rasping voice. His chest rose and fell strongly with his harsh breaths, and his vivid green eyes were alive with desire. "Siri . . . I'm not made of stone. I'm half mad with wanting you . . . Don't stop me this time, beloved."

"I can't stop . . ." She heard the voice that was hers and not hers, and knew it came from someplace deeper than her mind. "I have to . . . stop." Her body, yielding, swayed toward him; her mind, trapped in the chaos of its terrible conflict, fought the need to surrender in love and desire.

It was the confrontation she had hoped to avoid, and the pain of it tore at her. The full force of his need was focused on her, battering her mind and body, and her female flesh had surrendered at last. But her mind struggled to remember the price she would pay for her body's capitulation. If she could have, she would have told him then why this was forbidden to her; but she was physically incapable of speaking of it except as a last, desperate resort. Should he try to force her, she could speak; otherwise, she could say nothing.

It was her choice . . . her choice . . . Hunter or the Unicorns . . . to live fully as a woman, loved and loving, for a few brief weeks . . . to live the remainder of

a natural life alone but for a Summer that came once in ten
years . . . to love or not to love . . . to be woman or
Keeper . . . to live or to die. . . .

"Siri, I love you!"

. . . woman or Keeper . . .

"I need you so much—"

. . . Hunter or the Unicorns . . .

"—and I know you need me!"

. . . to live or to die . . .

"Goddammit, Siri, talk to me!" He was almost out of
control, fighting himself and wildly intent on obtaining a
response from her even if he had to force her brutally to
confront her own feelings against her will. The heat of her
naked body inflamed him, and he reached out with a groan
to persuade in another manner.

But the cry that came from her then chilled him; it was
soft and agonized, eerily inhuman. And he caught her body
as it crumpled bonelessly against him.

"Siri!" He lifted her into his arms and carried her
swiftly to the bank, suddenly afraid that he had finally
pushed her too far. Her wet body was light and completely
limp, and only the faint pulse he detected in her throat
reassured him that she lived. Without pausing to gather
their clothing, he carried her through the forest to the
cabin.

———

She awoke slowly, surfacing from a nightmarish world
that was cold and white with snow, and utterly empty. It
took several moments for her to realize that she was in the
bed that had been Hunter's since his arrival. She was
covered with the quilts and naked beneath them; her
clothing lay across the foot of the bed. She sat up slowly,
holding the covers to her breasts in a new and unconscious
modesty, looking around until she saw Hunter.

He was standing at the door, leaning against the jamb
as he stared outside, his body stiff. He was fully dressed,
and Siri hesitated only a moment before swinging her legs
from the bed and reaching for her clothes. She kept her
back turned to him, and realizing that she did so was a tiny
shock.

He didn't speak until she drew on her boots and stood, and it was obvious that he had been aware of her movements even though he had not turned to face her.

"Neat trick, that." His voice was flat. "I suppose some men might enjoy making love to an unconscious woman, but I'm not one of them. A wonderful defense, Siri."

I couldn't choose! She even opened her mouth to speak the words, but they simply would not emerge. "I can't change what I am," she managed finally, huskily.

He swung around then to face her, his face stone and green eyes violent. "I don't want to hear that again! What you're doing to me isn't pretty, but then, you know that, don't you? You know exactly what you're doing to me. Did I say I was half mad with wanting you? I was wrong. I am mad. There's no other explanation. I should have listened in the city when they told me you drove men mad, because now I know it's true! If I had a scrap of sanity to call my own, I'd climb out of this valley and put a galaxy between us. But I can't leave, Siri." His laugh was harsh. "God help me, I love you. And there's not a damn thing I can do to change that."

The hardness of his face and the ferocity in his eyes hurt her, but there was nothing she could say or do to change him. She was so weary and frightened. Although her loss of consciousness had stopped the confrontation, it had solved nothing. He still wanted her, she still wanted him, and there was still the choice that would destroy her no matter what.

She acknowledged that to herself then. If she chose Hunter, she would die. If she chose the Unicorns and that choice drove him away from her—as she had no doubt it would—there would be nothing left of her but an empty shell. Rejected by her one time too many, he would return to his world for good, she knew; no human man would remain contentedly in love with a woman he could not possess physically without a very good reason. And she could give no reason. Love would become hate, and he would be gone, never understanding why she had driven him away.

Never even knowing she loved him.

Boran summoned the sorceress several hours before dawn. He had returned with his second group of Huntmen, discovering they were laughably easy to control; it only required a fraction of his concentration to keep them as docile as sheep. Leaving them asleep in exhaustion after their rough entrance into the valley, he made his way swiftly but silently to the deepest part of the forest and summoned the sorceress.

And, as she neared, he realized in shock that his control over her was a newly tenuous thing. He frowned, concentrating, and felt the chaos of her mind. A grunt escaped him when he also felt the pain in her. Surprised and unsettled, he carefully probed her thoughts, discovering the source of her confusion and pain.

So! The other was demanding a consummation of his love, unaware of the cost to her. And her body had surrendered, but her mind had prevented that consummation. The resulting battle within her was throwing up a kind of shield against himself, Boran realized.

He waited until she stepped into the clearing and then focused all his mental energies on retaining his control over her. But when he went to meet her, he saw that a curious transformation had occurred. The woman who faced him was his creation—and was not. Moment by moment, she wavered between Keeper and awakening girl. She smiled at him, yet her black eyes were wary, disturbed. Physically she was a little stiff.

Without saying a word, Boran poured into her mind all the sexual power he could summon. He used their past meetings, used his mental imagery of the fantasies he had indulged in, mentally caressed her awakened senses. He allowed his constant desire to flood her mind, forcing her to mentally "feel" his arousal, the potent male need for release in a female body. He shifted his intense gaze to her breasts, and the power of his mind made the look a physical caress that brought her nipples instantly erect and visible beneath the black cloth. He heard her gasp, and his gaze moved lower to fix at the base of her belly, and he thought of a silver-furred triangle and damp heat.

He stepped closer even as she closed her thighs

tightly, and when he looked at her face he found that something in her was still resisting him. Suspended somewhere between Keeper and woman, she was fighting arousal, fighting him. And there was something else in her face, something new. A serenity he had never seen in her, an utter calm.

"I want you, princess," he said softly.

"No." Her voice was detached, distant.

"Yes. And you want me." He reached out slowly with his good hand, tracing his index finger around an erect nipple in a steady circle. "Look how you want me."

"No." She didn't draw away, and her eyes remained fixed on his face, frowning a little, vaguely disturbed. "The Keeper cannot. Siri will not."

He continued to caress her breast, now cupping the firm flesh and squeezing gently. But he was frowning, both unsettled and fascinated by her division of herself. He knew, of course, why the Keeper "could not" surrender to desire, but he was curious as to why Siri "would not." "Why will Siri not?" he asked calmly.

"She loves another."

His hand stilled, and Boran fought a sudden rage. "Does she?" His voice remained calm. "But I don't ask for her love, princess. I don't require it. I want only her body."

Siri tilted her head to one side, still frowning, apparently unaware of the hand on her breast. She seemed puzzled. "She cannot give her body except in love," Siri told him slowly. "Even though you love her—"

Boran stepped back jerkily. "What?"

"You love your creation." Her voice was still eerily detached. "It is—and is not—her. You love Siri as she would have been, without the Unicorns. Hunter loves her as she is."

The rage Boran felt warred with coldness as he realized how much she had shaken him. Furious, he reached out with both hands, his right hand grasping cloth and his stiff left hand hooking under the material. With one movement, he tore open her bodice, snapping the laces, until she was bare to the waist. Roughly, he grasped both her breasts. "*This* is what I *love!*" he said harshly. "A female body, princess, nothing more. The way a stallion *loves* a mare, and a dog *loves* a bitch!"

She didn't move, didn't seem to feel the pain of his cruel hands. "Siri will not give you her body," she said, in a voice that was curiously gentle. "And you cannot take it."

Boran was tempted. But he was certain of two things, even in his rage. One, that it would indeed have to be rape and, two, that it would be more pleasurable if Hunter watched. He slowly regained control over himself and stepped back again, releasing her bruised flesh.

"Who are you?" he asked suddenly.

She tilted her head again, her frown deepening. "I am . . . the Keepers," she told him slowly.

"Keepers? More than one?"

"All Keepers."

Curiosity dimmed his anger. "Where is Siri? Where is the Keeper of the Unicorns?"

"Here."

"Why doesn't she speak?"

"We do not allow it. She is . . . torn. You would harm her. The Guardians will not permit this. She must decide."

He was frowning. This was unexpected, and potentially troublesome. "You have never interfered before. Will you again?"

"No."

He relaxed.

Oddly, she smiled. "There will be no need. You are warned, Boran. She has powers even she does not suspect. Her body will not be taken against her will."

Boran banished a flicker of doubt. He was, after all, invincible. And he had so nearly taken Siri before; she would spread her legs for him at his bidding. He knew she would be his very soon. Her powers his. Her virgin's blood his. And the unicorns, the Triad, his. "Take your precious Keeper back to her bed," he ordered carelessly.

She turned away, soon disappearing into the darkness of the forest.

He stared after her. "*Love!*" he spat softly. He began to make his way back across the valley, angry and unsettled.

He, love a woman? Any woman? It was laughable!

And he laughed. But nothing human would have found the least bit of amusement in the soft sound.

———————————

Siri woke with a start just after dawn. She sat up and slid stiffly from her makeshift bed, her eyes going instantly to Hunter where he slept in the bed across the room. They had not spoken after his outburst yesterday, and Siri had no idea what to say to him today. There was nothing she could say, nothing that would change what was.

She stood up, her body stretching automatically, and then winced and looked down at herself. Her hands lifted to her breasts, finding them tender, and she frowned at the broken laces. How had that happened? And when? She went to find fresh laces, removing the torn ones and tossing them into the fireplace absently. And she pulled her bodice open before replacing the laces, staring down at the bruises mottling her breasts.

Coldness swept through her. What had happened? She remembered nothing, and the bruises had not been present when she had regained consciousness yesterday and dressed. She relaced the bodice slowly, trying to think. And that was when she became aware of the blankness again.

Catching her breath, this worry replacing everything else, she crossed quickly to the table and sat down, drawing the cards forward. She shuffled the deck with the automatic, instinctive gesture of someone looking to a ritual for sure comfort. She laid out the pattern briskly and then stared down at the cards, seeking that comfort.

There was none.

Frowning, she studied each card of itself and in relation to the cards nearest it. What she saw was a meaningless jumble of cryptic symbols and disjointed warnings.

There was danger, but it was unnamed. There was blankness . . . wrongness . . . threat. There was purpose, evil purpose. Green eyes . . . but something wrong with them. She couldn't *see* what was wrong with them. And a face that was half angel and half devil . . .

wavering . . . shimmering like heat off a rock . . . an angel face . . . no . . . half devil . . . slipping away . . . a twisted smile . . . a dead, beckoning hand. . . .

Siri rubbed her eyes hard and stared down at the pattern again. Nothing. What had she seen? She couldn't remember. As if a veil had been drawn across the inner eye she depended on. She saw the symbols and knew what each meant, but she could see nothing specific, nothing concrete.

But she felt the wrongness, like a chill of death.

Hesitating only a moment, she rose and crossed quickly to the open door. She didn't try to summon the Unicorns, but instead sent out the piercing sound of warning. She didn't try to touch Cloud's mind, except to fling a quick, wordless request for him to do what he could to hide the cave opening himself. Then she blanked her mind instantly, trying to sense what the wrongness meant.

"Siri?"

She half-turned to see that Hunter, awakened by her warning, was dressing quickly, his face taut and his green eyes fixed on her. The anger of yesterday was gone; today there was only swift concern and the instant desire to help her.

"Something's wrong," she explained evenly. "The cards make no sense, but something's wrong."

He was strapping on his knife, his gaze intent and searching. "Huntmen?"

"I don't know!" There was a wealth of bewilderment and anxiety in her cry. "I just don't know. We'll have to set the traps and patrol. Carefully. Whatever is threatening may already be in the valley."

"I love you," he said, needing to say it, needing to repair what hasty words might have damaged.

She went still for a moment, gazing at him, and then the Keeper was turning away briskly to claim her weapons. Once outside the cabin, they stood for a moment scanning what they could see of the valley. All appeared peaceful, but the sky remained gray and still, and not a whisper of wind or a single note of a bird's song disturbed the silence.

"Now even I feel it," Hunter said. "There's something

very wrong here."

"We'll have to split up," she said, "and check the traps as quickly as we can. We can meet at the Crystal Pool when the traps are set. The Unicorns are hidden; Cloud will see to it that the brush hides the cave opening."

Hunter didn't argue, feeling a sudden, driving need for haste. "Be careful," he said softly as they parted.

It took nearly an hour for them to check the traps. Each worked quickly, the senses of two trained warriors probing their surroundings guardedly, warily. When they met at the pool, both were tense.

"I've never known the valley to be so silent," she said as they worked their way back toward the meadow.

"If the threat comes from Huntmen," he agreed, "they must be unusually strong and determined."

"Perhaps these are after the Triad."

Hunter stopped. Astonished, he asked, "What?"

Siri hesitated, then said, "According to ancient legend, a man's strength and power can be tripled by the possession of three horns. Age—the horn of an old Unicorn; Strength—the horn of a Unicorn in his prime; and Youth—the horn of a young Unicorn. Not many remember that legend, but some have."

Before Hunter could respond, they were both frozen into immobility by the sense more than the sound of presence. With a shared glance, they began moving again, more slowly, more cautiously. They moved only far enough to peer through concealing trees into the meadow—and the danger then became palpable.

Six Huntmen stood out in the meadow, close-grouped, conferring among themselves quietly. They carried no packs but went armed with the usual spears and knives; one held a crossbow. There was a peculiar sense of unity here missing from the earlier group; these men were stonefaced, and there was no obvious mockery among them, no jeers. No bravado.

Hunter felt a chill. He was looking at Death awaiting only a victim, and he knew it.

So did Siri. Crouched in the underbrush beside

Hunter, she studied the Huntmen intensely. Faced with clear danger, she didn't think again of the wrongness, the blankness she still felt; the assumed the Huntmen were responsible for that. She felt Hunter tense beside her, and her own body stiffened as two men left the group and headed determinedly for the forest.

"They'll probably split up inside the woods," she whispered. "So we will too. We have to reduce their numbers or we don't stand a chance."

Hunter nodded silently. There was so much he wanted, needed, to say. He said nothing.

They faded back into the forest, parting with a last glance so intense it startled them both: Siri because her own emotions had risen up so powerfully in that instant; Hunter because he had seen mute longing in her eyes. But neither could afford to think of that.

The silence of the woods closed around them, ominous and heavy. There was a need for speed and both knew it. The other Huntmen could easily circle to get behind them, catching them in the center of a deadly circle. Aware of that possibility, they wasted no time in pursuing their adversaries. The two men had, as Siri had predicted, separated upon entering the forest; both were uncommon woodsmen, moving with silence and stealth.

But they were up against two warriors trained from youth and driven by a purpose no greedy mind could ever match.

Siri took her man within moments of leaving Hunter. It was a brief, silent battle, the man the more powerful of the two but Siri too quick and skilled to be defeated. It cost her a few bruises and the ache of strained muscles. But she won.

Hunter was just as quick, the fear of having Siri out of his sight and in danger making him a deadly foe. He wasted no motion and no pity on the body left for the animals to drag away.

They met where they'd parted shortly before, both still too tense and wary to think much of personal concerns. They were committed to their war, and both were conscious of time rushing. Gripping their weapons, still silent, they moved on.

Instead of returning to where they'd first seen the

Huntmen, they moved through the forest away from the
path to where the woods curved out from the cabin.
Compared to any other vantage point it was no better or
worse; they still couldn't get close enough to use arrows or
spears. But that turned out to be a futile point as they
arrived at the forest's edge and gazed across a deserted
meadow.

Both froze instantly, straining with quivering senses to
locate the missing Huntmen. Siri whistled softly, chancing a
call to the feathered inhabitants of the forest, and an
answering cry filtered through the trees to them. One cry.

She frowned as she turned back to Hunter. "One is
searching near Bundy's cave."

"Maybe he'll be roasted."

"Only if he's incautious—and somehow I don't think he
will be."

Hunter nodded, accepting. "The others?"

"I don't know." Siri rubbed fretfully between her
brows. "I can't sense them, and the birds don't see them in
the forest. They must be at the narrow end of the valley
among the canyons. Perhaps they think the Unicorns are
hidden there."

After a moment's thought, Hunter shrugged. "We
know where one is; let's get him. No—*I'll* get him. It's your
turn to wait and watch."

Siri smiled a little, knowing when not to protest. But
she was still gazing at him, troubled. "I wish I knew—"

"Where the others are?"

"Yes. I still feel that wrongness, that blankness.
Hunter, be careful."

"You, too," he advised, touching her cheek briefly.
Then he paused before turning away. "I'll meet you back
here," he added meaningfully.

"All right." She accepted and understood his worry.
But how strange to have someone worried about her! "If
I'm not here, it'll be because the other Huntmen appeared
and came too near. If that happens, I'll work my way back
around to Bundy's cave."

He hesitated for another second, knowing that he was
leaving her disturbed, and unsure of what that might mean.

He didn't doubt either her survival instincts or her skills, but his own instincts were clamoring a warning.

But he left finally, spear in hand and knife loosened and ready in its sheath. He threaded his way among the trees, keeping cautiously to cover as he searched for another who searched. And he wondered about the "wrongness" that Siri found so troubling. He accepted her description of wrongness and blankness but found it difficult to understand, even though he himself felt the changed atmosphere of the valley. Still, it was enough that she was worried.

Enough to worry him. Enough to distract him.

Enough to almost get him killed.

The Huntman burst from the tangled undergrowth in a murderous dive, his outstretched hand bearing a knife long enough to daunt an enraged snowcat.

The knife missed Hunter by scant inches as he dodged, his own knife instantly in hand. He had no time to use the spear, for his powerful opponent lunged again immediately, knocking it away with the bow he held. Spear and bow fell and were trampled underfoot as two pairs of strong arms fought for the space to thrust a deadly knife.

And then there was only the desperate straining of muscle and balance, greed and need. Clothing tore in grasping fingers, sweat slicked flesh and dripped blindingly into eyes. Grunts of pain sounded as knees and booted feet sought crippling blows.

They were evenly matched, both tall and broad-shouldered, both strong. The Huntman weighed a few pounds more, but Hunter was driven by a need to win that the other could never hope to equal in his simple greed and anger.

Hunter would win because he had to.

The only price he could not pay for more time with Siri was his life.

Or hers.

"You'll . . . lose," he panted, his knife moving nearer to a convulsing throat even as he held the other's knife at bay.

"No," the other rasped harshly.

"You lose!" Hunter repeated as the knife inched closer to its target.

The other man's muddy brown eyes, fierce with rage, went suddenly, oddly, opaque. And then glittered with a wild triumph. "No, Morgan," he hissed balefully. "You lose! *She* loses!"

And Hunter's knife, with a strength born of chilling unnamed fear, found its target.

He crouched there by the fallen Huntman for a moment, breathing raspingly. His muscles ached with the strain of combat, and his mind was clouded and useless until his heart slowed its pounding.

Then the Huntman's peculiar triumph registered and Hunter felt again that chilling finger of fear tracing his spine.

"You lose! *She* loses!"

He had been so certain.

Too certain.

Forgetting everything but Siri in that moment, Hunter caught up the bow, spear, and knife left by the enemy, slammed his own knife home in its leather sheath, and raced through the woods with the reckless speed of driving anxiety. And when he came at last to the place where she'd promised to wait, there was only her bow, splintered and useless, lying on the ground.

Beyond anger and fear and despair lies a fury, a heedless, berserk ferocity far, far over the brink of madness. It shatters civilized control and leaves behind it icily cold, utterly uncaring determination. Words cannot reach that place, cannot touch it; all fail-safe mechanisms built over aeons of evolution to cage the beast are irrevocably gone. And that beast, that raging beast, demands violent action.

Beside himself with rage, Hunter watched the implacable, suffering stranger to whom words meant nothing and the explosive release of action everything. They had her. And how they could hurt her.

Siri . . .

―――――――――――

When Hunter had disappeared into the woods, Siri leaned against the tree at her back and stared broodingly toward the deserted meadow. When Hunter found his target—and she never doubted that he would—there would be three left. She listened for a moment, hearing nothing, no disturbance in the forest or meadow. Sensing only *wrongness.*

Uneasiness made her shift her weight restlessly. The last ones, she thought firmly, would be no problem. And then they could release the Unicorns from their hiding place and be safe again. For a while.

Until the next time.

She became aware, suddenly, that her hand was tapping the bow restlessly against her leg. The uneasiness was stronger now. Frowning, she focused a mental question and thrust it at her subconscious, into the well, since her conscious mind could find no answer.

She was tensing even as the answer came, tensing and stepping away from the tree, bow lifting.

Too late. Too late.

She knew the answer as pain lanced the back of her head, as she fell to the ground. Knew that her mindless prayers had been answered, that she would not have to choose between Hunter's life and those of the Unicorns. Knew as blackness closed over her in a smothering blanket why there had been wrongness in the valley and a blankness she'd been unable to see through. And she tried and failed to hold clear thoughts as cold agony hit her, tried to scream the mental warning she had no strength even to whisper.

Not six Huntmen.

Seven.

Instinct kept Siri silent and still when she awoke. She was aware first of the midday sun burning down on her, and of the rock beneath her cutting into her arms where they were bound behind her back. The ropes were tight, cutting off her circulation, as were the ropes around her ankles, and she could feel the swollen uselessness of her hands and feet. Her head throbbed from the blow that had knocked her out, and judging by the bruised soreness of her body, she'd been dumped unceremoniously where she lay.

On hard, hot granite.

Behind closed eyes and an unaware face, her mind struggled with that fact. Granite. The ridge! The ridge by the gorge where she's first found Hunter. At the narrow end of the valley where, she remembered desolately, there was no cover for Hunter to use in approaching unseen. No vegetation. No unevenness in the land itself.

No chance.

The Huntmen had chosen well.

Marshaling her strength, Siri reached out, desperately, for the one mind in the valley she so badly needed to touch. Nothing. Blankness. Not the emptiness of no life, but the blank solidness of a curtain she couldn't part.

There was something at work here she had never encountered before. An astonishing mental power, capable of disguising its own presence in blankness and capable of blocking off her efforts to reach Hunter. And she wasn't strong enough to fight it.

Desolation stabbed her, desolation and tearing fear. She couldn't even warn Hunter or prepare him for what would come. Couldn't explain that the cards had been right after all. Couldn't apologize for an eventuality she had not been able to foresee.

Couldn't even say good-bye.

She felt tears squeeze between her lashes and trickle down over sun-heated skin, but no sob escaped her. She lived many myths, but Siri knew better than to expect a miraculous saving from the situation. She had been born and raised to rely on her own abilities, her own skills. And for all her faith in Hunter's abilities, she knew only too well that he could not, unseen by her captors, approach where she lay.

Her mind was curiously still and silent, her emotions numbing slowly. She regretted the loss of her life as any sentient being would regret death. She regretted that she would see no more Unicorns, no more Summers. She regretted that she had not told Hunter she loved him. And, more than anything else, she regretted that she had not said good-bye to him.

She had said good-bye to the Unicorns yesterday, but

not to Hunter. And that hurt her more deeply than
anything had ever hurt her in her life.

"Hello, princess."

She felt the point of a knife beneath her chin and
opened her eyes slowly to stare up at him, her mind
suddenly whirling with confusing images. Friend . . .
seducer . . . enemy . . . She saw nothing but blinding
sunlight for a moment, then a head and massive shoulders
blocked the light and she saw him.

And Siri shrank back in horror.

The right side of his face was classical perfection, the
strong and handsome face of a mature angel. Dark-haired
and green-eyed, he was beautiful. But the left side of his
face, from brow to the base of his neck, wore the skin of a
demon. Horribly blackened, hardened, his flesh was furrowed and pitted. The left corner of his mouth pulled
downward in a permanent, grotesque sneer. And the green
eye on that side was covered with a milky film, blinded.

And she remembered.

Smiling, Boran said, "I was going to let you remember
only once I was inside you, princess, but this is better.
You'll know what's happening to you, you'll feel the pain
and horror and disgust as I take your precious virginity."

An animal cry of protest lost itself somewhere in her
mind, and Siri felt a sudden raging bitterness. How
desperately she had fought to resist her feelings for Hunter,
never considering the possibility that some hideous Huntman would make a mockery of her "choice." Everything
that she was rebelled violently.

"Don't you like my face, princess?" he asked softly, his
voice deep and incongrously beautiful; it matched one side
of his face but never the other side. White and even teeth
showed in his twisted, triumphant smile. "I couldn't let you
see it before now, because I wanted your willing coopera-
tion. And you did cooperate, princess. Do you remember?"

A bitter bile rose in her throat as Siri did indeed
remember. She remembered his hands on her body, his lust
in her mind. She remembered going to him like a trained
animal called to heel, stripping off her clothes for him, lying
down for him . . .

"Spreading your legs for me," he murmured gently.
"I've tasted your lovely body, princess. I've petted you like
a favorite bitch fawning at my side. You went crazy for me,
remember? You moaned and writhed, and begged me to
pleasure you."

Siri fought to swallow the sickness enough to speak,
and though her voice was husky, it was clear. "No. That
wasn't me. That was some poor, mindless creature you
trained to want you."

His smile died, and even the angel side of his face
hardened abruptly. "You, princess. Your body."

"But not my mind." She found a small, scornful smile
somewhere and a tiny laugh. "You haven't the courage to
try and take me in my right mind."

He was still for a moment, and then his smile
reappeared. "In due time, princess. I want your would-be
lover to watch. He knows we have you, of course, but I
couldn't let you warn him. A little trick I picked up on
another world. I put a blanket of darkness around all of us
as easily as I controlled your mind."

"Hunter doesn't know where the Unicorns are hidden."

"So the Keeper can lie?" He laughed. "I'm disappointed in you, princess. Such a pitiful lie! He knows. Unfortunately, his knowledge of their hiding place is buried in his
mind, and I can't get at it. But he knows. And he'll tell me.
Or he'll watch you die very slowly. I'll take you first, of
course. I want your virgin's blood. And then my men will
take you. If that doesn't kill you—and it probably will—
then I'll allow them to finish you. They enjoy torture."

"And you don't?" she snapped, holding on to anger
because she couldn't let herself think of anything else.

He went still again, staring down at her. For an
instant, something flickered in the clear green eye, and
then it was gone. "No, I—" He shook his head abruptly.
And smiled. "I enjoy pleasure. And I will find a great deal of
pleasure in taking you while he watches."

Siri had long since realized that there was more here
than simple greed. This man wanted Hunter to suffer, that
much was plain. It was also clear that he believed in the

ancient legends about the power granted a man who took a
Keeper's virginity. But he also wanted the Unicorns.

"Hunter won't break his word to me," she said finally.
"The Unicorns are safe from you."

Boran chuckled. "Oh, he'll talk. When he hears you
scream in pain and watches me take you, he'll talk."

She swallowed dryly, feeling the knife's point cut into
her slightly. Could she thrust her body forward and
upward, ending it now? She wanted to in order to spare
Hunter, but there is that in even one resigned to death that
resists until the last possible moment. And she wanted so
badly to see Hunter one last time.

"He won't talk," she said tiredly. "His promise binds
him."

Boran shrugged. "Think what you like, princess. I
know. When he hears your agony, he will talk. And then
you'll both die."

"Why do you want him to suffer?" she asked suddenly.

But Boran was unwilling to part with his reasons. He
put his knife aside and reached to begin fondling her
breasts. "Such lovely breasts you have, princess. Has your
would-be lover touched them as I have? Has he suckled the
sweetness of them as I have? Has he seen them grow hard
with wanting him as I have?"

Siri felt physically ill at his touch, her flesh crawling
coldly and her stomach churning. The smooth mockery of
his soft voice sickened her even more, as did his questions.
But she tried not to think or feel, aware that he read her
thoughts with pathetic ease. Instead, she nudged her
subconscious, desperate to find some weapon to fight his
intentions.

It never occurred to her that because Keepers had to
be virgins there would exist some final, extreme weapon.
But it seemed the Guardians had planned well. Without
her conscious volition, words welled up and escaped her
tight throat.

"You cannot take me, Huntman."

Boran went still, hearing in her voice something
ancient and certain. And her eyes were unfocused, turned

inward. He forced a laugh. "You can hardly stop me, princess."

"I have stopped you. Be aware of your body."

He pulled his hand away from her as though she had burned him, and then slowly reached down to cup himself protectively. But it was too late. The sexual arousal he had felt almost constantly was completely gone; his member was flaccid.

Boran had never felt such rage—or such fear. That she could steal his manhood with such ease was a stunning shock, and because his sexual organs were so often used as weapons, he felt as momentarily defenseless as an archer without his bow. And then rage overwhelmed all else.

Harshly, he said, "If I didn't need you as bait, sorceress, I'd kill you now. But be assured, you will die slowly. And you won't go to your death with your maidenhead intact. You may have stolen my manhood, but I will improvise."

Siri's surge of triumph faded, and she felt cold.

Very cold.

Ten

(The beast was a tortured, mindless thing.)

Hunter was aware, in some distant, sane part of himself, that he kept moving. He combed the forest methodically, searching. And if Death had been on the wing when Siri had hunted, today Death wore the boots of a tortured man whose faint hope gradually disappeared.

They had her.

(The beast quivered, racked by unendurable pain.)

He kept going. He searched the base of The Reaper near the dragon's cave and near where the Unicorns were hidden. He quartered the ground all around the Crystal Pool. He scanned the meadow without leaving the shelter of the trees. And when his footsteps turned toward the narrow end of the valley, his tormented mind worked in agony.

That was where they'd be, of course. The hard granite of that place had literally branded itself into his very flesh when he had fallen; he could remember in his earlier exploration of the valley that it was the perfect spot for an ambush.

Or for a merciless Huntman to wait with his captive.

Hunter wouldn't let himself think about what would be demanded of him in return for Siri's life. In all logic, the Huntmen could not afford to allow either of them to live no matter what happened. There was the faintest chance that Siri would live for a while longer, bait for Hunter, while they tortured her before his eyes.

(The beast crouched tensely.)

There was no crystallized realization in Hunter's mind that he would not be able to bear seeing what they would do to her; there was only the sound of his very soul crying out in silent agony.

He heard his own voice suddenly in his mind.

"I'd prefer a clean death."

And hers.

"So would I."

And he heard the harsh rattle of his understanding like an animal trapped in his throat.

(The beast screamed fearfully.)

He couldn't do it. He couldn't kill her himself to spare her torture. He would never have the strength for that. And the Huntmen would never allow him to get near enough, he told himself frantically, desperate to avoid facing the truth of her warning; she had known this might happen.

He pushed it out of his mind, knowing that the decision, were he given the time and opportunity for even that, would be made through instinct and not through intellect.

Hunter leaned against a tree for a brief moment, survival training causing him automatically to take stock. He had one spear, two knives, and a bow that was useless without arrows and wouldn't have done him much good anyway; it was not a weapon he was skilled in. He tossed the bow aside, trying not to remember Siri's bow lying splintered where she should have been.

Then he straightened, positioned his knives more firmly—one in its sheath, the other in his belt—and took a more balanced grip on the spear; if the opportunity arose to use it, he wanted to be ready. He began walking, moving through the trees fringing the forest out into the meadow. There was no other way. No way to cross the gorge and get behind them. No cover to use in approaching unseen.

He thought like a warrior and knew where they'd be. On the ridge. To his possible advantage, there was only a rather large boulder some little distance from the ridge, he remembered. He wouldn't be able to throw his spear far enough to reach the ridge, but at least . . . At least what?

At least that final run won't be so long.

It gave him little comfort to know that he would kill as many of the Huntmen as he could. No matter what happened, no matter how many arrows or spears or whatever did reach him, he would feel at least one Huntman's dying throat in his hands.

He walked slowly, steadily, making for the boulder he could only now see. Unhurried, appearing calm. His green eyes focused on a point beyond the boulder and a crumpled, bound figure lying on the ridge, growing plainer as the distance between them closed. There was a knife at her throat, a Huntman crouching behind to use her as shield as well as bait.

(The beast lunged mindlessly.)

And other Huntmen nearby. He noticed in passing that there were four of them almost hidden behind the rocks.

(The beast growled hungrily.)

His mind toying absently with that extra enemy, Hunter walked on. So there had been seven, not six. Had that seventh one been the wrongness Siri had sensed? Not that it mattered now.

Not that it could ever matter now.

(The beast paced its cage.)

He didn't even think about the fact that he had four to kill now. That didn't matter either.

The Huntman holding Siri allowed him to reach the boulder. A mistake, Hunter thought, detached. Something rippled across the surface of his mind, but he was detached from that too and barely noticed. His inner gaze was frozen, his outer gaze fastened onto black eyes that looked at him with a calm that was agony. She was bruised, her clothing disarranged, and blood trickled from the knife's point at her throat.

(The beast howled in mortal anguish.)

Hunter firmly closed the door against that inner beast, leaving it caged, crouched and ready to spring. But not yet. Not just yet.

"No nearer, Morgan!" The one holding the knife at Siri's throat shouted hoarsely, but it was the hoarseness of greed about to be realized, not fear.

Hunter stopped, the boulder between them. His eyes measured the distance he would have to cross to reach them, and he knew that even wings lent him by sympathetic gods couldn't close that distance in time to save Siri.

(The beast growled and lunged in its cage, desperate to be loosed.)

Not yet.

He didn't want to hear what the Huntman would say, knew what he would say but didn't want to know. And had to hear. Had to hear what he would give his life not to hear, never to hear.

"Make your choice, Morgan! Tell me where the unicorns are hidden or I'll cut her throat!"

(The beast screamed . . . shrieked . . . bellowed . . . its silent anguish rising in a crescendo of raw torment.)

The man's words went through Hunter like a flaming knife, cutting in agony and then cauterizing, leaving numbness. But beneath the surface numbness the beast howled in mindless despair and grief and misery, its anguish very nearly destroying the cage holding it captive.

Very nearly.

Hunter wasn't ready for the choice, could never be ready. Siri had spoken of the agony of being forced to choose between the flesh of her flesh and the flesh of a living myth. Now, in a stark, torturing reality, Hunter was being forced to choose between the flesh of a living myth . . . and Siri. Not the flesh of his flesh, but the heart of his heart and the soul of his soul.

Had he apologized to her for his harsh words of

yesterday? No. And he wished he had. He wished now he
had.

There was always a chance, a faint, almost vanishing
chance, that the Huntmen would free Siri if they were
given the Unicorns. It was that chance, that dim possibility,
that tormented Hunter. But he knew with an awful, tearing
certainty that there was a third price he could not pay for
more time with Siri.

The lives of the Unicorns.

There was something Siri was trying to remember.
There was, she thought vaguely, something wrong with
this. The Huntman crouching behind her with the knife.
There had been another, hadn't there? *Half angel, half
devil?* No. No, it was gone now. And it couldn't have been
important, or she would have remembered.

She pushed that puzzle aside as Hunter came closer.
She could feel the tension of the Huntman as he waited for
his answer, but she had eyes only for Hunter. His lean face
was a battlefield, she realized, a battlefield frozen in time.
Armies fought there blindly, viciously, endlessly. Opposing
sides of rage and fear warred brutally.

She was dead no matter which he chose. Did he
realize that? She reached out desperately to touch his
mind, fear lending her the strength to break through the
strange blankness she sensed like a curtain between them.
And black, screaming agony washed over her, drowning the
warning she would have sent.

The cards' prophecy!

It had never been her agony she had seen, her choice
to make, but Hunter's. This very scene had been intended.
If only she had known that! If only she had been able to *see!*
They could have prevented this somehow. But it was too
late now, and she could only try to reach out to Hunter and
ease his pain, voice agreement and understanding for his
choice. He was too intelligent and too loyal, she knew, to
make the choice the Huntmen wanted.

She reached out to him, but Hunter's own violent
emotions now curtained his mind in blackness.

He was suffering alone in his mind.

Hunter wasn't thinking. Instead, he was seeing a dying man's flashes of life and being in his mind's eye. His childhood. Young adulthood. The Quest that had taken him through the galaxy. The valley. Siri. The Unicorns.

He focused eyes that felt hot and painfully dry on Siri's face, her beautiful, beloved face and the eyes that were so calm and understanding.

God forgive him.

"Siri, I'll keep the faith," he called to her hoarsely, the words tearing from him and leaving raw, bloody wounds. "I'll keep my promise."

Though it would destroy him.

And in that moment, moved unbearably by his torment, Siri made her choice. If the gods decreed that she would somehow survive this day, all that she was would be forever his. "I love you," she whispered, knowing he didn't hear, wishing desperately that she could shout the words to him. . . .

Hunter felt hollow, empty, not even the sudden glow in her eyes or the soft smile curving her lips able to help him in that moment. His male instinct told him that he had betrayed her by choosing the lives of the Unicorns over hers, but a deeper and newer instinct insisted that by choosing her he would have betrayed everything she was, everything he loved in her.

In that moment, he didn't know which instinct to trust.

But it didn't matter.

There was nothing left in him.

He had chosen.

(The beast gnawed at the bars of its cage.)

"Siri . . ." he whispered, numb. But his legs were tensing under him, his grip on the spear tightening as he gathered himself in readiness. It was time, his mind told him, deadened, suspended. And—

(The beast fought free at last and demanded with a berserk scream the release of action.)

Only that would soothe a savage, mindless grief.

Another howl split the air, this one from the enraged Huntman as Hunter's words were absorbed. He looked at the woman he held so cruelly, at the man whose stony face denied any change of mind or heart. And his blind rage defied logic in its need to strike out. His knife lifted high in the air and then began the deadly downward arc that would end in Siri's breast.

But the knife was halted in midair, even as Hunter's instinctive lunge forward had halted, even as the half-hidden Huntmen's leader barked a sharp order.

By the sound of Death.

(The beast howled savage victory.)

The sound sliced through the still air of the valley. Enraged, triumphant, savage, uncannily beautiful, it echoed off the granite walls of the ridge, writhing among the living as if it were a sentient thing itself. Challenging all who heard to beware the relentless avenging fury of an unstoppable force, an irresistible law of nature. The ancient magic of the sound paralyzed, holding its listeners in a primal terror of the unknown.

The unreal.

The impossible.

Cloud followed his trumpeted cry, thundering across the meadow with the sound of a hundred instead of one. The frozen watchers could sense the vast herd at his back, the ghostly representations of a huge family decimated by the cruelty and greed of man. Myth alive on thundering hooves, the sunlight flashing off golden, lethal horns. Myth coated in pure white. The spirits of ancestors and brothers and children brought to life for just one deadly purpose.

To avenge the dead.

The illusion—or delusion—lasted only brief moments, and then they could all see only Cloud bearing down on the ridge in fury. But even that held the Huntmen spellbound for scant seconds longer.

It was nearly enough time.

Hunter and Siri had the advantage then, because both were accustomed to the sight of living myths and so were easily able to overcome the sense of unreality and doom. Although they were both elated and fearful to see the stallion, they acted instantly.

Running forward, Hunter's arm snapped in a long smooth motion to send his single spear flying. The Huntman with the crossbow, who had risen to his feet in astonishment, crumpled silently to the ground.

Siri, aware of her captor's slack grip on her and his inattention, used every protesting muscle she could command to fling herself forward, rolling out of his reach. Her bruised body cried out in pain, but she was too worried about Cloud to pay attention to her aching self.

"Cloud, no!" she cried desperately.

Her voice snapped the remaining Huntmen from their spells, but before they could react, the furious horned stallion was upon them. Their attention was entirely taken up with remaining alive. They dodged the long golden horn on Cloud's first pass, the two of them separating to attack the Unicorn from either side, knives raking the pure white coat that was instantly stained with scarlet.

Time focused. The valley held its breath as myth struggled against man. Myth held the upper hand. Myth bent on vengeance. Myth made terrible in rage. Myth fighting for the future of its race.

All her consciousness fixed on the battle, Siri nonetheless wondered fleetingly where the other one had gone. There had been four here. Or . . . No, not four. How had she come to think that? Only three. She shook her aching head a little, bothered, but she could think of little except the scarlet-stained Unicorn fighting for his life.

From the corner of her eye, Siri saw Hunter racing for the Huntman his spear had killed, and she realized that he was going for the crossbow that might stop the bloody battle occurring just a few feet away from her.

She knew there wasn't enough time. There would never be enough time.

Cloud was bleeding in a dozen places, his breath rasping harshly within seconds, the labored sound an accompaniment to the scuffles of boots and the scrapes of hooves on rock.

Siri was unaware of the tears coursing down her cheeks, aware only of the pain of Cloud's mortal wounds. But the stallion was unwilling to die just yet, and when it seemed that he would fall at any moment, he turned in midstride to lunge suddenly and fatally at the enemy. Two lightning strikes, left and right, and their tactic had become their downfall.

Only when the Huntmen had been tossed aside and kicked viciously into the gorge did Cloud sway, then drop to his knees and fall heavily onto his side.

Hunter reached Siri almost instantly, dropping the crossbow with a clatter on the rock. His knife in hand, he began cutting the ropes binding her hands and ankles.

"Can you—?" he began hoarsely.

She shook her head. "No. No . . . he's dying," she managed to say in a choking voice. "But I have to be with him. I have to touch him."

Neither of them was thinking about anything other than Cloud in that moment. There would be time later to feel joy in still being alive and together, time for gratitude when grief had gone.

Hunter carried her to Cloud's side. He could feel the pain in her, the physical pain of her injuries and the agony of returning circulation in her swollen hands and feet, the mental pain of the severing of her bond with Cloud. And his own mind was dazed with grief and pain, with the loss of a noble creature he'd only begun to know.

"Cloud . . ." She forced a swollen, deadened hand to lift and rest on the stained neck as she stared down into dimming black eyes. She took what pain she could into her own aching body, easing his last moments, grief hurting her far more than anything else. Then she let her hand fall into her lap, seeing through her tears the stained coat whiten brilliantly for a heartbeat before fading, wavering, turning to dust.

Only the long golden spiraled horn remained.

Prices.

Cloud had paid the price for more time for them.

Boran had lost control, and his awareness of that was a crawling chill of fear in his mind. Oh, he had been able to control Siri's mind up to a point, had been able to blank her memories of him, even after the bitch had emasculated him. He had even managed to alter Hunter's memories so that he would not remember the presence of a seventh enemy. But when Siri had stolen his manhood, the shock had weakened his abilities. One of the bastard Huntmen had nearly ended her life in a single thrust, and that had been no part of Boran's wishes.

Goddamn the woman! What witch's powers lay hidden in her mind waiting to ensnare him? What else would he lose if he confronted her again? Hurrying cautiously from the bloody battlefield behind him, he felt the lifeless shaft of muscle that had once throbbed with power, the limp sacks of his seed shriveled, and bitter curses tore softly from his throat. Had she, in truth, castrated him forever? Was he cursed by her to never again know the pleasure of thrusting himself into the slick heat of a female body?

He had to know. For the moment, he put aside his drive to acquire the Triad and destroy the Keeper and his rival. He would leave the valley, return to the city long enough to find some whore to bed.

And if Siri had indeed ruined him—

You love your creation. He brushed that memory aside, impatient. Love was an emotion reserved for children and fools; it weakened the mind. He was not weak. But his failures enraged him. He had failed to seduce the Keeper, had failed even to rape her.

But he would not fail again. He would attain the Triad. He would destroy Hunter. And if Siri had indeed emasculated him, she would be a very long time in dying.

It was Hunter who picked up the horn and gently laid it in her arms before putting his own arms around her and holding her close. He didn't even think of the incredible sight of a dying creature vanishing into dust. It was a part of the valley and the Unicorns and so was right. "I tried," he whispered into her hair. "But by the time I reached the crossbow it was all over."

She heard his pain, the quiet fury of his inability to stop what had happened, and her love for this man helped to ease the burden of grief. "You couldn't have stopped it," she murmured. She shifted slightly and winced as the pain of cuts and bruises stabbed her.

Immediately Hunter rose with her in his arms. "We

have to get you back to the cabin," he said worriedly. He could see her weariness in the pallor of her face beneath the bruises and feel, even in the gentle care of his embrace, the shrinking of abused flesh. "Siri, did those bastards—did they—"

"I'm all right," she said softly, understanding. She looked down at the horn she held and fiercely blinked back tears. "But you're wounded." She reached out a hand to touch the jagged slash on his upper arm but didn't complete the action as he spoke.

"No, don't try to heal that." He hadn't even realized that the Huntman in the woods had managed to cut him. "It'll heal. And you're too drained."

Tiredly she rested her head on his shoulder. "We'll put Cloud's horn in the cabin and then go to the Crystal Pool."

"Why there?"

"The waters have healing properties."

They were both speaking in normal tones, the horror they had gone through numbing them, cushioning the bitter grief.

He nodded slightly, carrying her across the meadow with a steady stride. Just before they reached the cabin, he saw her gaze toward the wide end of the valley, but she made no sound to summon the herd.

"Do they know?" he asked, aware that her thoughts were for the remainder of the herd.

"They know Cloud's gone. I think they'll remain in the cave for a while; it's their custom to grieve in private for the death of a Leader." She looked up at him as they entered the shadowed interior of the cabin, seeing very clearly despite dimness that today had taken an enormous toll on Hunter. He looked abruptly older, his face gaunt with strain and the release of strain, pulled tight with grief. Her heart ached for him, and she searched, in a sudden and unfamiliar shyness, to find the words to tell him how she felt about him.

But the words wouldn't come, not then. When he set her on her feet, she went to lay Cloud's horn high on a shelf, leaving it there after a final, lingering touch. She turned back to Hunter and nodded, and they moved wordlessly from the cabin.

Once at the pool, they began to undress, and she realized that neither of them was looking at the other. Hunter was troubled by something, she knew. And she was wrung out emotionally, feeling grief and anger at Cloud's death, weariness and pain. And a terrible, yearning love for Hunter. She was too tired to think, vaguely conscious of a small blank place in her mind and a half-conscious need to remember . . . something.

She slipped into the cool water, feeling the physical pain ease immediately, the weariness fade away. With no desire to swim, she found a flat rock deeply submerged and rested there, allowing the water to lap about her shoulders and neck, splashing some absently on her face to cool the heat of the hours spent unprotected in the sun.

Hunter moved slowly through the water to join her, still silent, his face closed. After a glance, Siri left him to his thoughts, knowing that he would speak of whatever disturbed him when he could.

The cool water seemed to drain away aches and pains, replacing them with a sense of physical well-being. Birds began to twitter softly high in the trees, stirring finally after the intrusion that had kept them silent for so long. The clearing darkened slightly as afternoon wore on and evening neared. The Moonflowers began to open, tentatively, almost as if embarrassed by their colorful glory.

Siri left his side once to dive in the deep end of the pool, returning with two rootlike plants. She showed him silently how to peel the wet bark to get at the crunchy, tasty interior, and they ate in continued silence.

Hours passed in peace. The sun set. Since she had never learned to share her pain with another, Siri dealt with the wrenching grief of Cloud's death in her own quiet way. And because the harsh life of Summer had taught her much about death, she accepted his sadly and silently said good-bye to her lifelong friend. The memory of him was tucked away in her mind, protected and treasured, never to be hurt again. And though a part of her would always grieve for the loss of so noble a creature, she accepted what was.

With that accepted, she found herself aware once more

of Hunter's nearness, and the effect his presence had over all her senses. And she had made her choice.

Forbidden! Outcast!

It was a faint, distant voice, a warning she could no longer heed. The Unicorns or Hunter. Loneliness or love. Life or death. Keeper or woman.

She had chosen.

In giving Hunter her love, she would lose the trust of the Unicorns, and she ached already for that loss. But she would do everything in her power to save the Unicorns, no matter what. She would protect them, somehow, until another Keeper could take over. The Unicorns would make her Outcast, of course, but she would be required to remain until Fall. And, since this had never happened before, she might be required to remain long enough to train another Keeper.

She and Hunter might have years together before she was forced to leave the valley . . . and die.

She wondered then if she would be able to bear his leaving her now or ever to complete his own journey. There was a part of her that wanted to cry out against that, painfully conscious of how little time they would have. But another part of her recognized and understood that it was vitally important that he return his people's knowledge and history to them.

So little time they had.

She glanced at him, suddenly disturbed by his silence and closed face. Did he still want her? Or had the choice forced from him taught him the price of loving a Keeper? What could she tell him? *I won't be Keeper for long, my love. Just a woman. Just a woman who loves you.*

"You're troubled," she said suddenly.

After a moment, Hunter nodded.

"Can you tell me?"

"I don't know how." He hesitated, then blurted gracelessly, "I feel I betrayed you!"

She understood. "By choosing the Unicorns? No, Hunter! Choosing *me* would have betrayed me."

"That's what I told myself. But—"

"Man's dreams must live, no matter what," she said softly. "I only hope . . ."

He looked at her. "What?"

She couldn't speak of it, still. After she had broken her bonds, she could, but not before. How cruel of the Guardians! Siri drew a deep breath, but her voice emerged again softly. "If—if I had died today . . . I would have died loving you."

Hunter went still, gazing at her with his very breath suspended. The filtered moonlight showed him that her face was a little shy, a bit hesitant—but glowing. And her black eyes were bottomless, glimmering. He lifted a hand slowly to touch her cheek, his thumb brushing quivering lips, and the events of the day faded in a sudden, dizzying rush of love and desire.

"Siri?"

She turned her lips into his palm briefly, aware of hot tears in her eyes, a sweet ache in her heart and body. "I was never meant to love," she whispered. "But I love you, Hunter."

He rose to his feet, his hands finding hers and pulling her up gently. He didn't think he was breathing and his heart hammered in his chest. The sight of her with the water lapping about her waist, her naked breasts gleaming wetly, went to his head like an aphrodisiac from the gods.

But he forced words past the lump in his throat, because he was, even now, afraid there was something elusive standing between them. "You said . . . you wouldn't be my lover. You said you couldn't change what you were." His lips twisted wryly. "Those words are branded in my mind."

She slipped her arms up around his neck, her breath catching when she felt the hard strength of his chest against her breasts. "You changed what I was," she murmured huskily. "I want to belong to you."

Hunter hesitated for a brief moment, then groaned softly as he lifted her wet body into his arms. "I love you, Siri," he told her deeply, carrying her from the pool.

And she felt that she floated as he carried her through the night into the cabin.

Siri didn't think of loss, or of surrender. She didn't think of the price she would pay for this night. She thought only of love and longing, of the wild awakening of her body, of all her senses . . . of her soul. Just as Hunter and the Unicorns had softly, gently changed places in her heart, so did she become woman first, and Keeper second.

Nothing in her life had prepared her for the love of a man.

In the still quiet of the cabin, only two hearts beat to disturb the silence. Moonlight spilled through the open doorway and pooled about the wide bed with hazy brilliance. A gentle, sweet-smelling breeze wafted in to touch and caress the two still beings lying together in growing enchantment. Green eyes and purple gazed deeply, saw completely. The moonlight wrapped about them with wispy, insubstantial arms, just as it had embraced the magic of a Unicorn Dance.

His hand brushed a strand of her hair from her brow with infinite slowness, and the spun-silver threads seemed to cling to his fingers with a life of their own. The moonlight appeared to shift, almost blinding them with radiance as her hair became a nimbus of iridescence and her eyes glistened with luminous intensity.

It was a sight the gods would have denied to mortal eyes, had they that power; it was given only to Hunter, now, to see how love transformed his woman . . . warrior . . . Keeper . . . lover . . . into something resplendent, something wondrous.

She was almost translucent, the seductive shape of her woman's body blurred into softened enchantment. Love aglow, entrapped within its frail human shell, beckoned with a siren's bewitching smile, a child's innocent touch, a woman's knowing laughter.

She was breathtaking.

A very old instinct told Hunter that he would never again see her in quite this way. Whatever the future held for them, this first joining as lovers would never be repeated, never be duplicated. He knew there would never be less between them; he knew there could never be more.

Siri watched, lost in the stillness that surrounded

them, as the moonlight veiled him in dazzling brilliance. In wonder and in love, she felt the winging of her senses, felt the strength of a woman's need to know her man. Her breath came quickly; she was unable to breathe. There was a roaring in her ears; there was a great silence. She saw with stark clarity; she was blind.

She was loved.

Loved.

She welcomed his mouth when it closed over her own. So warm and sweet, a slow caress that pulled a whimper from her throat. She felt his tongue tracing the sensitive inner surface of her lips, then slipping inside her mouth to explore in a stark thrust of preliminary possession, and a shiver passed through her body. His lips hardened, slanting across her mouth, his tongue driving more deeply and twining with her own in an erotic duel.

Her fingers found and clutched his shoulders, frantic to hold something solid in the dizzying whirl that had become her world. His skin was hot and smooth, the muscles coiling like living animals beneath her touch.

His power and tenderness moved her unbearably, his strong male body an alien, fascinating, beautiful thing so different from her own. The very texture of his skin beneath her fingers seeped into her being and became, curiously, her own skin. His beating heart matched the rhythm of hers, surrounded hers, became hers. The softness of his breath left her lips.

He lifted his head at last with a harsh sound, and his vivid green eyes moved down over her body slowly. One large hand reached to touch her flat belly, and her muscles contracted convulsively as she bit her bottom lip to hold back some faint sound struggling desperately to escape.

"Don't hold back," he said thickly, seeing her struggling not to give in to her senses. "Let yourself go, beloved. Let yourself feel. I want to teach you all the pleasure of love." His head bent suddenly, and his tongue stroked the hard pink tip of her breast, and Siri gasped as a wave of hot need shuddered through her wildly.

"I—I feel . . . I can't control it," she whispered unsteadily.

"Don't try," he told her in that thick, strained voice. "Let it control you, beloved." His face was taut, his eyes blazing, but the curve of his lips was tender.

"I—I've always controlled," she managed, biting back another wild moan when his hand slid up over her midriff to warmly cup her straining breast.

His eyes softened, and Hunter bent his head again to nuzzle his lips across the flushed skin of her breast. "Not this," he murmured hoarsely. "No one controls this." He lifted her hand from his shoulder and placed it on his chest. "Feel my heart beating for you?" He caught his breath, half-closing his eyes when her fingers moved convulsively in the dark mat of hair covering his chest. "I can't think for wanting you," he groaned. "I can't control my need for you."

And she knew it was true, knew that he was as much a prisoner of desire as she was. Accustomed to controlling her world and herself, Siri abandoned that control consciously for the first time, giddy with the freedom of it. And she was suddenly, furiously impatient. "Show me," she gasped, her nails digging into his skin, the heat of her body something she was wild to dampen. "Take me, Hunter!"

"Shhhh," he whispered, the hand at her breast lifting to cup her cheek as he kissed her lips gently. The strain in his face was growing, but there was a sudden flicker of harried humor in his vivid eyes. "Don't tempt me, dammit. There's nothing I want more, love, but I have to go slowly. I don't want to hurt you."

That hadn't occurred to her. "Will you?" she asked, blinking dazed eyes at him trustfully.

He groaned. "God, I hope not." But compelled by her trust, he had to be honest. "I might hurt you—I don't know. The first time . . ."

Siri saw his worry, and it moved her unbearably. "Just teach me to feel these pleasures," she whispered. "I love you, Hunter."

Had she only known, her total love and trust did nothing to ease his sudden burden. As desperate as he was to lose himself in her, to take her as he had ached to do all this time, he was very conscious of the importance of guiding her through an experience she had absolutely no knowledge of. If he was rough or awkward in his own need, he could easily ruin things for her.

Reining his own impatience as tightly as possible, he murmured, "Close your eyes, beloved. Just let yourself feel." And when she obediently closed her eyes, he swallowed hard and forced his mind to concentrate only on pleasing her.

It was, in truth, what he wanted to do. The only problem was in convincing his body to remain patient. He managed it. Barely.

Siri felt his lips cover hers again, and she opened to him with a kittenlike sound of pleasure. With her eyes closed, she could only feel, and the moist warmth of his agile tongue sent hot shivers all through her. Unconsciously, her body moved, and her tongue responded to his as though with a will all its own. She felt him draw her tongue into his mouth, stroking it with his own, inviting her to explore, and she accepted the invitation eagerly, with growing ardor.

When his lips moved finally to trail down over her throat, she heard his rough chuckle and realized that she herself had made a sound of disappointment when his mouth had eluded hers. But the frustration was brief, because the pleasure of his lips moving over her flesh was exquisite. She could feel his teeth nip in tiny bites, his tongue soothe, and her head moved restlessly on the pillow as heat swirled all through her.

His hands surrounded her breasts gently, the long fingers tightening and relaxing in a rhythm that stole what was left of her breath and yanked a moan from her throat. Her own fingers threaded through his thick, silky hair, holding him to her, and she arched in impatience against him. His tongue was gliding between her breasts, down one slope, into the damp valley and up the other slope, teasingly avoiding the tight pink tips.

"Hunter," she moaned, "I need—I need—"

He breathed warmly on one straining bud, then flicked his tongue over it again and again. "Tell me what you need," he whispered thickly. "Don't be afraid to tell me, love." But she didn't have to, and his lips closed over her nipple, drawing it into the heat of his mouth strongly while his tongue swirled.

Siri couldn't believe the molten pleasure of that caress, and was hardly aware that her breath escaped her in little pants and her heart was pounding, smothering her. She moaned when he moved to the other breast, lavishing it with his lips and tongue, his hands still squeezing gently. One of his legs slid between hers, drawing them slowly apart, the fine hair covering his flesh a sensual abrasion against her soft inner thighs. And she felt a faint, distant shock, a sudden awareness of surrender and submission.

Forbidden . . . Outcast . . .

She shook her head to throw off the ancient warning, but it was the instinct of an innocent female body that tightened the muscles of her thighs in an equally ancient fearful response.

He was murmuring wordlessly against her skin, and one hand left her breast to stroke slowly over her quivering belly until he found the soft silver down at its base. His fingers moved gently among the pale hairs, tearing a gasp from her throat, tightening her muscles even more. But his touch was insistent, knowing, and when he found the damp heat of her womanhood, new instincts burst into life. Her thighs relaxed slowly, then tensed again, but this time because they were parting for him, obeying the gentle pressure of his leg.

Time slowed, inched almost to a halt. Every second was a brief eternity, to be treasured and held for as long as possible. He could feel her heartbeat beneath his lips; the increasingly frantic flutter of a caged bird's wings. Her smooth skin wore the sheen of polished gold and shared the warmth of light itself. Like a lodestone, her body drew his touch.

His arms cradled her in strength and gentleness; his touch was the shatteringly tender and passionate touch of love. Unhurried, each movement achingly slow, he learned the secrets of her body. And she was awakening, responsive; there was no effort now to smother the sounds of passion. Her husky moans and sharp gasps were spurs to his own passion, and every muscle of his body was rigid with the effort of control.

Their bodies responded to one another as if with an old, tender, passionate memory, a certain knowledge.

The moonlight shifted, now veiling them in brilliance, now lighting each, starkly real, for the other to see. The soft breeze caressed them in sweetness.

"Hunter . . ."

"Yes, beloved," he murmured harshly, his breath rasping. He had lifted his head from her breasts now and was watching her, his fingers still moving in a steady rhythm over her slick, throbbing flesh. Her body was tensing, her hips beginning to lift to his touch, and her feverish eyes fixed on his face with the sudden, breathless panic of a female body reaching desperately for the satisfaction of release.

In an agony of need, her body strained at the brink, and she hadn't the breath to ask him why he was doing this to her. It was a sensation beyond anything she had ever know, a sweet, wild, mad spiraling of all her senses, a coiling of tension that felt as if it had to break her into countless shattered pieces and fling her into the winds. And then she did break, her body convulsing against him, a cry torn from her throat as wave after wave of pleasure swept over her body, her senses, her dazed mind. And the tension drained from her in a rush, leaving her limp and shaking.

"You're so beautiful," Hunter murmured in a strained voice, nuzzling his face between her breasts while his hands stroked her body gently. "So passionate . . ." A guttural groan escaped him. "God, give me patience!"

She was stroking his damp back with trembling hands, and felt the coiled tension of all his muscles. Still drifting in the lingering soft ripples of pleasure, she was nonetheless aware that Hunter had shown her only a part of lovemaking. And with the wonder of what he had shown her, she was utterly unafraid of what was to come. Her body was already renewing its need, and she sensed that his was almost out of control.

"Love me," she whispered, lifting her head to press her lips against his hard shoulder. "Love me again . . ."

He drew a ragged breath as he lifted his head, and his eyes were wild. "Siri . . ." His mouth found hers fiercely, driven, and her instant response made his already pounding heart beat like a savage thing fighting to escape his chest. Spring-coiled tension stole into fragile human bodies, winding tighter and tighter, compelling, insisting, driving. His muscles were rigid with intense restraint, and he thought he'd burst with the feelings.

Siri was with him again, her body moving against his, her hands stroking over his shoulders and chest. And her need was impossibly greater than it had been before. There was a terrible, empty ache deep inside her, and she moaned wordlessly, trying blindly to draw him closer. "Hunter . . . please . . ."

He was breathing as if he had run some long, desperate race, trying fiercely to control his body even as he gently widened her thighs and slipped between them. And only the sudden, almost unconscious shock in her face enabled him to retain some faint measure of control. "Siri . . . ?"

She fought a last silent battle with a ten-thousand-year-old taboo, until the ancient voice stilled in defeat. She held his shoulders fervently and her legs cradled him as she felt the warm hardness of his body seeking entrance. "I love you," she murmured, conscious now only of the need to belong to him.

He lowered his head to kiss her deeply, then watched her face intently for any sign that he was hurting her as he began a slow, careful pressure. Never before forced to hold back and take care, Hunter discovered a wild pleasure in the very restraint he had to exercise. The slick heat of her flesh against his caused savage ripples of pleasure to course through him, and feeling her body open to him slowly was a caress unlike anything he had ever known.

Siri's eyes widened in wonder and in the purely female shock of possession. She could feel her body stretching to admit him, feel him moving deeper, filling the emptiness that had ached for him. The throbbing hardness of his body was alien for a stark instant, but then she could feel the acceptance of her own body, and the coiled tension and heat that had remained suspended began to build again.

Hunter half-caught his breath in relief and pleasure as the heat of her body sheathed him tightly, completely. She had taken all of him, was, even now, moving sensually against him, and the pleasure was unbelievable. He was mesmerized by the wide dark eyes fixed on his, by the tremulous, wondering smile curving her lips, and he kissed her deeply as he held himself still deep inside her.

Siri moaned softly, her limbs holding him with lithe strength, and when he began moving she nearly cried out at the sensations, the silken friction of their bodies driving her need abruptly higher. What he had shown her of lovemaking had been only a prelude, she realized dimly. The emotions and sensations of before were pale things, and her body responded to his now with a wild desire that nothing could have prepared her for.

And Hunter, the need for caution and care seared away in the fire of her response, lost the last threads of his restraint. He wanted more of her, all of her, everything he could possibly hold of her. He could never get enough, but the drive to try gripped his body, his mind, his soul, in urgency. He buried himself in her again and again, raw sounds of pleasure torn from his throat. And it still wasn't enough.

It would never be enough.

Exquisite torment trapped them in its toils, carrying them ever upward in a mindless ascent. They rose, bathed and blinded in moonlight, held aloft by a scented breeze, ensnared by each other. She was woman incarnate; he was man personified; they were lovers enchanted, bewitched, set free.

They were one.

It was a sharing so total, a joining so complete, that they were transported beyond anything either of them had ever known. And both knew, dimly, that it was granted to mortals to touch that wondrous place only once in their lifetimes. This first time between them was a treasure.

There could never be more.

There would never be less.

The moonlight had crept away softly, but the scented breeze remained, a reminder of a trip to gossamer enchantment. The cabin was quiet now, and contained only mortals who would hoard a special memory close to their hearts. Lovers.

They didn't sleep for a long time, but lay entwined in breathless wonder. It was Siri who spoke first, her voice shy and wondering.

"Is it . . . always like that?"

Holding her close, Hunter continued to stroke her spun-silver hair tenderly. He didn't quite know how to answer her. He could answer from his own experience, but there was more to her question than simple experience versus innocence. A whispery little voice in his mind murmured in answer to his own musing, and he didn't even wonder from whence it came.

"No," he answered finally in that certainty he didn't bother to doubt. "No, it's never been like that before. And it will never be quite like that again."

"Because there can never be another—first time?"

He nodded, watching her intently, hoping in a deep and secret place of his heart that she was not disappointed but, like him, would cherish a magical memory from another plane of existence.

Her eyes glowed in purple wonder. "How lucky we are," she whispered, and he knew that she shared his feelings.

"I love you," he said, the utter stillness of his voice filled with more raw power than an exultant shout could have claimed.

She pulled herself forward to kiss him softly, then lay with her head pillowed on his broad shoulder. "I love you, Hunter. I didn't know what it would be like to love a man; I didn't know I could love a man like this. But I've never been more happy than I am right now. I'll never regret loving you."

Hunter listened as her breathing became deep and steady, knowing that sleep had finally claimed her. He held her securely, the old fear of waking to find her a dream haunting him. Because her last words held the sound of a vow, and he wondered with a pang why she should feel the need to deny possible regret.

Stoically, he placed that pain far back in his mind to share the pain of knowing she loved the Unicorns best, that he was second in her heart. He could only love her, unreserved, undemanding, holding on tightly to the knowledge that she had chosen him, that she loved him as much as it was possible for her to love a man.

It would be enough.

It would have to be enough.

Siri woke slowly. She was conscious of gray dawn light filtering into the cabin, the sun obviously reluctant to provide the bright dawn to which the valley was accustomed. Birds called to one another deep within the forest, oddly timid, oddly repressed.

Then Siri remembered.

Prices.

She slipped from his embrace carefully, gently, then sat on the edge of the bed and stared down at his sleeping face. The gray light was stark and critical, but it couldn't alter the face of her lover. The strength and character and beauty of him would challenge and defy even the unloving light of honest dawn.

The memory of their night of love held her spellbound for long moments, then she shook her head slightly, dispelling the mist. Not because her thoughts were unwelcome, but because such treasures were meant for the innermost heart and not the incredulous mind.

No, she didn't regret her choice. She regretted only that the choice had been demanded of her. And now the consequences had to be faced.

Siri shied away from that. She didn't want to face the Unicorns; for the first time in her life she dreaded the sight of their glossy white bodies as they greeted the morning out in the meadow.

How long would she and Hunter have together?

She wondered, as he had once wondered, what god or gods would demand such a thing of her. Were women on other worlds forced to cut short life for love? She didn't know. She knew only that she could have made no other choice.

She gazed at her man, and in that quiet moment of love and contemplation a thought dropped softly into her mind, appearing without her conscious volition from the well of knowledge.

A Prince among his people.

It explained so much, she thought. The cool, level eyes and commanding voice. The nobility of face and pride of manner. The obvious wealth needed to set out on a years-long Quest. Somewhere lay a kingdom Hunter had left on a Quest to save his people. *And to gain a throne.* A throne he would abandon for her? She didn't know, couldn't ask. But she knew now that his world needed more than the knowledge he would take to them. His world needed him, their prince. Would he return to them for good?

Only time would tell.

She wondered, vaguely, at the tangled threads of destiny. She, Keeper of the creatures he had sought; he, his lost history rooted in this world, this Earth, searching the galaxy for myth and finding it alive on the planet his ancestors had nearly destroyed ten thousand years ago.

How much had been Fate—and how much had been their own free wills shaping destiny? Siri didn't know. She knew only that it was time to face her own destiny.

She left the bed and moved to the far corner of the cabin and the small cupboard cunningly hidden there. It was not a secret place, but rather more of a place for secret things. The clothing that had belonged to her father—retrieved long ago from The Reaper's sea-cave—was folded neatly on a shelf; she made an absent mental note to alter whatever she could for Hunter's use.

And there was Hunter's backpack, the one he had borne during his trip through The Reaper's defenses. She had never opened it, had, in truth, forgotten all about it. As had Hunter, she realized now. Or perhaps he simply believed it destroyed in his fall. She made another mental note to give it back to him in case there was anything in it he wanted.

She searched the shelves. She didn't even know what

she was looking for until she found it. Far back on a shelf, folded neatly, lay a tunic woven from the purest silk. It was long, starkly white, and possessed full, flowing sleeves. Special, the old Keeper had said, for special times.

Could there be a more special time, a more important time, than this?

Siri felt the cool smoothness of the silk and listened to it whisper as the material slid against her skin and molded her slender body. There was no superstition within her, merely an instinctive need to stand before the Unicorns clothed in the purity and joy of white. Though no longer physically innocent, she felt no shame in her love for Hunter, and she would not stand before her adored Unicorns in apology.

There was another tunic, a close match to the one she wore, among her father's things. It, too, was white, but it was decorated on the shoulders and sleeves with intricately woven colored threads. Her mother's hands had fashioned it for her father. She held it up briefly, then closed the cupboard and carried it across to the bed. It would fit Hunter.

She wouldn't let herself think about what she would do if the Unicorns denied her even the most minimal trust.

Still, there were no regrets. If that price were demanded of her for this time with Hunter, she would pay it willingly. She would make this time an eternity.

With a last, lingering glance for the man sleeping peacefully, Siri squared her shoulders and went out into the dawn. She moved several yards from the cabin, unconscious of the faint chill of the air but very aware of the chill around her heart. She sent out a soft, trilling call for the Unicorns and waited quietly to know what her own choice had cost her.

She stood, straight and proud, the white tunic glowing in the weak dawn light. And her love for Hunter kept the coldness around her heart at bay. Her eyes were deeply purple; the black eyes were reserved now for the warrior, and never again for the woman.

When she heard the first soft thud of hooves, Siri focused her gaze on the ground before her. But then she realized what she was doing, and lifted her chin firmly. They would accept or deny her. It was their choice now.

They came in a group, standing before her at last in a half circle. All were subdued, still strong in their grief for the lost Cloud. The two foals remained close to their mothers' sides. No creature stepped forward to cross that invisible line separating them from Siri.

She swallowed hard and fixed her gaze on Storm, the new Leader. Then, as Siri stared incredulously, dazed with delight, the stallion stepped forward to gently nuzzle her shoulder.

Eleven

Barely aware that she had stopped breathing, Siri stared into liquid dark eyes that were uncannily like Cloud's because they held the ancient wisdom the old stallion had possessed. Dark liquid eyes, old and wise, and infinitely trusting. With a muffled cry, she threw her arms around Storm's satiny white neck and held him tightly.

"Siri?"

She released Storm and turned quickly, seeing Hunter dressed in the tunic she had left for him. He looked both relieved and anxious; clearly, it had disturbed him to wake and find her gone. Even more clearly, he was disturbed by the tears flowing, unheeded by her, down her cheeks.

"What is it? What's wrong?" he asked quickly.

"Nothing. Nothing's wrong!" Siri could have shouted aloud in joy, and laughed. "Hunter, they still trust me!"

"Did you think they wouldn't?" he asked uncertainly, puzzled.

She smiled at him, reaching up to touch his cheek as he came to her. "It was a part of your people's knowledge

251

lost to you, and I couldn't speak of it. Hunter, only a maiden can guard and protect the Unicorns. Only a maiden can be Keeper. Physical innocence forms the bond of trust."

He caught his breath suddenly, and his eyes were vivid. "You mean you thought that because we became lovers . . ." Then he glanced past her at the quietly watching herd.

Siri was nodding, clearly incredulous. "I can't understand it. There are only two immutable laws governing Keepers, and that's one of them."

Hunter, still struggling with what had happened, didn't ask what the second law was.

The Leader decides.

Startled, both Hunter and Siri swung around to stare at Storm.

"I—I heard—" Hunter broke off to stare at Siri.

"You heard his thoughts?" She gazed at him questioningly.

Hunter nodded. "As if he spoke aloud."

She looked at the new Leader of the Unicorns, asking a silent, puzzled question, knowing that Storm would answer now as Cloud had answered in the past.

And Storm, the weight of new responsibilities lending him maturity and dispelling his arrogance, took another step toward them and answered. And Hunter heard the answer as clearly as Siri did.

The Leader decides. It has always been the destiny of Keepers that they never know the love of a man. This was decided long ago by the Guardians. In order that the Keeper be most effective, her heart must not be divided. She is apart from other women, out of reach of man.

But unbreakable laws await only those strong enough to break them. Love forms the bond; how, then, could love be its destruction? Always, the Leader watched and waited. In ten thousand years, the Leaders watched and waited in vain; the Keepers loved only their charges and scorned men. But Cloud knew that it was intended in his lifetime for one Keeper to know the loving touch of a man.

"He knew?" Siri whispered aloud. "But why didn't he tell me? Why was I forced to make the choice?"

Hunter looked at her for a moment, then at Storm to await the Unicorn's answer.

He was forbidden to tell you. It was necessary that both you and the man struggle to find your love. Cloud waited until both choices had been made. He approved your union with his life.

"All this was . . . meant?" Siri asked, stunned.

You saw it yourself in the cards, Keeper. You knew the man would be your lover. And we knew of the man before he came. Knew of his Quest. It was foretold long ago that a Prince would bond a Keeper to his side and his heart.

Hunter started slightly and glanced at Siri, but if she had noticed Storm's mention of a prince it didn't seem to surprise her. Instead, she asked another question.

"How is it that Hunter can hear your thoughts now?"

No man has touched the heart of a Keeper in ten thousand years. Storm's thoughts were curiously gentle. *It is a magic thing. And though he did not come to you seeking power, or an enhancement of his own abilities, both are a gift from the Guardians.*

Siri looked at Hunter, her eyes shining. And even though she addressed the Unicorn, her gaze was all for the man. "Hunter will always be able to know your thoughts as I do? You trust him as you do me?"

He has more than earned the trust of the Unicorns. And he has a home here always in this valley, if he wishes to remain.

The sun had come out finally, bathing the valley in the warm radiance of waning Summer. No grayness now. No oppression.

Neither of them noticed that the Unicorns had gone away quietly to graze in the meadow, leaving them to their privacy.

Siri was smiling mistily up at Hunter. "Is that what you want?"

"There's nothing I want more."

"You'll have to return your people's knowledge to them."

"Yes." They both knew that. "But I'll come back." He remembered that she had said she could never leave the

valley, and his realization that he would never sit on the
throne of Rubicon was distant. He would come back.

Siri clearly followed his thoughts, and her eyes widened in wonder. "Abandon a throne for me?"

"I love you."

Even in her awe, she realized there was something
else, something he wanted to ask her. "What is it?"

"When we became lovers," he said slowly, "you
believed the trust of the Unicorns lost to you. That was why
you fought so long, why you said—you couldn't change
what you were."

"Yes," she confirmed steadily.

"Then you don't love me less than you love them?"
Painfully, he added, "Not a very worthy question, beloved,
but an honest one."

"Hunter . . . Is that what you thought? That you
meant less to me than the Unicorns?"

"I can bear it," he said quickly. "I knew you loved me
as much as you could love a man. But that bond, that
lifelong trust with the Unicorns—I knew I couldn't equal
that."

"I chose your love," she said softly. "If the Unicorns
had demanded another Keeper, there still would have been
no regrets."

"But you would have lost them."

"I couldn't lose you."

Awed, Hunter could only stare at her for a long
moment. His mind worked sluggishly. "You . . . would
have had to leave the valley?"

Siri hesitated.

She would have died.

Turning her head to look toward the grazing Unicorns,
Siri said, "Sometimes mind-touch can be irritating."

A Unicorn's laughter touched their minds.

But Hunter was too shocked to feel humor. "You would
have died? That second immutable law you spoke of? You
said you couldn't leave this valley. You can't *live* outside the
valley?"

She smiled slightly, seeking to reassure him. "I would
have remained at least until next Summer in order to train a
new Keeper. We would have had years together."

"But you would have died," he said flatly, hoarsely.

Siri stepped close, sliding her arms around his waist. "We all die, Hunter. But in choosing to risk losing those years, I gained them instead."

He held her tightly, shaken by how nearly he had come to losing her—even though that loss would be years in the future. "I couldn't live without you," he said unsteadily, adding in a fierce tone, "I'll make damn certain you don't leave the valley!"

A point of interest, Storm mind-voiced idly. *Unless Outcast, leaving the valley will not harm her.*

"I didn't know that," Siri said, surprised, and she felt a sudden rush of delight at the new possibilities before her. "Hunter—I can go with you! I can see your world."

He smiled down at her, more grateful than he could say that she could be with him. "I want to show you my world. And others—"

As long as you return next Summer.

Hunter glanced toward Storm, his brows lifting. "Is he going to keep jumping into private conversations like that?"

Unicorn laughter.

Siri felt a joyous laugh of her own bubbling up. "It looks that way, doesn't it? He's much less serious than Cloud was."

"Cloud," Hunter murmured. "I'm so sorry about him. Does it make a difference, beloved? That he died for us?"

Serious, she said, "There's no taint, Hunter. No stain. Cloud did what he had to do."

The last of his burdens slipped from Hunter's shoulders. "I was so afraid . . ."

She smiled. "And now?"

"And now I feel as if someone has given me the right to paradise."

You're getting maudlin, Storm observed sternly. *Want a ride?*

"My life's ambition as a boy," Hunter confided gravely, "was to ride a Unicorn."

Laughing, Siri gestured toward the two Unicorns who had left the herd and now paced gracefully toward them. "You get Storm, then. Hang on tight. He likes to jump."

"Jump what?"

"Anything."

Weeks before, Hunter would have felt more than a little peculiar climbing up onto the back of a white creature he knew very well to be a thinking, reasoning being with racial memories older than his own. On this day, he gave the matter no more than a passing thought.

Storm led the way at an effortless gallop, Hunter's weight disturbing him not at all. Fancy followed, matching her mate in more than speed; his new maturity had sparked her own, and she was now a calmer, more dignified consort for the new Leader of the Unicorns.

They raced the wind and won.

Astonishing Siri as well as Hunter, it became obvious that the thoughts of all the Unicorns now touched them. And since the entire herd soon entered the game, it became wildly confusing—especially to the unschooled Hunter.

I'll carry you one day, Green-eyes.

Hunter nearly fell off Storm. "Who was that?" he called in astonishment.

Siri was laughing. "That was Rayne."

"But she's just a baby!" he protested. "How can she seem so—so mature?"

Racial memories, Rayne explained calmly.

"Oh," Hunter said somewhat blankly, then considered. "Little Joy, too?" he wondered, somewhere past astonishment.

Hello.

He tried to experiment. *Hello, Joy.*

"You're learning how to focus your thoughts," Siri called approvingly. "I caught that."

"Self-defense," he explained dryly, but with a feeling of elation.

Shall we go over there?

We'll follow the path.

"Siri?"

"Fancy and Storm."

"Ah."

Don't eat that, darling.

"Who?"

"Teen talking to Joy."

"I thought she claimed racial memories—no, that was Rayne, wasn't it?"

"Yes. Anyway, racial memories don't always tell them what they can eat."

"I see. And the endearment?"

"Is that a question?" Siri wondered innocently.

Hunter sighed. "Not really. Am I correct in assuming Unicorns call each other darling on the slightest provocation?"

Only when we want to.

"Storm?" Hunter guessed cautiously.

Right, Green-eyes.

Siri was laughing again. "It seems they've found a name for you!"

"What do they call you?" Hunter wondered.

"Keeper," Siri answered.

Darling, Storm corrected placidly.

Siri nearly fell off Fancy. "I didn't know that!"

Hunter chuckled. "I'm glad you don't know everything, beloved. It's very wearing on a man to think he's the only one asking questions."

Tell him about the Well of Knowledge, they heard Storm mind-voice. *He should understand that in addition to loving you.*

The two Unicorns slowed to a walk, moving side by side as they headed back toward the cabin and leavng their riders free to talk quietly.

"Well of Knowledge?"

Siri explained as best she could how knowledge was passed from Keeper to Keeper, augmented by the knowledge of Merpeople, Unicorns, and Guardians. She explained that answers to questions were found simply by asking her mind.

And Hunter shook his head at the information. "That explains a great deal I found bewildering about you, beloved. You know so much about life outside this valley. It almost seemed believable that you were ten thousand years old!"

"It wasn't that I didn't want to explain before—"

"It was just that it never seemed strange to you," he finished, answering her smile with one of his own.

She liked your questions.

"This," Siri said strongly, "has got to stop!"

Hunter chuckled quietly. "No privacy in an enchanted valley."

"That's putting it mildly."

"Well, I've no secrets," he said innocently.

She frowned at him. "Neither have I."

She wants a girl first.

"Storm!"

Hunter reached out to take his distracted love's hand, smiling tenderly. "A girl would be fine with me. As many girls as you like in fact."

She was suddenly troubled. "The danger in the Summer . . ."

Since he had considered the problem during odd moments, Hunter offered a practical solution. "We could hide them in the cave with the Unicorns. Or in Bundy's cave; he'd protect them for you, wouldn't he?"

She turned startled eyes to him. "It's so simple," she said slowly. "It would work—unless we had no warning."

"The cards would warn you. Granted, it's not a perfect solution," he admitted. "If something should happen to both of us . . . But, Siri, all parents deal with the uncertainties of bringing children into the world. We'll do the best we can."

They had reached the cabin, and now both slid from the backs of their mounts. After physical pats and mental thanks, they watched the two Unicorns return to the herd.

"They seem to be giving us privacy at last," Siri noted, aware of the silence in her mind.

"Good," Hunter said dryly.

"Just in time for breakfast," Siri said.

As they went into the cabin, he said suddenly, "I meant to ask you about this tunic. Your father's?"

"Yes. It fits you well. We should get our other things from the Crystal Pool," she added idly.

"After breakfast."

Yes, my love.

With a soft laugh, Hunter drew her close and bent his head to hers. "That's one mind-voice that sounds familiar," he whispered, kissing her with a gentleness that swiftly became something else.

Reluctantly, Siri finally murmured, "I thought you wanted breakfast."

"I want you."

———————

Not the same, but not less.

———————

"Can I talk to your mother the way I talk to the Unicorns?" he asked sometime later. They were sitting at the table, Hunter in his chair and Siri in hers, enjoying a very late breakfast.

"Have you tried?"

"No."

"You won't know until you do."

Wondering silently just how to go about reaching a Mermaid, Hunter found that his mind knew. *I don't know your name.*

My name is Shauna, Hunter.

Hunter blinked and stared at Siri. "I seem to have reached her."

Siri nodded, watching him with a smile.

You have a lovely daughter, Shauna.

Thank you.

I love her very much.

I know. Her happiness is mine.

Uncertainly, Hunter voiced a cautious question. *I don't suppose we could meet?*

No. Better not. Not yet.

I'm sorry. I only—

Don't be sorry, Hunter. I am what I am. Take care of her.

You're not—

Leaving? No. Not now. But you need privacy.

A door closed in his mind.

Hunter drew a long breath. "She seems . . . so sad."

"Mermaids live always with their curse," Siri reminded quietly. "But don't be depressed for her. Despite everything, the Merpeople are a happy race. They love life."

He nodded slightly. "When will she return to her people?"

"When Summer is over. She needs the protection of the deep sea in Winter."

"She remains here in Summer in case you need her?"

"So I believe. She says her visits give Bundy something to guard."

Hunter's thoughts, concerned as they were with a mother's love for her child, shifted in perspective. "Siri, about our children. Would our daughter be Keeper after you?" He didn't like to think of a time "after" Siri, but needed to ask.

"No, I don't think so." She frowned, thoughtful. "After today, I can't be sure of anything, but the Keeper of the Unicorns has always been the child of Mermaid and man. Our children will be welcome here, but another will be Keeper after me."

"Will our children inherit the mind-touch ability?"

"It's likely. Unless you and I cancel each other out and they end up being psi-null."

Shaking his head, he said, "Has it occurred to you that any offspring of ours will be an unusual mixture? You're the daughter of a Mermaid—"

"And you're the son of a king," she finished softly.

Hunter looked at her a bit restlessly. "I'd like to know how Storm knew that." He reflected for a moment. "On second thought, perhaps I wouldn't like to know."

"It seems your destiny was here," Siri said, rising from the table and going to get his backpack from the hidden cupboard. She carried the pack to the table, laying it before Hunter and reclaiming her chair. "I'd forgotten until this morning, but I put this away for you that first day."

"I thought it was destroyed," he said slowly, unfastening the straps and opening the pack.

"No. A bit battered, as you can see, but whole." She

watched him, seeing him steel himself oddly before reaching into the pack. And she wondered what, besides his conscious Quest, had driven him from the kingdom he had been born to rule. There was more, her awareness of fate told her that. He had been meant to come here, meant to find her and his myths and his people's lost knowledge; there was a reason for it all.

Hunter ignored the jumble of clothing and dried provisions inside the pack. He searched with one hand, seeking with touch rather than sight, until his fingers closed about a ring of cold metal. He pulled it from the pack and sat for a moment turning it absently, his gaze on it the accustomed one of long familiarity.

But Siri had never seen such a thing before, and stared at the ring in fascination. It was large to fit a man's finger and shone dimly with the dull glow of gold. The shank was wide, and set securely atop it was a carved stone. The stone, unlike any Siri had ever seen, was not one color but rather a myriad of shades. Black, red, green, purple, it seemed to reflect each color at once as it was turned in the strong hand holding it. The carving was enigmatic, curiously unformed, but it bit deeply into the stone to form a definite symbol that not even her Well of Knowledge offered to define.

"The symbol of your house?" she asked curiously.

Still gazing, unseeing, at the ring, Hunter shook his head. "No. Not really. It's ancient. A puzzle." He looked across at her with a sudden, rueful smile. "My interest in legends and myths comes naturally, beloved, considering that my own family history is riddled with both. Even some things as peculiar and unbelievable as your valley."

"And you were taught—"

"Told. As such things are traditional in my family, the legends are passed from each generation to the next. Most, of course, are simple tales of courage or daring or enterprise, of ancestors whose actions shaped the destiny of the family. Some tales, however, are puzzles. Like this ring. It's a secret thing. My father died before I was born, and although my mother was his second wife and his first wife was also expecting his child, he gave the ring to her and asked that she pass it to me should something happen to him. My mother took me out into the forest one day when I was little more than a child. She gave me this ring, which was not to be worn but only kept safe. And she told me of a legend which made no sense to me—a tale which has never faded from my mind. As if the telling locked it inside me in some manner I could never understand."

"Like my Well of Knowledge," she suggested.

He nodded, then stirred restlessly, his gaze dropping to the ring. "I've often thought," he murmured, "that I was the wrong son to give this to for safekeeping, that my half brother should have taken it. His mother was our father's first wife, after all. But I was officially firstborn, and my mother insisted that my father wanted me to have it, and that the ring was mine."

Siri waited and listened quietly, sensing that Hunter was carefully probing his own past, his memories, triumphs, and disappointments, seeking to assemble a puzzle that had been only disjointed pieces until now.

He stirred again. "It's an . . . impossible tale. Its roots lie too deeply in ancient times to retain any shreds of truth. Or so I've always believed. Now, I'm not so certain of that. And a part of me must have believed, because I've never worn it and always kept it safe. Only since entering this valley has it been out of my possession and out of my mind."

"It's a talisman?" she guessed softly.

"Of a sort. Supposedly, there is something protective or lucky about it. It was given long, long ago to the oldest ancestor my family claims from their new beginning. From a time when they were wrenching a civilization from a hostile world, using only the primitive means they had chosen to keep. The ancestor began as a soldier, and his name was Hunter."

Siri felt a curious suspension, vaguely aware that something, some memory or sliver of knowledge, had sat up alertly in her mind.

Hunter went on musingly. "I'm the only one of his descendants to bear his name. My mother told me that I was so named because the Wisewoman who attended my birth insisted. And my mother, wanting to avoid any taint of bad luck for her firstborn, agreed. But the name wore heavily on my shoulders after I was given the ring."

When he remained silent for a long moment, Siri prompted gently, "The first Hunter?"

Sighing, Hunter pulled his mind away from the faint detour it had taken unbidden, concentrating on following the spiraling trail of legend and reality toward some truth, some knowledge he only dimly recognized. "As I said, he began as a soldier. But he lived in violent times; it isn't easy to build a civilization with primitive tools and a diverse shipload of people. They were warring times, and a man may carve his own destiny during such an era in the history of a world. He wrought a kingdom with his wits and his sword, and held its reins in iron hands. And he was a good ruler, a wise ruler.

"With his kingdom at last peaceful, he began thinking of a successor, a hand and heart to guide when his own finally withered. Some unnamed compulsion drove him to travel far from his kingdom to seek a bride. There was much of that world unexplored, and he traveled far beyond the boundaries of what he knew, searching for a place he could not put a name to."

Almost hypnotized, Siri realized that Hunter's very words were ancient ones, that this "legend" had indeed been locked within his mind in careful words. This tale, she knew, had not changed in the telling for untold generations. Like her own beginnings as Keeper, it lay more than ten thousand years in the past. And the alert, waiting part of her mind voiced a calm recognition of truth.

"The king was accompanied only by the captain of his armies," Hunter went on. "When he and his companion came upon a towering mountain, he realized that he had found his journey's end. They rode their andars—creatures native to that world trained to carry riders—as far as they were able, and when they were forced to dismount, he left his companion behind to stay with the creatures and went on climbing alone. It took him days to reach the summit, but the goal was more than worth the effort. At the summit he discovered a plateau unlike anything he'd ever seen. It was forested with tall, graceful trees, and there were peaceful glades and sparkling streams.

"And a race of people lived there. They were not of the powerful, thickly set people he ruled; despite the world's high gravity, these beings were tall and slender, graceful in their strength and wise beyond his knowing. They lived in templelike buildings more beautiful than anything he'd ever seen in his travels. He was welcomed by them calmly and graciously, bidden to remain as long as he desired. Their king was a very old but still incredibly powerful man, with a flowing silver beard and ancient green eyes.

"The first Hunter remained there for a time. Their cool, shaded gardens soothed his restless spirit, and the wisdom of their conversation fascinated him. They knew . . . so much. And there was one in particular he sought out, finding in her gentle manner a balm and an odd strength.

"She was called Athene. Her skin was fair, her eyes green, and her hair black as darkness itself. She was serene and gentle, and the brusque soldier-king found a peace he had never before known in her company. He learned gentleness from her, the rough edges of him smoothed by her touch. He fell in love with her, and dared to ask the ruler of that place for her hand.

"The ruler bade him ask Athene herself and return to him with her answer, and Hunter did so. She answered him with calm certainty, saying that she would leave her mountaintop home for his kingdom, but warned him that her ruler would demand a price for her hand. Hunter felt that no price could be too costly for his love, and returned to the ruler to convey Athene's acceptance of his suit.

"The old ruler indeed demanded a price. He produced a ring." Hunter looked down at the bauble in his hand. "This ring. It would bring good luck to the family, he said, but there was a great deal more to it than the simplicity of a talisman. The ruler told him that there would come a time when the child of Hunter would be required to accept a task great with danger. The ring, he said, was called Omega, and Omega would summon when the time came. Omega was to be held but never worn until the summons, and it would summon only the firstborn of Hunter.

"Hunter was a man in love. Though reluctant to think of his firstborn on a dangerous quest, he was a soldier and king, and knew that there would be danger for his offspring, quest or no. He accepted the ring and the responsibility it entailed. And he carried his bride from the mighty summit of her mountaintop home and far away to his kingdom."

After long moments of silence, Siri said very softly, "His firstborn was never summoned." It wasn't a question.

Hunter looked at her. "No. Never summoned. After many long years, the soldier-king realized that the price he had paid was more complicated than he had known. He was wise enough to realize the promise involved all of his blood, and honorable enough—and grateful enough—to be determined that his promise to the old ruler be kept. It was his queen he went to for advice, as he had often done over the years. She advised him to pass on the ring and the promise, and to make certain as much as possible that the original promise was honored. So the ring was passed from firstborn to firstborn and never worn but only kept safe. Until it came to me."

"And when it came to you?" she questioned softly.

Hunter took a deep breath and set the ring on the table, staring down at it broodingly. "When it came to me, I thought it an amusing tale. Then. But I've wondered these last years. And I've never forgotten. Promises and quests. My Quest taught me a great deal. I came to realize just how badly my world needed . . . something. I *felt* I'd find the answers I was looking for on other worlds."

"And you did. You found the myths. And more than that, you found the roots of your people, their history. When they understand how nearly they came to destroying themselves, it *will* help them, Hunter."

He smiled a little. "I have to believe that." Then he looked at the ring. "But this . . . I was told that nothing confined Omega to the soil of one world, but only to the blood of one family. It's still my responsibility to pass it along. I had to take it with me when I left Rubicon."

"On your Quest for a throne?"

He looked at her and sighed. "As I said, I was officially

firstborn. But my half brother's birth hour was uncertain; there were no witnesses to the birth. Jason, our uncle, had no offspring of his own, and announced that he would decide in time which of us was to rule. But he died of a fever before he could make his decision known. The Council, unwilling to decide, announced that the next King would chosen by means of a Quest. The first of us to return with proof that Unicorns did—or did not—exist would occupy the throne."

"And your half brother?"

"I haven't seen him since we left Rubicon." His tone was abstracted; he looked back down at the ring.

Siri was quiet for a long time, watching him. He hadn't realized, she saw. Hadn't put all the pieces together. She reached carefully for words. "And if you had always been meant to leave your world? If your Quest for a throne was always intended to become something more?"

He looked at her, a little puzzled. "I've learned to respect your ideas of Fate since coming to this valley. But—"

"You heard Storm," she interrupted firmly. "The Unicorns knew that a prince would come; they were told so long ago by the Guardians. They knew you for that prince instantly—why else would they have trusted you as they did? Why else would Cloud have led me to you when you were so badly injured? Why else did he refuse to be hidden with the others when we knew you were coming?"

"There are countless princes—"

"But only one prince named Hunter," she insisted, her voice very soft.

"What has that to do with it?"

"Everything." She unlocked her hands and reached across the table to touch the ring with one finger. "This. And green eyes, Hunter."

"I don't understand."

"Your destiny and mine were intertwined long ago. Set for us in ancient times, when the Guardians traveled from one world to another. They lived on this world once, this Earth. They were a playful, *human* kind of a race, but very wise. And they lived for all to see on mountaintops within

graceful temples. They could—and did—summon the
lightning and the wind out of sorely tried tempers, and
sometimes interfered in the lives of humans."

He was frowning, trying to follow her. "Part of legend,
of myth. I remember some of the stories. So?"

"Don't you see the parallels? When you talked to me
once about myth, you mentioned some of the ancient Earth
myths. The gods and goddesses, remember?"

"Yes." A suddenly arrested expression flickered in his
eyes. "Do you mean that the first Hunter—"

"The Guardians travel," she said softly. "They live for a
time on one world, then move on to another. Is it so
impossible to believe they would have visited the adopted
world where some of your race struggled to build their
civilization again?"

Hunter drew a deep breath. "No. No, I suppose it's
possible."

"Possible? Think of that first soldier-king and his green-
eyed bride, the wife he won with a promise. *Think*. The
mountaintop home. The slender, fair people—on a high-
gravity world where they could never have evolved naturally. Hunter, isn't your family different in physical stature
from most of those in your world? Taller, fairer, and green-
eyed?"

His mind coping with possibilities, Hunter said almost
absently, "Yes, all of that. Only those of the royal house
have green eyes; all of us do, except those who married into
our family. And we're taller than most." Tension stole into
him, and disbelief swiftly fractured into shards as he neared
the core of truth within his own set of puzzles.

"Your ancestor," she said quietly, "the man whose
name you bear, took a goddess for his bride."

"No," Hunter denied instantly, unwilling to accept
that.

"That has to be it," she insisted. "She was a Guardian,
Hunter. Only godlike beings, beings so advanced and wise
they *seem* godlike to us, can plan and control the destinies
of generations to come. Is it so impossible that your
ancestor took one of the Guardian race for his bride? And
that his bride-price was a promise to aid when called? The

Unicorns knew, Hunter, and the cards told me part of it. That a green-eyed prince called Hunter would leave his world on a Quest and find a valley where myth walked. That he would come here to fulfill a prophecy made by the Guardians themselves. After ten thousand years of waiting . . . You were *meant* to come here, Hunter; it was a part of your destiny."

Hunter shook his head. "The Guardians could have had nothing to do with my leaving my world. Omega didn't summon me; I've never worn the ring, never felt anything at all from it."

"You forget." Siri smiled gently. "*The child of Hunter will be summoned.* Your firstborn, my love. Our firstborn. The Guardians planned well. The knowledge of aeons can be passed on through me, the wisdom of four races. And through you comes the strength of a warrior and the ancient lineage of kings descended from a unique soldier-king and a daughter of the gods."

Hunter tried to let all that sink in, finding to his astonishment that there was no resistance left in his mind. He believed because it was no longer in him to disbelieve. He believed because he *felt* it was true.

Slowly, he said, "but why will the summons come? What will it be about?"

"I don't know. Only time will tell us that."

Hunter sighed. "A woman set to be Keeper of myth by the Guardians; a man descended from Guardians, bound by a promise made generations before."

Looking down at the ring she still touched, Siri found then that her Well of Knowledge *could* define the cryptic symbol carved in the polished stone. "Omega," she murmured. "Letter. Symbol. The end. The last."

He looked at her, never questioning the knowledge. "The last? Last what?"

"I don't know."

"Could your mother tell us?"

Siri reflected. "Probably. But she won't unless and until she thinks we should know."

"Then we wait, beloved? And live?"

"We wait. And we live, my love."

Siri awoke several mornings later with a start, feeling a peculiar heaviness, as if a thick blanket lay over her. She slipped from the bed, careful not to wake Hunter, thinking the heaviness merely some residue of a forgotten dream. But the feeling wouldn't ease. She dressed silently, trying to breathe slowly, feeling her heart beginning to pound harder and harder.

What was wrong with her?"

Uneasiness haunting her, she stepped to the open door to gaze out into the valley, seeing the herd grazing quietly. She had the fleeting idea that they moved too slowly, as if in a dream, but then it was gone. She turned back to the silent cabin and found herself moving to the table, laying out the cards instinctively. But there was nothing there; nothing except the constant Summer warning to be wary.

She rose and moved about the cabin restlessly. Then, realizing what she was doing, she stopped in the center of the room and gazed about slowly and searchingly. There was something wrong, something she saw or didn't see that disturbed her. What was it? Normal items in their accustomed places, the shelves holding implements and folded clothing and—

Siri heard her breathing quicken in the still room. Where was Cloud's horn? She went to the high shelf and searched with her fingers, thinking, hoping that perhaps the horn had rolled back against the wall. But it wasn't there. Then, puzzled and disturbed, she searched the floor all around the shelves. Perhaps it had fallen?

No. The horn was gone.

Siri turned toward the bed, Hunter's name in her throat, rising to her lips. But she didn't call out. Instead, she moved again to the door and stood gazing out over the valley. All appeared peaceful. The sun was rising cheerfully, birds twittered brightly in the forest. The cards had warned of nothing specific, advised only wariness as usual. But she felt . . .

There was a tiny spot of blankness in her mind, her senses. It was oddly difficult for her to breathe, the feeling of heaviness clinging like a blanket. And she felt curiously weak, drained. The hand she held out before her trembled faintly, drawing a frown from her as she stared at it.

Was she only weary? Had the violent activity and emotions of the Summer finally caught up with her? She thought with a sudden smile that no Keeper before her had known the physically draining but definitely pleasurable activity of lovemaking. Even as the thought occurred to her, she felt another wave of weakness, a faint discomfort in her mind.

How strange.

She hesitated again, on the point of waking Hunter, but decided against it. She was just tired, that was all. Only partly reassured, she left the cabin, her steps turning toward the Crystal Pool. Rayne was probably there, she thought vaguely, since the foal was not near the rest of the herd. The small unicorn would most likely be delighted to join her in a morning swim; maybe that would clear her stuffy head.

She glanced at the herd as she passed, telling Storm mentally what she was going to do. And she was only partially aware that the stallion lifted his head slowly, that his acknowledgment seemed oddly distant and muffled, as though reaching her through a layer of thick cotton.

The quickly rising sun was well up when she entered the forest, its slanting rays brightening what would be shaded later in the day. She followed the path, her steps quickening without her conscious volition, even as she felt weaker, shakier.

She forced her sluggish mind to think about the missing horn, trying to explain its absence. Perhaps inquisitive Rayne had found the horn lying on the floor during one of her visits to the cabin and playfully made away with it? No. No, that didn't seem right. Rayne would hardly be disrespectful. Yes, that was the word. Disrespectful. Had Hunter moved the horn and forgotten to tell her? But why would he do that? Had she herself moved the horn and then forgotten? Forgotten . . . Something forgotten . . .

Siri ran a hand across her eyes irritably. Why couldn't

she *think?* It was as if something had curtained her mind, smothered it somehow.

The moment her hand left her eyes, Siri froze, her breathing and heart suspended, eyes going wide and black and agonized. Then a reckless fury launched her in a headlong dive toward the man bent over a frail, crumpled white body stained with scarlet.

A man with half the face of an angel.

And the cry that burst from her lips was wild with rage and grief and heavy with remorse.

"Rayne!"

Twelve

Hunter, waking to find Siri gone, rose and dressed quickly. He wondered if he would always be uneasy when she was away from him, or if the worry would trouble him only in Summer and only in the valley. Thinking of some of the worlds he'd walked on, he doubted it; if he and Siri visited those dangerous places, he knew he would worry about her. But the thought of her pleasure and excitement in seeing wonders unknown to her far outweighed his instinctive desire to protect her.

He smiled as he crossed to the open door, looking forward to seeing worlds anew through her eyes. The smile remained as he gazed out at the peaceful herd of Unicorns. Idly, he continued his ongoing attempts to become more adept in mind-touch; the Unicorns were easiest to communicate with, although it was growing easier to reach the cool, shaded depths of Siri's mind.

After a moment he frowned, wondering why the herd was ignoring him. No white, horned face turned inquiringly toward the cabin; no distinctive, curiously alien mind-voice reached out in response. Odd. Now that he considered it, he realized that *he* felt odd, somewhat shaky and weak. His mind seemed sluggish, and he had the impulse to rub his forehead hard although he felt no pain.

Very odd.

Then, before he could make a second attempt to reach the Unicorns with his mind, he heard Siri's voice crying out in rage and pain, the single word slicing fear through his body.

"Rayne!"

Hunter erupted instantly from the cabin. A part of his perception saw the Unicorns galvanized by the scream, saw gentle Dawn whirling toward the forest in a mother's instinctive leap toward her daughter. Though he wasn't sure what danger confronted them, Hunter instantly sent a ringing mental command, unknowingly blasting through the layers blanketing all their minds.

Storm! Hide them!

He saw the stallion quickly head off the distraught mare, turning them all toward another path to their cave— this one taking them away from the forest and the threat within it. Then Hunter pushed the Unicorns from his mind and ran, desperate to reach his love.

Siri's dive, instinctive rather than planned, carried them both several feet away from the limp body of the foal. Nearly blind with fury, she grappled with the powerful man, managing to hold off his bloody knife but unable to get it away from him. Then Boran sacrificed a moment of vulnerability to slap her viciously, the powerful blow abruptly draining the strength from Siri's arms.

Instantly, he snatched a leather thong from his belt and bound her wrists tightly at her waist, taking advantage of her dizziness and nausea. His heavy weight held her body still, and his knife was at her throat.

"You weren't supposed to come out here, princess." His incongruously beautiful voice held a curious blend of anger and entreaty.

Siri turned her head away sickly, grieving eyes searching for the fallen Rayne. Tears blinded her for a moment, then her vision cleared and her body arched in a desperate attempt to throw off the weight of the man. "She's still breathing! Let me go to her!"

"I can't take the horn if she lives," Boran explained, his one clear green eye inches from Siri's face. "I have to have the horn. Especially now. You stole my manhood, bitch. I need the Triad more than ever."

Siri looked at him, fighting her sickness at the sight of that horribly mutilated face. She could remember, but only vaguely, that he had threatened her with rape. And she had fought in the only way she had possessed. "You would have destroyed me," she whispered. "What I did—"

"What you did," he rasped, "was worse than destroying me! I went to the city, princess-bitch. I paid a whore to lie with me. And I— She laughed! She *laughed* at me! I wanted to kill her, but I . . . You took that away, too. All the way back here, I planned to kill you." He looked down at her, the hand still holding the knife rubbing lightly across her breasts. "I'll make you a *queen*," he said suddenly, hoarsely. "All will bow down to you!"

Siri turned her face away, sickened and afraid, realizing that his evil mind had splintered. In stealing his manhood, she herself had driven him over the edge into total madness. He hated her with a mindless, obsessed rage, yet he wanted her with a terrible hunger—and he was afraid of her.

In an eerie, reasonable tone, Boran said, "I just have to get this horn; I took the other from the cabin while you slept with—him. And I have King's horn. The Triad, princess! I'll get the talisman from him, and then we can leave this accursed place!"

"No." She swallowed, trying to speak clearly, forcing herself to look at him. Trying to fight the smothering blanket that, even now, this powerful man wrapped around her. "I love Hunter."

His twisted lips moved in a horrible grimace, and the single green eye blazed. "You spread your legs for him, didn't you, bitch-princess? I knew. As soon as I returned, I knew. *He* had you first!" Still holding the knife, Boran moved his thumb across her lips roughly, again and again, staring fixedly at what he was doing. "I'll wipe away the taste of him," he whispered. "And when you give me back

my manhood, I'll teach your lovely body to forget him.
We'll reign together, my princess. I'll be good to you, I
promise. I'll pleasure you as *he* never could. Just give me
back my manhood."

Through the bruised lips he was still roughly scraping
with his thumb, she whispered, "No, I won't."

Boran made a strangled sound, the knife once again
returning to her throat as he heard what was in her mind.
"Never undone . . . what is done, never undone. You
bitch! You turned me into a eunuch! Reverse your spell! Do
it, or I'll—"

"*Boran!*"

"I'll cut her throat if you move!" Boran snapped, his
head turning, the single eye glaring malevolently at
Hunter.

And Hunter stood frozen, the shocks piled one atop
the other holding him motionless. At his feet lay Rayne, her
stained side rising and falling pitifully with her labored
breathing. Feet away lay Siri, held down by the weight of
Boran's body, her hands bound, a knife at her throat.

Hunter felt another wave of weakness pass over him,
vaguely aware that it was Boran who caused it, that
somehow he was exerting some force over them all. "What
do you want?" he asked hoarsely, fighting that weakness,
desperate to get the other man away from Siri before he
used that knife.

Boran tilted his head to one side, as if listening to
distant music or a distant memory. "I want to see you suffer,
Hunter," he said slowly, reasonably.

"You were my friend!" Hunter burst out, bewildered.
"My *brother!*"

"*Brother!*" Boran's voice went suddenly brittle with
loathing. "*I* was firstborn! My mother bore me alone with
no tender Wisewoman's hands to help. Carried me back to
the palace though she could hardly walk herself. *She told
the Court when I was born before she knew of your birth!*
Firstborn, the rightful king after Jason died. But Tynan and
the other Elders couldn't stomach the thought of me on the
throne, could they, dear brother? They couldn't bear the
thought of a scarred king! So they invented their little

Quest and sent us both out into space, trusting blindly that you would return first."

He laughed harshly. "They were wrong. Brother? I hated you, despised you, and you never even knew. I planned your *death* and you never knew!"

Hunter's numb mind sought memory and answers, finding both. "The trial," he whispered.

And he remembered the trial by fire, the test of manhood that had been abandoned years before by a peaceful civilization. It had been Boran's idea to resurrect the old custom, his idea that they test one another. On the threshold of manhood, both young and arrogant, they had joined in what was supposed to be mock battle. Then an accident, a misstep by Hunter's mount, had knocked Boran into the fire—

"Yes," Boran hissed softly. "Jason would have chosen you as his successor, and we both knew it. So I planned. You were meant to die that day, Hunter. Instead, it was I who went into the fire, yet survived. Survived to see women faint at the sight of my face. Survived to hear the whispers advising the King to choose you as his successor. And he would have, because Boran would disgust the Court with his horrible face!"

"You said it was an accident," Hunter said dully. "You said you forgave me."

"And you believed me! I decided to wait until you assumed the throne. I knew you, Hunter. I knew you'd never place another above me. You'd be King, and I'd be your most trusted adviser. And I would kill you one day. But then Jason thwarted my plans by dying before he could name his successor. And the cowardly Council sent us from Rubicon."

Siri absorbed what was being said, but while Boran was distracted by his need to explain his hatred, she was forming a plan of her own. Bit by bit, she was drawing back the mental strength he'd stolen from her. Cautiously, she was calling on every resource available, pulling energy from the deepest corners of her body and mind. All she needed was a moment, an instant of power greater than this evil man could command.

Boran's sighted eye glittered balefully. "I followed you,

looking for my chance. If you were dead, I'd be King whether or not I found proof of unicorns. More than once, some alien weapon in my hand nearly killed you, but your luck was strong. So I concentrated on building my own powers, and I followed. When you heard of unicorns near the Huntman's city, I heard as well. I was here before you. I found King and the horn he possessed. And I had heard of the Triad, and the power to be gained by taking the Keeper. I knew I needed the strength of both to defeat you and return to rule our world."

Hunter fought to throw off the draining weakness he felt. "Siri's done nothing to you, Boran. This is between the two of us. Your revenge concerns only me."

Boran tilted his head again in the curious, listening gesture. "Yes. I meant to have her, of course," he said in a slow, distant voice. "It was amusing to control her. And I came so close to having her." He shook his head suddenly, and the green eye was glittering again. "You think I don't know you'd cut your own throat, consign your own soul to hell to spare her pain?"

"If you harm her," Hunter promised thickly, "I swear I'll break every bone in your body! And my soul will chase yours to the farthest corners of hell!"

Boran's single eye went distant again, and he frowned. "Hurt her? My princess-bitch? I have to have her, first. After I kill you, then I'll have her. I wanted you to watch while I spread her legs and buried myself in her, but she—" His mouth twisted. "She's a witch. She has great powers. But once I've had her, I'll command those powers. She'll be my queen."

"You'll die," Hunter vowed, muscles tensing in readiness, knowing that he had to act and hoping desperately that Siri, still and silent though she was, could somehow read his intentions, could somehow keep that knife at bay for the vital few seconds he needed.

And Siri chose that moment for the largest gamble of her life. Her fierce refusal to allow this evil man to harm either of them made her reach deeper within herself than she had ever done before. She was no witch, no sorceress, but she was the Keeper of the Unicorns, and she was enraged.

That rage was her catalyst, thrusting her focused energies in a deadly shaft of pure incandescent power aimed narrowly at Boran's one sighted eye. She poured into that blow every spark, every atom of willpower, loosing mental daggers of fury.

And it found its target.

Boran howled, agonized, his green eye as damaged as the seared side of his face. He dropped the knife and clapped his hand to his burned eye, never noticing that Siri rolled violently away from his writhing body.

Hunter was on him in an instant. There was no pity within him for this nemesis of his lifetime, no quarter granted to the enemy who would have destroyed his love and himself. Because of Boran, Hunter, Siri, and the valley had suffered.

Boran fought blindly, but with no lessening of his deadly warrior skills. Both men were weaponless, both meant to win.

Siri gained her feet shakily, weaker now than she'd ever been in her life after the explosive release of energy, weaker even than she had been after saving Hunter's life. But she was the Keeper, and her love and her duty sent her stumbling the few feet to Rayne. There was nothing she could do now to aid Hunter, and she trusted his skill and ability to defeat their enemy.

She fell on her knees beside the foal, horrified eyes fastening on the gaping, bleeding wound that was pouring out Rayne's life to stain the ground. Instantly, Siri reached out her bound hands to cover the wound, desperately aware that her energies were too low, that she hadn't the strength to heal so mortal a wound. But she poured everything she could summon into the effort to heal, sparing nothing of herself, sending her own dwindled life-force into the beloved foal's body.

Darkness surrounded her, clutched at her hungrily. She felt the agony of the foal shrieking along her nerve endings, burning, searing. A whirlpool of blackness sucked the life from her in a draining rush, and she couldn't feel her body anymore. . . .

They were equally trained and skilled, almost identical in size and weight, and both, for vastly different reasons, were enraged and driven to win. With his mind splintered, Boran's mental powers were not what they had been. Hunter could not take advantage of the situation, however; he was so unaccustomed to his own strengthening abilities that he never thought to fight with his mind.

It was brute strength against brute strength, and every driving fist and thrusting foot carried with it killing force. They stayed just out of reach of one another, neither willing to be caught in powerful arms that would crush the life from the victim. Fists became hammers in a brutal test of lethal strength.

"I'll have the bitch!" Boran hissed, ducking Hunter's swinging fist only by using what remained of his mental skill.

"I'll see you in hell first," Hunter growled, blocking a vicious punch and driving his own fist into Boran's stomach with the full weight of his arm behind it.

Boran laughed through pulped lips, gasping, his swings beginning to go wide, his blocks ineffective. "I've always hated you," he muttered, repeating the oath again and again. "Hated you! Always hated you . . . always!"

And Hunter leaped suddenly, driven to just *finish* it now, quickly, because there was something wrong and a terrible chilling fear writhed in his mind. He knocked Boran off his feet and they were rolling, locked together, on ground churned by boots and flecked with blood. Everything was still with straining for a long moment, and then a chilling, hollow snap cut through the silence and Hunter rose, trembling, to his feet.

He turned away from his fallen, motionless brother. A faint glint of something at Boran's neck caught his eye, but Hunter was too concerned to think about anything except Siri and Rayne. He moved quickly toward a Unicorn foal and a bound woman, and a raw sound of fear escaped his lips as he saw and understood.

Into the utter silence and darkness crept something Siri was only dimly aware of. Faint echoes disturbed her weary peace, soft and faraway, and she ignored the summons. But it grew louder, stronger, battering at her cowed, wounded self. It searched for her violently, urgently, seeking with hands imperative in their need. Siri curled up inside herself and drew the darkness around her, too tired to fight anymore.

She was floating on a gentle, peaceful sea. Though her eyes were closed, she could sense the clear blue sky above, and the breeze on her face carried the scent of salt and sunshine. How good of the gods, she thought happily, to have shown her the ocean of her world; she had always wanted to see it, although she had not realized that until he came. She felt calm, at peace. But then her peace was abruptly shattered by the sharp, oddly hoarse cry of a sea gull.

Disturbed, strangely uneasy, she opened her eyes to see dark clouds blotting out the sun. Fright and saltwater washed over her as the sea heaved beneath her body. With no more warning than that, the storm was upon her, and she thrashed about in the ugly green, white-tipped waves, desperately trying to fight a determined, hungry sea. The wind shrieked in her ears, momentarily drowning out the hoarse cries of the gull. And then the cries rose above the howling wind, only it was not a gull, but a harsh masculine voice, sharply commanding her to keep trying, keep fighting. She was aware of a compulsion to obey the rough commands, but the sea was dragging her down . . . down . . .

She cried out in terror, in silence, disappearing beneath the waves and tasting the slimy saltiness of seawater. For one timeless moment she felt the weight of defeat. The sea would win.

The harsh voice lashed at her, and for an oddly detached moment she marveled that the voice could reach her here in the green depths. Then something caught her, held her, and the voice was forcing strength into her aching body. It poured into her fiercely, reaching every corner of her tired mind, her battered self. She was moving up, up through the water, prodded by the relentless voice which would not allow her to . . . die. Yes, that was it. The angry sea wanted her death, but the commanding, urgent voice would not allow it. He wanted her life.

Coughing and choking, she fought her way to the surface of the sea, the harsh, strained voice growing ever louder and more commanding with every inch she gained. Finally she broke through, and was dimly aware of a strong arm extended to help her. With her last ounce of borrowed strength, she grasped the large hand, clinging desperately as he pulled her from the cheated sea and into the sunlight.

Siri was aware of silence first, a silence broken only by the rumble of distant thunder. She was puzzled; it never stormed in the valley. She felt weightless, and coolness surrounded her, lapping her tired body with a soothing touch. She enjoyed it mindlessly for a time, only vaguely aware that her body was growing stronger, her mind clearer.

"Beloved?"

It was a hoarse whisper, strained and uneven, curiously urgent at her ear. She pondered that for a moment, then her cleared mind allowed memory to rush in and she opened her eyes instantly.

"Hunter!"

He hugged her tightly, relief escaping him in a broken groan. "I thought I'd lost you," he whispered raggedly against her throat.

Siri realized then that she was truly floating—in the Crystal Pool. She was in Hunter's arms, held securely, his heart thudding in the distant-thunder rumble against her. And the Moonflowers were spilling glorious colors all around the pool. Night! She'd lost an entire day.

She turned in his tender embrace, her still-booted feet finding the bottom of the pool as she faced him. And her heart turned over. He was gray with exhaustion, strain cutting deeply into his lean face. But his eyes, his wonderful, vivid green eyes, were glowing down at her.

For a silent, thankful moment, Siri burrowed her face against him, holding on tightly to the love whose strength had been greater than her own. Then she remembered, and quickly lifted her head.

"Rayne! And—and Boran?"

"Rayne's fine." Hunter's voice was still a thick rasp, but he smiled and nodded toward the pool's edge.

Siri followed his glance, and relief lifted a burden. Little Rayne stood knee-deep in the pool, her anxious dark eyes fixed on Siri's face, her glowing white coat unmarred by blood or wound. And behind her stood the rest of the herd, all watching their Keeper gravely.

She looked back at Hunter. "Boran?"

"Dead." Bleakness darkened his vivid gaze. "Once a friend—always an enemy. And I never knew. I'm sorry, beloved. So sorry for bringing him into your life."

Siri hesitated, then glanced back over her shoulder involuntarily before looking at Hunter again. "Is the—body still there?"

"No." Hunter's frown was brief. "I was too worried about you to notice, but the animals must have taken him away." He couldn't help but think Boran's end a fitting one, even as his face tightened at the thought of what Boran had forced him to do.

Siri touched his cheek, silently comforting him, and tried to take his mind off that terrible betrayal. "What happened to me?"

You were dying. Storm's mind-voice was quiet. *He saved you.* Then, silently, the herd faded into the forest.

She stared up at him. "How—"

Hunter shook his head quickly. "I don't know. You were leaving me and I couldn't bear that. Rayne was all right, but you'd poured everything you had into saving her. All your strength. I wanted to give you my strength and somehow I did. I kept calling you with my mind and voice, searching for you where you'd hidden away. And when I found you, I held on as tightly as I could."

Siri held on to him now as tightly as *she* could. She thought of his fierce vigil, the endless hours of striving to find her, keep her, and there was nothing she could say to that, no simple words to utter. Instinctively her mind reached out to his, flowing gently into his, allowing the emotions that were too powerful for words to wash over them both, and heal them.

Because it had to be faced and put behind them, they talked much as they lay together later in their bed.

"He was my friend," Hunter said, the pain of betrayal in his low voice. "My brother. We grew up together, shared so much of our lives. His face was destroyed because . . . because of me. A misstep by my mount during a trial by fire. That he survived the accident, was a miracle."

"Or a testament to his hate," Siri offered softly.

"Yes. His hate. And I never guessed. It never occurred to me that he felt as he did."

Siri moved closer to him, giving comfort—and seeking it. "He—was here in the valley a long time. He—"

"I know, beloved," Hunter said gently. "I know what he did."

She lifted her head to look at him. "You know?"

Hunter touched her cheek gently. "It was in your mind. When I was trying to bring you back, I saw everything he'd done." He drew a deep breath. "My love, I don't know how you lived through it all. He was controlling our minds, making you do things, trying to seduce you. And I was battering at you, storming all your defenses like some animal—"

Siri pulled herself forward to kiss him. "Never an animal," she said softly. "And I'd go through all of it again as long as we loved like this in the end."

He drew her even closer, his eyes glowing. "Then I won't regret any of it, beloved. Anything is worth this."

Siri more than agreed.

For days they luxuriated in the sunlit warmth of their love. They lay together in the meadow, surrounded by the Unicorns, and basked in the waning Summer. They walked together, hand in hand, through the shaded, peaceful forest.

Bathed in eerie, beautiful moonlight, they watched in awed astonishment as the contented Unicorns broke one of their own laws and danced a second time in a single Summer.

And the bond between Siri and Hunter, forged in the crucible of love and agonizing choice, grew even stronger. The bond knit itself in tenderness and passion, knowledge and understanding, until two people were literally two halves of one.

And on a clear, fair morning as they sat together by the Crystal Pool, Siri's mother softly opened the doors of their minds with a gentle invitation.

I would like to see the man my daughter loves.

Siri and Hunter looked at one another for a long moment, sharing a thought it was unnecessary to voice aloud.

Mother? Isn't it dangerous?

No, child. Not now. His love for you is too strong to be set aside for another. It shields him from the madness.

I would be honored to meet you, Shauna.

Then come. Bundy will allow you to pass.

They rose and made their way toward the dragon-guarded entrance to the sea-cave. And Hunter was thinking of the creature he would soon meet, thinking and wondering.

"I remember the legend that a Mermaid is allowed to leave her sea and walk on land once in her lifetime. Is that when your mother found your father?"

Siri nodded. "Yes. To bear a Keeper, a Mermaid must fall in love with a mortal man, and he fall in love with a woman. Only afterward does he find out she's a Mermaid and must return to her sea."

"Then your father traveled overland to be here in the valley for your birth?"

"Yes. My mother was honest with him once she could tell him the truth. She explained the rules of Keepers, and told him that I would have to be raised here in this valley. Because she loved him, she warned him what could happen if he followed her. But he loved, and he followed. He had been a visitor here, not a Huntman but an explorer. He never believed Mother's race strange or unnatural, and I don't think he ever regretted following her."

"He'd be proud," Hunter said gently, "to see his daughter now."

"I like to think so." She felt the sudden heat of tears. "I never really stopped needing him."

Halting, Hunter drew her into his arms, holding her gently, wrapping her in his love and understanding.

Unsteadily, she said, "Mother never really got over his death. There's a Merman who adores her, but she's grieved so long. When I was old enough to try and understand, Mother talked to me about their curse. Their legends." She laughed shakily. "It seems we're all forced to contend with legends."

"What's theirs?" he asked quietly.

Siri knew that her mother was aware of the conversation and so would not expect them immediately in her cave. And she wanted to talk about this.

"When Merpeople first evolved, they were a happy, carefree race. They roamed the seas, unseen by man. They gathered knowledge and wisdom through their telepathy, but knew no curiosity strong enough to prompt a face-to-face meeting with other races.

"But one Mermaid was different from the others. She was intensely curious about men. Instead of seeking the depths when men passed over the surface of her sea, she began to follow and watch them. But when she surfaced beside their ships and tried to communicate with them, they fled in terror.

"Their fear frustrated her and, in time, angered her. And in her anger, she determined to make a man fall in love with her. So she found a creature of power."

"What kind of creature?" Hunter asked curiously.

Siri shook her head. "Not even the Merpeople are sure of that. But whatever this creature was, his power held little kindness. He asked her only for a ring made of coral, and when it was given to him, he promised to grant her two wishes. She asked that she be allowed to experience dry earth beneath her feet, and that she know the love of man."

Hunter felt the chill of foreboding. "I'm beginning to understand."

"Yes. She didn't phrase her requests very well, did

she? Experiencing dry land beneath human feet is not permanently shedding a tail, and knowing the love of *man . . .*"

"What happened?"

"As so often happens in the case of bargains, her victory became a curse instead of a blessing. And her price cursed her people. Before she could reach shore and gain the limbs she'd requested, she met a large shipload of men. And when she happily called out to them, they all abandoned their vessel to drown in the sea around her.

"She was shocked, bewildered. But she continued on to shore, and there walked upon human feet for the first—and last—time. She met a man and loved for a few days. Then compulsion drove her back to the sea and lost her the legs of humankind. And her love drowned when he mindlessly tried to join her.

"Grieving, she rushed back to the creature of power. But he laughed at her. She had gotten her wishes, he pointed out. She had felt earth beneath her human feet, and man would love her madly, endlessly, forever. She retreated to the depths, heartbroken. In time, she found a Merman to love, and bore him children. And discovered to her horror that her daughters shared her curse. Men loved them madly."

"So the curse was passed on. Endlessly."

"Yes. The Mermaids bore daughters cursed from birth to destroy any man who saw or heard them. In time, all Mermaids carried the curse. The Mermen escaped the taint, but they, too, were cursed in having to helplessly watch their womenfolk grow sad and haunted."

Hunter was silent for a long moment. "Yet the Guardians demand that the Keeper of the Unicorns be a child of Mermaid and man. How can they demand such a sacrifice?"

Siri sighed. "Bargains. Even the Guardians bargain and demand prices; we've guessed that. The Merpeople asked for protection against the predators of the sea—and were granted it. In the open seas, they're protected by dolphins. In landlocked or underground seas, dragons guard them. In return for that protection, they were asked to bear Keepers.

"But Keepers are at least not required frequently. Many Mermaids are spared that pain. The ones who are chosen must watch the men they love die. And for ten thousand years we Keepers have been doomed to be fatherless because of what we are."

Hunter, silent, comforting, hugged her gently.

After a moment, Siri stepped back with a faint smile, taking his hand. "Mother's expecting us."

"Thank you for telling me," he said quietly. Then, seeking to comfort, he added, "Perhaps the Guardians intend to put everything right one day."

"Perhaps. I hope so."

They reached the entrance to the sea-cave, finding the colorful dragon awaiting them somewhat balefully. His deceptively mild black eyes were half-lidded and his huge body completely blocked the cave from immediately inside the entrance.

"We were invited, Bundy," Siri told him severely. "You know that. Come out."

Bundy coughed a brief, hot flame, clearly indicating disgust, and began maneuvering his vast bulk toward the entrance.

"What's wrong with him?" Hunter asked warily, drawing Siri to one side of the dragon-blocked opening.

"He's disgruntled," Siri explained dryly. "Cave-dragons, unlike some of their brethren, strongly dislike sunlight. Bundy has to wait for us out here, and he isn't happy about it."

At last Bundy worked his awkward body from the cave. He was twice as large in the sunlight, his scales reflecting brilliantly and his bulk no longer squeezed into a cave at least one size too small.

After contemplating him for a moment, Hunter said, "Shall we go and visit your mother?" He took Siri's hand, trying not to wonder if he had really seen one of Bundy's mild eyes closing in a lazy wink.

They entered the cave. It tunneled through The Reaper's black stone base, narrowing as they walked until it was barely large enough for them to continue side by side.

The walls were smooth, as if worn by time or a gentle giant's hand. The floor was dry and just rough enough to give purchase to their boots. And it grew lighter as they walked, the very walls seeming to glow like those in the Unicorns' cave. Then they rounded a curve and stepped out of the tunnel, entering the chamber holding the sea.

It was vast. Tremendous. Incredibly huge. The walls glowed; the ceiling, impossibly high above, glowed. And within the day-bright glow was cradled a clear blue sparkling sea that could have held a small fleet of ships. A sandy beach curved all around the water, ending only where another tunnel could be seen.

The underground "river," Hunter realized. He noticed no movement other than that of the gentle waves at first, then saw something else. And he understood why a man— any man—could throw himself mindlessly into the sea to his death.

"Hello, Hunter."

Her voice was the origin of music. And she was stunningly, heartbreakingly beautiful. Silver hair fell in a soft curtain, framing her delicate, ageless face. Black eyes held the depth of oceans, the gentle wisdom and sadness of ages and curses. Her smile was serenity hard-won. And smooth golden flesh merged softly and gradually into light blue, satiny scales just below her waist, curving over the rock she sat upon to form a wide and graceful tail caressed by lapping waves.

"Hello, Shauna," he murmured. He understood now. The madness. But it did not, as she had promised, touch him. He saw and appreciated her beauty, but his heart was Siri's.

She gestured slightly, with that almost eerie, unconscious grace she had passed on to her daughter. "Come and sit down," she invited, smiling.

They did. Sitting, the two bipedal beings gazed in gentleness and understanding at the beautiful creature cursed to be loved to the point of madness by men.

"All peoples bear curses, Hunter," she said gently.

"What's mankind's curse?" he asked.

"Striving," she answered instantly. "Striving always in conflict. Never able to rest on the laurels of achievement."

He realized she was right. Mankind, of all creatures, was never content with what he had built, with what he knew. Always, there was a need for more.

"Dragons?"

"Their unreality," Shauna said with a smile.

"They live," he ventured, troubled by that.

"As myth."

"They exist."

"To those who see."

Hunter fumbled for understanding. "See with the heart?"

"See with the soul."

"But they guard. They frighten soulless men."

Shauna smiled again. "Fear stirs in a blind soul; understanding stirs in a sighted one."

Hunter allowed that to sink into his mind in silence. Dragons. Guards. Created out of fear. Nightmares. Out of the blankness of an unknown horizon. What had Siri said? That man had created myths out of ignorance, and destroyed them in . . . knowledge. Hunter concentrated on grasping the elusive answer, reaching out firmly. Unicorns were dreams of beauty, born in grace. Lovely dreams. They existed despite knowledge, because they were . . . magic. Not threatening. Not frightening. No challenge to science when Nature was filled with absurdities such as camels and giraffes. Merely magical, pleasant dreams. And they were guarded by the daughter of myth and—man.

There was something . . .

He looked fixedly at Siri, dimly aware of the presence of both mother and daughter in his mind, waiting quietly for him to find his way.

The daughter of myth and man. Shaped by her heritage to understand . . . both. The daughter of man, keeping his dreams alive. The daughter of myth, understanding the tremulous fragility of dreams. Keeper. Gatekeeper. *Gatekeeper.* Standing in a doorway, with a foot planted in two realities, two worlds. She alone held off extinction of myth. She alone preserved man's dreams from his careless abandonment.

He vaguely heard a deep sigh from his love, but his mind was still busy twisting and turning, in pursuit of the last enigma.

Dragons. In abandoning myth in favor of science, man had released first the dragons conjured from nightmare fear. The dragon threatened what was known to be true, to be real. No living creature could breathe fire. Ergo, dragons did not exist. *Could not* exist in man's world—or in his dreams.

They could only exist in myth. They guarded myths. *They were real only to myths*. And, Hunter realized, to him. Because he had sought and found a mythical valley filled with impossibilities. Because his love for the daughter of myth and man had opened an ancient, sighted part of his soul.

He looked at Shauna, who nodded gravely.

"Now I understand," he said. "The answer was before me all the time, and I didn't see it."

"You couldn't see it," Shauna said gently. "Not then. Now you've learned to see."

Hunter's hand tightened around Siri's, and he looked at her with wondering eyes. "You told me yourself—but I didn't listen. You said you were the only thing standing between the Unicorns and extinction—and you meant that literally. Myth, created by man, must be preserved by some part of man. But that part of man must also be of myth, to understand myth. The daughter of man protects his dreams for him."

Quietly, Siri said, "And you are descended from a Guardian, with their understanding buried inside you."

Smiling, Shauna said, "Together, you have forged a new beginning. For yourselves . . . and for all creatures born of myth. You share the final guardianship of the Unicorns."

"Final . . ." Siri stared at her mother. "No more Keepers?"

"No, child. You're the last of your kind."

"But—the Unicorns!" It was Hunter who protested aloud.

Shauna's laugh was happy music. "The Unicorns stand

at the threshold of their future. It is time for myth to be reborn in the hearts of mankind. It will take time, but even now the changes begin. Events set in motion long, long ago near their culmination. Hunter was more right than he knew. The Guardians will set all aright . . . in time. We Merpeople are released from our promise to bear Keepers, for they are no longer needed. And your children, with their combined heritage, will pay the debts of many myths. As it was written long ago."

Hunter was troubled. "That . . . dangerous quest my own ancestor agreed to?"

Shauna understood. "That is a part of the new beginning. Your firstborn will leave on a quest—just as you came here on a quest. It was foretold." Her voice was gentle, soothing. "But that is years in the future, Hunter."

"Mother . . ." Siri spoke hesitantly. "Why will there be no more Keepers after me? Keepers *must* watch the doorway between myth and man—"

"Not if man reclaims his myths. The doorway—the gate—was formed to prevent man's myths from slipping completely away from him. But soon man's myths must rejoin him, and that gate will close behind them. Men are troubled, Daughter, just as Hunter was troubled. Their worlds are rife with revolution and rebellion. They once sought myth in fear and ignorance; now they seek dream because they need something to temper the harshness of reality. They ache to know again the eternal youth and freedom of dreams. They have nearly come full circle to the unconscious wisdom of their own needs."

"I'm glad," Siri said finally, simply.

"So am I," Hunter said, indeed glad that man would learn to cherish his dreams.

So are we all.

They turned, startled, to see Storm standing quietly behind them on the sandy beach. His noble form seemed illuminated by the glow of the cavern, and his wise eyes were serene.

"Bundy let you pass?" Hunter asked.

Of course. I stand too near reality to be threatened by his unreality. Perhaps mankind will reclaim his nightmares as well as his dreams; only then will dragons challenge us in battle. But I think their day is past. They will never be as real as they were at one time.

Hunter felt a pang, thinking of his first meeting with Bundy. It was sad, he thought, that other men would not know that wonder and astonishment.

They will always be real to you, Green-eyes.

Shauna laughed softly. "Indeed, Leader. For now, however, you and I must see these two children wed."

Hunter was mildly surprised, though not at all displeased. "Is there a ceremony? I assumed, since no Keeper had ever wed—"

Shauna smiled at him. "A ceremony was planned, long ago, for you." She held out a hand as Storm stepped nearer, accepting into her palm the two golden rings that dropped from the Unicorn's mouth. "Made from the golden dust of the Unicorns' horns, given by them joyously."

Siri and Hunter gazed, awed, at the rings that had been woven from the dust of dreams.

Shauna's voice grew suddenly shy. "And I . . . ask that you also witness a ceremony involving myself."

"And me." There was a splash, and another form joined Shauna's on the wide rock.

He was a man from the waist up. Wide-shouldered, powerful. His hair was as dark as hers was fair, and his face as beautiful in masculine form as hers was in feminine traits. Bronze flesh merged smoothly into dark blue, satiny scales just below his waist. His lean face was neatly bearded, and blue eyes gleamed with humor and wisdom and love.

"Tork!" Siri looked at him in surprise. "I didn't know you were visiting Mother."

"All Summer," he confirmed cheerfully, the bass rumble of his voice as peculiarly musical as the Mermaid's. "And much good it did me! She's been frustratingly occupied with her troublesome offspring!" Laughing blue eyes belied the severe words and tone. "Now, however, she has at last got you settled. And my patience has run out!"

"You were never patient," Shauna told him lovingly. She smiled shyly at Hunter and Siri. "My mate-to-be," she

said, confirming the obvious, then anxiously asked Siri,
"You don't mind?"

"Mind?" Siri laughed delightedly. "I think it's wonderful!" She leaned forward to hug both Merpeople. "And
about time, too!"

Hunter, offering his own congratulations, saluted
Shauna's cheek gently and exchanged a warm and friendly
handshake with Tork, finding nothing at all peculiar in
either action.

When you're all finished, Storm inserted dryly, *we can
begin. The guests have arrived.*

And they had. All around the sea, seated on rocks,
leaning comfortably on the sandy beach, were a score of
Merpeople. They varied widely in coloring and features,
and spanned ages from a very old silver-bearded Merman to
an infant Mermaid cooing contentedly. They called out
greetings to Hunter cheerfully and congratulations to both
pairs of lovers, and all spoke to Storm with respect and
affection.

Hunter, fascinated, was deeply moved by the generos-
ity that enabled these cursed creatures to reach beyond
their own generations-deep sadness to embrace the joy of
the occasion. They were gentle and friendly, their beautiful
faces alight with happiness and their sad, deep eyes
shining. The Mermen were strong and clearly protective of
their mates and children; the Mermaids were somewhat
shy and gentle, and all were obviously grateful for the love
that kept Hunter safe from their cursed attraction.

And the ceremonies began, filled with ancient words,
promises of love and caring, spoken mentally and aloud, by
myths . . . and the child of myth . . . and the descen-
dant of a goddess.

Thirteen

Hunter and Siri barely noticed that the guests had gone, or that Storm had left the chamber. When they were finally able to tear their eyes from one another, they found only Shauna and Tork, their hands lovingly entwined, watching them with smiles.

Siri blinked uncertainly. "They've gone?"

Tork frowned at her reprovingly, his eyes dancing. "I make no allowances for the blindness of love, Daughter! Or for the ignorance of Keepers. It is the inborn tact of bridal guests which makes them speedily depart after the ceremony; they assume the wedded couples wish to be alone. And I, my patience tried sorely once again, wait for you two children to take yourselves off!"

Shauna, to everyone's amusement—including her own—was blushing.

Laughing, Hunter and Siri rose to their human feet.

"You won't leave this sea?" Siri asked.

"No," Shauna replied, studiously avoiding the warm, merry eyes of her new husband. "Not until Winter comes."

"But for now—" Tork said pointedly.

"We're going!" Siri laughed at him.

"Good," he said promptly, grinning.

Hunter and Siri left the sea-chamber hand in hand and made their way back to the entrance. They emerged into the sunlight and watched Bundy turn his bulk and squeeze it backward into the cave with a last wink.

They began walking through the woods toward the Crystal Pool.

"Wife," Hunter said, satisfied, content.

"Husband." Siri smiled up at him.

He stopped walking suddenly, enfolding her in a fierce, tender embrace. "Wedded by myths," he murmured huskily.

There was a glint of hot purple fire in her dancing eyes. "But very human for all of that," she said. "With human thoughts, human . . . desires."

"Like us."

"Very like us, my love."

His eyes glinted down at her. "I've never made love to a wife," he noted thoughtfully.

"Nor I to a husband."

With abrupt and lusty abandon, Hunter lifted her and tossed her slight, laughing weight easily over his shoulder, striding purposefully through the forest.

Summer waned.

Siri and Hunter spent every moment possible among the Unicorns, knowing their time with the herd was growing short. They often sat outside the cabin, just watching the herd, and on one such occasion, Hunter commented on the Leader and his consort.

"Those two have certainly matured."

Siri nodded. "It's a shame Fancy is barren. She adores Storm, and would give half her life to bear his foal."

"It's certain she's barren?"

"Cloud told me, and he knew."

Hunter, like Siri, fiercely resented any marring of their Unicorns' happiness. "That doesn't seem fair. She'd make a good mother, too."

Thank you, Green-eyes. There was something utterly content in Fancy's mind-voice, and a curious, muted jubilation.

The two humans looked at each other, sharing a sudden astonishment. Could it possibly be—?

Fancy? they voiced with one mind.

Delighted, feminine Unicorn laughter. *Next Summer, I'll bear Storm's foal!*

Siri gasped. *But, how?*

How do you think? Storm countered, amused.

That isn't what I meant! She was barren. Cloud knew. She was barren, Storm agreed calmly.

Then—? Hunter joined the mental questioning.

A blessing, the Leader told them, his own delight threaded through the wise mind-voice. *Conceived during the second Dance, when all things are possible. Now we await another birth. A golden birth, the final blessing of our future.*

"A golden birth?" Hunter looked at Siri.

"I don't know what it means." *Storm?* she asked. And was politely ignored. "He's not going to explain," she told Hunter dryly.

"That doesn't surprise me."

It was Hunter who realized one important fact, and he mentioned it to Siri one bright day while they were swimming lazily in the Crystal Pool.

"*Keeper* comes from the word *Gatekeeper*—right?"

Floating bonelessly on her back, Siri looked over at him as he made his way to the submerged rock he favored for a seat. "Right. Why?"

"You're Keeper of the Unicorns." His eyes were enjoying the sight of her floating in clear water and dappled by sunlight. "But you're not Keeper of anything else—no other myth, I mean."

"True. There are really no other creatures of myth in the valley that require a Keeper."

"Then," Hunter said slowly, "there must be other gates . . . and other Keepers."

"Because there are other myths."

"Pegasus. Centaurs. Elves. Shapechangers. And how many others?" He shook his head slightly. "If all of them are waiting for man to reclaim them . . ."

"Think of the Gates," Siri said softly, her eyes glowing. "All those Gates held and guarded by Keepers. All the generations of waiting."

"And all of them have to be, like you, the offspring of myth and man. I wonder how many other Keepers are aware that the changes have begun, that soon there'll be no need of Gates?"

Soon is a relative term.

They looked up, seeing Storm gazing down on them from the rocks where the waterfall began its downward plunge.

"You always jump into conversations," Hunter chided. He and Siri had discovered that it was much less confusing for them to speak aloud to the Unicorns whenever possible, and had adopted the practice.

Shall I leave? Storm inquired politely.

"No. You're here." Hunter looked at Siri. "Do you think he'd condescend to answer a few questions?"

Siri moved to join him. "We can but try."

Hunter stared up at the Unicorn, then muttered under his breath to Siri, "There's something very undignified about questioning a myth with no clothes on."

I don't need clothes.

Siri giggled.

"Very funny." Hunter frowned at the Leader. "We have questions."

I've never known a time when you didn't.

Hunter sighed. "We're wondering about the other Gates."

What about them?

"Well . . . they exist?"

They exist.

"And there are other Keepers?"

There are other . . . devices to guard the Gates. Not necessarily Keepers.

"But there are other Keepers?" Siri asked.

Storm rubbed his bearded chin absently against a rock.

"He's ignoring us," Hunter observed.

"Isn't he." Siri narrowed her eyes at the Unicorn. "Storm, if there are things you don't want to tell us, just say so."

There are things I don't want to tell you, the Leader said blandly.

"Why?" Hunter demanded.

Because.

"I wonder what Unicorn stew tastes like," Hunter said reflectively.

Terrible.

"We won't know unless we try," Siri said severely.

Humans don't understand humor.

"Neither do Unicorns," Hunter said threateningly.

Has it occurred to you two that there are some answers I'm forbidden to provide for you?

Somewhat mollified, Hunter said, "And that's one of them, I suppose."

No.

Hunter ran his fingers through his hair.

Siri choked on a laugh, and tried to sound stern. "Storm, just tell us if there are other Keepers."

Not at the moment.

"No other Keepers at the moment? Then I really am the last?" she wondered uncertainly.

No. The last Keeper of the Unicorns, but not the last Keeper. Another will be last.

"Storm—"

The last of the silver-haired, black-eyed Keepers will guard the Unicorns, Storm said in the curious tone of a litany. *But another will seek and keep creatures of the gods. And that other will be the final Gatekeeper, for there is one myth that will be the last to rejoin man's world.*

Hunter sighed. "I'm sorry we asked."

"I don't suppose he'd explain—"

Storm left the rocks to vanish into the forest.

"Obviously not," Hunter said.

Summer waned.

They had decided that as soon as the Unicorns left the valley, they would begin the trip to Rubicon. Hunter's ship was fast; it would take only a few months. He thought that the Council and people of Rubicon would accept a king who required a year or so each ten years in which to return to his wife's world.

And with their history returned to them, perhaps Rubicon would be healed. Perhaps. It was enough that Hunter would return to his world a richer man in many ways, enough that he had found much more than a myth in his Quest. He doubted the Council would be disappointed that he offered no proof either way of Unicorns' existence.

Unicorns would remain dreams.

Summer waned.

Siri slept peacefully, her head in Hunter's lap, beneath their favorite tree near the cabin. The sun was at its peak in the sky, shining down on another lazy day. She had napped often these last days, reclining in the sun or shade like a lazy cat. And she slept more deeply at night than she had in days past, curling up to him contentedly, reveling in the embrace that never loosened, even when he slept deeply.

Hunter, a bit drowsy himself, didn't realize at first that something was happening. But when he finally saw, he made no sound aloud. *Beloved? There's something . . .*

She stirred, the violet eyes opening slowly. "What, love?" she murmured.

"Look."

She sat up slowly, gazing in puzzlement as Storm and Fancy stood before them, obviously waiting. Fancy dropped a triangular bit of white before the two humans.

From Bundy. He regrets being unable to make his way through the woods.

They stared in bewilderment, both recognizing the smooth, unmarked ivory of a dragon's tooth.

Fancy dropped a second object. *From the Merpeople.* It was a necklace made of colorful coral. And then something dropped from Storm's mouth, a delicate circlet of gleaming gold even more finely made than their rings. A bracelet.

From the Unicorns, Storm said. *Made as your rings were made.*

"Why?" Siri at last found her voice.

Gifts. The Leader was placid.

Bewildered, Hunter asked, "Because Summer is nearly over?"

No, blind one.

"Then why?" Siri asked.

Both blind, Fancy observed merrily.

And ignorant, Storm added dryly. The Unicorn chuckles died into silence as the two white creatures moved gracefully back to their meadow.

Then, chidingly, two voices dropped into their minds. It was clearly a conversation between Tork and Shauna, and very clearly aimed at the humans.

Ignorant children! Tork scoffed.

They just haven't realized.

They never will, at this rate!

Siri frowned fiercely. *Mother! What does this mean?*

You know, child. The instincts are ancient, and buried deeply within you. Feel. Be aware of your own body.

Abruptly, Hunter began to realize what the gifts meant. And he could see dawning realization on Siri's expressive face.

You see? Shauna was speaking to her mate. *They do understand.*

About time, Tork grumbled.

Then the mind-voices were gone.

Siri's slender hands folded instinctively, protectively, over her still-flat middle. "Hunter . . ."

"A child?" He stared, feeling ridiculously dazed, into her wide, startled eyes.

"A child. Our child!" She rose to her knees, her arms sliding around his neck, her face alight.

Hunter held her tightly, the dazed feeling exploding into delight, into wonder. "Our child," he murmured huskily, kissing her with deep tenderness. And crowding

into his mind were also new realizations of responsibilities
and the awesome weight of parental hopes and fears. It was
terrifying. And he looked at her in sudden anxiety, the
dangers of giving birth uppermost in his mind. "To put you
through that, beloved . . ."

"I'll be fine," she said serenely.

"It scares the life out of me," he confessed raspingly.

She framed his face in gentle hands. "I'll never leave
you," she said softly, utter certainty firm in her tone. "I love
you too much to leave this life without you."

For that moment, it was enough. The fear would
trouble him again, he knew. In the dark predawn hours as
he held her in his arms. In the sudden, frightening
moments of understood mortality. In the naked time of
nightmares. In the deepest part of his soul.

But for that moment, it was enough. She carried a
living result of their love, and not even fear for her could
taint that.

Days passed.
Fall crept nearer on soundless feet.

Child, the cards.

Siri whirled from the doorway where she and Hunter
stood gazing out over the valley, her face ashen. She raced
to get the cards from their shelf where they lay alongside
the two horns reclaimed from Boran's pack, realizing in
sudden anguished guilt that she had not read them for too
many days now. Preoccupied with the peaceful serenity of
their life, she had forgotten the threat of danger.

Summer wasn't over yet.

And Hunter, tensely silent, didn't question as he
watched her rapid actions. She'd been somehow alerted,
warned, he realized. Perhaps by Shauna; he had long ago
grasped that there was some communication, deeper than
the mental, between Siri and her mother. She'd been
warned, and foreboding gripped him now with icy fingers.

Siri's fingers were unnaturally steady as they laid out the cards in the familiar pattern on the table. But her face was white, her eyes stricken. She stared down at the cards, blind for a moment in fear, her eyes clearing slowly. She forced her mind to see, to interpret and understand. To absorb cryptic symbols.

"No!" she moaned almost soundlessly, frantic eyes racing over the pattern again and again.

Huntmen. And a familiar blankness.

Already in the valley.

"Hunter!" She left the cards where they lay, spinning to face her love. "They're already in the valley. And—"

"What?" he asked, an icy chill skipping down his spine, because her face had gone impossibly whiter, her eyes unfocused as if all her senses were turned desperately inward.

"It's—blank again," she whispered. "Wrong."

Hunter felt so cold he thought he'd splinter if he even breathed. "He's dead. I felt his neck snap in my hands. He couldn't have survived that."

"I can feel him now." Siri looked blindly at Hunter. "His mind. As twisted and scarred as his face. He's *alive*, Hunter! Somehow, he's alive."

They stared at each other, both grappling with the impossible and finally accepting it, because it was Boran, because his hate had been so alive it could not be killed.

"The Unicorns—" Hunter's voice was hoarse.

Instantly, his mind joined hers in sending a frantic warning winging toward their charges. And they looked at each other in horror as both absorbed Storm's taut, warning reply.

Maya foals in the glade.

"We can't move her to the cave?" Hunter questioned tensely, reaching for and strapping on the knife he'd not worn for so long.

"No." Siri was collecting weapons also, a pitiful few weapons recovered from Huntmen. The bow that replaced her own splintered one. Arrows. One spear. A crossbow and three lone shafts. Her own knife. "No, she won't leave the glade now until the birth. Storm's taking the others to the cave; he'll do the best he can to hide the opening."

"We have to protect the glade," Hunter said, his tone grim. ·

"Yes. We can spare no energy for searching them out; we have to wait near the glade and protect it at all costs."

Hunter accepted the spear and crossbow from her, his green eyes dropping anxiously to watch her hand move with unconscious protectiveness over her flat belly. A cry of protest against endangering her or their child rose in his throat, blocked there, unsaid.

Their eyes met.

"We have no choice," she whispered, understanding, sharing his fear. This time, Boran would not be distracted by thoughts of possessing Siri or even of watching Hunter suffer emotionally. This time, only blood would satisfy his insane hatred.

"I know." He looked down abstractedly, a part of his mind noting that they were hardly dressed for battle in their comfortable white tunics. They were, at least, both wearing boots. His warrior-trained mind examined the possibility of any loss of movement or flexibility caused by the tunics. There was none. If anything, the garments offered them increased freedom.

He looked at her again, needing to say so much, having learned from the last time that the end could come too suddenly for final words. He hauled her against his side, ignoring the prodding of knife hafts and arrows and spear, holding her with a desperate fear.

"I love you," he said intensely, claiming her lips.

She held him with her own supple strength, flame meeting flame in their kiss, murmuring when she could, "I love you. We won't lose. We won't!"

Hunter hesitated, then turned quickly away from her. When he returned to her side, the talisman ring of his ancestors lay in the palm of his hand. "If there's any power in this," he said roughly, "we need it now."

Siri drew out one of the spare laces she kept for her clothing and quickly knotted it to fashion a necklace. In a moment the ring lay hidden inside Hunter's tunic, nestled against his chest.

And then they were out of the cabin and in the forest, racing with fleet speed lent by fear toward the glade where a Unicorn mare was giving birth alone. There was no more talk. No time for talk. No breath for talk. They separated at the glade, both circling the bramble-protected, almost impenetrable haven, moving watchfully, alertly, making certain no enemy had yet reached the precious spot.

The forest was utterly still, tense in waiting. No bird sang out in melodic happiness. No breeze disturbed the hot breathlessness of the valley. In the sun-dappled quiet surrounding the glade, the two humans paced warily.

Summer was nearly over.

Hunter searched the woods, his ears straining to catch the faintest betraying sound. He moved with sure instinct, never pausing for more than a moment in one place, his booted feet silent. His awareness of Siri, of the quicksilver coolness of her thoughts, was an ever-present thing, ingrained by love to become a part of him. Neither was he distracted by that sharing of awareness; it had become as natural to him as breathing.

It was his own thoughts that tormented him, taunted him, this grinding anxiety for the safety of his wife and child. Though Boran had been obsessed by Siri, perhaps was even now obsessed, her pregnancy made her a deadly threat to his hopes of ruling Rubicon. He could never rest as long as Hunter's heir lived.

Given a choice, Hunter might well have hidden Siri away, guarding her as fiercely as they now guarded the impending Unicorn birth. Given that choice, and disregarding her own nature and upbringing . . . but he couldn't do that.

In times of battle, women fought beside their men.

He accepted that fact in his mind, but his heart cried out, railing against the unfairness of this testing of womanly steel. Life tested them so harshly, he thought, and even the knowledge that his own woman was far better prepared for it than most did little to comfort him.

She should not have to do this!

It was cruel enough that she be forced to brave the long, harsh Winter alone and battle for her own and the Unicorns' lives in the brief Summer. It was cruel enough that her healing hands be stained again and again with the blood she was forced to shed. It was, the gods knew, cruel enough that she act as a gate between brutal man and the lovely myth she guarded.

But it was unpardonably, unthinkably cruel that she be forced into battle while carrying the seed of new life within her body.

Siri, too, was occupied by thought. Like Hunter, she was aware of his constant presence in her mind; like him, she was not distracted by it. Even more than he, she was comfortable with the mind-touch, to the point of barely being aware of it.

But she was fully aware of her own changed body. The hand not holding her bow at the ready moved often, unbidden, to protectively touch her middle. She felt a tendency to shield that part of her, to avoid any possible blow that would have, weeks before, been unthinkingly cushioned by lithe muscles.

And there was fear. A deep, instinctive fear for the child she cradled within her. Her awareness did not distract her from the dangers hovering oppressively over them. Instead, there was an enhancement of all her senses, those turned inward and outward. Energy replaced the lethargy of past days, flowing into her as if from a source she had never tapped before, never needed to tap.

And she was conscious as she had never been of the life waiting to be born within the glade. Last offspring of Cloud, her beloved friend.

The first two attacked alone, viciously, violently, single-minded in their determination and greedy blood lust.

There was no time for weapons other than knives, bare hands, and booted heels. No strength for anything other than forcing protesting muscles to their very limits.

Hunter spared a moment's thought for the thankful realization that these Huntmen were unused to prey that met them in fierce defense and fought violently, unused to

their quarry's skill. They should have rushed the glade,
overwhelmed their targets with two-to-one superiority. But
they had not. Thankfully, they had not.

And they had no weapons other than knives.

Boran had a knife as well—the knife of his powerful,
maddened mind. He was an expert tactician, and Hunter
knew he was out there somewhere. Waiting. Waiting for his
henchmen to wear them down, exhaust them.

Life struggled over death in the shaded forest, only
soft scuffles and panting curses marking the battle. Muscles
shrieked silently in inhuman effort, forced by need to
unknown strength. Agile skill and sheer raw power fought
mightily for victory.

And then it was over.

Siri? He couldn't see her.

Unhurt. And you?

Fine. He brushed absently at the blood of a deep slash
across his ribs, not even feeling the wound. There would,
hopefully, be time later for pain. If Boran allowed them any
time at all. If they were able to defeat him. Hunter knew he
was too tense, too tightly wound for a confrontation such as
the coming one promised to be. But there was nothing he
could do about that; his tension sprang from animal instinct
as well as knowledge.

Boran would come. In a hatred so violently powerful it
had defied death, he would attack his enemies, driven by
the bestial desire to tear limb from limb.

Hunter knew that.

He picked up his fallen weapons, moved once again,
prowling, his senses alert. Then a sudden thought. *The
Unicorns?*

We're safe. Take care.

He thought, idly, that Storm had turned out to be a
good Leader. He realized that his emotions had numbed in
battle, perhaps a safeguard meant to focus all energies on
his enemy, on survival. He prowled steadily, silently. His
warrior instincts told him that he and Siri moved at the
same pace around the glade, keeping it between them,
leaving as little as possible unprotected by at least one of
them.

He wanted to see her.

And he did, but not as he wanted to.

Two more Huntmen rushed him, carrying him off his feet in the strength of their coming. He rolled, gaining his feet again just in time to dodge a lethal slash of a knife. A booted kick sent one sprawling, leaving the other to close with Hunter in a murderous struggle.

And Siri was there, leaping at the fallen one, a single heartbeat too slow to keep him down permanently. Her black warrior eyes were flashing their warning of death, her slender strength a lethal force.

Hunter could no more keep his eyes off her than he could voluntarily stop breathing, but the sight of her spurred his own strength rather than distracted from it. He kicked the feet from beneath his adversary, drawing the knife he'd had no time to reach for until now and thrusting it home in a single merciless blow. He saw Siri struggling with her opponent on the ground, his knife scant inches from her throat. Then, with a surge of inhuman strength, her own knife found its target.

And it was while she was in that vulnerable position that Boran, master tactician, chose to strike. He was there instantly, kicking Siri's knife from her hand even as he dragged her away from her fallen victim. He pinned her arms, his knee pressed hard into the small of her back, arching her slender body. His knife was at her throat.

Even beyond his fear for Siri, Hunter felt his flesh prickle with a different kind of horror, an unearthly chill. Boran's neck *had* been broken in their earlier battle, and his head rested on one hunched shoulder; it lolled with his every movement, a thing apart from the body that no longer supported it. His once-good eye was seared, a blackened pit in the angelic side of his face. And Hunter saw the amulet then, glowing green as the blinded eye had once done, as if Boran's sight and all his power inhabited crystal rather than flesh.

Hunter knew Boran was blind, his eyes useless. But he was also aware that Boran could, somehow, see, because he could feel the inimical shaft of that vision—from the amulet.

"Boran—"

"Fetch the talisman, or I'll cut her throat!"

"The talisman? What are you talking about?"

"The ring, goddamn you! I was your childhood's shadow, remember? I saw Caprice give the ring to you. The ring that should have been mine. *I* was firstborn. With that talisman I'll be invincible!"

Hunter tried to think. "The ring has nothing to do with rulership, Boran."

"Give me the talisman or I'll cut her throat!"

"Don't, Hunter." Siri's voice was steady. "He'll kill me anyway. You know that."

Boran chuckled. "Don't you trust my word, princess?"

He leaned forward as he spoke, and Siri saw the pulsating green shimmer of the amulet as it swung outward past her cheek. His power. The amulet was alive with his power.

Ignoring his taunt, she tried to gain the time she needed to gather her own mental energies. "You should be dead. Even the Unicorns thought you were dead."

"Because that's what I wanted them to think," Boran told her, then added in a chillingly conversational tone, "Hunter, if you move again, I'll kill her."

Hunter, who had barely shifted toward them, went still.

In the same conversational tone, Boran went on, explaining his resurrection. "You blinded me, of course, and Hunter tried to kill me. But neither of you knew how powerful I was even then. The amulet saved me. It even gave me back my sight."

She had to aim all her energies toward his sight again, Siri realized. But this time her target was a crystal amulet. She needed time. "But how did you—"

"I want the talisman," Boran snapped to Hunter. "Now!"

"Let her go," Hunter demanded.

"Give me the talisman," Boran said, "and I will." On the insanely lolling head, slack lips twisted in a hideous smile. And, slowly, his head rolled to rest on the opposite shoulder until Hunter could see only the blackened, pitted side of his face.

Hunter reached to free the talisman from his tunic. He knew Boran wouldn't let Siri go, but a glance at her inward-turned eyes told him she was preparing herself for some attempt, and he wanted to give her that chance.

Boran stiffened visibly, and the amulet seemed to glow with increased brightness. "Throw it to me!" he ordered.

Hunter drew the necklace over his head and tossed it. He thought Siri might try to escape as Boran reached for the necklace, but she lay pinned, his knee at her back and the knife at her throat.

Instantly Boran slipped the necklace over his head, allowing the ring to lie alongside the amulet. And he didn't seem to notice, as Hunter did, that the talisman barely touched the amulet before sliding away from it jerkily, as though physically repelled.

"Let her go, Boran."

Boran laughed. "Fool! Do you think I don't know your seed took root in her belly? I won't allow your bastard to steal my throne!" He caught his breath in a horrible chortling laugh. "I'll cut it out of her belly, that's what I'll do. I'll cut it out, and then she can be all mine—"

The brutal threat caught the last tendrils of Siri's focusing energies and fused them into a desperate thrust outward, aimed at the amulet she couldn't even see.

Boran cried out and fell backward away from her to lie writhing on the ground. The amulet at his throat was darkened, but dim flashes of green fire webbed outward from the center.

Siri turned as Hunter lunged past her. Yanking the amulet from Boran's neck, snapping the chain, he threw it to the ground. It was Siri who found a large stone and carried it to her husband, both of them realizing, finally, what they had to do to destroy this evil.

The stone crashed down on the dimly glowing amulet, shattering it into shards of lifeless crystal.

Boran twitched once and lay still.

Then, in a moment out of time, Maya stepped from the glade. And at her side—

Twins.

They were gleaming gold, from tiny muzzles to minute hooves, long-legged and unsteady. Deep golden eyes, bewildered and afraid, looked on their first glimpse of a world outside their birth-glade.

The golden birth.

Epilogue

Fall.

She sat alone in the library, an old woman with old eyes, carefully transferring the last of the books to their most compact form. Satisfied, she gazed on the neat packages, nodding to herself. Yes, they would fit into his ship. And there would be no difficulty in reprinting the books on Rubicon.

Everything was ready.

"Maggie?"

Maggie O'Shea turned and looked at them with a smile, a tall, handsome prince and the beautiful Keeper at his side.

"Maggie," said Hunter softly, "there's someone I want you to meet."

Smiling, her ancient eyes glowing, Maggie said, "I've been waiting. I've been waiting such a long time."

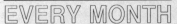

The first Delaney trilogy

Heirs to a great dynasty, the Delaney brothers were united by blood, united by devotion to their rugged land . . . and known far and wide as

THE SHAMROCK TRINITY

Bantam's bestselling LOVESWEPT romance line built its reputation on quality and innovation. Now, a remarkable and unique event in romance publishing comes from the same source: THE SHAMROCK TRINITY, three daringly original novels written by three of the most successful women's romance writers today. Kay Hooper, Iris Johansen, and Fayrene Preston have created a trio of books that are dynamite love stories bursting with strong, fascinating male and female characters, deeply sensual love scenes, the humor for which LOVESWEPT is famous, and a deliciously fresh approach to romance writing.

THE SHAMROCK TRINITY—Burke, York, and Rafe: Powerful men . . . rakes and charmers . . . they needed only love to make their lives complete.

☐ *RAFE, THE MAVERICK by Kay Hooper*

Rafe Delaney was a heartbreaker whose ebony eyes held laughing devils and whose lilting voice could charm any lady—or any horse—until a stallion named Diablo left him in the dust. It took Maggie O'Riley to work her magic on the impossible horse . . . and on his bold owner. Maggie's grace and strength made Rafe yearn to share the raw beauty of his land with her, to teach her the exquisite pleasure of yielding to the heat inside her. Maggie was stirred by Rafe's passion, but would his reputation and her ambition keep their kindred spirits apart?   (21846 • $2.75)

LOVESWEPT

☐ *YORK, THE RENEGADE by Iris Johansen*

Some men were made to fight dragons, Sierra Smith thought when she first met York Delaney. The rebel brother had roamed the world for years before calling the rough mining town of Hell's Bluff home. Now, the spirited young woman who'd penetrated this renegade's paradise had awakened a savage and tender possessiveness in York: something he never expected to find in himself. Sierra had known loneliness and isolation too—enough to realize that York's restlessness had only to do with finding a place to belong. Could she convince him that love was such a place, that the refuge he'd always sought was in her arms?

(21847 • $2.75)

☐ *BURKE, THE KINGPIN by Fayrene Preston*

Cara Winston appeared as a fantasy, racing on horseback to catch the day's last light—her silver hair glistening, her dress the color of the Arizona sunset . . . and Burke Delaney wanted her. She was on his horse, on his land: she would have to belong to him too. But Cara was quicksilver, impossible to hold, a wild creature whose scent was midnight flowers and sweet grass. Burke had always taken what he wanted, by willing it or fighting for it; Cara cherished her freedom and refused to believe his love would last. Could he make her see he'd captured her to have and hold forever?

(21848 • $2.75)
